Chronicles of Lim: Book One

ALL THE DISAPPEARING THINGS

L.M. Dodds

For Brendan. You and the boys are my favorite world.

1

ASRA

TREVESTEN, ~ 500 YEARS AGO

The maid's hips swung suggestively with each step down the fine, thick rug.

"You're far too good at that," Asra whispered as she crept down the hall. She wasn't in disguise. She had too many instruments, elixirs, and other objects necessary for this job to have them hidden under an apron.

Solvan's voice came out high and girlish from the peaches and cream complexion of the female they'd left sleeping peacefully in a closet.

"People think it's all in the hips, but it's the ankles that really make it work."

Asra snorted as they both stopped at an ornate set of double wooden doors. A lion's carved wooden face roared at them from the center, complete with drops of blood dripping from its overlarge teeth.

"I'd be willing to steal from him for this tacky art alone," Solvan muttered as he worked at the lock with both magic and skill. A strawberry blond curl fell into his face.

Asra said nothing. Her eyes darted to each end of the hall. Elwin and Brigid could only give them a few minutes. She flexed her fingers before brushing them down the many pockets of her jacket, silently naming the contents of each one and their uses.

Solvan blew upward as the curl fell forward again. Asra pushed it under his cap, thankful she'd kept her own dark hair short. It was practical for many reasons: easier to wash, it never got in her eyes when she was working, and less for anyone to grab onto in a fight.

The lock clicked.

A whoosh of air rushed past them as Solvan disabled the last of the enchantments. Breaking protective charms was difficult magic. It had taken the four of them years of practice. Solvan had been in and out of this house multiple times over the last month, disguising himself as various servants and other members of the household so he could study Mr. Kroten's locks.

The two of them hurried inside, closing the doors behind them.

Downstairs, the house was in an uproar as servants prepared for the Krotens' evening celebrations. Solvan had heard Kroten refer to Queen Sabine as a "hairy bitch" on more than one occasion. Throwing a party in honor of her birthday was just another way to show off his wealth and compete with his neighbors.

The Krotens' party would likely become more elaborate each time the queen turned twenty-five. This was only the second time, but the party was still more lavish than any of them had ever seen. By her seventh rishival, they'd probably have to build a whole second mansion to contain it.

Hundreds of pounds of flower petals had been delivered to carpet the floor. Mouth-watering smells emanated from the kitchen, honey-baked confections, roasted meat and vegetables, and mountains of tiny pastries filled with sweet and spicy mousse. She didn't need to ask Solvan to know he'd swiped as much as possible. A telltale clink came from under his skirt—a few bottles of beer, apparently, too.

But in Kroten's office, it was as quiet as a tomb, only the sound of their beating hearts.

The interior was just as gaudy as the doors. The endless regurgitation of bad taste was everywhere. A spotlight illuminated a pretentious painting of Kroten smashing two giant boulders that both of them immediately itched to deface. But there was no time to dwell on the garish decorations and stupidly expensive knick-knacks.

They were only there for one thing.

A gleaming red stone the size of a robin's egg sat inside a glass case on top of a pillar in the corner of the room. It pulsed like it was happy to see them. Asra pulled out a vial of yellow powder, poured it into her hand, and blew it onto the glass, revealing even more magical locks.

Solvan changed back into himself to make it easier to work. Asra pulled out half a dozen of her cleverly designed tools, and they worked quickly to disable one layer of security after the other.

A large crash sounded from below.

"Shit," Solvan hissed.

Elwin was posing as a delivery person, one of many moving in and out of the house. He'd positioned himself at the servants' entrance to this hallway.

He'd dropped a case of glassware to block the entrance when they'd arrived. That he'd dropped a second case was a bad sign. Once could be mistaken for clumsiness, two would be suspicious. If they hadn't yet thrown him out of the house, they would soon.

Finally, Asra popped open a vial of silver liquid. It moved and undulated in the glass, eager for its role. She placed it against the glass case, and it slithered out, running along the tiniest crack where the glass case met the pillar before seeping inside.

They held their breath as it appeared inside the glass, moving spider-like up the cushion before blanketing the stone. For a moment, nothing happened. Then, the silver liquid contracted, falling flat on the pillow, the lump of stone gone.

It raced back to the edge, through the cracks, just as Brigid's voice sounded from downstairs.

"No! No! No! This is all wrong! These flowers are all supposed to be red! The queen hates pink!" she shrieked, doing an excellent impersonation of the flamboyant decorator she was meant to be. The merchants all prided themselves on knowing insipid details like this, and the Krotens had hired Brigid on the spot when she'd slyly revealed that her cousin was one of the queen's chambermaids.

None of them knew whether the queen had chambermaids. Brigid had no cousins.

"Time to go," Solvan said, looking around to ensure they'd left no trace of their presence. Asra wished she could be there when Kroten came back and found his precious stone missing, with no evidence of how it had been removed.

She held out her hand, and the liquid climbed up her fingers, rolling into a ball and expanding until it melted to the sides, revealing the glowing red orb.

They raced to the door, closing it softly behind them. Solvan gripped her hand, extending his power to her and turning them into identical versions of the same maid. Asra quickly pulled strands of the blond curls out of her cap to hide the similarity.

Footsteps sounded on the staircase, and they quickened their pace. The flustered voice of Ms. Kroten floated up to them.

"How was I supposed to know that insufferable cow hates pink? I like pink!" she whined under her breath as she ascended the stairs. "It's not like she's even going to be here!"

Asra shook her head. She was too close. They wouldn't make it. She dragged Solvan as she turned them back toward the office.

Several pairs of feet padded quickly up the other end of the hall. The servants had cleared Elwin's obstacle. The fire in Asra's blood warmed with excitement. Tiny flames jumped at her fingertips, eager to settle this problem with heat and cinders. Her heart danced even as she forced herself to remain calm.

"Get under my dress," she whispered to Solvan. He didn't question her. The glamor slipped as he let go of her hand to hunch down between her legs. He made himself as small as possible as she floated him the tiniest bit off the floor. As soon as his palm touched her again, she changed back into the maid, her skirts wide as they hid him and his bounty. Asra backed up next to a small alcove that held a giant urn filled with fresh flowers.

Ms. Kroten strode into the hall, her dress a vivid fuchsia, just as two servants arrived from the other end of the hall.

"You there. Come help me change. Apparently," her voice became nasally and baby-like, "the queen hates pink."

If Brigid heard Ms. Kroten imitate her like that, she'd delight in slicing her dress to ribbons, probably while she was still wearing it.

Asra made as much of a curtsey as she could. "Yes, ma'am, I heard. I was just getting the hairpins."

The male servant, his hair a dark green, frowned at Asra. Was this maid not obedient? But he said nothing in front of his boss.

Ms. Kroten wasn't even listening. She'd already flounced into her room, still muttering about Queen Sabine.

Asra moved as gracefully as she could with her legs wide to accommodate Solvan. Just as she approached the room where they'd stashed the real maid, the male servant called out to her.

"Something wrong with your guts, Billie? Why are you moving like you're about to give birth to a troll?" The female with him looked at Asra with intense dislike. Not friends then.

Asra quickened her pace. "I'm not feeling well. Instead of focusing on my ass, why don't you"—she tipped her head at the female servant—"go help Ms. K change?" Then she looked at the male servant. "And you can get fucked."

The two didn't even bat an eye, proving her theory correct that while this maid might look pretty, she clearly wasn't sweet. Asra didn't wait to see what else they would do. She hustled into the room and slammed the door behind her. Solvan let go, tumbling onto the floor before bouncing up again.

Asra laughed, exhilarated at their near miss. Solvan went to the window, wrenching it open to reveal Elwin standing casually on the roof, hands on his hips, eyes raised in question.

"How valuable were those glasses?" Solvan asked.

"It was two cases of wine," Elwin grinned, holding out his hand for Solvan's bag of pilfered goods. "And, a lot."

Solvan climbed out onto the roof as Asra made her way to the closet. She waved another vial, this one tiny, with clear liquid, under the nose of the maid, who awoke with a start. Before she saw her, Asra ducked out of the closet and out the window, sending the young girl a note to attend to Ms. Kroten immediately. She didn't think the other two would do her any favors, and she wasn't trying to get anyone fired.

The three of them darted across the rooftop, shimmied down a drainpipe, and landed in the soft grass behind a giant topiary. Brigid instructed the Krotens to shape them all like towers "inspired by the turrets of Adnatia." They didn't look like turrets. Solvan and Elwin snickered like children.

As they snaked toward a line of trees at the property's edge, a sleek black jaguar flew past them.

They raced to catch up to Brigid. The four of them reached the property wall and scaled it easily. The cab they'd paid to wait was still there, the horses snorting and the driver relaxing in the sunlight.

As they opened the door, he startled, grabbing the reins and encouraging the horses to move as soon as the door to the carriage slammed shut behind them.

Brigid changed back, fanning herself and laughing. "Well?"

Asra held up the stone, and the other three murmured appreciatively. "First thing on the list, done and dusted."

A firework sizzled a path into the sky before popping and exploding into a hundred brilliant orange stars. Hands reached up to grab them as they floated lazily downward. The rest made tiny, plinking sounds as they landed on the cobblestones.

Asra leaned over the walkway, high above the street, watching children scoop the stars into their pockets, the orange glow still visible through the material. The smoke from the fireworks mixed with the smell of various food carts lining the streets. Sticky roasted nuts, spicy noodle soup, and cotton candy, all layered above the brackish scent of the nearby harbor.

"Damn it," Solvan said next to her. Asra took a long pull on her bottle as she looked over at him. He was frowning, one eye closed to squint into his drink, where several stars glowed from the bottom. "Now my beer is warm."

On the other side of him, Elwin and Brigid laughed. Asra handed him another from her bag, and he clinked it with hers in thanks.

"I say next time we try to get in." Elwin looked over the rooftops and bridges of the small port city, as if he could see all the way across Trevesten, to the party taking place at Adnatia palace. More fireworks went off, the crowd oohing and ahhing as the illuminated confetti blanketed the crowds below.

"She probably has every type of booze in Trevesten," Solvan said, putting a hand over his drink as another firework exploded.

"You mean in all of Malan," Brigid corrected. She handed her drink to Elwin so she could readjust her hair, gathering all the errant dark strands into a thick knot atop her head.

"And I bet the place is just rife with distracted partygoers who wouldn't notice a few missing valuables." Elwin grinned, restlessly bouncing on the balls of his feet.

"Indeed. A small price to pay for a good time," Asra joined in. "The food's probably pretty good, too." A couple tiptoed across the walkway beneath them, their arms out, attempting to make up for balance stolen by an evening of revelry.

They all nodded their heads in agreement as another explosion sounded. This time, red hearts filled the streets and tumbled down the rooftops. Soon, they would clog the gutters and make the roads impassable. Children, and the more tipsy adults, would lie down and make snow bats or fill up hollow necklaces and bracelets to wear as they celebrated. The brilliant shapes would all vanish by morning.

The celebrations for Queen Sabine's rishival were in full swing. Asra smiled, thinking of how the Krotens' party was probably far less festive right now.

Upon turning twenty-five, all fae regained the knowledge and memories from their past lives. The process, known as a rishival, varied in time but was predictably intense. Having all those memories shoved into one's head was not fun. The madness was terrifying, but the sickness was worse. The nausea made even the strongest fae hug the cool floor and hope for death. Considering they could live up to three hundred years in each life, the rishival in their seventh and final life could be positively brutal.

"Do you think it's possible?" Brigid asked her, her gaze calculating. "To get into the palace?" She leaned back into Elwin's towering frame and he wrapped his arms around her.

Asra stood up straight, stretching an arm across her torso. "Nothing's impossible. But it would take a lot of planning, years possibly." She began calculating the needs for such a job; travel, bribes, they'd likely need kippies for invisibility and persuasion.

"Who says we can't plan two big jobs at one time?" Brigid replied. She paused thoughtfully. "We couldn't sneak in, we'd need to be allowed. We could pose as guards or cooks or something."

Asra shook her head and switched to the other arm. "Not getting into the rishival dressed as a cook."

Brigid threw a handful of red hearts at her. "*Or something.*"

Asra laughed as she pulled hearts from her hair and clothes. "I agree with you. Sneaking in is out. But the party is filled with royals, ambassadors, other important types." She pursed her lips, thinking. Who were the less important fae allowed to move freely through the rishival?

"Entertainers?" she suggested.

"Yes!" Solvan said, pointing at her. "We just need to create an act so incredible the queen will have to invite us next time."

They lapsed into thoughtful silence, contemplating how they could mold their skills and magic into an appropriately spectacular display.

Elwin pulled Brigid into a dance. They skillfully navigated across the narrow walkway, neither of them making a single misstep despite the rickety construction. Elwin dipped her low and Brigid gave them a dazzling upside down smile.

Solvan pursed his lips. "Is that the best you can do? You're going to need to practice more." He stomped his foot, making the lanterns hanging precariously from the railing sway. "I will break you down and build you back up. You shall be my greatest creation." He clapped his hands. "Again!"

Brigid snorted a laugh as Elwin brought her back up. "You'd be an excellent tyrant, Solvan."

"He could certainly pull off the outfit." Asra smirked.

"Alas, I am but a poor Suka thief. Forever waiting to achieve the greatness I deserve."

"Don't make me throw you off this walkway." Elwin shoved him in the shoulder. Solvan gasped dramatically and fell over the side. He nimbly caught the railing with one hand and swung back up behind them.

"Seven." Asra clapped dutifully.

"Six point five," Brigid said as she threw an arm around his shoulders.

Several other fae joined them on the walkway, and they had to stop talking about heists and thievery. Of course, this was Oderon. It was one of the more sordid cities in Trevesten. There was a good chance the people next to them were just as criminal as they were. Still, one couldn't be too careful.

It was after one in the morning when the four of them left the celebrations for the small house at the end of a skinny side street. The house had belonged to Asra's grandfather, the first and only home she'd ever known. Before the others had moved in, it was cold and empty. She'd been jumpy, moving from room to room, searching for voices or a life that never appeared. Her neighbor had taken pity on her, checking in, ensuring Asra ate and slept properly.

She'd practically collapsed in relief when Solvan agreed to move in. It felt almost complete with Elwin and Brigid there.

Later, when the last of the fireworks had gone off and most of the remnants were fading from view, Asra considered the palace again. It would be fun to see a royal rishival. The luxury at that party would put the Krotens to shame.

She toed off her boots as she undressed for bed, pretending not to hear the fervent whispers from Brigid and Elwin's room. While it wasn't impossible for her to plan two jobs at one time, her thoughts were focused on only one.

Asra unrolled the map across her desk, turning to the sixth page. The mapmaker had given Sverresen a rectangular shape, despite nobody really knowing what it looked like.

They would be smarter than the ones who had tried to go before. The ones who didn't return.

Asra rolled the red stone around in her palm. It warmed at her touch. They still had a lot more preparation to do if they were going to survive a round trip to the sixth world. Sverresen was out of reach.

For now.

2

SABINE

TREVESTEN, ~ 500 YEARS AGO

The food was abysmal. Sabine discreetly spit the bizarre concoction into a napkin and dropped it onto an abandoned plate. It was clear she hadn't been discreet enough when a server immediately bustled by and collected the plate and a few empty glasses. The uniformed female gathered everything up into a cloud of debris that trailed behind her.

"Thank you," Sabine said.

The server curtseyed before slipping past Sabine and into a hidden door in the wall that led to the kitchens. Sabine took a delicate sip of her wine, eyes scanning the room.

Gold and blue decorations, the official colors of Adnatia, filled the massive ballroom. Giant golden snowflakes fell endlessly from the ceiling, disappearing just before they reached the heads of her guests. Blue silk covered every surface, spelled to look like ever-moving water, swirling and pooling onto the floor. Every table had crystal cloches containing miniature sparkling fireworks.

The revelers outside were sending off their own magic and colorful explosions into the sky. In front of her, a fae juggled dozens of objects he'd lifted from obliging partygoers. Another fae was creating amazingly lifelike candy creatures. A child giggled as her candy lion roared when she licked it. Sabine questioned the appeal of eating something that appeared to be living, but the candy purveyor had a line twenty fae deep.

Sabine knew she was queen. The tattoo on her wrist, a circle with an arrow through it, proved that. And unlike Sukas, non-royals, she got to keep her name. But she wouldn't remember everything or recognize everyone until after she completed her rishival. This was only her second life, so she hoped that and the combination of healing elixirs would make hers manageable. No matter how painful it was, she was grateful. The rishival was a gift to the fae from the Allmother. It required a significant amount of power; power trolls, sprites, and others didn't have.

She supposed it would never get any less strange, having so many people know you, know things about you that you didn't know. After the rishival, Sabine would understand who here were genuine friends and who had just been buttering her up all these years. Pandering, so she might overlook any prior transgressions. She would also discover who might have used her lack of memories for political maneuvering.

Her eyes found a prime suspect for the latter across the room. Lord Connery was dancing with Lady Elestra, and Sabine had to work hard to keep the scowl from her face. He was so unbelievably obvious about it. Sure, they were old family friends, and Lady Elestra was honestly one of the nicest fae she'd met in this life. But he was clearly just dancing with her so Sabine would notice.

Connery's blue eyes, enhanced by his navy and cream-colored coat, were full of mirth as they laughed at something Elestra said. His smile was honest and typical of the friendly nature he'd shown her from the first moment they met two years ago.

Her advisors had explained the history of Connery's family. He was on his first life. His mother, Corinne, despite already being married, had found her mate and gotten pregnant with Connery. Her husband attacked her when he found out, and she handed him a humiliating defeat. Now he was licking his wounds somewhere in Eloisha. The family remained, and Connery's siblings would do anything to ingratiate themselves with the palace after their father's disgraceful behavior.

She forcibly averted her eyes, which unfortunately fell on Ambassador Venten, the emissary from Boralta. She'd had extensive lessons on the territory to the north of Trevesten, and its mercurial leadership.

She smiled politely as Venten approached her.

"Enjoying yourself, Your Majesty?" Ambassador Venten tipped his glass of wine at her, the amber liquid catching in the light. He wore a slim black coat over a gray shirt. His tie was in the Boraltan style, a flat multi-strand braid down his chest.

She didn't dislike Ambassador Venten himself. Sabine simply had no interest in any discussions regarding alliances and treaties until she completed her rishival. Boralta was convinced that more interaction between their people was the key to creating more nyssar, new fae life, and growing the fae population. It wasn't a new idea. Every leader in Malan had to consider it. Boralta had been sending her letters since before she could walk.

"Of course," Sabine said. "Aren't you?"

"Absolutely." He smiled, showing a row of straight white teeth with slightly elongated canines. "I'm impressed with your restraint. I was far more uncouth at my rishival. I believe by the end of the night, I'd expressed my undying affection toward nearly everyone and everything." His eyes twinkled with amusement.

Sabine gave him a small smile. "I suppose that is the downside to my position. But I am enjoying the festivities all the same, regardless of my ability to confess my love to the room's inanimate objects."

Venten chuckled but didn't let it go. "I noticed you are not dancing."

Sabine refused to look at Connery. "I have been dancing. Now I am simply enjoying the view."

"And is the 'view' worth your attention?" he said, his eyes lowered over his drink.

Sabine bristled and dropped her voice. "Very little is worth my attention until after I regain my memories, Ambassador Venten."

The Boraltans did not tattoo their royals, so they could continually return to their families like Trevesten did. Instead, Boralta held a contest, a match designed to see the most gifted fae ascend to the throne. A fae's natural power followed them and accumulated through each of their seven lives. The Boraltan's contest was consistently won by fae who were in their seventh and final life. Sabine thought it was interesting, but it meant inflexible curmudgeons often ruled the Boraltans.

The current curmudgeon's two-hundred-year term was ending soon. Another reason she saw no reason to deal with Boralta's entreaties just yet.

Venten nodded in apology. "Of course, I will be honored to call on you again when that time comes, if you permit it."

"Still lurking about, Venten? Don't you Boraltans need to hibernate?" Morgan's voice was like a blade, her beautiful sapphire dress swaying with each step. The fae age slowly, and despite being two hundred and seventy-five years old, she also had more than enough power to preserve her youthful appearance. Her eyes narrowed on the Ambassador.

He held his hand to his chest. "Princess Morgan, I didn't see you there. It's difficult to notice anyone at all next to your sister's beauty." His eyes were full of innocence, but he gave her a wicked smile.

Sabine repressed the inappropriate urge to roll her eyes.

"Yes, she is beautiful, and your batlike presence is ruining the effect." The words shot out of her perfect bow-shaped mouth as she smoothed the bodice of her gown.

"Now I'm a bat? I thought I was a bear?" Venten's voice had become silken.

"Either way, you belong in a cave. Now shoo." Morgan waved her hand as if Venten were nothing but an annoying insect.

"In alia vita." A small smile played on his lips as he bowed and strode away into the crowd.

"The Boraltans are breathing down my neck every second of the day. Could you have possibly found someone less complicated to bed?" Sabine spoke to her sister while giving a feigned smile to Lady Moranne, who bowed to her from across the dance floor. The notoriously rude female was wearing an orange dress that completely washed her out.

"Where would be the fun in that? I'm going to die soon. I'm not wasting my time on uncomplicated bores." Morgan said the words as if they were nothing, but they gutted Sabine.

Looking at her sister, one could never tell Morgan was reaching the end of this life, her first life. Her power was nearly as great as Sabine's. They were very close. She had only been sixty-two years old when Morgan was born.

Although Sabine knew Morgan would be reborn and the tattoo on her wrist, the twin to her own, would bring her back to her rightful place at Sabine's side, it still made her sad. Morgan would be a child again, not the wise and barb-toothed female that stood beside her now. Sabine would have to wait at least twenty-five years before Morgan regained the memories of their time together in this life.

She was about to respond when a familiar shadow came over her. She turned to see Connery, his face full of promises, standing beside her. He bowed deeply to both of them.

"Would you care to dance, Your Majesty?" Connery smiled, and Sabine's insides squirmed. He had to know how he looked. How all the females looked at him with his broad shoulders and powerful jaw. His face was a little flushed from the warmth of the room, and his hair had become windswept from all the dancing. As if noticing her perusal, he brushed his hand through it. She couldn't stop the slight twitch of her lips.

Sabine had read everything in the family archives. The ruling family of Trevesten specifically advised against pre-rishival romantic entanglements. They tended to be, at best, embarrassing and, at worst, catastrophic. Her own notes from her prior lifetime confirmed it. Nevertheless, Sabine's hand somehow found its way into Connery's as he led them out onto the dance floor. Morgan melted into the crowd, no doubt to find Venten and continue their verbal sparring somewhere more private.

It was a lively and popular tune. Sabine couldn't help her grin as he expertly led them through the dance. He held her close to pull her into a small lift. When she was tight against his body, he whispered into her ear. "I take it the food is not to your liking?"

His tone was teasing, and the feeling of his breath sent a shiver down her spine. She gave him a raised eyebrow—was there anyone who hadn't seen her spit out that pastry?—and a smile before he flung her away into a spin. She sailed back into his arms and he pressed a firm hand against the small of her back.

"I don't suppose you'd let me visit you tonight?" His fingers curled, lightly stroking her through her dress.

"Are you sure it's me you want to visit?" Her voice sounded annoyingly jealous. He spun her away again.

Connery gave her a mildly scolding look that made her skin heat. "My dear queen, who else is there?"

3

LIM

LASHIA, 2705 POST WEAKENING, PRESENT DAY

The giant hunk of meat stared at me from the counter. I repressed the urge to ask what it was or where it came from. The dishes rattled as Emir crashed through the backdoor, carrying another unidentified carcass. He let it fall next to the first, a look of pride on his face.

"You see this? Unbelievable! All of it"—he slapped one of the carcasses—"only twenty marks!" His grin was wide under his bushy mustache, his forehead sweaty with exertion and eyes round with excitement.

I pulled my lips into my mouth and let out a slow breath through my nose. I sniffed delicately. It wasn't balara meat, thank goodness. I couldn't look Derek in the eye for a week after that. Not that he spent any time looking anywhere but his feed trough, anyway. Balaras were like the worst crossbreed of a horse and a donkey. They looked like large donkeys but had very little work ethic, the joke being that they'd evolved to be so lazy nobody ever strapped them to a cart again. Derek certainly fit the stereotype.

We had quite a few new creatures, evolving from out of the muck, adapting to the world nature had all but wiped clean thousands of years ago. My own terrifying pet had only been seen in the last two hundred years. Emir had once brought me one of those dog-sized rats. Meat was meat, I supposed, but even I'd grimaced a bit at cooking that. I sniffed again but still had no clue. A type of large bird, maybe? At least it was fresh.

"Did you get the vegetables I asked for?" I leaned against the counter, my arms crossed.

Emir's grin faltered. "Well, I owed Tomas a little money…" At my look of disappointment, Emir backed up, his hands up in surrender. "Don't give me that look. I got most of it!" He went scrambling out the backdoor to his wagon. The door slammed open again, making the hanging braids of garlic and dried chilis swing from the ceiling. Emir set a large reed basket next to the meat.

I peeked inside and sighed. "What did you pay for this, then?" Half of the vegetables were hovering between sad and inedible, and the other half weren't much better. I'd need to use most of this today to make it worth anything.

He puffed out his chest proudly. "I got a deal for the whole bundle, meat and veg!" He began pulling things out of the basket, showing me each one and singing its praises, "See! Perfectly good head of cabbage, just cut out the black spots. And these apples are excellent, only one or two bruises." He stroked his mustache and squinted a little at each item as if he were evaluating a priceless piece of art.

I scoffed and wrinkled my nose. "You're really not selling it as well as you think you are." He put his hand to his chest and gave me a look of mock innocence. I pushed off the counter with my hip. "Fine, please go get the rest of your riches."

Emir grinned and sauntered out the door. What would it be like to have my pick at the market and not have to rely on Emir? After all this time working for him, it was probably less about him not trusting me with the money as it was not wanting me to know how little he had to spend. Emir always owed money to someone. Playing cards every night will do that. More often than not, he'd surprise me with some great deal on something scavenged from a pit. I was always squeezing by with just enough to keep this restaurant, *his restaurant*, running.

I pulled down a jar of salt, scanning my other options. Seven long shelves contained all the herbs, spices and preserved fruits and flowers I'd painstakingly accumulated over the years. Jars of dried chamomile, dill, and orange peels. Bottles filled with different vinegars and powdered roots. Emir was forbidden from touching anything on the entire wall.

Technically, we lived in New Marée, named by the first people who had settled here when the oceans had risen so far, it was actually near the coast. But the water had receded again, and now everyone called it "New Marais," or just "the swamp." A whole lot of wet, dense air and soft ground that grew more mosquitos than food. The rare good soil was in high demand. A few things would grow out back. But we mainly had to buy or forage our produce to feed the hungry fishers, tradespeople, and other motley groups that frequented The Peregrine.

Emir began unpacking and putting things away, humming cheerfully under his breath. I salted the meat and then grabbed my cleaver to break it down into more manageable pieces. Couldn't very well put 'mystery bird' on the menu board, so meat pies it would have to be. I could sauté some mushrooms in a little bacon fat and thyme, throw in some leeks, and make a nice, thick gravy. I was thinking about the peppery pie crust I'd use when something whooshed through the air and smacked the wall behind me.

I twisted as a ball ricocheted from the wall to the counter to the stove. As it lost momentum, it rolled in progressively smaller circles of filth before resting atop the drain in the floor.

Emir laughed as he came back up from the cellar, yelling out the open window. "You crazy things, your sister is going to cook you for that!" He pulled his head back in as a smaller head appeared below, her eyes barely making it over the windowsill. Emir ruffled her hair fondly.

"Ayla..." I groaned, pushing the heels of my palms into my eyes. If I'd had nails long enough, they would have pierced my skin.

"We're sorry, Lim." Large brown eyes blinked slowly at me. There was a beat, and then she quickly gestured to the ball, her capacity for remorse apparently exhausted. "Can we have it back?" The other kids, my twelve-year-old brother Keen among them, whispered and giggled behind her.

Except that my eyes are green, and hers are brown, Ayla and I look incredibly alike. We have my father's dark hair, the same freckles dusting our noses, and, according to my father, the same way of pushing our lips to the side when we're trying not to smile. Neither of us was smiling now. She kept quiet. Ayla didn't have Keen's easy charm. She just waited me out, confident that I would eventually give in.

I stuttered an exhale. "Please go play elsewhere." I picked up the ball and threw it through the window. She ran backward and her small hands deftly snagged it from the air.

"Thanks, Lim!" Keen shouted from somewhere outside before many tiny feet stampeded away. The juvenile shrieking trailed off into blessed silence. Keen would undoubtedly be out front. He was a natural leader and peacemaker, always ready with a joke to diffuse tense situations.

Keen was the first to make me a big sister. I adored him immediately. At fifteen, I'd been an only child long enough, and he and his chubby fingers were a wonderful surprise to me and our parents. Two years later, Ayla came marching into the world. Keen's eyes were also brown like Ayla's, but he'd gotten our mother's lovely auburn hair.

I frowned at the muddied walls and floor. Last night's careful cleaning undone. I reached out my hand, stretching my fingers toward the mess. "Abracadabra!"

Nothing happened, of course. Emir shook his head at me in mild reprimand. "None of that. And you better not let anyone else see you doing it." He strode out of the kitchen and up the back staircase to his apartment above.

I rolled my eyes at his back as I pulled out the mop, bucket, and vinegary cleaning solution I'd made from bitter purple fruits. I filled the bucket at the kitchen's enormous sink, dishes from the morning's prep still waiting to be washed. Above it was a window to the side yard where I could see several of the chickens had taken refuge from the children.

I took out my annoyance at Emir's comments on the mud. He didn't mean 'anyone,' he meant 'Tals,' like him and probably most of the patrons of his restaurant. I cleaned every bit off the walls, shelves, surfaces, and finally, the floor.

After putting away my cleaning supplies, I pushed my hands and arms under the tap, rinsing off the last little flecks of mud. I glanced at the glowing blue cuffs circling my forearms. Neither the mud nor the water had any effect on them. Nothing did.

The cuffs restrained a Jinn's magic, magic that no Jinn had used in centuries. Regardless, Tals got jumpy whenever any of us so much as alluded to anything magical or fantastical. I'd drawn a picture of a unicorn once in school and my teacher had made me burn it in front of the entire class. Unicorns never walked this earth even when magic was allowed but, sure, traumatize a child for no reason.

I put the bucket and mop back in the supply closet. My frustration got the better of me and I slammed the door closed, the wood making a satisfying crack I felt deep inside me.

I finished making two more drinks and set them down in front of the couple at the far end of the bar before immediately turning to make two more. Emir was holding court at one of the bigger tables. His boisterous laughter rose above the clattering of silverware, the clinking of glasses, and the noisy chatter that filled the room. Tonight, it was even louder, as Emir had booked a band for the evening. People listened as much as they shouted to be heard above the music.

The doors opened to allow in another group of people, machinists, from the look of oil permanently staining their nails. Emir waved to them and they all sent back cheerful greetings before grabbing a table. Elias, the server, swept over to them, and I began filling the beers I could hear them ordering.

One of my regulars, Aiden, was in tonight, perched on what he considered "his stool." He was regaling what looked like a first date with a story about a prank a friend had played on him. The woman was laughing so hard she was nearly crying. The man was laughing too, but also trying to figure out how to get his date's attention back on him. He gave her a look of wistful admiration, which made me want to help him out.

"Aiden, what do you think of the band tonight?" He turned away from the couple as he assessed the musicians, who were only just getting started. There was a piano player, a guitarist, and a singer—they were all siblings with round faces and curly hair. The guitarist gave a cheeky wink as he warmed up the crowd.

Aiden spun back to me. "Did you know that all the musicians used to have electric instruments - everything was electric? You could hear them from miles away when they would perform. Playing to crowds bigger than all of Lashia." He tapped his legs to the rhythm of the music and stroked his full beard.

People loved to talk about the before times, the amazing art, the incredible technology. I would have given my left arm for electric lights in here, maybe in a few years. Some of the other boroughs had electricity now. In the capital borough, Eudora, they even had electric streetlights. As it was, I spent a lot of time lighting the lamps on the tables and the two beautiful but giant chandeliers hanging from the ceiling.

"So I've heard." I gave a small smile to the man and nodded surreptitiously at an open table. He didn't squander his opportunity. He quickly hopped down and escorted his date and their drinks to a place where he could try to earn some undivided attention. She gave him a smile that assured me she was more than happy with the new arrangement.

Aiden turned back to the band, his knee bouncing along to the music. He gave some folks coming in a wave and spilled beer down his shirt in the process. I dropped some glasses in the dirty bus bin and threw him a towel while I craned my neck to check the kitchen orders. The meat pies were selling well. Audre, who was working the line, flipping burgers and finishing what we couldn't cook in advance, gave me the universal symbol for drinking. I passed her a glass of cider and she smiled gratefully at me.

The door opened again, and Emir's son, Leo, stepped inside. He grinned at this father before bounding over to the bar. My stomach gave a little flip as he set his honey-brown eyes on me.

"How you doing, Leo?" I found something to do with my hands.

He gave me a sly smile as he sat down on a barstool and propped his chin in his hands. "Beautiful Lim, when are you going to get out of this place and run away with me?"

I rolled my eyes and pretended his words hadn't affected me in the slightest. "Don't you think your father would have a problem with that? Unless you think people will pay him just to socialize and not to eat?"

Leo gave an easy laugh, glancing at his father, who was indeed chatting with a new table. "Too true. What would he do without you?"

I just shook my head. "The usual?"

Leo nodded, and as he took the glass of beer from me, his hand closed over my fingers, sending warmth up my arm. He winked and hopped off the stool to join some friends.

I began wiping down the bar, stopping to take a bite of the sandwich Audre passed me.

"Seriously though," Aiden said to me, his merry but slightly unfocused eyes peeking out from his impressively robust facial hair. "When are you going to get out of here? Be the boss?"

"Starting a restaurant takes money," I muttered around a mouthful of ham, my eyes not quite meeting his. 'It also takes time, energy, and confidence I don't have,' I thought to myself. Making rodent taste good was not a reason people went to good restaurants.

The door banged open and a group of four men walked in, their faces weather-beaten. One man wore a mean little smile on his face, and the others looked equally unfriendly, which wasn't all that unusual here. Emir's restaurant catered to the less illustrious citizens of Marais. I could see yellow cuffs on one man, but I didn't really need to see it to know they were all Tals. I self-consciously tugged on my sleeves, which were always rolled down in public. The man in front surveyed the room, and his eyes examined me before sliding toward Aiden. His mouth tightened, and beside me, Aiden sat up a little straighter, using his large body to block me from view. Emir saved us from further scrutiny by jumping out of his seat and calling out.

"Jared! Welcome! Welcome! A round of our best whiskey, Calimea!" His nervous energy kept me from retorting that we only had one kind of whiskey; these men were likely here to collect a debt. I also pretended it didn't bother me that he'd used my full name in front of people who obviously had a problem with Jinns. I passed the drinks quickly to Elias, who brought them over to their table. One man leered at Elias, who gave him a terse smile before slipping away.

As they sat down, Jared muttered something to Emir, who waved it off good-naturedly. Emir's response carried over to me. "She's a good worker, only one I can trust with my recipes, y'know."

A chill went down my back. People made jokes about us. Sometimes they even got a little rude. But something about Emir's reaction made me think the man had made more than a snide comment. I rubbed my hands on my apron, trying to calm myself. This was nothing, nothing at all. I'd grown up here, and my family was here. I was used to it. But if I ever did open my own restaurant, maybe I'd do it in one of the bigger cities, Eudora or Chelsea, somewhere I could blend in.

4

LIM

LASHIA, PRESENT DAY

I handed Audre the last dish for her to dry. I arched my back, stretching and pulling my arms up over my head. Audre put the kettle on, and I pulled down her favorite tea, a blend with sweet pink petals and star anise.

The last guest had gone home at one a.m., and Elias, Audre, and I had been up until two cleaning up. We'd left some dishes for this morning, baselessly hoping that Emir, who'd gotten a blissful nine hours of sleep, might do some of them before we came in. No such luck.

I poured boiling water into the teapot and added the tea, the room filling with the flowery licorice fragrance. Audre closed her eyes over her mug and inhaled. We were both about to take a drink when the backdoor opened, bringing in the overpowering smell of roses with it. The sickly scent filled my nose, and I repressed a gag.

"Does Emir know you two are standing around instead of working?" Sydney crossed one arm across her slim waist and bent her other at the elbow so she could play with her frizzy blond hair. She brushed her chipped, red nails through the ends.

"Good morning to you too, Sydney," Audre replied, not bothering to look at Emir's sister until she got her first sip. I saluted Sydney with my mug but said nothing. She was exhausting but mostly harmless.

Sydney huffed. "You two are really lucky my brother likes you. Most places wouldn't bother with all the trouble you cause."

Audre snorted while I rolled my eyes. "Jinns don't cause trouble." I sighed. Nothing different about us but the color of our cuffs for hundreds of years. But ignorant jerks like Sydney still feigned fear that, at any moment, we would turn them all to dust.

"Oh really? Well, a lot of other people seem to think differently." She rummaged in her bag before pulling out a crumpled piece of paper and sneering as she shoved it at us.

My eyebrows knitted in confusion as I opened it. Audre leaned toward me, pushing up on her toes to read over my shoulder.

Are Jinns taking over your neighborhood? Are they infecting your work-place? Do you wish you and yours could live in peace and not under the constant threat of magical violence? Stop living in fear and join the Sun Guardians!

Someone had written a time and date for a meeting place along with the symbol of a sun.

Audre and I shared a look. "What is this even supposed to mean?" I asked Sydney. "The Tals are going to get together and what, talk about how we can't be in their club anymore? None of us can do shit," I waved my arm at her, bare since I'd rolled up my sleeves to do the dishes, blue cuffs fully on display.

Sydney snatched back the paper and shoved it back in her bag. "It's because of you we have to wear these!" She gestured to her own arms, where yellow bands glowed under her pale pink shirt. "You don't think that's a little unfair? That we're punished for something you did?" She crossed her arms across her chest, glaring at us. "We shouldn't have to suffer for your crimes."

"Suffer?" spluttered Audre, angry disbelief flaring in her eyes.

"The Tals were the ones who decided *everyone* had to wear cuffs, Sydney. Your people are responsible for making you suffer the horrific indignity of having to wear those cute little bracelets."

"They never would have had to do that if Jinns hadn't been so evil! The Tals weren't the ones just murdering people for any little slight!"

Audre's face had a mercenary tilt, she was about to say something that would either make Sydney cry, Emir yell at us, or both. Emir didn't care much about his sister, but appeasing her was easier than having to deal with her incessant whining.

"Emir!" I yelled, tired of Sydney's mouth. "Your delightful sister, who continues to blame us for the actions of a bunch of jagoffs who died a billion years ago, is here!"

Sydney's face flushed with anger. She used a bony elbow to push past us.

"It's also not our fault you don't look good in yellow," Audre called after her as Sydney stomped up the stairs. Audre made a rude gesture at her back. "Honestly, the nonsense they come up with. Do you think it would solve all of this if they could just change the color whenever they wanted?"

"Good idea. You should go to that meeting and suggest it. Be sure to ask them to remove your cuffs so you can use your super powerful magic to take care of it for them." I opened the door to let Sydney's terrible perfume out.

Audre barked a laugh and threw a dishrag at me. I smiled too as I caught it, but inside, I felt a little queasy. Although this push by the Tals to have their cuffs removed was new, the constant fear-mongering was not. I'd seen flyers like that before. And once, in the market, someone had painted "Go home Jinns," on a wall, that same sun underneath. Go home to where? I'd thought. Nobody was from here.

Marais was one of the less populated but much larger—and therefore spread out—boroughs. Each borough had a few thousand people. It was incredible we had that many, considering how few remained after the Weakening. Some accounts referred to it as a reckoning or rapture, but that made it sound too much like a single event.

The death of our natural resources had been happening for some time, but in those last one hundred years of the common era, things deteriorated rapidly. The hurricanes became catastrophic, winds faster than planes could fly. Tsunamis and tornadoes that fell from the sky as often as rain. Mother Nature wiped out entire cities in a matter of hours. Those who could, migrated. They moved to the parts of the land that were the most sheltered, that still had some resources, trying to survive day to day until the earth stopped screaming. There was another dark age and the surviving records paint a grim picture. All the technology was dead. Survivors were isolated. People existed—you could not call it living—just existed in this way for generations.

The environment slowly took itself back, purging itself of noxious gasses, letting the surviving flora take back the buildings and bodies into the ground. Most animal and plant species died, but enough survived the erratic environment that we have some again, for food, clothing, to rebuild. They are not quite the same either though, changed for their environment.

Living thousands of years in a brutal environment, all while knowing what humankind had been capable of, had its repercussions. That's the leading theory anyway, that the knowledge of what was without a way to reclaim it for so long caused a sort of evolutionary break. Some of us, Jinns, developed powerful abilities.

But hundreds of years ago, Jinns, having used their magic to do some spectacularly shitty things, were overthrown. Now, the government applies blue cuffs to every Jinn child to restrain their power. Tals receive decorative yellow cuffs, simply to make it easy to verify everyone's registration. I was used to Tals proudly displaying their yellow cuffs. Apparently, now they resented us for those too.

I tried to push away the thoughts of Sydney and her stupid flyer. Working for Emir afforded me a little protection. It was one reason I'd stayed here so long.

The customers dwindled, so Emir told me to take a break. He took over for me at the bar, overpouring and messing up the cocktail ingredients, but I wasn't about to complain.

I was happy to see Leo sitting with my two friends, Indie and Simon, in a booth near the band. The musicians were playing something low that made my bones hum in a happy sort of way. I plopped myself down next to Indie and took a sip of my drink—a fermented concoction I was still playing with. It was still too bland, more citrus perhaps. I made a disgruntled noise, remembering that Emir had used the last of it yesterday, making a truly inedible cake. Audre and I had to force down an entire slice each before he strode away, beaming with his success. Derek had enjoyed it, though.

"Finally got away, huh?" Indie smiled at me, her eyes glowing in the candlelight.

Leo, on the other side of the table, grinned at me, his arm thrown casually over the back of the booth. "It really was a packed house, Lim. You should be proud. My dinner was excellent." He patted his belly approvingly.

"I'll give your compliments to the chef," I said, jokingly referring to Emir. Underneath the table, I could feel Leo's leg lightly leaning against mine.

Two days ago, he'd been helping me in the pantry. He reached for something above me, and I could swear he had this look, like he might kiss me. But he walked out when Emir's footsteps sounded on the stairs. If Emir had noticed my flustered look when I walked out with the butter, he'd said nothing. Just thinking about it again made the color rise to my cheeks.

"You all aren't even listening! Do you hear that glassy tremolo tone? It really compliments the vulnerability in his voice," Simon shouted at us, his eyes plastered on the band, his lanky frame practically buzzing.

The three of us shared a look of total incomprehension.

Leo laughed and threw his arm around Simon's neck. "He's right, show some appreciation for the art!"

I smiled into my drink, content for the moment. Leo's eyes were watching the movement of the piano player's fingers, as if he could memorize the movements for later. We dated for a little while when we were teens. Keeping it a secret from his Jinn-hating family had seemed romantic at the time.

He was my first kiss, my first a lot of things. He was a riot, always fun, always with big plans. Convinced me to climb through ruins and build forts in the woods. His sandy hair glinted under the bar lights and his body was close enough that I could smell him, sunshine and salt. The electricity of being close to him still tingled inside me.

I'd gone away to school in Eudora for a few years, learning to cook, and when I came back, he was dating someone new. They'd eventually broken up, but there'd been others since. Lots of others. Aside from flirting, nothing ever happened between us again. Leo traveled a lot for work, and once, Sydney had teased him about having a girl in every borough. I wasn't sure if she'd meant it or just said it so I would hear. I guess we hadn't hidden our relationship as well as I thought.

Emir was nice enough to me, but that didn't mean he wanted Jinn grandchildren. Emir's other siblings, especially Sydney and her equally horrible husband, Marco, would never allow it. Magic passed through the maternal line. Although it was common enough for a Jinn woman to give birth to a Tal, none of them would risk it for me.

"Next weekend me and Simon are going to see 'Beyond the Ruins,'" Indie shout-whispered into my ear. "The papers are calling it a 'moving and traumatic retelling of our origins.'" I turned away from Leo and gave Indie an exaggerated grimace.

"That sounds like it'll make your sides hurt from laughing."

This was no doubt Simon's pick for entertainment. He was very into knowing all the trauma of our origins. Indie chuckled and glanced out the window. She tensed slightly, and I followed her gaze. A group of people were walking down the street—stumbling down the street would be more accurate. There was a man near the front wearing black pants and a dark coat, and while the others were jumping around, hanging off trees, and generally being idiots, he looked driven...and mean.

Leo, noticing our expressions, turned his head to the window, his eyes narrowing in question. The man stared at The Peregrine with venom in his eyes. Nobody else in the restaurant had noticed. The musicians kept playing, and people went on drinking and talking. The group outside had almost passed the restaurant when, before I could even open my mouth to warn anyone, the man in front picked up a rock and hurled it through the window.

"Fucking Jinns!" he yelled as the glass shattered. I ducked as the shards flew onto the table and pulled Indie down with me. On the other side, Leo and Simon also pushed themselves under the table. The group outside howled with laughter. My heart was hammering in my chest, but I stood up. They ran off into the night, still laughing at our fear.

Emir ducked under the bar and ran toward the front door, throwing it wide. He looked like he might yell something, instead, he just spit on the ground before stomping back and assessing the damage.

Audre had come flying out of the kitchen, a knife in one hand and a spatula in the other. We shared a look, but I just shook my head tightly. She stowed her utensils and stormed off to get a broom.

"Is anyone hurt?" Indie asked. There were murmurs, chairs pushed back as the customers stood up from their tables, shaking glass from hair and clothes. Everyone looked around, but it appeared there were no injuries. The glass spared anyone who wasn't directly in front of the window. The rock left only a slight scratch where it had slammed into the bar.

I walked over and picked it up. Leo came up behind me and grabbed it from my hand, appalled. He stared at the rock like it might explain its trajectory.

"What the stars is wrong with people? He could have really hurt someone!" He held up the rock to show Emir. Emir gave Leo a look to tell him to shut up. He began making jokes with the customers, offering them a free drink and trying to bring back the convivial atmosphere. He might have been a terrible business owner, but even Emir knew people didn't want to visit a restaurant where you might end up with a rock to the head.

"Well, that's one way to say 'last call.'" Aiden had climbed out from under the bar and was eyeing the inside of his glass, trying to judge if it was still safe to drink.

I shook my head at him. "Better safe than sorry."

Behind him, Audre had returned, and she plucked the glass from his hand and dumped it out. "What she means is don't be stupid."

Aiden grinned and clapped her on the shoulder. He started overturning chairs onto the tables so Audre could sweep.

Indie, one of only two doctors in Marais, was checking people over for glass. She told everyone to shake out their hair and clothes outside and to be sure to check their shoes as well. Simon and Elias were pulling the dishes and glassware off the table.

I helped the rest of the customers outside as the band finished packing up. Indie and Simon made their goodbyes as well. As she left, Indie gave me and Audre a look like she wanted to speak more, but now wasn't the time.

Leo and Emir went outside and returned a few moments later with wood and nails to board up the window. Once we'd cleaned up the broken glass, I fell automatically into the nightly closing rhythm with the rest of the staff.

About an hour later, I made my way home, technically my parents' home. I climbed the stairs to my attic bedroom, stepping over Brax's giant feline body as I opened my door. His eyelids fluttered, and he heaved himself up, stretching deeply and pushing out his razor-sharp claws before following me inside. I followed the doctor's orders, carefully removing my clothes and shaking them off out an open window. Stepping into the shower, I gently combed through my hair for glass. My finger found a tiny piece, and I hissed at the cut before holding it under the water until the blood stopped.

5

SABINE

TREVESTEN, ~ 500 YEARS AGO

Sabine watched from the window of the tiny house she'd commandeered. She'd paid the occupants handsomely. Right now, they were likely enjoying oysters on the beach.

She let her eyes slide to Connery beside her. He stood with his feet planted in a battle stance, hands near his weapons. He was prepared for a fight, but if everything went to plan, there'd be none. There was no moon, and velvety darkness filled the streets. The male who called himself only 'Jack' had planned well. But there was enough light in the small room that she could see Connery's face. She'd know it even if she couldn't see it.

Two weeks after her rishival, the Allmother had blessed them with a mating bond. He would love and support her through all their long lives.

Despite the stress of this evening, and the weeks leading up to it, she let herself indulge in a brief fantasy. She imagined what it would be like to have him all to herself on one of the many islands off Trevesten's coast. How wonderful it would feel to have him massage sweet-smelling oil into her skin after baking in the sun all day. He noticed her glance and gave her a questioning look.

His voice sounded in her mind, another indicator of the strength of their bond. "Everything okay?"

Tension twisted in her gut, the fantasy evaporating in an instant. "Yes. Fine. Do you think he'll be on time, or will he make me wait?"

Connery's eyes found the window again, sifting through the dark shapes to see the city he knew so well. "He'll make us wait until he thinks it's safe."

Sabine repressed an exasperated sigh. She wanted her sister back now. She also wanted to see her plan work.

Jack had demanded two thousand gold pieces in exchange for the location of her sister, Morgan. Sabine had known there was something wrong when Morgan still hadn't appeared a year after her death. It wasn't always precise. She knew someone who hadn't appeared again for three years after their death. The fae considered the continuation of their people to be of utmost importance. The crown gave great incentives for females who had lots of children. Because if there were no children, then those fae who had not yet had their final life could not return.

She snuck another look at Connery. Any children they had would be nyssar. Others could also produce nyssar, but for mates, it was guaranteed.

There were hundreds of royal families, but Sabine's had ruled Trevesten for millennia. When anyone gave birth to a child with a royal tattoo, they were required to inform the royal's family. The family that bore Morgan would have seen the circle with an arrow through it and known they were caring for the Princess of Trevesten. Sixteen months after Morgan's first death, Sabine received the ransom demand.

Anger licked up her insides. How dare he try to extort money from her? Connery had wanted to play it safe. He sometimes got a little annoyed with her scheming. But she always came out on top. Two thousand gold pieces was nothing to her, he'd pointed out. But it just infuriated Sabine even more to know Jack had likely chosen that amount for that reason. It was a trifle, easily parted with, no reason to get too invested in his capture. A tiny thrill of anticipation went up inside her. She couldn't hold back her grin.

"Sabine," a low growl split the silence in the room. She turned to see Connery's face, alive with apprehension. "What have you done?"

"Nothing." She wiped any expression from her face. Connery never needed to find out.

Movement down below captured their attention. Jack was on time. They'd left the gold, as directed, in a flowerpot hanging outside a cafe. The pot was one of many hanging from a large outdoor patio. It was a clever choice. There were multiple avenues of escape, some of which led into the forest, others that led to the harbor. Jack had specified that Morgan's location would appear in a flowerpot once 'his associate' had safely retrieved the money. If he saw any guards, tails, or anything suspicious of any kind, the pot containing her location would remain empty.

Sabine's guards had searched every pot before they placed the gold, but nothing had been out of the ordinary. She'd requested proof that Jack truly knew of Morgan's whereabouts. He'd sent a lock of her hair. After the healers had tested it and shown it to be true, Sabine's need for vengeance had only grown. He'd cut her beautiful hair! Connery had calmly pointed out that it was the safest form of proof, but Sabine heard nothing over the roar in her ears. The beast inside her brayed for his blood.

Claws extended now from her fingertips as she leaned over the windowsill, trying to catch the movement again. Connery pulled out a spyglass that worked in the dark, scanning the patio and surrounding streets. But there was no need for squinting, a male ambled up the street, bold as brass. He even sang a little tune as he crossed over to the patio. He stumbled a bit and fell over the fence surrounding the patio, making an excessive amount of noise. The pots he'd upset swung back and forth, hitting one another and causing a small waterfall of flowers.

Sabine didn't like it.

The male pulled himself to his feet and leaned on the fence for a bit, catching his breath. Finally, he lurched toward the pot with the money and pulled out the sack. He held it triumphantly in the air. "Oh ho! Sneaky bastard was telling the truth." He promptly dumped the gold into a sack of his own, tossing the original aside.

Sabine held her breath, frozen. Beside her, Connery's mouth was agape. All this secrecy and darkness and Jack had sent this buffoon to collect the money? The buffoon in question climbed back over the fence, ignoring the very obvious opening on the other side, clutching the money to his chest. He wandered back in the same direction he came, this time singing louder. Halfway down the street, somebody poked their head out and told him to shut up. He merely chuckled and continued on his way.

Once he was completely out of sight, Sabine and Connery wasted no time. They both leapt from the window of the home and raced over to the flowerpots. Each of them stood on one side, waiting.

It was over an hour before one pot made the telltale snicking sound of a message appearing. Sabine got there first. She tore open the note.

Morgan is in the care of Ms. Lucy Bligh.
Lucy is a simple fae, go easy on her.
Jack

Sabine supposed it was too much to ask that a lowlife like Jack give her an actual address, but they'd easily find Ms. Bligh. She'd have Antonio track her down tonight.

There was another snicking sound, and a note appeared out of the air. Connery caught it, but she snatched it from his hands, hoping it contained what she wanted. She'd deal with the look of suspicion on Connery's face later.

The entire street was alight when Sabine and Connery arrived. A dozen guards surrounded the location where Jack had brought her gold. Except it wasn't gold. Jack had chosen gold because it resisted all magical enchantments. So she'd spelled a bunch of fake coins instead. It had been difficult. They had to have the same weight and the same look, of course. But she'd also had to layer a tracking spell on top. Either spell would fade eventually. Without knowing how long it would take for Jack to take possession, it was a gamble.

But he was here. The male who'd dared to keep Morgan from her. Sabine was alight with the anticipation of seeing her guards march him out of the house. She wanted to see the look on his face when he saw her. When he realized how stupid he was to have challenged his queen. Sabine and Connery stood back. As queen, especially without Morgan secure in the palace, it would be folly to wade into the fight herself. But her claws were back, itching to be used.

A window shattered as a guard flew through it. She rolled for a bit before laying immovable on the stone street. Another guard retreated from inside, his hands covering his eyes in pain.

A figure appeared on the roof. Jack's eyes met Sabine's, and he shook his head at her like she was a child who'd disappointed him. Rage coursed through her veins at his patronizing expression. He sprang from the rooftop, nimbly running from house to house. The guards gave chase,

several of them following his path and the others swarming the surrounding streets.

"I think not," Sabine growled as she sprang into her animal form. Her
bear was black and blended perfectly with the shadows as she raced after
him. Connery became the wind, rushing alongside and around Jack,
relaying the male's location to her through their mind connection.

Jack threw a small object behind him and it exploded into razor-sharp
powder. Sabine dodged, but it still sliced into her skin. She didn't pause,
she could heal herself later. Several more guards fell back, injured. Jack
tried to send throwing knives toward Connery, but in this form, he was
impossible to touch. The knives clattered loudly to the rooftops after
they sailed straight through him.

Connery was the only one not injured when Sabine at last closed her
mouth around Jack's leg.

He'd been standing with his back to her when Sabine walked into their
bedroom. The muscles of his back were tight and his hands gripped the
windowsill as he stared out into a starless night.

She knew he'd be upset that she'd kept her plan from him. If she was
perfectly honest, she wasn't sure it was even going to work until it did.
Sabine grinned inwardly. It had worked beautifully. They'd gotten her
sister out, and even if things had gotten a little dangerous, she didn't
mind some chaos.

Connery turned to look at her, and she wiped any evidence of her grin
from her face and her mind. He was calm, too calm. Shit, he was furious.
Sabine didn't think she'd ever seen him so angry, not at her, at least. There

was also something else in his eyes she didn't recognize, but it made her heart twist painfully.

"Secrets again, my love?" He was preternaturally still, as if it was taking everything he had to control himself.

Sabine couldn't feign remorse for such a successful endeavor. "You know why I had to. It was the best chance we had to catch him... and it worked." She risked a step toward him. When he didn't move away, she added a slow smile. "We won."

He said nothing, and she ventured another step, her eyes wandering over his beautiful face and down his strong body, which was still as taught as a bowstring.

He still had that strange look in his eyes, but he didn't stop her as she came toward him and ran her hands up his chest. Her fingers danced along his collarbone, making languid circles over the tattoo there—a flame with two lines through it. His breath became heavier, but still, he did not speak or wrap his arms around her.

"Do you remember our discussion," he said the words with pained emphasis, "after the trip to Eloisha? And after the one to Boralta? And again after our visit to your uncle? You promised you would stop keeping me in the dark about things. Stop telling me what I wanted to hear when you were going to do something different all along? Do you remember the way you looked at me and swore to stop treating me like just another hired soldier, an assistant to do your bidding without argument? Do you?" He raised an eyebrow at her, and the air in the room trembled.

Sabine stepped back and tossed her head in exasperation, opening her palms to him. "Yes, but..."

"And tonight, you did the same thing. We agreed to do this in the safest way possible. No traps. You had no idea where your only sister was or what was happening to her and you risked it, just so you could win. So you could prove to Jack how clever you are. The opinion of a Suka grifter meant more to you than your promise to me." His jaw hardened, and she could hear him grinding his teeth. "I'm not sure why I'm bothering to ask again, but do you not understand how that makes me feel? I'm your mate, your equal, Sabine. You treat me like a plaything."

"Connery"—she moved closer to him—"you're not my plaything, but I'll be yours tonight if you like." Sabine curved her lips into a slow grin as she laced her fingers around his neck and whispered into his ear. "Let me show you how well I can follow your instructions."

A note appeared on the dresser. Sabine frowned but released him as he immediately stepped away and picked it up.

"You're needed. Your sister is awake."

Relief crashed through her. Morgan had been out cold and no amount of assurances that the toddler was just tired from her rescue had appeased Sabine. Connery dropped the note back onto the dresser and looked at her expectantly.

Sabine sighed. "Okay...but when I come back, I'm going to make things up to you." She gave him a soft kiss on the neck, letting her breath trail down his skin. His eyes showed that familiar hunger, but he only nodded. She didn't push. He was still mad, and she had broken her promise. Perhaps he'd gain some perspective while she tended to her sister.

Sabine walked down the hall to her room, and as she opened the door, she tried to identify what she'd seen in Connery's eyes.

Morgan raised her head as Sabine came in, a toothy smile breaking across her cherubic face. The returning smile that formed on Sabine's face turned into a frown. Her hand stalled on the doorknob.

It was sadness.

"Sorry, give me a minute, Morgan." Sabine didn't bother shutting the door. She rushed back to their room.

It was empty.

A note lay on her pillow.

You know why I had to

C

"Connery!" she yelled into his mind and aloud, "Connery!" But there was no response in her mind, and in the room, only silence.

6

LIM

LASHIA, PRESENT DAY

On Tuesday, I found myself west of town, in the largest expanse of swamp. I was in a small boat I had built for this purpose. It had long, curved wooden slats on the bottom, which made it easy for me to pull it across the sandbars in between each pool of water.

The chattering of tiny insects filled my ears as I leisurely rowed my boat over to a small leather ball floating on top of the water. I put the ball into the boat and began pulling the rope attached to it, finally bringing up a metal cage. Inside, three small crustaceans scuttled around, drawn to the trap by a trout head. They joined the others I had collected in a small bucket, along with a few more trout heads to assuage my guilt, as I continued on to the next buoy. One after the other, I pulled up the buoys, emptied the trap, refilled it with bait. Occasionally, I jumped out of the boat to pick up and catalog any flora, fish, or shells I'd not seen before.

I examined a palm-sized mollusk. It resembled an oyster in shape but was smooth with a faintly pink exterior. Grabbing my knife, I cracked it open, but no pearl. No flesh either, just glittering pink sand. I popped the shell in my bag and carried on.

After my fifth trap, I pulled my boat onto another sandbar and sat down to take a break, fanning myself with my overly large straw hat. A blurry film of clouds covered the sun. The heat had abated a little. Fall was coming, but taking its time as usual. I took a drink from my canteen. The cool water was delicious after hours of sweaty work. The smell of salty water and ripe fish permeated the damp air. I pulled a bit of dried beef out of my bag and a few small fruits and chewed on them while I watched the horizon.

The swamps were endless. There was nothing else to the west or the south. If I squinted, I could make out some shapes to the north, but whatever it was, it was either very tiny or very far away. I wondered how long it would take to get out of the swamps if I headed west or if, indeed, I ever would. Perhaps I would just end up in the ocean.

I'd been to the ocean in the east once, when I was in Eudora. A few of us had gone and camped on the beach. The waves were loud and exciting and I could easily picture how the water had boiled and stormed and flooded the coasts until most everything was underwater. The swamps didn't feel safe exactly, but I knew them. I felt comfortable here on my own, wading through all the secret shallow water.

Something winked in the sand about fifty feet away. I brushed off my dress and shoved the last piece of fruit in my mouth as I stood and wandered over. There was a lot of treasure still to be found. Entire cities had been abandoned, covered in ice or mud, but as the seasons retreated to something survivable, scavenging became a way of life. Eudora was founded in its location mainly because of the enormous library they had found there. It was almost entirely underground, but the former guardians had the foresight to take the books off the shelves and store them in fire and waterproof boxes.

The object was metal, silver maybe. I dug around it carefully and pulled it out. It was... a mask? No, a plate. I brushed off more of the sand with my sleeves. It was about the size of my face and had lovely, intricate designs etched into the surface. Flipping it over, I could see similar designs on the bottom. My skin flushed. Glancing up at the misty sun, I reminded myself that I'd been out here for hours. I'd likely not eaten or drank enough, or both. Putting the plate into my pack, I went back to the boat.

By the time I reached home, I was feeling much better. For good measure, though, I drank several glasses of water and made myself a sandwich—some cured pork and greens with pickled onions.

After I unpacked my bag, I inspected the plate again, rolling it around in my hands before placing it on my dresser. It was oddly familiar, like a toy I'd lost or a book I'd read before.

The shower felt wonderful on my dry skin. As I stepped out of the bathroom, something made me do a double-take in my mirror. I swiped the steam aside with my hand. For a moment, I could swear something was off, but couldn't put my finger on it. My skin had gotten some color. Perhaps that was it. The sunburn made my freckles stand out and my cuffs a little paler.

Brax sat up to attention. His ears twitched and turned, listening. My father's voice called up at me from the bottom of the stairs.

"What is it?" I yelled, drying my hair with a towel.

"It's Sasha, she's gone into labor!"

I threw on some clothes and raced outside. We climbed into my father's wagon, and he urged the animals on as fast as they could go.

Indie's practice included a reception area, her office, an operating and delivery room, four hospital rooms, and the family room. When we arrived, my mother and Leo were already there. Leo paced back and forth, his fingers interlocked behind his head. His hands came down to grip my shoulders when I wrapped my arms around him.

Sasha was Leo's half-sister, born to a Jinn woman Emir had dated before he'd met Leo's mother. The siblings were close, having bonded over the unreliable people in their lives. Sasha's mother left when Sasha was two. We couldn't prove it, but strongly suspected Sydney's influence. Leo's mother had run off with a merchant from one of the northern boroughs when Leo was a teenager. The man who'd gotten Sasha pregnant had bolted the minute she'd told him about the baby.

Simon and Indie had made this room a soothing place, filling it with comfortable chairs and worn rugs. There were wooden puzzles on the walls to keep one distracted and a play area in the corner for younger children. She and Simon had done so much to keep it from being sterile and scary. The room had a large internal window that was currently covered with gray curtains. When opened from the other side, it would reveal the delivery room. Leo's eyes continued to dart to the curtains at every sound.

"How long?" I asked. I could tell Leo wanted to continue his pacing, but he settled for kneading my shoulders. It was a little painful, but I said nothing.

"Her water broke a few hours ago," my mother replied from where she sat at the table, knitting. Hours? I knew it could take time to have a baby, but surely this was excessive.

Sasha screamed, and we froze. We could hear her yelling in pain, Indie and Simon murmuring to her. Meanwhile, my father was calmly leaning back in his chair.

"Did someone tell Emir?" My eyes snapped to Leo.

"She asked me not to," Leo said, blowing out a breath. I could understand that. Emir would either bring more panic or try to turn the whole thing into a party. Either way, he'd be chaos Sasha didn't need right now.

I stepped away from Leo, wringing my hands while he resumed his pacing. "How are you sitting there so calm?" I demanded of my father, watching him twirl his hat slowly in his hands.

"She's having a baby, not a dragon." He gave me a comforting smile. "Besides, don't you want this kid to be born into a world of hope and excitement? Instead of these"—he motioned at me and Leo—"anxious faces?" Sasha screamed again, and I couldn't muster hope or excitement.

A sick feeling settled in my stomach, and I paced a bit myself. Leo sat down. Then stood up. Then I sat down. My parents shared a look when I got up again.

Finally, after another half an hour, Sasha's screaming stopped. My mother stopped knitting, my father stopped twirling. There was complete silence.

A cry went up in the other room. It was the cry of a child with two very healthy lungs. The four of us released a collective breath, and my father dabbed his eyes with a handkerchief. He and my mother rose and gave Leo their congratulations. I locked eyes with Leo as we reached for one another. His arms wrapped around me, and his head briefly dipped into the curve of my neck before he bounced back at the sound of Simon opening the door.

Simon gave us all a big smile as he wiped down his hands with alcohol. "Congratulations, Leo! You've got a beautiful niece! Nearly nine pounds!"

Leo whooped. The rest of us clapped and cheered. My father threw his hat into the air and caught it.

"How is Sasha?" I said, my wide smile almost hurting my face.

"Mom and baby are both doing great. Indie is just doing the baby's health tests. Give us a second to clean up and I'll open it up for viewing."

We waited another half an hour, all of us immediately cheerful and continuing a discussion we'd all had before about possible names. Simon pulled open the curtains. Sasha lay on the bed, holding a tiny baby girl with a gentle feathering of light brown hair. Sasha's face was red but beaming. The baby seemingly spent all her energy being born and was now fast asleep.

A little while later, Indie came out. She looked exhausted, too. Her coppery skin was damp with perspiration, but she wore a beautiful grin.

"Congratulations again, Leo. Sasha will stay here for the next few days. Me, Simon, and my nurses will look after her and the baby to make sure everything is good before she can go home. She'll need some help. Is she staying with you?"

Leo's forehead wrinkled. "Staying with me? No, I don't think that's what she was going to do. Is that what she said?" Leo's constant movement paused.

"Don't worry, little brother," Sasha said as Simon wheeled her down the hall. She wore a fluffy blue robe and slippers and held the baby tight against her chest. "I wasn't planning on moving in with him, but I won't be on my own. Celeste will be with me. She's going to help me raise her." Sasha jutted her chin a little in pride. I'd suspected there might be something between her and the curvy blond but figured she'd tell us when she was ready.

Leo looked visibly relieved. "I would have let you move in, you know—I just didn't think." He ran his hand through his hair, grimacing. Sasha just shook her head and returned her gaze to her gorgeous little girl.

My parents stepped over to offer their congratulations and some baby clothes and things they had stored away. It hurt that they had not chosen to save them for me. But, considering there was very little chance I would need them until well after Sasha was done with them, I let it go. Indie flashed me a look that said she knew exactly what I was thinking.

I gave her a wan smile and asked, "Does she have a name?" We all stared at the little scrunched face, her mouth moving as she slept.

"I think so. I'm feeling all powerful now without a husband's opinion to worry about—trying not to let it go to my head." We laughed. "I think I'll call her Priya." There was much cooing and clapping as we huddled around them both.

"We need to let Mom get some rest, as Priya is going to want to eat again soon," Indie said, diplomatically kicking us out. She looked happy and beautiful but noticeably relieved. I wondered how difficult this birth had really been. She gave Simon, who had just appeared again from the back, a look of pure love and contentment. He embraced his wife and kissed her on the head.

"I'll be back shortly." He glanced over at Sasha. "Do you want me to wake you if you're sleeping?"

"Yes, please, I want to see." She pulled her robe tighter. The atmosphere in the room immediately chilled and a strained silence replaced our previous merriment.

7

LIM

LASHIA, PRESENT DAY

Leo's eyebrows lifted. "Oh, that fast?" His gaze was open, unaware of the shift in the rest of us.

"Yep. Indie delivered another infant early this morning. When Sasha went into labor, we alerted the registrars. They asked to do them both together." Simon didn't wait for a response. He kissed his wife and left out the front door.

My eyes darted to Indie, offering her a smile to break the tension. "Congratulations on another successful delivery, Dr. Kyo. Was it a boy or a girl?"

Indie couldn't hide the pride in her voice, although she waved her hand like it was no big deal. "A boy, eight pounds, three ounces."

We lovingly surged toward Sasha and Priya as we all made to say our goodbyes. "We'll come and see you again tomorrow, Sasha," I said. "I'll bring you some food, only stuff you can eat with one hand." She laughed. Her eyes crinkled into a smile, but I could see the slight wariness behind it now that the registration was imminent.

We gave our hugs to Sasha and more adoring looks to Priya. My parents let Sasha know they would bring the baby things directly to her house in a few days. Leo, however, didn't move to leave. He was still bouncing with energy.

"Can I stay? I'd like to see," he asked Indie. Indie looked at Sasha in question.

"I don't know Leo." She held Priya tighter to her chest, and the wariness appeared in full force. She knew Leo was only curious. After a moment, she shrugged.

Indie put her hands on the wheelchair handles and narrowed her eyes at Leo. "She's going to rest. Afterward, once they're here, she can decide if she wants you in the room or not. But it will be her decision. You will not do anything to threaten the comfort or health of Priya, your sister, the other family, or the safety of this practice, understood?" I'd never heard Indie speak to anyone like that. And yet, it sounded like she'd had to say it several times before. The look on her face said she was deadly serious, and Leo quickly nodded.

"Whoa! Aye-Aye Captain," Leo gave his sister and Indie an incredulous smile, "I've just never seen it. You won't even know I'm here." He mimed buttoning his lips.

Indie arched an eyebrow but said nothing as she wheeled Sasha away to her well-deserved rest.

"Can we give you a ride, Calimea?" my father asked.

"No, I'll stay. Thank you." I'm not sure why Leo's interest in the registration bothered me. Who wouldn't want to see the only allowed magic?

After my parents had left, I turned to Leo. "Hey, they won't be here for a while and we haven't eaten. Why don't we go across the street and get something? We'll be able to see them from the window." I motioned to a small café across the road. Leo grinned and swung an arm around my shoulder, an arm he removed as soon as we were outside.

We sat down at a sidewalk table with a good view of Indie's office. I ran my finger longingly down the thick paper menus. Emir would never spring for paper menus. The cost was too exorbitant. I made do with our chalk slates. Besides, with Emir's inconsistent shopping habits, our menu was too small and varied. More often than not, we just told the customers what was available.

"What do you think she could do? If they didn't cuff her?" Leo had finished his fish pie and was drinking a beer, his eyes thoughtful. I was picking at the rest of my stew. It wasn't bad, it just wasn't good. It didn't taste like much of anything. I didn't look up at him.

"I don't know." I kept my voice down. Leo didn't understand how dangerous a conversation like this could be. When we were in school, we'd get punished for even talking about what powers we might have. "I mean, do you think there's even any left?" I put my fork down and signaled the server. Perhaps cheese could save this meal.

Leo turned to me, eyebrows raised. He thankfully waited until I finished speaking to the server, his head cocked. "What do you mean, 'is there any left'?"

I puffed out my cheeks, thinking. "The theory is that we evolved magic because our tiny human brains couldn't cope with not being able to do all the things technology once made us capable of. We have technology again, albeit not anywhere near what we had before." I gestured at a passing bus. It was a patchwork of scrap metal and was probably being held together by spit and willpower, but it was one of a dozen we had in Lashia. "Don't you think that might have an effect?"

Leo's eyes looked away, unfocused, as he considered my comments. "Hmmm," he said. "I guess that makes sense." He shrugged, unbothered.

I hoped it was the end of that discussion when the server appeared. She dropped a small cheese plate in front of me, her yellow cuffs contrasting sharply with her dark skin. I stabbed a small piece of hard goat's cheese and shoved it into my mouth.

"Do you think"—Leo tapped his bottle thoughtfully against his chin—"if none of you really have any magic anymore, we could remove everyone's cuffs?"

My eyes widened before cutting to the couple who'd passed by our table. I gave them a polite smile. When they were gone, I leaned across the small table. "Leo, for stars' sake, keep your voice down."

"What? Why?" Leo whispered as he brought his head close to mine, looking around in confusion.

"Just...do you mind if we have this discussion some other time, not when we're sitting on a sidewalk? I mean, you won't even put your arm around me in public." I silently added, 'let alone much else,' at the end of that sentence. Pursing my lips at him, I took a grim satisfaction from the look of sheepishness that crossed his face. "So clearly, you have some idea why."

A surprising amount of anger sparked inside me, pushing at my skin. I could feel the color rising in my chest. All of this was so stupid. We were all just playing pretend, pretend differences, pretend magic. The edges of my fork dug into my palm as I looked away from him.

Once, Indie was holding a Jinn baby for the registration—the birth had been hard on the mother—and she'd felt something move slightly beneath the child's skin, just a ripple, just for a moment before they put the cuffs on. I'd been in awe when she told me later. Looking back, it had probably been nothing. Just wishful thinking that Jinns used to make ourselves feel special, and Tals used to justify treating us this way.

"Calimea?" Leo said softly, "I'm—"

"Leo!" His head whipped around to where I had spotted the registrars just as they walked into Indie's.

We jumped up from the table. Leo threw some money down, and we hurried across the street. Upon entering the family room, we found three men silently waiting. Indie came out from the back to see the five of us awkwardly staring at one another.

Two of the men wore identical black suits. Their faces were entirely devoid of expression. The other man was tall and muscled. He had dark eyes, bronze skin, and a full mouth held in a soft smile. He wore short sleeves, revealing his green cuffs, unique to registrars because they alone could use magic. I had never seen the cuffing performed before. When Keen was born, I stayed with Indie, and when Ayla was born, I stayed home with Keen. I'd seen the registrars around town, of course, usually escorted by two accompanists like these. Most people avoided interacting with them outside the registration.

Another moment and Simon came out not with Sasha, but with a young woman with dark blond hair and delicate features. She was wearing a robe cinched tightly around her waist and holding a baby bundled in a soft cream blanket. A man with inky black hair and a hard glint in his eyes, presumably the father, stood beside her. Simon left and returned promptly with Sasha and Priya, who was wrapped in a white blanket with blue flowers.

Indie's voice was strong and clear as she said, "Good evening. I am Dr. Indira Kyo. This is my nurse, Simon Kyo. These are the Martins and their guests"—she gestured to Sasha, Priya and then to Leo and I—"and the Whitmores." She gestured to the other family.

The registrar stepped forward and, in a gentle voice, introduced himself. "Hello, my name is Chiwel, and this is Bill and Dan." He pointed to each of the men with him and then paused. "Or maybe this is Dan and this is Bill. I'm not sure, honestly they look exactly alike."

Bill and Dan said nothing at this attempt to break the tension. I'd never seen faces more blank. The rest of us gave small smiles or nods, but the Whitmore man clenched his jaw and tightly gripped the back of his wife's wheelchair. Indie gave Chiwel several drops of alcohol to rub on his hands, and he continued on, unperturbed. "Can you please unwrap the children so I can see their arms?"

The mothers removed the children's limbs from the warmth of their wrappings. Priya flexed her impossibly small fingers and, for a moment, I considered Leo's question. What was she capable of right now?

The Whitmore man made a spitting noise and my head snapped up. All of us were looking at him now except for his wife, who didn't take her eyes off her baby boy. Without thinking, I took a small step in front of Sasha and Priya.

"You're one of us," he snapped at Chiwel. "Don't you ever get tired of being a traitor? Marking one of your own for no good reason?" The rest of us sucked in a breath. Even Leo gave a little 'tch' at the man's outburst. Chiwel only gave the man a dismissive glance before returning his attention to the children. Boldly, he approached the Whitmore boy first.

"He won't feel a thing," Chiwel said softly to his mother. He carefully took the boy's hands in his own, his large thumb pressed gently into the child's palm. A flare of light went up from the registrar's fingers, and for a moment, I didn't breathe.

Indie presumably saw this all the time, but her face held the same amount of wonder as mine. Tears gathered at the corners of my eyes and a lump formed in my throat.

Real magic.

As the light dimmed, two yellow bands appeared on the boy's forearms. I'd known the minute the father had made his spiteful comment to Chiwel that they were Tals. Registrars and accompanists were always Tals. The government didn't trust Jinns with any magic. They could somehow provide this specific ability to select Tals so they could perform the registration.

Bill or Dan stepped across and handed the woman a piece of paper before handing an identical one to Indie. The man snatched the paper before his wife could touch it, although I noticed she didn't even raise her hand to try. He promptly wheeled her back to her room.

Chiwel then turned to Sasha. Her breathing was a little unsteady. Beside me, I could feel Leo's excited energy. Priya was fast asleep, unaware of the tension lingering around her. Chiwel reached out and again reminded us that Priya wouldn't feel anything before cradling her hands, just as he'd done with the Whitmore boy. But this time, when the light dimmed from his fingers, two glowing blue bands appeared. Leo exhaled, an awed smile in the sound. Chiwel gave Sasha a small nod. Bill or Dan was there again with the paperwork, and only a moment later, Simon wheeled them both back to her room.

"Thank you," Indie said. She tucked away the documentation that would allow her to maintain her medical license. It was proof of her compliance with the rules that had existed to keep the peace for hundreds of years. Chiwel only nodded. As he passed me, his eyes slid to mine, and then down to my own cuffs. His brow furrowed slightly, but he said nothing as he walked out.

8

ASRA

TREVESTEN, ~ 500 YEARS AGO

"Will it still work if he's dead?" Solvan toed the male's boot, his body still and silent. Asra didn't really think the other fae had hit him that hard. He went down like an anchor. They'd carried him back here, where he now lay in a rather ungraceful position on her floor.

"He's not dead," Brigid replied, sliding a knife from her waist. She approached him cautiously. Beside her, Elwin tensed, his hands going to his own weapons. Brigid pushed the sharp point of her knife into the male's exposed shoulder. Other than a small trickle of blood, he didn't react. She reached over and put her fingers on his neck. "Still beating. Slower than Solvan in the morning, but beating."

"You know it." Solvan pretended to preen in front of a mirror, and Brigid laughed.

Asra rifled through the man's coat. The little packet of glittering green powder she found explained his sorry state and poor reflexes. "We'll need to worry more about whether it still works with this shit going through his veins." Asra tossed the substance to Elwin, who caught it in one hand.

"My, my, what would the queen say?" Elwin held the packet up to the light, examining it. It practically glowed, a siren song to those looking for an expensive high. "Are the royals so bored with all their wealth and power, they need to resort to this?" Elwin made a chiding noise and shook his head at the still-unconscious male.

"Indeed," Asra agreed, frowning. "But if he's out here, as far as one can be from the palace, I'm guessing he's trying to avoid notice. That, and his little habit, should very much work to our advantage." Asra caught the powder as Elwin tossed it back and pocketed it. She wondered how far gone he was on hush. He might be their only shot. It was his business what he put in his body. As long as he was clean when she took his blood.

"I'll take first watch. You three go have fun."

"Oh well, if you're sure," Brigid said in phony hesitancy. A popular minstrel was performing at their favorite tavern. The three of them bolted from the room without another word.

Asra tied the male to the bedpost and settled into an armchair. She pulled out a book but kept one eye on the motionless figure. Solvan lifted the male's coat from the table last night while he'd been involved in a very heated game of cards. His shirt was gone, ripped from him in the tussle, which gave her an excellent view of his chest.

Her eyes trailed over the muscles, the various freckles and scars that marred his otherwise smooth skin. She settled on what she valued most about him and his chest, the tattoo just below his collarbone. A flame with two lines through it. As a royal, that tattoo would follow him through all seven of his lives and guarantee they were filled with the finest Trevesten had to offer. But to her, that indelible mark meant a significant bit of gold. They probably wouldn't even have to steal it this time.

Asra's eyes traveled down from his chiseled face to his expensive boots. "What in the stars are you doing here, anyway?" Asra murmured to herself as she watched him.

They'd been trying to find someone for months now. Kidnapping was out of the question. Only a few royals deigned to set foot in Oderon, and it had been proving impossible to find one willing to help a group of criminals like them. They needed someone desperate. They'd scoured the gossip rags, hoping someone's scandal would bring them low enough that Asra might approach them. When they began considering inventing such a scandal themselves, this male suddenly appeared out of nowhere.

A little while later, Asra had dozed off. There was a subtle change in the air and she quickly twisted, knocking the now awakened male onto his back. She drew her blade before he could even blink, holding it to his throat as she sat astride him.

"Who are you?" His voice was more annoyed than afraid.

"I'm the person who saved your ass from being beaten to a pulp by four disgruntled card players who thought they'd found an easy mark." Not technically true. They ran when he'd gone down, but a white lie was the least of her crimes.

His face paled, and his head fell back, eyes squeezed shut in pain. "If I promise not to try anything, would you mind getting off me? I feel quite ill."

Asra stood up, but kept her knife out. He struggled up before immediately collapsing back onto the bed, elbows on his knees and head in his hands. She strolled over to the carafe on the dresser and poured him a glass of water. She could have also mixed in the healing elixir but figured she'd rather have him a little off his game for this discussion. Asra still wasn't sure how she would convince him to help without exposing them all and ending up arrested.

She didn't recognize him from the society pages or any of the birth or rishival announcements. He might have been a nyssar. Or he might have just been one of the many royal families she didn't know or care about. It wasn't necessary to keep up with the goings on at court when you were a thief and had no children. He sipped the water gingerly while she waited. She was excellent at waiting.

Finally, he looked up at her. His eyes were bloodshot and hollow. "Well? Are you going to tell me who you are?" Asra arched an eyebrow at him, and he let out a breath. "Deepest apologies. My name is Connery. It is wonderful to make your acquaintance. With whom do I have the pleasure of speaking?"

She gave him a sly smile, the kind she usually gave to smug bastards before helping herself to their valuables. "*Lord* Connery?"

He shook his head. "Oh, that's your game? Ransom?" He abruptly stood from the bed and walked to the dresser. He poured himself another glass of water, watching her as he swallowed it. She didn't miss it, the way his eye twitched when he said 'ransom.' This was a fae who definitely didn't want anyone to know where he was.

She pulled out the elixir and tossed it to him. As he caught it, a look of eagerness crossed his face before being replaced by disappointment. He was expecting something else. He recovered quickly, uncorking it and downing the entire bottle. At her raised eyebrows, he said, "I assume if you'd wanted me dead, you would have done it last night."

She tipped her head to him. The color was returning to his face, and he'd managed to say that last sentence without looking like each word was causing him physical pain. "My name is Asra."

"Pleasure." He gave her a mocking bow. "Asra, do you happen to know what has become of my shirt?" There was no flirtation in his voice, no attempt to question whether she'd removed it or he'd willingly removed it for her.

"You were relieved of it during your friendly game." She spun the knife in her hand. No magic, just skill, and his eyes flicked to it, assessing.

He let out another sigh. "Not one for polite conversation, are you? Not that I wish to deepen our acquaintance too much, but you could be slightly more forthcoming." He poured some of the water from the carafe into a small basin and splashed it on himself, a few droplets trickling down his chest.

She let him see her eyes as they wandered obviously down his body. His face hardened. Touchy.

"I can get you another shirt. But actually, I am interested in getting to know you a little better. Specifically, why a fae like yourself"—she used her knife to motion to his tattoo—"is brawling in a tavern in Oderon. Gambling debts? Running away from an arranged marriage?"

At that, he balked and his eyes turned stormy. Bullseye.

She waved a hand. "On second thought, I don't really care, but it makes me think you're here because you don't want to be found, and I wondered whether I might be of some assistance there." His scowl deepened, but his silence said he was curious.

"How about some breakfast?" she asked cheerfully.

His face didn't soften. "First, I can get my own shirt from my own room. Second, I'll not be sharing any food with you until you give me back my belongings." His eyes cut to his coat hanging on the back of her armchair.

"Of course, Lord Connery," she said in a sickly, ingratiating tone. She grabbed the coat while keeping her eyes on his and tossed it to him.

Connery immediately rifled through the pockets, glaring at her when he found them empty. "Where is it?" he gritted out.

"You know that stuff won't just kill you? It'll make you stupid." His eyes were lethal, and she let out a long sigh. "I'll make you a deal. You agree to sit with me and my crew and hear our proposal, which will include you helping us in exchange for us helping to hide you from whatever it is you're so desperately trying to avoid. If you decline our proposal, you agree not to say anything to anyone about us or what we've discussed. We'll agree to never mention having seen you and I'll give you back the hush."

Connery looked at her, running through the words in his head, looking for traps. "Agreed." He held out his hand, and Asra shook it. Sparks passed through their skin as the power sealed their bargain.

Solvan sat on the kitchen counter while Brigid and Elwin were curled together on one of the table's benches. Asra carefully unrolled the map onto the scarred kitchen table. Brigid and Elwin placed various items on the corners to hold it flat.

The map was a work of art. Asra had stolen it over twenty years ago from a ship headed to Eloisha. It had seven layers, each with a colorful illustration of the 'known' worlds. Not all were truly known because the fae in their world, Malan, the third layer, had only returned from visits to three others: Kysalt, first; Harena, the second; and Tulo, seventh.

Sverresen's illustration was predictably vague. Scholars could prove there were seven worlds and that they layered on top of one another like the map showed. Each world had a distinct climate and magical signature. After that, everything got murkier. Folktales and legends formed the basis of the rest of the knowledge about Laloten, fourth, Mokame, fifth, and Sverresen.

Asra had spent years gathering those stories, comparing them against one another, sifting for the truth. The four of them had been everywhere, interviewing fae who specialized in traveling by portals, storytellers, and the wisest scholars. Asra had notebooks filled with every detail and she was now confident that they knew as much as they were ever going to about Sverresen. A world purportedly filled with wild magic.

Now, they were gathering the ingredients she would need to create a kunli, a device to open a portal between the worlds. The male who possessed one of those ingredients stared at the map, lips pushed to one side and eyebrows knitted in concentration. He'd been remarkably attentive as she'd summarized all of their hard work.

"Bet you've never seen one like that?" Solvan said from the counter-top. He had one of his bladed stars out and spun it dangerously in his palm.

Connery's eyes darted to Solvan, at his star, and then back to the map. "No, never one so beautifully rendered." His fingers reverently touched the thin, almost transparent pages.

Asra flipped to Malan, pushed aside the fourth and fifth layers, and placed it on top of Sverresen.

"These," she said, pointing to four different places in Malan, "are the places we believe are the best entry points to Sverresen. We need locations that have some element of untapped power. The kunli will draw on that power, as well as the power we imbue within it, to transport us through the layers between, and into, Sverresen."

Connery nodded and gave them all a frank appraisal.

Asra was holding her breath. They only needed a little blood from him, and she'd be one step closer to completing this dream that had latched onto her as a child and would not let go.

All fae had some level of ability besides the unique gifts they received after each rishival. But they didn't always need or want those gifts. Trevesten had mostly outlawed the sale and collection of magic because many of the fae who tried to do it met with disastrous results.

But Asra, she had a genuine talent for it. A place where the magic was wild and theirs for the taking was just her sort of place.

"You're all insane, you know that, right?" His face gave nothing away. Her mouth quirked.

Solvan hopped off the counter. "I told you, pay up." He held out his hands to Brigid and Elwin.

"Not so fast." Brigid held up a finger.

"Yeah, Sol, he's simply stating a fact. Insanity is a requirement for this group." Elwin leaned back, his arm wrapped around Brigid.

Connery glanced briefly at the two mates and Asra was sure she saw something like anger flash in his expression.

Solvan huffed and rolled his eyes. He turned to look at Connery, hands on his hips. "Well, your lordshippieness, what's it gonna be?" Brigid grinned, and Elwin barked a laugh. A 'shippie' was what they called the more ignorant merchants and royals who hired boats in Oderon. So named because they knew nothing about the different names and types of vessels or which would be suitable for their purposes, and could therefore be grossly oversold.

Connery frowned, and the air in the room shifted. He was definitely going to have to get used to being treated like a Suka and not a royal. Asra suspected nobody had ever referred to him as anything but his proper title, said with reverence and respect.

She said nothing but waited. A warm, furry body wound its way through her legs under the table. One of Yas' cats.

"So I give you my blood. You use it to build a kunli and sail off into the sunset? Where does that leave me? Aren't I supposed to get something out of this?"

"It will take us at least two years, maybe longer, to gather the rest of the ingredients for the kunli and supplies for the trip. During that time, I'll let you live here, hidden from whatever it is you're running from. We're very adept at keeping out of sight. You might even learn something. And," she fished the glittering packet of hush from her pocket, "we won't judge you for your special hobbies."

Connery's eyes widened in anger, and he reached for the packet. Asra opened her palms and revealed her empty hands. Elwin shook the packet before tossing it to Solvan. Connery lunged at him, but Solvan didn't have it anymore. Brigid gave him a feline smile as she deftly flipped the packet from finger to finger.

Connery's face heated. "That is mine," he snapped.

The fae were always expecting magic, so it often paid not to use it at all. Over the years, they'd found their skills at sleight of hand nearly as valuable as their power.

"As long as you're clean when you give me your blood." She waved an empty hand in front of Connery before reaching forward and plucking the hush from his pocket. She held out the packet to him. He snatched it and glared. "Think about it. We could be very good for you."

9

LIM

LASHIA, PRESENT DAY

It was late, the house quiet, my family all sleeping soundly. I grabbed a glass of wine and a plate I'd made myself of leftovers: a roll, some cheese, a small piece of chicken, the last scoop of sauteed greens. Brax followed me upstairs, leaning against me in what he pretended was affection but was really an attempt to upset my balance and make me drop my food. His head came up to my elbow, and he rubbed against it, practically smirking at me. Keen mumbled in his sleep as I passed his room.

I got to my room without donating any of my food to Brax's mouth and set my plate down in triumph. Too triumphantly, apparently, as a large crack appeared right down the center. The food slid toward the center and I glanced around for something else I could use. I swear Brax laughed—hoping I would go back downstairs, leaving the food unguarded.

"Not a chance, you dirty thief." I grabbed the silver plate from the dresser and carefully transferred all the food onto it. Brax huffed sullenly and began cleaning himself.

Balancing the plate on the covers over my stomach, I nibbled on my odd assortment of food. I willed the wine to calm my agitated mind as my thoughts bounced between Leo, Sasha and Priya, and the restaurant.

I'd gone to see Sasha, bringing her enough food to last a week. My mother assured me that nursing women must be fed at all times or the baby will take all their nutrients and leave them malnourished. "And downright cranky," my father had chuckled under his breath.

I'd held Priya, inhaling her new baby scent, and thought about what Leo had said at the cafe. The registrars had magic somehow, but only enough to give us all our cuffs. Did the government ever test any of us? Just to see if we still had any power at all? And what if it turned out we didn't?

And even though I'd never used my power and would never get the chance, the thought made me sad.

There was a crick in my neck when I awoke, as well as a slightly weird feeling. The crick in my neck I could explain. I had seemingly not moved from my original position. The plate was still sitting in the same place on my stomach, my hand having slipped nearly off of it, and Brax was securing my legs with his enormous head. I rubbed my eyes and pinched the bridge of my nose. I ran my tongue across my teeth. I'd forgotten to brush them. Gross.

Tossing the plate onto my nightstand, I stood up, displacing Brax, who didn't even open his eyes despite my rather forceful shove. Trying to give the impression of a woman who did not fall asleep with unfinished cheese on her stomach, I brushed my teeth thoroughly and braided my hair. I stared at my hair in the mirror, again contemplating whether I should cut it all off. I flipped the braid over my shoulder and froze.

The ground felt unstable beneath me. I reached out my trembling arms and stared at them—in the mirror, then back at them, then back in the mirror.

My cuffs were gone.

I rubbed my arms. Nothing, there was nothing there. My eyes cut to the silver plate, but nothing had changed about it. It still looked the same. The remnants of my dinner were gone, but I suspected that was more Brax's doing. My thoughts ran back to when I'd first gotten it, how strange I'd felt. The paleness of my cuffs after handling it. I hastily threw on a long sleeve shirt and trousers before stumbling down the stairs and out the back door.

Indie, I had to see Indie. Maybe I was just sick or something. I threw a saddle on Derek, who neighed at the early morning intrusion. Hopping on, I tapped my heels against his sides, but he remained stubbornly motionless. I tapped them again, harder this time. Nothing.

"I will give you a bucket of apples if you just move." Derek looked back at me, blinked, and lay down in his straw. I scrambled off to avoid being crushed. "You would literally die without me, you ungrateful animal." He'd always only been willing to help me to a point, and being awake this early, before being fed no less, was not that point.

I slammed my hand against his paddock. Derek responded to this by rolling over to his side and going back to sleep. "Well, clearly, my gift is not one of persuasion!" I hissed into the empty yard, reminding myself that the rest of my family was still asleep.

I'd often considered getting a bicycle but had just never bothered. I walked, took Derek, or, in really dire circumstances, I'd spring for a carriage. Taking my father's balaras wasn't an option. The entire barn would erupt with noise if I walked in.

The yard was secluded and shrouded in the early morning haze. My parents' farm backed up to a cluster of bald cypress trees. Their closest neighbor was over a mile away.

I put my hands out in front of me, feeling ridiculous. Maybe I hadn't always paid attention in history, but even I knew what the Jinns before me could do; elemental magic, mind control, changing their appearance or the appearance of others. I concentrated on that weird feeling. Did I even need my hands to do this?

First, I concentrated on the water, the dew on the leaves, the puddles among the yard, willing it to do...something. I concentrated so long and so hard my jaw hurt. Nothing. Okay, maybe not water. I snapped my fingers, hoping for sparks, but was a little afraid of starting a fire. Purely for scientific purposes, I tried to give myself a slightly nicer ass, but that also failed. I focused on the wind, the earth, the plants. I even gave animals another try, but considering my luck with Derek, it was only a half-ditch effort.

It was now nine a.m., and I was tired, hungry, and sweaty. I gave up and went back inside. Perhaps my theory was correct, perhaps magic was gone and these stupid cuffs were just ornamental bigotry.

"You okay this morning?" my father asked while the two of us ate breakfast. Upstairs, I could hear my mother trying to cajole Keen and Ayla to get ready for school.

"Fine," I mumbled around a mouthful of smoked trout and buttered toast, chewing like an insolent toddler.

"If you say so," my father said, his brown eyes giving me a look that said he'd get it out of me, eventually. I was about to just tell him when my siblings clamored downstairs, squabbling about missing homework. In the cacophony of cries for lost shoes and lunch requests, I slipped out the door and made my way to work.

I was in the kitchen cutting onions when a drop of water appeared on the cutting board. And then another. I touched the back of my hand to my face for evidence of tears but found none.

Emir shouted from upstairs. As I glanced up, I noticed a growing wet patch on the ceiling. Fat beads of water were lining up and preparing to fall onto my food. I swiftly moved everything out of the way and ran to the closet to get a bucket. Emir's shouting continued, filled with expletives.

"I'm coming, hold on!" Once I was certain the bucket was in the right place, I tore upstairs.

Emir was up to his ankles in water. It poured uncontrollably from a broken shower pipe. His face was mottled red, and I noticed an inordinate amount of sweat beading on his skin. I ran over to the access cupboard, turning off the water at the source. Emir was pulling in towels and bedsheets and anything he could to soak up the water. I ran and grabbed more towels. Any more water, and the ceiling would cave into the kitchen.

The water slowed, the last drops trickling loudly in the silence. Emir leaned on the wall, his chest heaving. He turned to face me, revealing a brutal gash on the left side of his head.

"Emir, what the hell?" I involuntarily reached out a hand to him.

"I tripped, hit the pipe." He was still short of breath. There was so much blood. It leaked down the side of his face and seeped into his shirt.

"Can you get to the chair?" I motioned to a worn armchair just outside the bathroom door. Emir turned, gripping the walls for balance, his feet squishing across the sodden floor. He collapsed into the chair and leaned his head back.

"I'm going to go get the first aid kit and send for Leo. I'll be right back." Emir didn't even nod, and I didn't like the ashen pallor of his face.

I ran downstairs and straight into Audre.

"Oof, where's the fire?" she said, clutching her shoulder.

"Emir fell. He's got a huge gash on his head. Can you get Indie right away? And Leo?"

Audre didn't even respond. She ran right back through the door and took off on her bike.

I grabbed clean towels and the first aid kit from the kitchen before running back to Emir. He placed the clean towel I gave him against his head while I fumbled with the first aid kit. He said nothing, which made me worry more than anything else. I tore open the box and found the antiseptic. Pouring some onto a rag, I gently pulled Emir's hand away and had to stifle a gasp.

My stomach lurched at the sight of the deep wound. Cleaning it before I could stop the bleeding was futile. Instead, I pressed the rag against his head and hoped to all the stars in Lashia that Indie would get here soon.

The door slammed downstairs, but it was Leo, not Indie, who appeared in the doorway. His face paled. Emir managed a weak smile for his only son.

"He said he hit his head on the shower." I tipped my head toward the bathroom. Leo's eyes widened at the soggy mess inside.

Leo knelt down next to his father, taking his hand and giving him a grin. "You know the water is supposed to stay in the shower, right, Dad? Did you start drinking a little early today?"

Emir huffed in a weak imitation of a laugh. "Slipped...on...pen," he rasped. I replaced the towel with a new one, trying not to show Leo the extent of the blood. I didn't want Emir to see it in Leo's face.

"That'll teach you. Leave all that pesky reading and writing to the smart people next time. Stick to what you do best, gambling and lying about who does the cooking around here." Leo winked at me. Emir gave another little puff, and I forced a laugh for his sake. "Here, let me do that, Lim," Leo said, reaching for the towel.

I stepped back to change places with him.

Leo's eyes went round, and he froze as he pulled the old towel off. There was genuine fear there. Without thinking, I pushed up my sodden sleeves. Emir let out a strangled sound, his eyes going wide at the sight of my bare arms. Leo looked at his father in alarm.

"Dad? What is it?"

Emir wheezed, his gaze going to mine in accusation as he clutched his chest.

By the time Leo's eyes darted to me, I'd frantically shoved my sleeves back down. Bile and panic rose in my throat.

Emir's face went from red to purple as he flexed his fingers.

And then he was gone.

I poured Leo a drink; he knocked it back in one. Audre arrived with Indie right after Emir had passed. Indie tried to resuscitate him, but his heart remained stubbornly silent. She'd called the coroner, who was upstairs with her now.

"I'm so sorry, Leo," I said again, my voice catching. Emir was not perfect by any definition, but he was good to me and he loved his kids. I suddenly thought of Sasha and Priya, and my heart broke. "Do you...want me to tell Sasha?"

Leo sucked in a breath as if he too had just realized what this news would do to Sasha. Like me, Sasha had some protection because of Emir's presence in her life. The thought popped into my head that I was going to have to find another job. Guilt consumed me, not just for that selfish concern but for the part I'd played in Emir's death. I would never forget the look on his face when he saw my arms. It wasn't just shock; it was betrayal.

"I'll tell her. I'll go once they're finished here." Leo reached across the bar and squeezed my hand. I worried he'd be able to feel the lack of my cuffs and was relieved when he stood up. Indie and the coroner descended the stairs and walked over to us.

"I'm sorry for your loss, Mr. Martin," the coroner said. I wondered how many times he'd had to say it. "Do you know if your father had any wishes regarding his remains?"

Tears swam in the corners of Leo's eyes, but his voice was steady. "He wanted to be buried at Donfor." Leo named the mountain to the north of us, so named by the locals because it was where most of Marais buried their dead.

"Very well. I can have him taken to the funeral home where they can prepare him." He handed Leo a card with the funeral home's information, which was entirely unnecessary since there was only one. Leo nodded tightly.

The coroner went back upstairs with two of his assistants, and we all waited in silence as the three of them retrieved Emir and carried him downstairs on a gurney. They'd draped a sheet over his face, but as they passed, Leo stopped them. He pulled the sheet back and kissed his father on the forehead. Indie gripped my hand. I took a shaky breath and several tears slipped down my cheek. I wiped them away with the back of my sleeve, but it was still soaking wet. Indie handed me a tissue with her free hand, and I dabbed my face.

He turned to us when they'd gone. Indie stepped up to him, and they hugged. "I'm so sorry again, Leo," she murmured. He nodded and gave her a sad smile. She gave me a bracing look before leaving out the front door herself, back to the patients she'd abandoned when I'd called her away.

His shoulders slumped. "I'd better go tell Sasha." He grimaced. "And my aunt and uncles."

Terror seized me. If any of them found out…I bit my lip and gave Leo a quick nod. "I'll clean up. And I'll ask my dad to fix the shower."

Leo brushed the wet hair out of my face, his gaze contemplative. He let his hand linger on my neck. An ugly thing twisted inside me. I didn't deserve to comfort him.

The door flew open, two fishers in the middle of a conversation walked in. They froze, noticing the empty chairs. I wondered if they could smell Emir's death, feel his true absence.

Leo sighed but gave them a kind smile. "We're closed today, I'm afraid." They quickly retreated, muttering their apologies. He took a piece of paper from behind the till, wrote something on it, and hung it on a nail on the front door.

Emir Martin has passed away. Closed until further notice.

Audre was in the kitchen, her hands clasped around a cup of tea. Blood didn't bother her. But her mother had an open casket, and apparently, one dead body was more than enough for her.

The two of us went upstairs and began cleaning Emir's room, dumping all the wet things out the window into the washbasin by the backdoor. I dried the floor and opened the windows to air out the room. The chair had a smudge of rusty red blood on it where Emir had leaned his head. I rubbed it off, choking back tears and nausea.

Whenever I did laundry and my back ached from all the lifting and scrubbing, I dreamed of having an electric washing machine. But now, as I cleaned all of Emir's sheets and towels, I only dreamed that nobody would ever know I'd killed him.

10

LIM

LASHIA, PRESENT DAY

Donfor gave me the creeps. I'd seen the ancient graveyards in Eudora, the dead there had given up. Life expectancy in Marais wasn't long and the ghosts here felt young and angry. Even when I stayed on the path, far from the burial plots, it affected me. The ground of the mountain felt like one big lumpy grave, and one day, it would writhe beneath us, and we'd all tumble in. The dense fog, infused with moss and pine, only added to the effect. I couldn't even see to the edge of the mountain, only the treetops were visible.

My parents left Keen and Ayla at home. I didn't want them here with Emir's relatives. Indie, Simon, and Audre stood next to me, all of us in the darkest clothes we owned. I'd done my hair, tried to pin it into something respectable, the kind of hairstyle an innocent person would wear.

Emir was popular. There were so many people here, most of them people I'd seen at The Peregrine. Leo stood nearest to the grave, holding Sasha's hand. Her eyes were red, Priya in a sling against her chest. Sydney, Marco, and Emir's other brother, Tarik, stood on the opposite side of Leo, furthest from Sasha. Sydney wore a tight black dress and dabbed dramatically at her cheeks. I rolled my eyes. She spent half her time complaining about her brother and the other half complaining to him. There was no real sadness on any of their faces. I could sense their discomfort, though, their indignation that Leo preferred to stand with Sasha.

"Should have told him to wrap it," I muttered under my breath.

"What did you say?" my mother whispered. Next to me, Indie raised her eyebrows and Audre smirked.

I took a breath. "Nothing, sorry."

Leo gave a wonderful speech. He peppered it with funny anecdotes about Emir's drinking, gambling, and dating life. Sasha said nothing, tears tumbling down her face while Leo's arm held her tightly around the shoulders. One by one, the mourners passed them and threw an offering, usually a flower but sometimes a note or other token, into the grave, "for Emir," they murmured as they passed.

When it was our turn, the others dropped in sprigs of goldenrod. I held my offering tightly, trying to breathe back the tears. I didn't want Leo's family to see me cry. The pretty pink shell I'd found fell onto the coffin. My outstretched hand bore tiny pricks of blood where I'd been gripping it. "For Emir," I forced out, my cheeks dampening against my will. Leo's honeyed eyes were deep with sorrow but also with something that filled me with both happiness and shame. Before he could say anything, I turned and walked away.

"Are we sure all these people even knew Emir?" Indie asked me.

She and Simon kept me company at the bar while I served endless free drinks at the wake. Although many people were telling fond stories about Emir, we'd definitely gained a few additions from the gravesite.

Sydney, Marco, and Tarik installed themselves at one of the corner tables and kept demanding more drinks for 'Emir's friends.'

I snorted in response and slid another drink down the bar. Aiden caught it, having given the guests a surprised once-over himself. It shocked me to see him in a suit. I wouldn't have thought Aiden even owned a suit, let alone one that fit so well. He raised the drink to me in thanks. This would probably need to be his last drink. Aiden never got sloppy drunk, but there was a point at which I could tell even a man of his size might get taken advantage of. I didn't need anyone deciding to relieve him of his belongings after what had already been a pretty shit day.

Audre had stayed only long enough to help me set up. She hadn't been as close to Emir as I was and she didn't want to hang around with, in her words, "a bunch of drunk bastards who would've dropped Emir in a heartbeat if the booze stopped flowing."

A feeling of unease that had nothing to do with my missing cuffs writhed inside me. Even if I could keep it a secret, could I stay here? Would Emir's family be here every night? Would they be willing to buy the ingredients I needed? I couldn't expect Leo to be the go-between. He had his own courier business. People often paid him to deliver more valuable items personally, so he was gone a lot.

Along with plates of cheese and dried fruit, there were towers of sandwiches. I'd placed them strategically around the room so that people would congregate away from the bar, away from me. Indie, Simon, and Aiden were the exceptions.

Simon snagged the pickles from Indie's sandwich while she took the cheese from his and doubled it on her own. They sat so close to one another, so familiar. Envy sparked deep inside me. They'd found each other immediately. We'd all grown up together, but Simon and Indie had always gravitated to one another. Indie noticed me watching them. She lifted her fluffy black lashes—another thing I envied—in question.

I shook my head. "I should have made your sandwiches separately. So I wouldn't have to watch you mutilate them in front of me." Simon grinned, halfway to taking a bite, but Indie's eyes narrowed. We still hadn't had the chance to talk properly since Emir's death, and she knew I wasn't telling her something.

"Later," I mouthed, pouring another round of beers. I took a sip of my tea, wishing I, too, could afford to drown my sorrows in wine. But I needed a clear head. A fine rain was falling outside, the sneaky kind that soaked your clothes before you even realized it was raining. Inside, the restaurant was warm, almost stuffy. I longed to kick all these people out and air the place out properly.

Cheers went up as Leo opened the door, standing aside for a dark-haired man with piercing blue eyes. They both took off their soaking coats, and Leo ran a hand through his blond hair, sprinkling rain droplets onto the floor. The man tipped his head to me, smiling kindly. I returned a confused smile of my own. I'd never seen him before, but Emir's siblings recognized him immediately.

"Mr. Dale!" Sydney shouted, shoving her brother out of their booth so she could get up. She was unsteady on her feet as she walked over to him, her blond hair glowing in the candlelight. "Thank you so much for coming." She held out her hand and gazed at him from under her eyebrows. I'm sure she meant to be flirty, but in her inebriated state, she just looked sleepy. Dale shook it politely.

"I'm very sorry for your loss." He looked at her as well as Tarik and Marco, who had also risen. They all shook hands, and he said, "is there somewhere more private we could talk?"

"Of course, we can go upstairs to my father's rooms," Leo replied. "Would you like anything to eat or drink? Lim makes a mean shrub if you'd prefer something non-alcoholic." Leo motioned to me.

Dale's eyes alighted on me again and his eyebrows rose almost imperceptibly in recognition. "Yes, I would appreciate that. Perhaps we could go upstairs, and she could bring it to me in a few minutes?"

"Calimea, we need to speak privately for a few minutes. Afterward, bring Mr. Dale a shrub and a sandwich," Sydney said imperiously, as if I hadn't been right next to them during this entire conversation. Marco smirked at me, but Tarik said nothing, his eyes dark and his expression hard. As they made their way to the stairs, Leo gave me a wink and then rolled his eyes at his aunt's behavior.

I could only get out a brief "will do" before all of them made their way up the staircase next to the bar. I didn't even breathe until they crossed the short interior balcony above me and went into Emir's rooms. My heart was hammering in my chest and my cheeks flushed. I went hot and cold at the same time. Leo hadn't seen. Leo hadn't seen. I repeated it to myself over and over again. There was no reason for anyone to suspect me of anything.

"Aren't losing any time, are they?" Simon said, polishing off another sandwich. His plate held a pile still waiting to be devoured.

Indie blew an errant coppery brown curl out of her face. "Nope, little vultures probably felt it the minute Emir drew his last breath." Indie grimaced at my surprised look. "Sorry, Lim."

"No, I—What do you mean? Who is that?"

"The lawyer," Simon replied.

"They're about to find out what Emir really thought of them. Or how much he gambled away." Indie sipped her wine thoughtfully.

A rousing rendition of "One-Eyed Clyde" broke out in the corner. The mourners waved their drinks in the air as they lamented the dragon's foolhardy attempts to steal a star from the sky. Simon perked up, and both he and Aiden turned to join in. I smiled in spite of myself at their tuneless caterwauling.

Indie winced as they hit the high note and hopped off her stool. "You make the drink. I'll grab the sandwiches."

"Unacceptable," Sydney shouted, loud enough to be heard through the wall. I knocked hard so they could hear me above her shrill voice, and Leo quickly opened the door. I held up the drink and plate full of sandwiches, hoping I could drop them and get out.

Every pair of eyes turned to me. The five of them were scattered around Emir's sitting room. Dale sat at Emir's desk, still covered in stacks of papers, bills, and other reminders that he'd been living in this room only days before. I'd taken away all the empty teacups and pint glasses when I'd cleaned up the soaked towels and linens. I had been afraid to touch anything else, despite the number of times I'd rifled through that desk, looking for something Emir claimed he couldn't find. Marco sat on the couch while Tarik leaned against a closet, arms crossed and face filled with threat.

Sydney shrieked again at seeing me. "You have got to be kidding me. This is a mistake!" Her chest heaved. "She manipulated him!" She pointed an accusing red nail at me, and my eyebrows shot to the top of my head.

Did they know? Manipulated seemed like a strange euphemism for murder.

Dale sighed. "His will was signed and witnessed by two people as well as myself." His face was calm, much calmer than mine probably looked. He casually crossed an ankle over his knee as he weathered Sydney's reaction.

"What people?" growled Tarik from the corner. The brothers looked similar, but his eyes lacked any of Emir's warmth. A vein was popping in his forehead.

Leo, noticing that I was still holding everything, gently lifted the glass and plate from me and brought them over to Dale, who smiled gratefully. He took a sip and looked me in the eye. "Hmm, he was right. This really is delicious." He put the glass down. "Ms. Revin, I had an ulterior motive for asking you to wait before coming up."

My stomach dropped and my hands went clammy. I clasped them behind my back. "Call me Lim, please." I was grateful my voice held steady. "And what is that?"

Sydney marched over to me, but Leo stepped between us before she got too close. She was near enough that I could see the lipstick on her teeth. "What did you do to him? Did you fuck him too?" Her voice was poisonous. Gone was the grieving sister.

"Aunt Sydney!" Leo shouted. "That's enough. Back the hell off!"

"You don't speak to your aunt that way!" Marco yelled as he stood up, his eyes bulging from his oddly juvenile-looking face.

Dale cleared his throat. His voice came out soothing as much as it was commanding, a man who was no stranger to this type of conflict. "As this is your house now, do feel free to ask them to leave." My eyes widened in disbelief. "I was truly hoping they'd be done with their pointless yelling before you arrived, but it seems not."

If I hadn't been frozen in shock, I would have laughed. "I don't understand?"

Leo turned to me, still with one eye on his relatives, hands on his hips. His eyes held only affection. "My father left you the restaurant, Lim, the building and the land."

I blinked slowly. "But what about you?" I dropped my voice to a whisper, "Sasha?"

Leo's face softened at my concern. "He left us some money, but obviously, neither of us were going to run a restaurant." He let his hands fall, his voice comforting. "We were the witnesses, Lim. We always knew it would be you."

Tarik pushed off the wall, and Leo turned to face him, protecting me again. "We have lawyers too," Tarik threatened before pushing past Leo and storming out. Sydney and Marco followed.

"Slut," spat Sydney as she pushed past me, her frizzy hair looking near-electrified now.

I stumbled back, and Leo caught me, his hands holding my shoulders. Leo's chest was warm against me. It made me want to lean back and close my eyes. I wanted to turn to him, to have him wrap his arms around me and envelop me in that sunbaked scent of his. But I didn't. From here, I couldn't see the chair where Emir died, but I felt it lurking on the other side of the wall. Emir's bloody face as he was dying and the horrified look in his eyes as he noticed my missing cuffs flashed through my mind.

"That was unnecessarily dramatic." Dale's voice startled me out of the horrible memory. He took a bite of his sandwich. "Thank you for this again. I haven't eaten all day." He chewed thoughtfully before swallowing and asking in a tone that belied simply curiosity. "Were you sleeping with Emir?"

"What?" The word tumbled out of my shocked face.

"No!" Leo practically shouted.

Dale nodded, taking a drink. "I apologize for being indelicate. I ask because that's the most likely way they would challenge the will. Undue influence and all that. But it would be very hard for them to prove, even if you were."

"Well, she wasn't," Leo said, a look of disgust on his face.

The ridiculous theory helped my anxiety subside. At least, of all things, I was not guilty of that. But even without a guilty conscience, my mind was racing. Emir had really left me the restaurant?

"Of course, if you two are together, that could also come up." Dale wiped his mouth with an expensive-looking handkerchief he pulled from his pocket. Everything about him looked well put together. The shine of his boots, the tailored suit, a blue shirt that brought out his eyes, even his hair was perfect, despite having been out in the rain.

"That's not—" I spluttered, trying to find the words. "We're not sleeping together." Next to me, Leo exhaled and paced to the closet.

"No, we're not. But we have."

"Leo!" My face was red. "That was a long time ago." The irony did not escape me that I'd been waiting years for Leo to acknowledge what we meant to one another, and now I wanted him to shut up about it.

Leo stopped his pacing and came over to me, pulling my hands into his. "I know. But Sydney knows I care about you. And if she can't prove you were"—he made that disgusted face again—"with my father, she might say you manipulated me into doing it." Out of the corner of my eye, I could see Dale nodding as he picked up another sandwich.

I pulled my hands out of Leo's and wrapped them around my waist. "That's an unbelievably long game. Seduce you and then sit around and hope for Emir to die?"

"Unless you killed him," Dale said. I whipped around to face him, that panic clawing up my chest again, heat running through my body.

Dale casually took another drink, but I felt like he was watching my every move.

"I didn't kill him." I put every once of certainty I had into that sentence. "Leo was here too. He saw what happened." Dale only nodded ambivalently, but I didn't buy it.

Leo put his hand to my face, pulling my chin toward him. "Hey." He gave me that smile that usually made my toes curl. Part of me still reacted to it, even though I was terrified. "We know you didn't, Lim. We're just being prepared so we can help."

Dale got up, collecting his bag. He approached me, holding several sheets of paper. I recognized Emir's handwriting immediately. How many times had I seen it on notes left for me in the kitchen? Suggestions for bizarre flavor combinations he'd thought of or requesting something special for whichever girl he was seeing that month?

"Here are your copies. I'll deliver your sister's myself and retain one for safekeeping." I felt like someone else as I took the papers and shook Dale's hand. He gave me that kind smile again, but this time, his eyes examined my face carefully before making his way downstairs.

11

SABINE

TREVESTEN, ~ 500 YEARS AGO

"Your Majesty?"

Sabine's head snapped up, her eyes meeting Antonio's. His face was the picture of calm, an unbothered soldier with endless faith in his queen. But she knew him too well. His thumb rubbed against the pommel of his sword. The tiniest tell. He was concerned about her. She was concerned about her too—nothing seemed to work lately. Connery had now been gone for over a month, her mind empty of his voice. She'd thought for sure he would return in a week. Then she was sure it would only be two.

She wasn't sure of anything anymore.

The mating bond was supposed to mean something. It was a tether between two people so strong they were of one mind. Her power had also been acting erratically since he'd been gone. The Allmother no doubt punishing her for being so stupid. She'd thought she was so clever, but clearly she wasn't, not even after all these years of life.

Her eyes roamed over the people in attendance, knowing that while they might show her respect now, behind closed doors, they mocked and pitied her. They all knew her mate had left her. Their whispers floated to her.

How selfish must she be to squander such a gift?

Was she defective in some way?

A familiar heat burned behind her eyes, the sign of the tears that would not stop. He'd given her so many chances and she'd taken them all for granted. She deserved this. She knew she did, but knowing it was justified only made her devastation worse.

Antonio cleared his throat. She did her best to look attentive and waved her hand for the trial to begin. Those in attendance shuffled in their seats in anticipation. The place was packed with fae. They sat in the seats behind the advocates and the benches high up in the gallery, looking down on the proceedings. There were even fae gathered outside, waiting to hear the verdict. Their excited voices carried through the large stained glass windows that threw vibrant colors across the floor. A little inconsistent with the seriousness of the proceedings, but the palace of Adnatia was nothing if not unique.

There were journalists reporting on the trial. Fae that had the ability to transfer their thoughts directly to a notebook they held in front of them. There were royals, here for the show or simply to be seen, and all manner of other creatures, their eyes wide with anticipation. Only one person sat behind the Defendant in the row reserved for his guests. It was unsurprising, since she expected that most of the Defendant's associates were probably criminals.

She rarely attended trials, only when they involved royals or a dispute between a citizen of another territory. She should have been paying attention. After all, this was the male who'd stolen her sister.

Knivan Crowley, or 'Jack' as she'd known him, sat next to his advocate, calm but interested. They had given him clean clothes and the opportunity to shave, so the face she'd so recently seen covered in a month's worth of beard was now bare. His dark hair was still a little long, curving down into his silver-gray eyes. For a moment, her blood boiled at the memory of Crowley baiting her into paying for her sister's safe return. But her near-constant state of despair quickly snuffed the emotion out.

The court was called to order. The judge spoke, her voice clear and commanding. "Knivan Crowley, you are accused of kidnapping and extortion. Her Majesty, Queen of Trevesten, has already given her testimony regarding your ransom demands. I understand you wish to present a witness regarding the charge of kidnapping?"

"We do, your honor." Crowley's advocate, a male named Reuben, stood. "The defense calls Lucy Bligh."

The female sitting behind Crowley stood, tripping slightly as she made her way to the witness stand. Someone, probably Reuben, had attempted to make her look presentable, but everything was a bit off. Her hair had come loose from the simple updo, she seemed unused to walking in the shoes she wore, and she'd failed to take off her coat. But she walked with a self-important air and primly took her seat on the witness stand.

Reuben gave her a kind smile. "Ms. Bligh, what relation are you to Her Royal Highness, Morgan of Trevesten?"

"I'm her mother." She sat up straighter but gripped the pockets of her coat.

"When was Her Royal Highness born? In this life?"

"She's two," she said proudly.

"Yes, thank you. What is her actual date of birth?" Reuben coaxed.

Bligh's eyes darted around the room. "September twelfth." She nodded at Reuben, but before he could ask another question, she continued. "I remember because I was supposed to get paid for the work I'd done for Ms. Nidern, but she said she had to give it to me on the fifteenth because her husband had to do a kippie first."

Sabine sighed internally. 'Kippie' referred to power a fae could sell or purchase. Whether it was power the fae would take into their person or external spells and enchantments, Trevesten had strict regulations on the purchase and sale of magic. One could purchase a few abilities legally, healing for one. She herself had absorbed power from Trevesten's strongest healer. But there were always people willing to bend the rules for a new ability or boost in their own power. And something in the way Bligh said it made her think that Mr. Nidern wasn't selling his magic legally.

Unregulated magic sales could be simple scams. A fae thought they were absorbing enough to turn back the years on their appearance but received only a lackluster hair color change. They could also be danger-ous or lethal. Some daranas Sabine had confiscated were so poorly made she couldn't understand why any fae would dare risk touching them. Sabine vaguely wondered why Mr. Nidern felt he had to sell his power before forcing herself to refocus on Bligh.

"So I told her I would come back on the fifteenth and get it, and as we were talking, the baby started squeezing and I knew it was time." Bligh rubbed her stomach absentmindedly and there was an answering pang in Sabine's own. As mates, she and Connery would have been blessed with a nyssar if she'd gotten pregnant, a completely new fae life. She forced herself to calm her breathing and shove down the anguish at the thought of never having a child with him.

"Thank you," Reuben quickly interrupted. "Ms. Bligh, was anyone with you when you gave birth to the Princess?"

"No. Why would anyone have been with me?" Bligh looked confused. "I didn't know before I had her. I didn't know anything before that. I told you before when we were in your office. I didn't know she was a princess. I have twelve different children I look after during the week.

Twelve. also had a mark on her, but it doesn't look like Mary—I mean Morgan's, but you know it's hard to keep track. I used to have fourteen kids, except two of them moved to some place in the north." She held up her hands as if she would begin counting off the other children when Reuben intercepted her again.

"Ms. Bligh, after the Princess was born, you saw the royal mark on her wrist, didn't you? The circle with an arrow through it?"

Sabine ignored the eyes that she had turned to her, trying to glimpse the same mark on her wrist. She'd worn long sleeves today. She would have considered anything else unfit for the formality of court.

"Yeah..." Bligh's voice was timid.

"And did you inform anyone of her identity? Did you try to contact Her Majesty?"

At this, Bligh turned to look at Sabine as if she'd just now realized the queen was there. Then her eyes fell on the jury members. Some gave her curious looks or tight smiles. Bligh's gaze wandered. She seemed to have forgotten the question and looked as if she was waiting for someone to tell her what to do.

"Ms. Bligh? Did you tell anyone that you'd given birth to the Princess?"

Bligh's eyes snapped to his. Her expression changed in an instant from calm to angry. "I'm not living here. I don't want to live here." She looked at Sabine. "I don't want to live with you. I know what happens. You'll come and steal me away, and I won't get to live in my house anymore, won't get to take care of the children." Bligh became increasingly agitated, pulling at her coat and rubbing her hands.

Sabine's mouth thinned. Since they'd discovered Morgan's mother, they could not get her to move to the palace. For most fae, giving birth to a royal was amazing luck. The family lived in or near the respective royal household and their every needed was provided for. Bligh had taken the money. She didn't even seem to object to the guards Sabine provided to protect her and her home. She chatted to them about her various charges, made them cups of tea, and was happy enough, as long as they never mentioned the palace.

Reuben looked at the judge, and she nodded, allowing him to get closer to Bligh. "Nobody is going to make you leave your home. We just want to know whether you told anyone about Princess Morgan after she was born."

This seemed to calm her down some, but she still muttered, "You can't just take people" before she composed herself. "I told him." She pointed at Crowley.

"You told Mr. Crowley?"

"Well, no, I told that friend of his, Bennie or Baron or whatever, he bought me a drink and I told him. He"—she pointed at Crowley again—"showed up the next day. Told me I could get in a bunch of trouble for keeping her to myself. I told *him* I didn't want to go live in the palace too." She gave Crowley a disappointed look. Remorse crossed Crowley's face briefly before it returned to stoicism.

"And when was that?"

"When Emmet started walking."

The picture of patience, Reuben tried again. "Would that have been about a month ago?"

Bligh nodded, distracted again. Sabine didn't need this demonstration. She'd met Bligh and understood that her intent was never to hide Morgan but to protect herself. Sabine had immediately declared no charges were to be brought against her.

Crowley, on the other hand, deserved everything that was coming to him. The evening of Crowley's capture dominated her mind. It consumed her like a fever and she would never stop replaying it. She went over and over every look she'd shared with Connery, the warning in his voice. She heard herself, so flippant, so dishonest. Shame beat her until there wasn't a single part of her that didn't feel regret. She still didn't know how Crowley had discovered her trick. The guards found every last piece of the fake gold, all the spells still intact.

Antonio cleared his throat again, and she collected herself as the judge released the jury to deliberate.

They took longer than she thought they would. On the charge of extortion, they found him guilty. But not on the charge of kidnapping. Crowley had never removed Morgan from Bligh's home. A technicality if she'd ever heard one, but Sabine accepted it. She was going to give him the same choice either way, Tarkana or execution.

He chose execution. From the moment she'd faced him and he'd gone down fighting, she knew he would.

12

LIM

LASHIA, PRESENT DAY

I tossed and turned that night. I wasn't sure how to tell my family about Emir, about my arms, about any of it. Brax tried to snuggle close to me but gave up, hissing, as I managed to dislodge even his enormous body with my movements. He retreated to the couch in my room. I sat up, covered in sweat, wondering if I should just sell the place. Sydney, Marco, and Tarik would make my life a living hell. And who would even go there now that Emir was gone? I didn't have his way with people. I couldn't charm a table full of rowdy patrons. People would find out about me. Of course, perhaps if I could prove I was magically impotent, they'd leave me alone.

'Probably not,' said a snarky voice in my head.

I rubbed my hands against my eyes and again saw Emir's chair. It was a red overstuffed thing. I'd seen him use it to put on his shoes or read the paper if there was nobody in the restaurant to talk to. Nausea rolled through my stomach as I remembered the way the back of the chair had pushed into me as I'd tried to stop the blood. I could practically feel the material against my skin, my bare feet on the floor as I sat in it.

I opened my eyes.

I was in Emir's room, sitting in Emir's chair, still wearing my night-clothes. I leapt out of the chair and ran out to the sitting room. The clock said it was after four. The night was nearly dark as pitch. With my cuffs gone, the only light came from a waning moon. A mouse scurried across the floor, and I instinctively jumped back, calling for Brax.

A high-pitched shriek escaped me before I toppled back over the couch. Brax crouched down, peering at me through the gap between the couch and the floor. Did Emir ever clean under here? He inspected the room while I scrambled to my feet, his whiskers flicking as he sniffed the air. He stepped toward Emir's bed and placed his paws on it, preparing to climb up.

"Brax, no!" I shoved him aside. "What in the stars is happening right now? How are you here? How am I here?" My forearms were dark without their previous blue glow. I turned to Brax. "Did I bring you here? You weren't here when I arrived, were you?"

Brax raised an eyebrow at me in a stunningly human expression. He couldn't tell me anything, even if he knew the answers.

"Right, okay," I said to the empty room. "I did this. I can undo it." My gaze locked on Brax, and I pictured my bedroom.

And he was gone.

I took deep, gulping breaths. Could I move anything? Anywhere?

A mug sat on Emir's desk. Focusing hard, I visualized it moving to the table in front of the couch. Nothing happened. I tried again with a piece of paper, but again, nothing. No inanimate objects? But I was still wearing clothes, thank the stars, so perhaps if I touched it? I grabbed the mug and focused on Emir's bedroom.

It was instant, effortless. My grin split my face, then quickly fell as my eyes caught on Emir's chair.

I closed my eyes, and when I opened them, I was home.

I was out of bed the next morning before the sun had fully risen. I'd probably had only two hours of sleep, but my skin hummed with energy. Stealthily, I crept down the stairs, after giving a dubious-looking Brax instructions to stay put. For an enormous beast capable of ending the life of anything in Lashia, he certainly still embodied a house cat's typical apathy.

"What are you doing?" Ayla's voice cut through the silence.

"Agh! Stars Ayla, you're going to give me a heart attack!" I winced at the reference, and Ayla saw it.

"I'm sorry." She shuffled out of her room, still wearing her daisy-patterned nightgown, her hair tangled from sleep. "Mom said you wouldn't go to work today. I thought you would stay home with us?"

"I'm not going to work," I said, pushing her hair behind her ear. "I'm going to see Indie. Don't you have school today?"

Ayla narrowed her eyes in an expression of disdain far beyond her years. "It's Saturday." She folded her arms across her chest and raised her chin. "You don't look sick."

"I'm not sick. I'm going to see her because I...want to talk to her."

"About Emir?"

Ayla never called Emir 'Mr. Martin,' none of the kids did. He'd always been kind to my siblings, to all the kids who played in the neighborhood. Unless he was hungover. Then he gave them whatever cookies or treats he could find in the kitchen to go away so he could recuperate in silence.

"Yes." It wasn't technically a lie. "But I'll tell you what, if you let everyone sleep until eight, I'll tell you something you can share with them. You'll be the first person in the family to know." Ayla's eyes lit up.

She was always hungry for secrets. "Do we have a deal? No making noise, no 'accidentally' opening Keen's door by mistake. Let them all sleep until eight?"

Ayla nodded solemnly and held out her hand. We shook on it. I told her what Emir had done, leaving me The Peregrine. She hugged a tired-looking stuffed bear to her chest in excitement. I could already hear her sing-song voice at the breakfast table, teasing the others about how she knew something they didn't. She magnanimously let me pass as well as borrow her bicycle. I wasn't about to try Derek again.

By the time I got to Indie's, it was almost seven, and I was drenched in sweat. Indie and Simon lived in a small blue house with a wide front porch. It was set far back from the road but only one street away from the busier street where she had her office. I wheeled Ayla's bike up the little gravel path before leaning it against the porch. Simon answered after my second knock.

"Lim!" he said, surprised. "What are you doing here this early?" He was already dressed and holding a steaming cup of tea. The rich blend filled my nose as Simon waved me into the house with his free hand.

Their place was immaculate. There were no piles of papers or clothes strewn about. Handcrafted gifts from their younger patients decorated the surfaces. The bookshelves were full and neatly alphabetized. On the very top shelf, certificates and recognition from Marais for their work with the community. The wood floors creaked under my feet as I made my way to the kitchen, where I could hear Indie moving about.

"Oh, it's you. I was about to have to hurt someone for showing up here at this hour without a baby falling out of them." She gave me a quick hug, and I inhaled her cinnamon and citrus scent. She scanned my face. "What's wrong?"

I told them about Emir's will and the siblings' reaction.

"I'm not surprised," Indie said. "Emir owed you a lot, and he cared about you in his way." I furrowed my brow at the last part of that comment. She just continued, "But you did not come over to sweat on my kitchen chairs at the crack of dawn just to tell us that."

I shook my head slowly. Then I got up. I needed to move, to do something with my hands. Indie and Simon shared a look, communicating silently in the way of couples who have been together for a long time. They continued to stay quiet as I raided their fridge for breakfast ingredients.

I set an omelet at each of our places, earthy cheese, butter, and lots of dried chilis. I had cooked, and they had listened. The two of them reacted in tandem, one shushing when the other one gasped, one nodding vehemently while the other shook their head just as hard. It would have been funny was I not describing how I accidentally broke an ancient law that was the foundation of our society. And that I had no idea how to fix it.

"So," I said, finishing up my omelet, "any ideas?"

Simon had been staring at my bare arms since I'd rolled up my sleeves to show them.

He steepled his hands in front of him. "During the war, the Jinns who aligned with the Tals helped them create things to combat the other Jinns, to negate magic. This might have been something a rich Tal used to serve food—to ensure anyone who dined with them wouldn't be able to use magic against them. The plate might have nullified the magic that applied the cuffs." He squinted one eye and pursed his lips in contemplation.

"But I can use my power now. I haven't touched the plate since I used it, but if I kept touching it, you think it would take all of it?" Panic laced my words.

Simon shrugged. "Didn't you say you left your hand on it all night? Probably takes longer than that, but best to stop touching it with your bare skin just in case. I don't think it would work to stop your magic completely. Like I said, this was probably just used as an extra tac-tic—probably when dining with their own Jinn allies. Not a lot of trust happening back then. But the cuffs were not your magic. They're..." he seemed to be searching for a more scientific word, but said, "a blanket on top of yours."

A little thrill went through me at the thought of 'my magic.' "Do you think it would work if they tried to cuff me again?" We all pretended not to imagine what the government recuffing me might look like.

"I should think so. But it stands to reason the plate could undo it just the same." Simon got up and began perusing his bookshelves, looking for something. He stood on his toes, peering behind the books.

Indie was silent during this exchange, but now she inhaled and said only, "show me." Her deep brown eyes were intense, and she looked like she was bracing herself.

"Me or one of you?"

Indie exhaled and looked at me with amused contempt. "You first, obviously. I'm not trusting my body or my husband's with this"—she waved her hand at my arms—"until you prove it's safe." She crossed her arms and raised her chin. "Also, if you end up splitting yourself in half or something, I'll need Simon to help examine your body."

"Ever the scientist." I smirked, relief running through me. I knew that Indie and Simon wouldn't react badly, but a weight lifted, even with her staring at me with intense scrutiny.

Indie's shriek and Simon's weird "Gah!" sound carried to me where I stood in their bedroom. I laughed out loud.

"Oh my stars, Lim, where are you?"

I appeared in front of her.

Less shrieking but still satisfying, as they'd obviously jumped up from the table in surprise.

"I can't believe it!" Simon abandoned his search for whatever he'd been looking for and was now examining me from all sides. He even went so far as to check my pulse and peer into my pupils.

Once he'd made a third lap around me, he announced, "Okay, do me!" and held out his arms as if I was going to physically pick him up.

"What? What happened to the scientific method?" I crossed my arms.

Indie grabbed a stethoscope and joined him in the examination. She gave a casual wave with her hand and said, "he'll be fine. I'm going to need to take your blood."

My lips curled at this abrupt and assumed invasion of my privacy. Indie was clearly itching to get something under a microscope.

I turned to Simon, and he was gone. Indie stared at the spot he'd been. He appeared again a moment later.

"I CANNOT BELIEVE IT!" He yelled in delight. "I WENT TO THE BATHROOM!" The two of us burst into laughter at his beaming face.

Indie's expression turned suddenly serious. "How are you going to hide it? It'll look odd come summer, and are you planning on just never dating again?"

"Like my dating life has ever been super active?" I scoffed, but I understood the direness of her question. Cooler temperatures were coming, but this was going to become complicated once spring arrived. I paused, rubbing my finger on the table in little circles. "Would either of you ever want to..." I flipped my hand in a 'you know' gesture.

They looked at each other for several moments. Simon broke the look to frown at the ceiling while Indie's eyes glanced at my arms.

She reached out and touched my skin. "I was starting to think all of it was just another lie." I frowned at her, confused.

Simon put his hands in his pockets. "I always wanted to know." There was childlike hope in his voice. We'd had these conversations in secret, our answers constantly changing.

"We could be arrested," Indie said, but there was a distinct lack of conviction in her words. Still, she reached out and squeezed my hand.

"Yes," I said in a smaller voice. Who was I to even offer this to them? I'd put them both in an impossible position. "I could still go to the authorities. Tell them what happened, hand over the plate. They'd probably go easy on me." I shrugged. I had no idea whether they would go easy on me. Despite my suspicions, this was unprecedented. Those horrible Sun Guardians would lose their collective minds if it got out.

"That would probably work." Simon's voice was dejected. The two of them seemed to sense their only chance at ever knowing their power slipping away. A heavy feeling settled in my chest as I thought of them watching each registration, the magic appearing before their eyes but never being able to experience it themselves.

I suddenly had an idea. "I know. I could ask Dale—that lawyer. He would have to keep it confidential, right? He was Emir's friend. And he might at least be able to give me some idea of what might happen to me. And until then, I'll just keep the plate. Just in case."

The two of them didn't even hide their relief. "That's a good idea." Simon nodded eagerly. "Very practical."

The three of us stood grinning at one another for a moment before I broke the silence.

"Can you imagine dozens of people being able to do this? Moving from place to place like that." I snapped my fingers. "All because our ancestors couldn't handle not being able to use airplanes or cars?" I shook my head, my voice like an overexcited child.

Simon frowned, and Indie tipped her head at me in question. At my confused look, they glanced at one another before Simon spoke.

"You know how the teachers would shut down too much discussion about our magic?"

"Yes..." I nodded slowly to Simon, wondering where he was going with this.

"While there are some specific instances of very rapid revolution, the Biston betularia, for example—"

Indie cut him off. "Honey, let's condense this. We have a patient in twenty minutes." She began gathering their things while Simon continued to speak. I waited patiently for him to continue.

"The records are not great, but the first documentation of any Jinns in Lashia is from about five hundred years ago. And since the Weakening was only twenty-seven hundred and five years ago, that's really not long enough for anything to evolve."

"Huh?" My brows knit together and I cocked my head. "What are you saying? How did we get our magic, then? And all the weird animals?" My head whirred, dropping in pieces of my meager knowledge of the origin of Jinn power. Our education, my parents' education, it always taught the same thing. Humans' frustration at not being able to send instantaneous messages or build rockets caused an extreme evolutionary event.

"Not sure." Indie stepped up, handing Simon his bag while she slung hers over her shoulder. "The records of the first two thousand years after the Weakening are basically non-existent. But what they told us is almost definitely not true."

Simon gave another glance at the bookshelf. "I have something I think is an earlier account, but can't find it right now. Everything else starts immediately before the Treaty. Wars, bloodshed, and then the cuffs."

While I was still trying to process all of this, Indie clapped her hands together. "Right, well, now that's settled. I'm ready for my turn. Can you send us to the office?"

My mouth fell open. The two of them were remarkably trusting of my abilities for only just having learned about them. I thought for a moment. The office was closed still, but better safe than sorry. It would need to be somewhere there wouldn't be any people.

"Abracadabra," I said for dramatic effect and put them in their supply closet. I could almost hear the curses.

13

LIM

LASHIA, PRESENT DAY

The ingredients on my shelves felt foreign, like I'd never seen them before. I took down a jar of dried lavender and immediately put it back. The rosemary I swapped it for tugged at a memory I couldn't place. I chopped it finely before mixing it with my dough. I brushed the dough with sunflower oil and sprinkled more rosemary and some salt on it before putting it into the oven. The heat caressed my hand, the flames already high from the wood I'd been feeding it since I got here. It was late afternoon. I wasn't going to open the restaurant, but I couldn't stay away.

The thought that maybe I should sell went through my head again. Let some new owner deal with Emir's siblings. Even as I considered it, a gloom fell over me at the thought. I would hate that. And who was I to inflict Sydney on some innocent buyer? This place wasn't anything special. It was a backwater restaurant in a backwater place, but it was mine and I'd put a lot of work into it.

There was a knock at the backdoor. "Come in," I called.

Leo pushed in, freshly showered and softly smiling. My insides squirmed at the sight of him, but I just said "hi," in what I hoped was a calm, and completely non-magical, voice. 'Good morning' would have been entirely inappropriate.

"Hi," he replied, coming to stand far too close to me. His fingers found my face, and he tipped it up toward him. "How are you doing?"

"Shouldn't I be asking you that?" His thumb grazed my chin a little before a shadow crossed over his eyes and he stepped back.

"I'm not sure I believe it. I keep expecting to hear his voice." He rubbed his chest and his gaze floated to the stairs.

"Me too." I gave him a small smile. "I keep waiting for him to come barging through that door with weird fruit he bought from some guy's coat pocket."

Leo laughed. He looked at me again, and I bit my lip involuntarily. He shook his head like there was water in it. "I need to go to Eudora for work. Probably be gone a week."

He came toward me again, this time letting his hands rest on my shoulders. Each point of his fingers was like a brand on my skin. "I'm worried about leaving you here. I don't want Sydney and the others to make anything difficult for you."

My fingers pressed gently on his chest and I suddenly remembered my conversation with Indie. Leo would never be able to see me naked. The reasonable part of me scoffed at the thought. Leo wouldn't be seeing me naked for several reasons that had nothing to do with my cuffs. I sidestepped out of his embrace. Hurt flashed in his eyes, but I gave him a bracing smile.

"If there's a possibility that they could use our...friendship as a way to mess with your father's wishes, it's probably a good idea for us to keep our distance. At least for a bit," I tacked on, seeing that hurt deepen. "Right?"

He nodded slowly and ran a hand through his hair. "Right, of course, you're right. I don't want to mess this up for you."

"No, Leo." I couldn't help reaching for him, my hand finding his. "I don't want to mess things up for you either. If Sydney convinces everyone I tricked you to get your father to write that will, the whole thing will be in jeopardy. And I won't see you or Sasha lose a single mark of your inheritance." A stab of pain went through me. Emir had only seen Priya once before he died.

Leo smiled. It lit up his face as he pulled me into a hug. He lowered his voice, and it skittered across my skin as he spoke. "Always so practical, Lim. Always looking out for everyone else." My breath hitched as he prolonged the hug. His breath was warm on my ear as he spoke. "Someday soon, I'm going to get you to show me your spontaneous side." Warmth slid along my body until it focused itself between my legs. Leo pressed a quick kiss to my forehead before releasing me.

Mr. Dale, it appeared, had done his job well. None of the attorneys in Marais would represent Sydney, Marco, and Tarik, and word was that they'd gone to seek help in another borough. Other than having to briefly avoid Tarik's notice at the market, I hadn't seen them at all since the wake. I hoped pretending they didn't exist would somehow keep them away.

Leo had been gone over two weeks now, delivering packages and letters up and down the coast. In his absence, I took the time to truly make The Peregrine mine. I'd planned a new menu and found some more comfortable chairs to go by the fireplace. I'd scrubbed the restaurant from top to bottom with help from Audre and my family.

Ayla and Keen had a great time dumping all the silverware into the sink, throwing every napkin and towel in a pile to be washed, and removing every bottle and knick-knack from behind the bar so I could clean. I'd found coins, old tabs with items we hadn't served in months, and several pencils. I even found a hidden stash of Emir's favorite candy, a horrible salted licorice that nobody but him could stand.

I'd also been experimenting with and learning about my ability. In order to send myself or anyone to a place, I needed to have been there. And I needed to be near a person to send them somewhere, but I could pull someone to me from anywhere. Indie and Simon had spent some time with me in the uninhabited areas around Marais, testing my accuracy and distance. There didn't seem to be a distance too far, but Simon believed my speed was fractionally slower the farther I had to travel. But I also discovered that my magic waned. The more I used it, the less accurate I became, as well as taking a toll on me physically. Despite not actually walking to any of the locations, by the end of the day, I was exhausted.

My parents' reaction to my arms was predictably concerned.

"You sure it was this plate that did it?" my mother asked. "Not something that was done to you?" She reached for the plate when I'd first put it down. I'd stopped her before she could touch it and now she cradled her hand, like the thing had snapped at her.

"Yep, pretty sure." I shrugged. The two of them continued to stare at the plate accusingly. The midday sun streamed in through the open window, illuminating the designs. There were tiny flowers, animals, and intricate symbols I didn't recognize that looked like writing.

"What's the plan?" My father stood back, still frowning at the plate. I'd waited until Ayla and Keen were at school since they would presumably demand I immediately remove their cuffs and none of us were prepared for that fight.

"No grand plan, other than hiding my arms for now. Oh, and I'm going to see Emir's lawyer and figure out if there's anybody else this has happened to—maybe he can assure me it would just be a slap on the wrist?" Both my parents visibly seized on that hope, baseless as it was. Neither of them had ever heard of this happening, either.

"That's a great idea," my mother said with sudden eagerness. "Why don't you make something to take with you? Lawyers work long hours."

I rolled my eyes at her obvious intention.

"It's wonderful to see you again, Lim, please come in." Dale stepped aside and motioned to one of the plush chairs in front of his desk.

I suddenly felt like an idiot with my cake, which either made it look like a bribe or something someone's mother would do. I smiled at Dale's assistant, Betty, who had greeted me at the front door and given me a warm welcome. She gave me a little wave back before returning to her work.

"I, uh, brought this. I don't go many places without food." Dale's eyes lit up as he took the cake from me. His eyes really were amazing. They reminded me of the calm, deep water of swimming holes. He wore another nice suit, charcoal gray this time, but no tie.

"Thank you so much. I routinely forget to eat when I'm at work. It's a source of constant anxiety for my mother."

I smiled and self-consciously tugged at my sleeves. Of course, I'd immediately made him think of his mother. I sat down in one chair, and instead of sitting down at his desk, he took the one across from me. The cake judged me from the table between us.

"To what do I owe the pleasure?"

I inhaled and caught a whiff of forests and leather. "Mr. Dale—"

"Bastian, please," he interrupted me.

"Bastian." But I didn't go on. I chewed on my lip. "Do you...If you..."

Bastian's voice was filled with concern, "Lim, are you in any danger? Is someone threatening you?" There was an irresistible look of intent in his eyes. He would evidently take it seriously if anyone were threatening me.

I gave an awkward laugh. "When you have a chimera for a pet, people don't threaten you that often." Why did I bring up Brax? I was stalling.

Bastian's eyes flew open. "What? You have a pet chimera?" Seeing him unguarded. That was worth it. He was always so composed, and the look he gave me now, honest and excited, I liked it.

"Yes, Brax. He's a rug with a heartbeat, but certainly looks terrifying." Brax didn't follow me around town or anything, but his existence in my life was common knowledge among our friends and neighbors. News spread fast in Marais, and when he'd shown up to my father's farm two years ago, more than a few people dropped by hoping to spot him. Chimeras were rare and generally avoided densely populated areas. He was the most attached to me, but he would accept belly rubs and head scratches from the rest of the family.

"I've never seen one up close. We learned all about new species in school, of course, but a chimera," he whistled, "that I would love to see."

"He doesn't really like crowds, but I'd be happy for you to meet him." Great, now I sounded like I was inviting him to be alone with me. "Anyway, no, no physical danger."

Bastian returned to lawyer mode, his expression serious. "Is this about Emir's siblings?"

"Oh, no. They haven't bothered me. Thank you for that, by the way." I paused again, then hurriedly said, "No, I'm here because I may have accidentally broken the law." Something about this office, the thick books and Bastian's perfect suits, made me feel like an imposter. Like I didn't belong here. I didn't even know him, and yet I somehow valued what he thought of me, not just what he thought about my crime.

"Ah, I see." Bastian gave me that kind smile again. He must have perfected it during so many meetings like this one. "Have you been charged with a crime? Any reason to believe you might be arrested soon?"

"No. I don't think so. A few people know, but nobody else. And it really was an accident."

"And you want to know what would happen if the police discovered your transgression?" I nodded quickly in response. "Well, in this hypothetical situation where you have committed a crime. Is it very serious? Did you take someone's life?" His shrewd eyes focused on mine, but he still wore an expression of understanding.

"No," I answered automatically, thankfully. I didn't need to be bringing up Emir...yet. "But it is serious."

His fingers lightly touched my arm, and I nearly pulled it away. "Nothing you say leaves this room. You paid me"—he nodded at the cake with a small tilt of his lips—"so I'm your lawyer now."

I inhaled deeply through my nose. "Right, thank you." I pushed up my sleeves. Bastian just stared. And then blinked and then stared some more.

"How?" he breathed.

"Do you really want to know?" I squirmed, and his eyes snapped to mine.

"Hmm, maybe not just yet. You said this was an accident?" There was definite amazement in his voice.

"Yes. I didn't set out to do this. Woke up, and they were gone. I sort of worked backward to piece it together." It was one thing to tell Indie and Simon or my parents, but exposing myself to this total stranger was a real risk. My hands were suddenly damp.

Bastian sat back in his chair and crossed his leg over his knee. And then recrossed it on the other side. It was the most discomfited I'd seen him. He continued to stare at my arms.

"Hey," I said, "my eyes are up here." His eyes shot to me, actually horrified he might have caused offense, but broke out into a grin when he saw my smirk.

"You know, I thought there was something different about you when we met. I just never imagined it was going to be this."

Something inside me perked up at that, but I just gave a small laugh as I rolled my sleeves back down. I could feel Bastian watching me as I did so, making the same deliberate examination of my face as he did in Emir's sitting room. He rose from his chair and went to the bookshelves, scanning them until he pulled out a tattered-looking volume.

"The registration laws are old, as you're probably aware. One of those things that was put in place so long ago, there won't be a lot to go on when it comes to what might happen today." He opened the book and placed it on the desk in front of me. The print was tiny, but there it was in black and white.

All persons shall submit to registration within twenty-four hours of birth. Those possessing any magical ability, as determined by a Qualified Registrar, shall receive magically restrictive blue cuffs. Those possessing no magical ability, also as determined by a Qualified Registrar, shall receive yellow cuffs.

"I will start looking into it. Who knows, it's possible you're not the only one." He leaned forward, resting his forearms on the back of his chair.

"Yes, I think you might be right." I absentmindedly rubbed my forearm where my cuffs used to be. It was something I'd not previously given voice to, even to myself. It sounded so inflammatory.

Bastian's eyebrows lifted. "Oh, why do you say that?"

"Just a feeling. It was," I paused, considering why I came to this understanding, "it was too easy what happened to me. I'd be surprised if it hadn't happened before."

Bastian nodded, and I could see the internal debate within him, whether or not to ask me how I did it.

"Actually, that's not the only thing," I added before I could lose the nerve, wiping my hands on my skirt. It had to come out. If I didn't tell someone, the truth would involuntarily come bubbling up from me when I least wanted it to. I sucked in a breath. "I killed Emir."

Bastian went still. I immediately wanted to go back to when we were talking about Brax and cakes and not murder. I closed my eyes and just started talking. From the moment I'd arrived in the restaurant to the moment Indie had pronounced Emir dead, it all spilled out of me in a rush. Then I shut my mouth, my heartbeat loud in my ears, afraid to open my eyes.

Bastian's skin was cool as his hands enveloped mine. I'd clasped them together tightly as I spoke, and now he gently pried them apart.

"Lim, open your eyes, look at me."

I couldn't. I couldn't see the horror on his face, or pity, or reprimand, or whatever it was that would change the way he'd looked at me when I'd arrived. But peeling my eyes open, I found only compassion in those rich blue irises.

"You didn't kill Emir," he said softly but with finality. I shook my head and tried to pull my hands away, but he held them tightly. "Was Emir looking normal before he saw your arms? Was he the picture of health before that day?"

I saw blood pouring down Emir's face, the sweat beading on his forehead. "No, not really, but—"

"No, Lim. You don't need to find a way to be responsible. Emir was likely shocked, but a regular, healthy person"—he pointed a little mockingly at himself and the corner of my lip quirked—"would not have died from that shock." He held up a hand as I made to interrupt. "Yes, even a Tal, even if he was hurt by it. Healthy people don't die from surprise."

I inhaled deep into my chest and exhaled the whirlwind of fear and tragedy storming inside me. When I pulled my hands away, Bastian sat back in his chair. "Thank you," I said, my voice stronger than I thought it would be.

Bastian nodded. "I know that must have been awful for you. But I can tell you cared about him. I never believed you killed him. I asked mainly to gauge Leo's reaction because he was right. Sydney might have tried—might still try, to challenge the will. But I'm confident neither of you had anything to do with Emir's death—his lifestyle just caught up with him." Bastian dropped his shoulders a little sadly.

I swallowed. I would wonder later why he had not said that Emir had cared about me, especially considering he barely knew me and he'd known Emir pretty well. The silence was awkward. "So"—I stood up—"do you want to know what I can do, or would you like me to keep that from you as well for now?"

If I'd had any doubt before that Bastian was a Jinn, the look of pure excitement on his face would have erased it.

14

LIM

LASHIA, PRESENT DAY

When I opened The Peregrine for the first time since Emir's death, I wasn't sure what to expect. Audre was doing her best to lighten the mood, juggling kitchen utensils and showing off unnecessarily fancy knife skills. Elias had come back and was going about his duties like it was any normal day. I'd even hired a small two-person band to play in the corner. I hoped they wouldn't be playing to an empty crowd. There were usually so many fires to put out when Emir was in charge. Without them, I almost didn't know what to do with myself.

I looked up a little too eagerly when the door opened. It didn't surprise me, but I was still relieved to see Aiden's frame fill the doorway.

He ducked his head as he entered. "I wanted to be the first one here for your big night." He gave me a big smile from under his bushy black beard, his hazel eyes crinkling under his hat.

"Thanks, Aiden. I should have known I could count on you." I poured him his beer like an eager schoolkid.

He clinked his glass with mine. "You really have nothing to worry about, Lim. People didn't come here just because of Emir." Aiden's eyes got unusually thoughtful. "People are drawn to you."

I cocked my head at him, the corner of my mouth turning up. Sometimes, before he'd started drinking, or just in more particularly lucid moments, it was like the sun breaking through the clouds. And I could see what he was like, without the crutch of the alcohol.

"To you and your food of course." He took a long pull on his beer, his other hand drumming nervously on his leg.

I chuckled and passed him the bowl of spiced peanuts I kept at the bar.

It turned out he was right. Most of the regulars returned, and even a few fresh faces.

Just as I was finishing up a round of drinks, Bastian Dale walked in with three other people. No suit this time. He was wearing a pale blue button-down shirt, the sleeves rolled up to his forearms, accentuating his own blue cuffs, gray trousers, and brown boots. My eyes caught Elias touching his not-insignificant bicep. Bastian smiled at him, revealing a dimple in one cheek I failed to notice before.

Right as Bastian and his group sat down, the front doors pushed open and Leo burst into the restaurant, my heart lifting at the sight of him. Several people waved and called to him, but he headed straight for me.

"Well, hello, stranger. Did you miss me?" Leo shrugged out of his jacket and hung it on a peg on the wall, his white knit shirt hugging a slim but muscled torso. I caught myself admiring him and looked away.

"Hello to you too. I didn't know you were back."

Leo was about to reply when his eyes caught on Bastian's group. The two of them nodded politely to one another. "What's Dale doing here?" Leo turned back to me. "Is Sydney making trouble?" Anger slid into his voice. A part of me purred a little at it.

"No, he said he hasn't heard anything from them. Just here for the food!" I may have said the last part a little too exuberantly, but Leo didn't seem to notice.

"Of course he is! I'm just surprised he's willing to hang out with us riff-raff." Leo gave me a sly grin that made my stomach flip before pushing off the wall and making his way through the bar to greet his friends.

I poured a deep purple glass of wine and handed it off to a passing server. Couldn't find grapes anywhere in Marias, so I made do with the smaller and more bitter descendants of raspberries and blackberries, which luckily grew in abundance. I had plans to expand the drinks menu. Emir had never been a fan of cocktails. He considered any establishment that had more than three, 'uppity nonsense.'

"Did you see?" Elias' face beamed as he ducked behind the bar. He pulled some money out of the till to make change.

"See what?" I said, looking around for signs of a tussle or other chaos that sometimes erupted when people had too good of a time.

"That lawyer is back—I only got to see him for a second at the wake and he is just as gorgeous as I remembered."

Elias' face was too earnest, and I couldn't resist. "You think?" I furrowed my brow and pursed my lips, as if trying to remember Bastian's face and whether it could be considered objectively attractive. I gave Aiden a bemused look and shook my head. "I really can't tell. What do you think, Aiden?"

"Hmm...isn't one of his eyes a lot bigger than the other?" Aiden didn't break. He squinted at Bastian, his face a perfect look of serious contemplation.

"Was that it? I thought his face had a weird green tinge." I wiped out a glass.

"Oh yeah, you're right. It's not that one of his eyes is bigger, it's that they both bug out like a fish's." Aiden shook his head in a pitying way. "Poor guy. It's nice that you can see through it all to the beauty underneath, Elias." Aiden smiled at him proudly.

Elias gave us both a withering look that reminded me viscerally of my mother. "You are both hilarious." He threw a napkin at Aiden, who caught it as he stifled a laugh. Elias whipped his head to me. "With that sense of humor, I can't understand why you're so very single."

"Ouch! I'm not 'very' single," I grumbled. "I'm just plain 'single.'" Elias rolled his eyes. Leo's distinct laugh sounded from across the room, and I glanced over at him.

Elias cleared his throat loudly, and my eyes snapped back to his. "You need to give someone else a chance." His voice was low, rapid, and meant only for me. "You cannot go on living in this no-man's-land." He waved his hand in Leo's direction. "Pun very much intended."

My mouth popped open, but Elias just gave me a pointed look before strolling back to his tables.

Aiden was studying his beer intently. Traitor.

I shook off Elias' comment and grabbed the full bus bin on my way back to the kitchen. The kitchen ran beside the bar, but I had to walk into the dining room to get to the entrance. There were several small skylights in the ceiling, wooden slats that I had to raise and lower manually as the weather permitted, but it was a cool evening and the smoke easily wafted through them along with the smell of roasted meat and baked bread. As I walked toward the kitchen entrance, I caught sight of Bastian and his group again.

He sat with three other people. Two women and a man. I recognized two of them—the older woman, she'd been in before—for New Year. Curly silver hair, an easy, merry smile. She seemed like the ranking member of the group, and I pegged her for something rich—the pasta, perhaps. The other woman was Betty, Bastian's assistant. She'd be a red wine, steak frites. The man was unfamiliar. He was tea, chicken salad—no croutons. I dumped the dishes in the dishwashing area and went to peruse the tickets—I quickly found his table and hummed at my little victory. I'd gotten their orders correct, except the other man had gotten the croutons after all—perhaps it had been a long week. Bastian had ordered the chicken and dumplings.

I turned to their table again to see Bastian looking at me. His mouth turned up at the corners as he turned back to his companions. The silver-haired lady had seen it though—she raised her hand in a wave and somehow, without really beckoning, made it clear that she wanted me to come over. I made my way through the tables, saying hello to various guests and snagging Elias to let him know table eight needed more bread. Bastian's party was all smiles when I arrived.

"Good evening. Good to see you, Bastian, Betty. How are you all doing tonight?" I said with a bright smile, trying to channel some of Emir's bravado.

"You're the owner of this lovely place? Calimea Revin?" The older woman spoke first.

I smiled in acknowledgment. "Lim, please."

The woman's eyes lit with excitement in response. "I'm Grace," she continued, "Bastian's mother. I think you know Betty, and this is Peter." Betty and Peter both gave me friendly smiles.

"It's very nice to meet you. How has everything been this evening?" Speaking to customers was not my usual role, and I hoped I sounded professional. Sometimes I'd come out to speak to my friends or family, but never to just anyone, not like Emir did.

"Everything has been delicious. I cannot remember when I had a better meal," Bastian replied with a slight smirk.

"Hey!" Grace put her hand over her heart, and I suddenly saw the resemblance. They had the same mouth. "I suppose I can't be offended. I was never any good at cooking and his father was worse. Definitely nowhere near this!"

I chuckled. "Thank you for that, but the next time you pay me a compliment," I said out of the corner of my mouth to Bastian while giving Grace a placating look, "please do it without insulting your mother."

Bastian laughed out loud next to me, and I let myself really look at him, suddenly conscious that I'd been deliberately trying not to do so.

He eyed me appreciatively. "I will bear that in mind. My mother has been here before and had been suggesting I try it. After that cake, I figured I should come back under better circumstances."

A blush climbed my chest at the mention of the cake. "I'm glad you did. It was actually my mother's recipe made with pumpkins from my family's farm."

"That's so lovely, spending so much time with your family." Grace looked delighted.

Betty and Peter chuckled. Bastian rolled his eyes and gave a long-suffering sigh. "Very subtle, mother."

Grace just shushed him. And it was my turn to laugh. I didn't miss the way Bastian's eyes had dipped to my mouth for a brief moment before he caught himself.

I had the sudden urge to escape before any of these people discovered how limited I truly was at small talk. "Let me get you another round of drinks. On the house." There were some affected protests, but I just waved them off and made my way back to the bar. I ducked under the bar and poured them another round, handing it off to Elias to deliver.

The crowd became rowdier as the night went on. I barely had time to look up from the bottles, glasses, and ever-changing faces before it was

ten, and while the bar was still lively, the dining area was near empty. I
had not seen Bastian's group leave.

I hummed happily while folding an endless pile of napkins. Aiden had
been right. Everything had gone well. The people of Marais showed up
just as they had before. They drank and laughed and enjoyed my food.

It was bittersweet, but this morning, I could almost ignore the bitterness, the itchy feeling under my skin reminding me of how I got here.

Someone knocked, three sharp, loud bursts.

Dropping the folded napkins into their bin, I walked across the floor.
It was early. The weak light washed the tables and chairs in gray tones.

"Good morning," I said, opening the door to find a man with short
gray hair and a slim build staring at me.

"Good morning, Ms. Revin. My name is Detective Andrews. Would
it be alright if I came inside?"

A plug pulled. My insides were spinning, circling the drain. This was
it. One good night and I was going to be arrested. Somehow, I pulled the
door open for him without shaking. As I closed it, I schooled my face
into polite disinterest.

"How can I help you?"

What would it be? Imprisoned for killing Emir or removing my cuffs?
Perhaps I could serve the sentences concurrently. Bastian could tell me.
Shit. I shouldn't be talking to Andrews without Bastian. Or would that
make me look more guilty?

"I was hoping to ask you a few questions about Emir Martin. About
his death."

I walked away from him, keeping my pace slow. Ducking under the bar, I motioned to the still-brewing teapot.

He nodded. "Thank you. Milk and honey, if you have it."

I busied myself with making his tea. "Go ahead."

"How long did you know Mr. Martin?" He placed a small notebook on the bar and opened it.

"Practically my whole life. His son, Leo, and I went to school together."

"You had a relationship with Leo Martin, did you not? A romantic relationship?"

He didn't look at me as he asked. He sipped his tea, hand poised to write.

"Yes, when we were kids, teenagers. Not since then." My hands were clammy, but I didn't dare wipe them on my apron. I fell gratefully on the pile of napkins again, folding each one precisely so they wouldn't run out during this conversation.

"Did you know Emir had left you the restaurant?"

I shook my head. "No. He never told me." Andrews opened his mouth, but I cut him off. "Neither did Leo or Sasha."

"Odd that they didn't tell you, isn't it? He's your ex-boyfriend, and she's your friend. Don't friends tell each other secrets?"

I slid a palm down the napkin, thinking of Sasha and Priya's tiny face. "Emir was somewhat unreliable. I'm only guessing, but they probably didn't tell me because he could have changed his mind at any point."

For every good thing Emir did for me, for my family, there was an equal letdown. Each time he was kind to my siblings or gave my father a drink on the house, there were times he broke dishes trying to carry them from the kitchen while drunk or wasted our meager ingredients playing late-night host to his friends.

A tear fell onto the napkin I was folding. Working with Emir was like being in the middle of a seesaw, never knowing which side was going to go down. I wiped my face and looked up at Andrews.

He was watching me closely. "I'm sorry for your loss. Do you think you could take me through the morning of his death?"

"I was here around seven a.m., started prepping vegetables. Water started falling from the ceiling. That's when I heard Emir yell for me to come upstairs. When I got up there—"

"Did you go straight upstairs? When he called?"

"Yes," I said, bristling. "I grabbed a bucket to keep the water from falling onto the counter, but then, yes, I ran upstairs. Water was everywhere. Emir was trying to stem the flow of it from the shower. I turned it off at the valve."

Red eddies in the water. Sweat on his forehead, his mustache.

"That's when I saw he was bleeding. He told me he'd slipped and hit his head on the pipe."

"Was he dressed?"

"Sorry?" My brows knitted.

"Was he dressed? Or was he prepared to get into the shower?" Andrews' notebook was somehow already full of writing.

"He was dressed. Despite what Sydney thinks, I've never seen Emir naked, nor did I ever try to seduce him. He never tried anything with me either," I tacked on at the end, my lips pulling to the side as I frowned. "That's why you're here, right? Sydney wants you to prove I killed her brother?"

"I'm not a private detective serving individual citizens. I'm only here to get the facts. But as you've brought her up, why do you think she believes this is foul play?"

'Because she's a hateful bigot' was probably not the most helpful answer.

"Because she thought he should have left it to her. Despite neither of them liking each other all that much."

"You paid attention to their relationship?"

I rolled my eyes. "One doesn't need to be an expert in human behavior to see two siblings interact and know they barely tolerate one another."

"Sydney hasn't been very nice to you, has she?" Andrews asked, sipping his tea but never taking his eyes off me.

My skin bristled. "Sydney isn't nice to anyone she can't use."

"But particularly rude to you, correct? And the sous chef, Audre?"

"Audre had nothing to do with this—she wasn't even here when it happened."

"But you were. You were the only one with Emir when he hit his head on a shower valve, despite not having actually been showering. Of the two doctors in Marais, you called for the one that was farthest away."

A weight dropped into my stomach. I didn't even think about the other doctor. And he was closer. The magic hummed inside me, begging me to escape, but I forced myself to meet Andrews' eyes.

"And the only witness to Emir's statements that he slipped at all, that it was an accident, are you and your ex-boyfriend. An ex that is one of the two witnesses, the other of which is your friend, to Emir's will." At this, Andrews glanced around like he'd see Leo lurking somewhere. "If you're me, don't you think that's a little suspicious? If you were me, wouldn't you be wondering how a man slips on a pipe and ends up dead? People slip and fall all the time. They don't usually die."

Andrews' words weren't angry. He wasn't upset about any of this. He was trying to bait me. Emir's red face, wheezing in shock, swam through my mind.

"They don't," I gritted out. "Normal, healthy people don't die from a simple fall. But Emir wasn't healthy. And this wasn't his first fall, not by a longshot. I found him passed out drunk more times than I can count." A buzzing strength ran up my skin. "Emir didn't give me this place. I *earned* it for every time I've had to clean up his vomit, lie for him when a debt collector came by, and by being an amazing fucking chef."

I ducked back under the bar and strode to the door, opening it wide for Andrews. "Now, if you'll excuse me, I have a restaurant to run."

15

ASRA

TREVESTEN, ~ 500 YEARS AGO

Asra wiped the sweat from her neck. The cramped storeroom under the bakery was ideal for her less salubrious activities, but it was sorely lacking in airflow. It had an entrance through the bakery, as well as two other exits behind where she currently sat. One of those exits led straight to the docks and the other to one of the bigger marketplaces, where a person making a hasty escape might easily melt into the crowd. She wasn't really expecting to need it today, though. Brigid, Elwin, and Solvan were all stationed at the other exits and Connery was with her.

Asra floated the pitcher of water next to her to fill the two water glasses on the table. Connery caught his from the air.

"Thank you," he said, downing it.

She sat at a small rectangular table while he leaned against the wall to her right. He'd been with them for over six months now. As usual, he had a hood pulled low over his face, his clothing nondescript. When he'd first agreed to work with them, they'd teased him that regardless of what he wore, he would stand out if he didn't stop walking around like he was better than everyone else.

"I am not going to slouch," Connery growled.

"Nobody is saying you need to slouch, you whiny little—"

"*Solvan.*" *Asra's lips twitched as she cut him off. Solvan was perched on the back of the sofa, throwing bladed stars at the wall across from them. Each time they landed, with deadly precision, they made a soft thunk. It annoyed Connery, which was, of course, why he was doing it.*

Solvan had been raised without family in this life. He'd never known his father. His mother had been on her seventh life when she had Solvan and died shortly after he was born. He, of all of them, resented Connery the most for his cushy upbringing. Asra thought he might be warming to the male, though. He'd at least stopped using his glamoring abilities to do unflattering impersonations of Connery.

"*Look, watch me,*" *Brigid said, straightening her spine and looking down her nose at all of them as she gracefully floated across the room.* "*That is not the gait of a low-magic Suka from Oderon. That is the gait of a pretty boy who has never even had to use his very extensive power because everything is done for him.*"

Connery scowled but was silent.

"*Now watch Elwin.*"

Elwin prowled across the room, his eyes wary. He leered mischievously at Brigid before sinking down into a chair, head slightly bent and hands within easy reach of his weapons.

Connery clenched his jaw so tightly, Asra was sure he was going to crack a tooth. He inhaled through his nose and looked like he might strangle them all. Asra gave him a wry smile, and he exhaled, making his way across the room in a passable impression of Elwin.

"*See, there you go,*" *Brigid praised.*

Next to her, Elwin pushed his lips up and nodded in agreement. "*Not bad.*"

Connery looked at her, almost embarrassed. Asra just nodded and ignored the skittering she'd been feeling under her skin for weeks now.

Cool air rushed around her and pulled her from the memory. She tipped her head back and repressed a moan. "Thank you. That is such a relief."

"Not just a pretty face," Connery grunted, crossing his arms over his chest.

Asra tilted her head toward him but did not meet his gaze. "Your face is the least attractive thing about you." She could feel Connery's smile as he adjusted his position.

He'd spoken only a little about Sabine. Understanding that having the queen's estranged mate as a member of the group could put their activities under additional scrutiny, he had given them the basics early on. The queen's actions had driven him away, and he came to Oderon to move on, or wallow. She wasn't sure about the last part. The queen had kept it from the paper for months and then portrayed it as a mutual parting until they both 'matured,' but anyone could read through the lines.

Sabine had fucked up.

Asra turned to him. "I mean that, you know."

His eyes were almost clear, the steely fog just hiding at the edges. His fingers flexed. It was the third time since they'd been down here. He'd need another fix soon. He seemed to take only small doses throughout the day and a slightly larger dose at night to sleep. Brigid had tried to pry, but he'd shut down any discussion on the matter. Solvan had only half-jokingly theorized that he used hush to dull the pain of having to hang out with us Sukas after living so long in luxury. But Asra had other suspicions. She kept her mouth shut for now. He would tell them when he was ready.

Connery's head snapped to the stairs as they heard footsteps descending. Asra, who had done this many times, casually appraised the male who appeared.

He had a round, friendly face and an excellent head of pale, wavy hair. Asra could tell from here that it had a slight blue tinge to it. She cocked her head and motioned to the knife in front of her. The male sat down nervously and picked up the blade. He pricked his finger and let the tiny drop of blood that appeared fall into the bowl of liquid she'd set before him. It swirled slowly and inconspicuously at first but then picked up speed, changing from red to a pale green.

She opened a vial and let a drop of her own blood fall into the bowl. The pale green circled around it, consuming it until it was gone. After a moment, the green shifted, pulling back, and the two blood types separated. The air behind her vibrated. Connery was watching in interest.

"Not enough work at the prison?" Asra asked him. Damaris were rare and, for obvious reasons, unpopular. They were usually employed as guards or used as enforcers for debt collectors. The other fae were deeply suspicious of their power, and it made it difficult for them to find other work.

"I don't want to work there. I'm a tailor." He sized up Connery in the corner. "That coat is too tight for you. I could let it out if you like."

Asra didn't take her eyes off the male, but behind her, Connery replied,

"I appreciate the gesture, but I'm in no need of a tailor at present."

Asra pressed her lips together to keep from smiling and rolling her eyes at the formal response. They'd need to work on his speech again, too.

"I'll give you ten for fifteen," Asra said. Ten gold marks for this male agreeing to return and drain his power fifteen times, which would take an equivalent number of years off his life.

"Thirty for twenty-five," he responded. At her raised eyebrows, he added, "I don't need this to do my work. I've enough power for the rest of it without this ability. I'm trying to open my own shop." He practically glowed, and Asra couldn't help the smile that tugged at her lips.

After they shook on it, she placed the gold on the table in front of him, then pulled out the darana. It was one of the best she'd ever made. Asra had tried stars, cubes, and even a sphere shape, but this round disc worked the best.

"Nothing else on top?"

The male shook his head. Like draws to like, and a darana will take a power provided by a darana before a fae's natural gifts. She was fine with taking it as well, but she wasn't about to pay for some cheap thing he'd bought off one of the less reputable dealers.

The metal glinted as he allowed it to absorb his power and store it for her future use. After he finished his final donation, it would be enough to sell or trade his special ability to hundreds of fae. Depending, of course, on how much or how little she gave them.

Giving an ability also meant donating a smaller layer of base magic. But since all the fae had some level of these general abilities, like floating objects or sending messages, there was no real demand for it as a separate product.

Before she could say another word, he scooped up his gold and, with a bob of his head, hustled away.

"I can feel you thinking back there," Asra said as she hid the darana again and readied the table for her next customer. She stretched her legs out in front of her, crossing them at the ankles.

"Does it ever go badly?" His question held only the barest hint of judgment.

Asra paused. She didn't trust Connery, not completely, not yet. "I'm very careful."

"And this is how you'll use me?"

Asra winced at his phrasing. "No, not like this." She glanced up the stairs to check no other customers were coming. "The kunli, the device I'm building to transport us from Trevesten to Sverresen, requires many different components to work. It has to be crafted with a certain type of metal, with specific markings, and imbued with an elixir. That elixir requires the blood of a royal, among other things.

"This"—she circled her hand to indicate the customers—"is because we need to be prepared. We don't know what is there, what we might need as currency, even if the magic is wild. There may be keepers of the magic. We don't know if they'll part with it willingly or if we'll need to use...other tactics. I'm planning to collect a variety of things that may help."

He was silent for a long moment, but when he spoke, it was not to comment on the 'other tactics' but to ask something that surprised her. "Do all of you share power?"

She turned to him again, hoping to pull a little more out of that head of his. "Yes, why do you ask?" Brigid, Elwin, and Solvan had been happy to trade a bit of power with her. It made them a better team.

They couldn't take too much or too many powers. Some fae had a greater capacity, but at a certain point, the magic would become unstable. They also didn't like to keep too much extra in them, in case the guards showed up and they needed to absorb the magic quickly. An empty darana didn't have as harsh a penalty as a full one.

The small portion she'd gotten from Solvan wasn't enough to change into someone else. But it allowed her to disguise certain parts of her appearance. She couldn't shift into a sleek jaguar like Brigid, but it gave her excellent night vision and quick reflexes. Elwin's power made her slightly more resistant to injury and illness. And they appreciated her ability as well—who doesn't like fire?

Another set of footsteps descended, and she had to curb her further questions, which all revolved around what Sabine really did and whether he would go back to her.

Asra nearly reared back after watching the blood of her next customer, a thin female with mousy brown hair, consume the test blood. It didn't change its rusty color like the fae before, but Asra could see the faint echo of her own, underneath but hidden. She forced herself to keep her gaze even as she eyed the fae. She was also willing to sell a lot more than Asra asked. Connery seemed to feel Asra's apprehension and tensed.

The female laughed bitterly. "Pretty sure I couldn't take the both of you. Do we have a sale or what?"

When she left, they both exhaled.

As they walked back through the streets of Oderon, Connery said, "I knew we'd be dealing with a certain kind of fae, but stars." He gave a little shudder.

'Indeed,' thought Asra, but there was no doubt her power could come in handy. Especially if they needed to steal the magic in Sverresen. They could go back more than once. Asra grinned to herself. Solvan might never have to lift another money bag. Brigid and Elwin wanted a place of their own and kids. She thought about what she wanted and her eyes involuntarily slid to Connery as he opened the door to her house, stepping aside so she could enter first.

"Better, try again," Brigid coaxed. "Use the counterbalance. If they're noticing you on the left, they're not noticing you on the right."

"I really think you've almost got it." Yasmin, Asra's friend and neighbor, had also joined the fun. She cracked her neck to the side. Her shapeshifting did a number on her if she stayed too long as a bat.

Connery blew out a breath in exasperation but planted his feet again like he was ready to attack.

"I believe in you," Elwin added cheerfully, scoring Connery's latest attempt on a piece of paper after conferring with Brigid.

"I believe in you less. But even a monkey could learn this, so figure it out," Solvan said over his shoulder, but there was no malice in it.

The simple. The three of them all had something of value—a moneybag, a dagger, and, in Asra's case, a necklace. Brigid and Yas walked around, touching them like they might be jostled in a crowd. The two females shook their hands as friends or pretended to be shop owners from whom they'd purchased goods. Connery's job was to steal the valuables with no one noticing.

The windows were thrown wide to let the night air and the sounds of the street filter in. Asra could see Yas' cat sulking outside after having been stepped on one too many times during this performance. She could hear the continuous pounding of feet on the elevated walkways.

The first several times he'd done it, they'd been blindfolded. Now he was attempting it while they could see. A small pile of coins sat on the table. Asra's attempt to make the game more interesting and ensure they gave him a fair shot. Whenever they thought he'd stolen the object, they could raise their hand. But if he hadn't yet, they had to pay up.

Asra sauntered around the house. Discussing mundane things with Yas or allowing Brigid to strong-arm her into buying a fictional pair of boots. Connery bumped into her, but she didn't feel the weight of the necklace leave her pocket. She supposed she could have worn it, but stealing a necklace off someone's neck was something they wouldn't normally do. The absence was just too quickly noticed by people who wore such expensive jewelry. Now, watches were another matter. She fluffed the cushions on the couch and even washed the dishes, all while Connery peeked in and out of her vision. His hand brushed her arm or shoulder, pushing into her as he passed.

Brigid and Yas began clapping loudly, and her hand went to her pocket. The necklace was gone, replaced by several small stones. Elwin whooped, and even Solvan provided some disgruntled applause. They'd also lost.

Connery found her in the kitchen later, preparing dinner. His presence was warm at her back as his arms came around her neck. She stiffened, but he held the necklace up in front of her.

"Touchy little thing, aren't you?" he said as he pulled the ends of the necklace back. His fingers trailed over her skin in a way that she was certain wasn't necessary. Little tendrils of feeling followed his fingers, his air and her fire combining like wisps of smoke that caressed her skin.

"Nothing good has ever come from someone putting their hands around my neck."

Her ear tingled as he huffed with laughter. He was certainly taking his time with fastening the clasp. Asra didn't even wear this necklace. She'd stolen it on a whim and hadn't gotten around to selling it. It had three strands of creamy pink pearls. Something a young royal might wear to an informal dinner.

Instead of stepping back, Connery placed his hands on her shoulders and turned her gently to face him. His eyes were striking, blue water surrounding warm islands. There was a stronger veil from the hush in them tonight, keeping his eyes from their true state. She smiled and tried to sort through the torrent of emotions that were running through her.

"I'm glad I could be the exception." His fingers traced each strand of the necklace. Dangerous, very dangerous. The way he smiled down at the pearls unnerved her. He was there and not there at the same time. He glanced up at her and Asra stilled. She shouldn't allow this. Not while that mist of green shrouded his eyes and his mind.

She stepped back. "I think royals would love this game. They'd bet way too much money and ruin life for pickpockets everywhere. It'd be all the rage." Asra toyed with the strands of pearls, chasing the warmth he'd left there.

Connery cleared his throat. "You're probably right. But they wouldn't be as good at distraction as Brigid and Yas. It's a game that requires skill from everyone, not just the thief, to be truly good."

"A team effort." She smoothed her hands down her sides. The move momentarily drew his eyes down her body.

Connery gave her a small nod.

She turned away from him and went back to making dinner.

16

LIM

LASHIA, PRESENT DAY

Another two weeks went by and the restaurant continued to do well. I settled into a routine. Audre and I prepped and cooked in the morning. In the afternoons and evenings, I worked behind the bar, and Audre worked in the kitchen with Jake, the new sous chef I'd hired. Elias continued on as my best server, and even Keen began helping out, bussing tables and running food.

And finally, I moved into Emir's rooms.

I kept delaying it, moving things out, packing it into boxes for Leo and Sasha, or cleaning the place. I dithered over paint colors and told myself it still needed airing. The chair still haunted me from the corner of the room. Leo promised he'd take it, but he was often away for work, and it would be wrong to throw it out. I finally asked Aiden to help me one early evening. As he loaded it into his wagon, he said the guys at his work could always use comfortable chairs. I barely heard him as I put as much distance as I could between me and that constant reminder of the look Emir had given me in his last moments.

When it was gone, I could finally breathe in the apartment. I'd moved in the next day.

Emir's siblings seemed to have gone quiet, mostly. I'd heard nothing more from Detective Andrews. But after I'd been open for about a week, Audre and I showed up to find the word "whore" written in bright red paint on the window.

"You know, you'd think that with prostitution being a perfectly respectable profession, it wouldn't hurt as much," Audre had said, standing next to me outside the restaurant with a hand shielding her eyes from the sun, "but it's got bite."

My lips twitched. "Perhaps she thinks my product is inferior."

Audre laughed. "That's because all the men she knows clearly have an eye for a scarecrow with a bad dye job and too much perfume."

I snorted. "A girl can dream."

Audre went to get the cleaning supplies while I approached the window and ran a nail across the paint. It flaked off easily. I'd been on tenterhooks waiting for their retaliation. I'd expected her to show up and make a scene or spread horrible rumors about me. Nightmares of her letting rats loose in the restaurant or getting one of her friends on the council to make up some rule about why I couldn't open plagued me.

"Honestly, this is probably a good sign," Audre said, continuing our conversation as if she'd never left. "It means that her and the two other assholes aren't having any luck with their legal battle."

That's what worried me. Sydney might not do any permanent damage if she thought she still had a chance to own this place. But the minute she and Tarik—I didn't count Marco because I was pretty sure he had no independent thoughts of his own—exhausted their legal options, they'd be truly dangerous.

Sunday was market day. The weather had turned cool and bright and brought relief from the endless haze that so often trapped us in a muggy cocoon. The smell of flowers from the stall next to me was wonderfully overpowering. I was happy and full from the many foods I had sampled shopping and was enjoying smelling each type of flower in turn, dreaming of the teas and cakes I could make out of them.

I held Derek loosely by the reins. He pulled a small cart behind him, already filled to the brim. Along with my father, there were a lot of very resourceful farmers in Lashia. People who had taken plots of land that had formerly been nothing but wasteland or swamp or ash and slowly nurtured them back to life. Some things had made it through, like our tiny lemons; other things were new, with new names and uses. I was admiring a strange looking blue flower; it looked almost like an iris, but with several bright yellow poms in the center.

A voice beside me spoke. "A dozen of those for the pretty lady." My head snapped up to see Leo exchanging money with the vendor. She handed him a bouquet of the strange flowers—Pomme de Flairs, she called them. He turned to me and held out the bouquet, a slow smile on his face. His sandy hair had gotten longer. I resisted the urge to reach out and touch it.

"Thank you," I said in surprise. "What are these for?" I asked, letting my good mood deepen at the sight of him.

"Can't I do something nice for my favorite chef?" He let his gaze blatantly roam over my body.

I rolled my eyes, but my cheeks flushed. I smiled into the flowers as I smelled them. Leo took Derek's reins from me and pulled him along while we walked back toward the restaurant.

"What have you been up to?" I turned to half look at him. He was wearing a grey t-shirt and jeans and had his brown leather bag slung over one shoulder. He gave a small nod to the man running the newsstand as we turned the corner and The Peregrine came into view.

"Working. I've been negotiating a deal in Chelsea," he named the northernmost borough. "A partnership. So I can stop having to go up there myself and can spend more time here." He gave me a smile that seemed to hint at how that time could be spent.

He was making plans to be in Marais more? I wondered for the first time whether I could use the plate to put my cuffs back on. What good was my power if I always had to hide it? If I couldn't be with anyone? There was a tiny spark of irritation at the thought, but mainly, it didn't sound that crazy. I had a vision of Leo greeting customers, dealing with the ones that got too handsy with me and Elias, engaging in the small talk for which I had so little talent.

Leo pulled the back door open for me, and we walked into the restaurant. He shook hands with Jake, who seemed to already know who Leo was. I wondered how much Audre had told him. He called out a greeting to Audre, who only waved her spatula in acknowledgment while she quickly got out the lunch orders. Leo helped me unload all of my purchases, using every opportunity to touch me. I got so frazzled; I told him to get out, and I'd bring him some lunch at the bar. He gave me a lupine grin as if he knew exactly how much he'd affected me.

When I brought his food to the bar, he was chatting with Aiden, who was finishing his lunch and reading the paper.

"Here you go," I said, sliding him a bowl of potato and leek soup and some fresh bread. "Have you been by to see Sasha and Priya?"

He grinned broadly in response, his chest puffing out a little. "She looks like me, don't you think?"

I hid my smirk. She definitely took after Sasha. "I'll be glad if she takes after your side and not the sleazeball that abandoned them." The thought of abandoning a woman when she was pregnant with your child was incomprehensible to me. It had broken Sasha's heart, and nothing made me happier than to see her with Celeste now, someone who really loved her and Priya like they deserved to be loved.

Leo 'hmmmd' in response. "Yeah. What an idiot. Nobody thinks ahead anymore. If he didn't want a Jinn baby, he should have used protection."

My mouth dropped open a little. I'd said the same thing about Emir. But for some reason, it sounded different coming from Leo. I grappled for a way to respond, but I wasn't sure what was irritating me about his words. Aiden's eyes rolled toward us.

Leo dipped a hunk of his bread in his soup and took a large bite, chewing contemplatively. "I mean, look at my dad. Never planned a damn thing in his life. If it weren't for me, you and Sasha would have gotten nothing."

Aiden turned slightly to give us the illusion of privacy for this conversation, but I was confident he was listening to every word.

"What did you say?" I hated how small my voice sounded.

He looked like he might try to backpedal but let out a breath in resignation, a consoling smile on his face. "Lim, you know Emir cared about you. But you had to know that none of it was his idea. To your credit, it only took me suggesting it to him once, and he went running off to Dale. I also suggested that if he left Sasha nothing, people would think he was too poor to do so." Leo winked at me. "And, of course, pissing off his siblings was also pretty high on his list. He snorted and shook his head wistfully. "He would have loved to have seen the look on Marco's dumb face when Dale told him about the will."

"I don't understand." The edges of my vision dimmed. "Why did you tell him to leave it to me in the first place? Why not you?"

"Emir would have drunk this place into the ground if he left it to me because he knew how good a living I make. But I knew that if he left it to you, he'd feel some responsibility to keep it afloat." He rapped his knuckles on the bar. "And it worked. He didn't destroy the place, and now you're a business owner!" Leo grinned at me as if he'd announced a way to ensure peace between Jinns and Tals forever.

"I don't know what to say." My head was spinning. He'd done this for our benefit, to help me and Sasha, but it was so calculated. Indie's comment about Emir caring about me 'in his way' popped into my head. He cared about Sasha and me, but not to the point of doing anything about it without being manipulated into it.

Leo reached out and clasped my hand in his, lowering his voice to a whisper. Something in me squirmed, knowing Aiden was two stools away, listening to how Leo had tricked Emir into giving me this restaurant. "I knew it would be easier for us to stay friends if you owned the restaurant. I conduct business here all the time—no reason for anyone to give us a hard time." He gave me a bracing smile as he took a long drink from his beer. He turned around on the stool, his elbows coming to rest behind him on the bar, a man supremely pleased with himself.

When Leo said 'stay friends,' a cog slowly and heavily rolled into position, pieces dropped into their places.

Something very hard wrapped around my lungs, and I struggled to take a breath. "Leo, what's the deal you made in Chelsea?" Ice filled every part of me. Leo didn't notice my eyes turn to chips as they stared him down. He was too busy waving to two of his friends who were having lunch.

Beside me, Aiden dropped the pretense and put the paper down. His eyes flicked to mine as he took a sip of his iced tea. I could almost hear him asking me if I needed help. But I didn't need help. All this time, a house had slowly been collapsing around me and I'd been ignoring the escape route.

Leo didn't even look at me as he said, "Stovi Martinez has a daughter. He wanted to make sure his money stayed in the family." Leo brushed a hand through the air as if Stovi's daughter was nothing more than an unexpected rooster you might get when hatching eggs. "She'll mostly stay in Chelsea." He finally noticed my silence and swung back around. His caress was like a wet snake. "Lim, don't worry. She's used to Jinns. She said it wouldn't bother her at all if I had Jinn friends."

I pulled my hand back, feeling gross. "How understanding of her," I said flatly. "Will Sasha and Priya be invited to the wedding?" My voice seemed to come from a deep, long untouched place inside me. Leo really looked at me then, perhaps realizing that he'd misread this conversation. "How about me? Can I bring a date?"

How could Leo know so little about me, about Jinns, after all this time?

Leo's eyes widened, his voice patronizing as he leaned over the bar toward me. "Lim, where is this coming from? You know how it is. I thought you liked this." His hand waved between us. "Things don't have to change."

I blew out a long breath, but I said nothing. Next to me, Aiden was coiled like a spring. Leo seemed to have noticed him, too. It was all fine and good for Aiden to hear him boast about his clever plans, but now he seemed to regret having an audience.

"You're right, Leo. I'm sorry." My voice was even. The deep place expanded, flooding me with a sense of calm.

Leo looked at me warily but finally sat down, nodding in finality. "Apology accepted."

"That'll be twelve marks," I said innocently, my irritation retreating like the tide from New Marée. I rolled my neck, feeling the strain this conversation, and this relationship, had on me slip away.

He paused, his drink halfway to his mouth. I channeled Ayla and continued to give him a wide-eyed look, the look of someone who couldn't imagine not getting what they wanted. And I waited. I was excellent at waiting.

Leo looked to Aiden but found the man dropping his own payment on the bar, and a little extra. He begrudgingly took out the first coin he'd ever had to pay in this restaurant, *my* restaurant, and placed it in front of me.

17

LIM

LASHIA, PRESENT DAY

I whacked the dough down onto the table, stretched it toward me, folded it over itself, and then repeated the process again, and again, and again. Kneading bread was an excellent way of processing my emotions. And the way I felt, it was lucky that I had several more loaves to knead after this.

The conversation with Leo was still, days later, filling me with shame. Anger crawled up my throat like it would choke me. I wasn't mad at Leo. He'd never asked me out or made any mention of us being together since we were kids. And he'd certainly never hidden how he felt about us being seen in public or in front of Emir. However nicely he treated me, if he'd wanted to be with me, he could have. And I just ignored that fact for years.

I was furious at myself for being so stupid and cowardly. Deep down, I'd always known it would never be anything. But I'd let myself fester with this ridiculous fantasy. I'd let the thought of Leo surround me like a fence, keeping every other man away, keeping every other idea of happiness away. For what?

I shifted the first loaf into a small basket, covered it with a towel, and moved it to a high shelf. I dumped the next mass of dough out of its basket and started again. Behind me, Elias was filling small honey bowls for the tables. Audre was caramelizing several pans of onions, and Jake was shredding roasted chicken.

The rain was plinking down onto the roof of the henhouse, playing on the small pond I had dug out back. Out the window, trees and bushes greedily soaked up the water. I focused on them as I tried to stop myself from angrily replaying every single time I'd just heard what I wanted to, avoided really looking at Leo's actions.

Something hit me in the back of the head.

"You losing it, lady? I said your name three times." Audre's face was filled with amusement, her head cocked in question.

I picked up the towel she'd thrown off the floor and huffed. "Can't a girl have a daydream without people thinking her mind is in trouble?"

Audre's eyes turned shrewd. "Who are you daydreaming about?"

Elias grinned, "Oh, I know this one! Tall, devastating blue eyes, probably reads a lot." Elias pretended to fan himself with a leaf of lettuce. His last words to me about Leo popped into my mind. He would revel in telling me, 'I told you so.'

"Is it really? Are you seeing the lawyer?" Audre asked, giving me a surprised look.

I looked at Jake for help but found him looking as interested in this gossip as Audre.

"Stars at night, no, I was not daydreaming about him." I glared at Elias, vowing to keep Leo's confession to myself. "You three are worse than my mother." She shared Elias' opinions about my love life and had dropped more than a few hints that perhaps I needed a follow-up consultation at Bastian's office. The three of them laughed as I marched off through the doors to ready the bar.

The night was again busy, and it drove all thoughts of Leo out of my head. But it was not so busy that I didn't notice when Bastian walked in, just with Betty tonight. Surprising relief flowed through me. Instead of a table, he led Betty to the bar. I smiled at both of them. Were they dating? Dating your assistant was too much of a cliche, surely? As they walked over to take their seats, Elias acted out something obscene behind him, and I struggled to hide my embarrassment.

"Hello again. How are you both tonight?" I passed an order through to the kitchen, then wiped down the bar in front of them.

Betty beamed at me. "We're doing great. Not 'we,' I'm doing great. Bastian is however he is."

I gave a startled laugh. "Alright, well, I'm glad to hear that. However are you Bastian?" I liked the way his name sounded when I said it. Bastian smiled at me like he agreed, his cheek dimpling. He wore a navy sweater that brought out his eyes. His dark hair curled ever so slightly at the edges.

"I am also doing great, thank you. How are you?"

"I am great as well"—my lips twisted—"what can I start you off with?"

"I think I'll try one of these cocktails—what do you recommend?" Betty pushed her lips out as she studied the cocktail menu. This was the second time I'd seen them at dinner. She was certainly comfortable with him.

"How about the Sand Dune?" It was a refreshing drink made with these tiny and tangy fruits that grew near the swamps.

"Sounds wonderful." She passed the menu to Bastian, but he didn't glance at it.

"And what would you recommend for me?"

"I think you ordered a cider last time, didn't you?" I chewed on my lip, thinking. "The one you ordered was a little sweet. Would you like to try something drier?" Bastian opened his mouth to respond, but Betty beat him to it.

"How did you remember what he ordered?" She said conspiratorially.

"I can remember what most people order. Also pretty good at predicting what people will order, but only with food." I shrugged. It was not an uncommon talent among restaurant workers. I started preparing Betty's drink, muddling the fruit with mint.

"Why do you think that is?" Bastian's eyes twinkled playfully.

"I think people order food based on what they like. They order alcohol based on how they want to feel."

"So you're better at knowing what people are really like?" Betty posed.

Bastian's gaze was intense and caused my body to tighten in response. The way his eyes roamed over me in admiration, I almost checked to see if I was still wearing clothes.

"Hmm," I murmured, my cheeks reddening, "I'm not sure I've thought about it that way." I passed Betty's drink to her and looked at Bastian. "How would you like to feel, then?"

He gave me a smile I felt in several places. "I'd like to feel relaxed, but not so relaxed I can't work tomorrow."

I grinned. "Wise choice." I poured him a very dry cider made with fermented berries. He sighed appreciatively after his drink, and I couldn't help noticing his hair again. It looked very soft. I had a momentary vision of what it would be like to run my hands through it.

"How is your furry rug?" He inquired. Although he was two seats down, Aiden was clearly eavesdropping and spit out his beer. Betty dissolved into silent hysterics, and Bastian was supremely confused. I vengefully considered swapping Aiden's beer for juice.

"BRAX," I announced loudly, "is doing well." I quickly tried to fill the silence with something mundane. "Last night, he caught something

I don't think I've seen before, but he ate most of it. I just found some weird-looking feathers, almost golden."

Betty wiped away some tears with her napkin and composed herself enough to say, "That's right, you have a chimera!" She glanced around like she might spot him, and I wondered how much Bastian had told her of my visit.

"He doesn't like crowds," Bastian and I said at the same time. We exchanged an awkward smile. Brax was probably upstairs, making himself at home on my bed.

Aiden's eyebrows shot up until they were practically under his hat. Unfortunately, I couldn't smack him without raising suspicion.

Betty smiled, looking very pleased with herself, but said only, "Next time then."

"Would either of you like some food?" I asked to change the subject.

"How about you just bring us what you think we would like?" Bastian suggested. Betty had just raised her glass to her lips and simply bobbed her head in agreement.

"Of course." I wrote their meals down, a meat pie for him and a braised fish for her, and deposited it with the kitchen. Several more customers sat down, and I moved down the bar to serve them, grateful for the distraction. I grabbed the bus bucket and collected some dishes before going back to the kitchen where Elias was waiting for the rest of his table's order.

"Ugh, why did you plant that idea about Bastian Dale? Now he's here and I'm all in my head." I violently speared a finished ticket on the small metal spike we used for that purpose.

"Plant the idea in your head? That he's attractive? A blind duck could see that he's handsome, Lim." Elias bumped my shoulder and said, "But

if you want to feel really awkward, you should know it's pretty obvious
he thinks you are too."

"What?" I mumbled. "A blind duck?" I speared another ticket.

Elias sighed. "Yes, actually, sometimes you really are." He picked up
the last of his plates, balanced expertly on both his forearms and swept
back into the dining room. I looked into the kitchen and found Audre
and Jake craning their necks toward the pass-through to the bar.

"Would you two stop that?" I hissed. Audre and Jake quickly resumed
their normal positions, pretending to look guilty but giving themselves
away with positively juvenile snickering.

"Sorry, Lim," Jake said innocently. "Just wanted to see if Elias was
telling the truth."

"Ugh," I mumbled again.

"Order up!" Audre looked at me with maniacal delight as she handed
me two plates—Bastian's and Betty's food.

The speed at which she'd provided these meant they were probably
meant to go somewhere else. But instead of arguing, I just gave her a
scathing look, grabbed the plates, and stalked away.

I mustered some cheerful nonchalance as I came up behind them.
"Here we are!" Setting Bastian's food in front of him brought me so
close I could smell him. I recognized that leather and woodsy scent again.
It was positively delicious, and I wanted to recreate it immediately. I
quickly pulled back before I did anything awkward, like deliberately
sniffing him.

"This looks amazing." Bastian was looking at me like he knew I was
just thinking about sniffing his neck. I quickly diverted my gaze to Betty.

"Can I get you folks anything else? Another drink?" I cringed internally. Did I just say 'folks'?

"The other bartender got us one—we're good!" Betty beamed at me.

Other bartender? I whirled around and noticed Aiden for the first time, standing inside of the bar, a towel slung over his shoulder, pouring wine for two women.

"Aiden," I said, my eye twitching, "isn't it time for your break?"

"I could use a drink. Thanks, boss!" Aiden didn't look even the slightest bit embarrassed as he ducked back under the bar and settled himself next to the women. I went back under the bar myself, giving him a look to let him know we would discuss this later but poured him a drink anyway.

I spent the next half an hour making order after order and running both drinks and food out to the tables. When I could avoid it no more or it would seem like I was actually avoiding them, I went to check on Bastian and Betty. Just as I approached them though, Betty hopped down from her barstool, gave me a little wave, and pointed toward the dining room in silent question.

"Just past the kitchen on the left," I said, indicating the bathrooms. I turned to Bastian. "How was everything?"

"It was exemplary, just like you predicted." He gave me a half smile that emphasized his dimple. "She's obviously left, hoping I'll pay the check, so I better oblige her."

"Oh, right, of course." I grabbed his tab from the register. He dropped the total, and then some, on top.

"Thank you. It really has been wonderful. I hope everything is still okay?" He glanced quickly to my arms.

"So far, so good." I handed him his change, but he waved it away. "Thank you very much." And before I could stop myself, blurted out, "It was really nice to see you again."

He looked like he was about to say something, then closed his mouth. His hand went to his chest, and he plucked his sweater a bit like he was warm. "It was really nice to see you again, too."

There was an awkward pause.

"I can't watch this," Aiden suddenly interjected, somehow once again standing behind the bar. His voice carried over the heads of the three people between him and Bastian. Bastian's eyes flew to him. "The Peregrine is closed on Mondays. There's that show playing at The Brixton—"

"Beyond the Ruins?" asked Bastian.

"Stars, no." Aiden groaned. "That funny one with the guy with the hat."

"I think he means 'Twelfth Night,'" the man closest to Aiden supplied helpfully.

"Yes, that one!" Aiden slapped the guy on the shoulder, nearly toppling him into his drink. "You're gonna meet her there twenty minutes before that show and then you're gonna take her somewhere for a meal she didn't cook." Aiden's large frame cut an intimidating figure as he crossed his arms, daring either of us to argue.

My eyes must have been three times their size, and I was probably redder than Brax. Bastian looked at me apologetically.

"Thank you," Bastian said genuinely to Aiden before turning to me, "I really should have been able to do that myself. I just panicked." He gave me a sheepish smile that turned my insides to mush.

He panicked? I was very close to jumping through the kitchen pass-through just to avoid this bizarre three-way attempt at romance.

"Panicked at what?" Betty said as she suddenly came up behind him. "Oh, good, you paid the bill." She looked at the two of us. "What?"

"Nothing at all." Bastian rose and helped Betty with her coat. I continued to stand there like a pointless statue. Betty waved and walked toward the door. Bastian turned to me and said hopefully, "See you Monday?"

"Seeyoumonday," I said, the words coming out weird and quick. As soon as they walked out, I turned a horrified glare on Aiden.

He held up the glass he was polishing as if he was tipping his hat and tsked, "You're welcome! Always glad to be of service." He high-fived the man across from him, who looked overjoyed to be part of this little drama.

"That. Was. Mortifying." I closed my eyes, still clutching Bastian and Betty's glasses. I turned and dumped them unceremoniously in the bus tray.

"Yeah, well, some guys are just not that great at seduction." Aiden sighed, shaking his head seriously. "But hey, give the guy a chance and maybe he'll make up for it in other ways." He gave me a look that said he was rooting for me but not entirely convinced.

"Yeah, he better give amazing foot massages or something." Audre half yelled from behind the pass-through, clearly sharing Aiden's sentiment. I jumped and whipped my head around to her. She and Jake had obviously been hanging on every word. A group of women flooded in, several of whom waved to Aiden and saved me from further discussion. Good, if he wanted to play bartender, he could make their damn drinks.

Behind my closed eyes, the memory of Bastian sitting at the bar flooded in, his muscular forearms and sweater pulled up just slightly at the sleeves. I tried to recapture the smell of him. What was it? There was a low note there I couldn't place.

I fell asleep that night, methodically thinking of all the spices in my pantry and which might match the scent of Bastian Dale.

18

LIM

LASHIA, PRESENT DAY

Monday dawned, and I was beyond nervous. I wore dresses all the time. My apron dresses had big pockets and were very practical. Who has time to put on more than one thing in the morning? But this dress was...a dress. I'd bought it a year ago but had never had any reason to wear it. Too much for family gatherings, tending bar, or cooking. It was a deep green, almost black. It had long sleeves, one of its main selling points tonight, a square neckline, and while it wasn't tight, it followed my form to just above my knees.

My hair was loose. I didn't have much jewelry, but I put on some small gold earrings, which I thought looked pretty good. I kept the makeup simple but couldn't resist doing a little flick at the edges of my eyes with some dark eyeliner.

I'd painted the walls in the apartment a soft gray. Brax had appropriated the couch in the little sitting room. He currently lounged on it, flicking his tail and occasionally yawning. There was even a smaller guest bedroom—Emir had used it as storage—that I cleaned out and painted a dark turquoise. I'd put a large mirror in the my bedroom where Emir's chair had been.

"How do I look?" I twirled around in front of the mirror. Brax yawned again, showing all of his very sizeable and sharp teeth. "I'll take that as a thumbs up." Would I be this nervous if it weren't for the magic? If I was just the same with cuffs and no magic? I thought of Bastian and his fingers, and his dimple, and his scent, and yes, I would still be extremely nervous.

Thinking of Bastian's fingers, though, made me remember how supremely stupid I'd been about Leo. A small, sick feeling took root in my stomach. I briefly wondered if I should cancel, but a voice in my head, which sounded uncannily like my mother, shrieked in opposition.

"There." I added a delicate gold necklace and smoothed down my dress in the reflection. "Good."

Brax made an expression suspiciously like an eye roll.

The Brixton was a theater. Lashia had cinemas, but they were rare. Although the library found in Eudora had many films and TV shows, by the time they could recreate the technology to watch some of them, many of them had deteriorated beyond repair. The technology to create films existed again, but it was new and clumsy. For those who had seen the "real" films, it just couldn't compare, so there'd been little progress in improving it.

I had been to the movies when an exhibition came to Marais. They showed a movie each night for a week and two on Sunday. Simon, Indie, and I had watched them all, slack-jawed and mesmerized. There was a film about an orphan girl who fixes an entire household, including the sick-but-not-really sick little boy, just by planting a garden. As someone who saw firsthand the healing powers of things that grew from the ground, it resonated with me.

The Brixton wasn't large. But it had two stacked exterior balconies punctuated by regal-looking columns that reached the roof. People were

outside, chatting and enjoying hot drinks and wine before the play started.

As I approached the theater, I tried to spot Bastian. There were several
people standing alone, clearly waiting for dates or friends. I scanned the
crowd again and found him, his head reaching above a group of older
ladies who had him surrounded. He was all smiles, shaking hands and
chatting. It seemed to come so naturally. It had gotten easier for me, but
I was still better with food than with people.

Bastian looked up and around and spotted me. My smile was soft and
nervous. What I wouldn't give for some of the ladies' confidence. His
eyes widened as he took me in from head to toe. My breath hitched a
little at the blatant appraisal. He wasn't the only one. The ladies had also
all turned to me and were giving me sweet, knowing looks. He made his
apologies, and they politely waved him away.

He was wearing another suit, dark blue this time, and it fit his broad
shoulders perfectly. As he came closer, the scent of dark couches and
hearth fires enveloped me. He stopped when we were about a foot apart
and smiled, showing me that dimple.

"You are beautiful."

Smiling, I said, "Thank you." I reached out and felt his lapel. "You
look nice in a suit."

"It's the main reason I became a lawyer," he said, completely
straight-faced.

I laughed, more at ease. "What about the admirers?" I gestured with
my purse to the ladies, who were now huddled around the ticket booth.

"Those aren't bad either." He grinned and continued to stare at me in
a way that made my insides squirm and warmth creep up my chest. "I
already bought our tickets. May I escort you inside?" He offered me his
arm.

I put my hand through it and brought myself alongside him as he walked toward the entrance. I was incredibly conscious of everywhere my body was touching him. My fingers rested on his bicep, my shoulder braced against his, even where my hair brushed against him. I melted a little at each point of contact.

We walked through the lobby and several people called out to him. He waved at them but made it clear he was not stopping to chat. He led me toward the bar where he bought us some drinks and a program, and then up to our seats in a small balcony box. Neither of us made a move to readjust when the cozy seating kept our arms pressed firmly together.

The play was amazing—my sides and cheeks ached from laughing. I wasn't sure who the guy "in the hat" was that Aiden had mentioned because most of them were wearing hats and also because I couldn't picture Aiden at the theater.

Several times during the play, I caught Bastian looking at me. He made an exaggerated show of pretending not to and turning his attention back to the performers. He was certainly not hiding his feelings, despite the bizarre method by which we'd ended up on this date. Was he always like this? Maybe this was how normal dates were? Elias hadn't been entirely wrong. Since coming back from Eudora, I hadn't been on a single date.

When the play was over, we walked outside into the cool air.

"I have a place in mind for dinner. It's just around the corner. But if you hate it, please just tell me. You're the expert."

"I won't know unless you tell me." I let myself slide a little closer to him, emboldened by our proximity during the play.

Bastian opened his mouth to speak but stopped. A rumbling noise came from around the corner, raised voices shouting and chanting. All around the theater, conversations paused, heads turned. A woman grabbed her children and marched decisively off in the opposite direction. Most everyone else stood in confusion, waiting as the commotion grew steadily closer.

The noise intensified, and suddenly, about fifty people came pouring in from the other side of the street. They were carrying torches and shouting the words printed on their banners and signs, "Go home, Jinns!" Their expressions were angry and dangerously frantic.

"We need to get out of here," Bastian said, his grip on my hand tightening.

We were at a distance where I wasn't scared but close enough that I didn't argue. Bastian pulled me close and looked around. We started quickly making our way to the opposite end of the street. There were now plenty of other people around us who had decided that being elsewhere was the best choice.

Bastian pulled out a whistle and began blowing it in short, deliberate bursts—some kind of code. The rioters began smashing windows and throwing in their torches, destroying what they could find: mailboxes, planters, even the small trees that had been so preciously planted. Flames grew inside the empty storefronts, escaping outside to climb the cloth awnings.

Bastian's whistled code was being repeated from multiple directions. People came rushing out from houses and from adjacent streets. Some wore uniforms, but others just wore black and white armbands, the police and reserve officers.

I chanced a look behind me and was shocked to recognize the man who'd thrown the rock at The Peregrine. He unfortunately noticed me, too. His eyes narrowed and his face contorted in anger I would have thought impossible for someone to feel for a stranger.

"Get that bitch!" he yelled to the others. A group took after us. We sprinted down an alley and made several turns. I had the frivolous thought that my dress was going to be ruined.

Firefighters appeared, their numbers steadily increasing with the amount of smoke rising into the air. I had to concentrate so I wouldn't lose Bastian, despite our clasped hands, among all the people running beside us.

Stars, the smell of smoke was suffocating. I squeezed my eyes for a moment and deeply hoped the theater, its occupants, and the group of ladies were safe.

Bastian gripped my hand tighter. "Just a bit further. I think there are enough responders to contain them now. We just need to get away from the fire." His whistle blasts were no longer being repeated though. Nobody else was coming.

We rounded a corner and came face to face with a small group of rioters, led by that angry Tal. His eyes darted around like a snake's tongue, testing for threats in every direction. But his voice came out certain when he barked, "Grab them!"

Bastian gripped my hand tighter, turned, and ran down another street, then another corner. The smoke became thicker each way we went.

"I think we've turned around!" I yelled over the shouting, the popping of the fire and now constant whistles.

"I think you're right!" He ran back the way we came just as someone hurled a large trash can filled with fire at us. We both stumbled back as it crashed only a few feet away, its fiery debris spilling out onto the street and filling the air with the smell of burning and rotted food. The man who had thrown it yelled to someone we couldn't see,

"They're over here!"

He stepped from behind a corner. He'd torn his jacket, and he was panting. I didn't need to look to know it was the man from before. His eyes lit up menacingly at the sight of us.

I grabbed Bastian and ran toward an alley. I pulled him back behind a dumpster and said, "Let's go my way."

And there was silence.

Bastian stumbled as he stood upright. I'd brought us to the field behind my parents' house. I couldn't be sure the man from the riot wouldn't look for us at The Peregrine, and my parents' place was pretty remote. He stepped back and looked around, bewildered.

"We're at my parents' house." The lights were on in the house, but it was otherwise pitch black. I put my hand in his and started walking toward the house. I had the fleeting thought that it was much too soon to be introducing Bastian to my parents. My father's balaras brayed in greeting, setting off a cacophony of farmyard noise.

The back door opened with a quiet creak. My father walked out to us, holding a lantern.

"It's just me, Dad," I announced above the din.

"Are you alright?" He eyed our disheveled clothing in surprise as he raised the lantern. We must have smelled like a bonfire.

I nodded. "Is anyone else here?"

"No, just us. Ayla and Keen are asleep. Your mother is inside."

Bastian was still unnervingly silent.

"Mr. Dale." My father nodded to him. "Would you like to come inside?"

"Thank you," Bastian said. If it surprised him that my father knew his name, he didn't show it. It must have been a habit because he straightened his suit jacket and re-buttoned it. "It would be a pleasure."

My father looked like he might laugh, but I shook my head behind him and he just said, "Pleasure's all mine," and led the way into the house.

As we trooped into the living room, my mother's eyes widened in shock.

"Calimea? What have you two been doing?"

"I'm afraid our date took a turn for the worse," Bastian said. "There was a riot outside the Brixton. Some truly unpleasant people tried to attack us." My mother's mouth dropped open. "Lim saved us." Everyone turned to look at me, but before I could open my mouth, my mother said,

"Drinks! All that smoke, and you're probably hungry too. Calimea, why don't you come help me in the kitchen?"

When the door closed behind us, my mother simply said, "Tell me."

As I washed up, I explained about the Tals, the man from the restaurant, and my spur-of-the-moment decision to bring us here. My mother, ever the hostess, started pulling out glasses and arranging them on a tray with an assortment of olives, pickles, cured meats, and bread. I went down to the cellar to get some cheese.

That man knew where I lived.

I willed myself to the yard behind The Peregrine.

Everything was quiet, no fires, no smoke, no sign of any angry Tals. I breathed a sigh of relief and went back to my parents' cellar, grabbed the cheese, and came back upstairs. My mother just raised her eyebrows.

"All good, for now."

We brought the food and drinks out into the living room. My father was sitting comfortably, reading the paper in front of the fire. Bastian had taken off his jacket and rolled up his sleeves. The shock had clearly worn off, and his curiosity was showing. I handed him a glass.

"Is there anyone you are worried about that may be in the danger zone? Anyone you think you might need to check on right now?"

Bastian shook his head. "I don't know anyone who lives in the area, but it might be good to know if it's over."

"The museum?" my father said questioningly.

I nodded.

I went to the roof of the museum specifically. We'd had science field trips up here as children. It was also where they'd first hammered in the purported theory on the development of our magic. It was high enough that I could see out over the theater and surrounding streets. There were still fires burning, but the group of Tals had clearly dispersed—their nasty banners abandoned in the street.

The fire brigade had appeared and was working on controlling the last big blaze. People were everywhere working on the few smaller ones, stamping out burning embers and throwing buckets of water. It was bad, but there didn't appear to be anyone panicking or screaming, and I was relieved to see the theater still standing.

"It's okay," I said when I returned. "Most of it is contained and the rioters are gone." I took a swig of my drink. "Seems like it's not just the law I need to worry about." My voice was weak. I was terrified to think about what would happen if more people found out that there was a Jinn without their cuffs. "The Sun Guardians are getting worse every day."

"There's only one of you—and they don't seem to be too bothered about the registrars having magic." My mother looked at Bastian as if he could make this true.

I didn't miss the quick clouding of Bastian's eyes. My father responded, "The registrars exist to restrict Jinns, and they're Tals."

Bastian took a breath but then exhaled. "He's right. The registrars have magic for a very singular purpose."

I took another drink, letting the cool wine soothe my throat. How the registrars received and maintained the power to cuff us was the most closely kept secret in Lashia. My eyes found Bastian's.

"I don't know much about them," he said, practically reading my mind. "The registrars show up in shifts, two or three every couple of years, and then they go back to Eudora, and a new set arrives. They always travel with two accompanists, and they shut down any conversations regarding their magic or how they 'return' it when they're done with their services."

"It *is* getting worse, isn't it?" I refused to look at my parents as I asked him. He didn't look away, didn't hide the answer in his eyes. When he didn't speak, my mother sucked in a breath beside me. "I thought maybe it was just me because I'm in more danger now, but it feels like they're so much angrier, and so much more organized." I bit my lip. "Why? Why now, all of a sudden?"

Bastian shook his head, his eyes hollow. "I haven't heard of any others like you, if that's what you're asking. I don't know what's suddenly riling people up so much." He gave a sympathetic look at my parents. I wondered if Grace worried about Bastian, in his profession, often dealing with irate Tals.

The four of us nibbled and drank in silence for a while, each of us contemplating what this meant for us and all Jinns. After we'd finished our quiet meal, he stood up and held out his hand. "May I walk you home?"

Seriously, how did this man still look good after all that? I was pretty sure I was covered in soot and my hair was probably frightening. But he smiled at me like we had just come from a romantic evening out and were now just sharing a quiet drink with my family and hadn't just survived a riot and a worsening world-view. Although it had actually been a very romantic evening until that last part.

I took his hand. My father retrieved his suit jacket, and he thanked them for their hospitality.

"Are you sure you want to walk?" I said, giving him a lopsided smile. His eyes lit up.

I put us in my sitting room.

He let out a breath. "How long does it take to get used to that?"

"I'll let you know," I said, chuckling. Kicking off my shoes, I groaned at the relief. Running in heels was something I hoped I'd never have to do again.

The restaurant was quiet. Brax was gone, out hunting whatever poor creature was about to see its last night.

"This is not a line, I swear, but I'm a little worried about you—that man recognized you. I'd like to stay. I can sleep on the couch."

I ran a hand down my neck, and Bastian's eyes tracked the movement. I hadn't even kissed Bastian and the thought of him being under the same roof as me, even if he would be a room away, was making certain parts of me hum. My nerves rattled. It was quite different to go from dreaming about a man you saw occasionally to having one right in front of you, offering to protect you from danger.

Bastian's eyes darkened, as if he could sense the direction of my thoughts.

"There's no need for the couch," I said to break the growing tension. "If you'd like to stay, I have another bedroom." Just as we stepped out into the hall, Brax leapt through the window. Possibly because the night had so many surprises already, Bastian only flinched a little before staring in unrestrained awe. Brax stalked over and wound around the two of us before retiring to the couch. "Besides, the couch is taken."

19

ASRA

LASHIA, ~ 500 YEARS AGO

The five of them surrounded the broken kunli. A crack ran straight through the middle of its short metal body, the red stone at its center now dull. The air was heavy with silence. Nobody wanted to speak the obviously terrible situation into existence. It had taken so long to gather the materials, to obtain the right magic, from the right people. The device itself had taken weeks to craft. It should have been strong enough to get them back and forth multiple times. The jagged edges of the lifeless thing laughed at their hubris. Asra's breath quickened, and she was moments from hurling the thing to the ground when deft fingers reached out and plucked it from her hands.

"Let's not panic just yet," Brigid murmured. She put the pieces back into their case and stored it in her pack.

Asra took a breath and exhaled slowly. The walls of the cave were strangely smooth. The air was unusual, too, stale and lifeless. She shared a look with the others. Something was definitely off. Brigid and Elwin cautiously approached the mouth of the cave, swords drawn. Asra held her hands in front of her, her fingers heating with power. Behind her, Connery and Solvan, weapons also drawn, were the last to step out into the light.

It was dusk. A filmy orange light filtered through the sparse trees, making everything look greasy. Asra wrinkled her nose. Even the smells were foreign. They were in the mountains, but a sulfuric smell dampened the scent of trees and moss.

The terrible feeling she'd had from the moment they'd arrived grew stronger in Asra's chest. All the hope and excitement they'd been feeling last night was slowly being consumed by this awful place. She could feel Connery's eyes on her, but she avoided looking in his direction, afraid of the anger and disappointment she'd see there. This was not part of their deal.

They continued to walk silently down the mountain. Water rushed from somewhere below, and if life existed in this peculiar place, it would be there. Asra steeled herself. All was not lost. Perhaps they'd just arrived in a particularly unsavory place in Sverresen.

The river was wide and shallow with filthy, sluggish water. After Connery used the air to push the sides apart to check for hidden danger, they picked their way across, boots squelching in the mud. Behind them, Asra expected to see the river pouring through a muddied ridge but found no explanation for its sad appearance.

A sickly-looking deer appeared upstream. Its fur was the same dull brown as the river.

"Feels like we'd be doing it a favor," Solvan said.

"We might as well. Can't be sure when we'll get fresh meat again." Brigid pulled out a bow, but a surge of air rushed passed us. The deer froze, made a small choking sound, and keeled over.

They all turned to Connery, who had his hand out, fingers curled toward the deer.

"Neat trick," Solvan said with genuine honesty.

Connery frowned. "It should have been easier than that."

"I complimented you once. Don't go fishing for more," Solvan drawled.

"No, I feel it too," Brigid said. "That thing weighing down my power. It's not terrible, but it's definitely not normal." She shared a look with Elwin, who took his sword and jabbed the tip into his arm. Usually, nothing would have happened, but this time, an angry red mark appeared before healing over.

Connery turned in her direction, but Asra looked away before he caught her gaze. She felt it as well. Like they were dragging their magic behind them instead of it flowing easily in their veins.

She held on to the hope that it was the journey, and not this place, that had weakened them.

After they'd broken down the deer and Asra flash-roasted it, they continued to make their way down the mountainside. The trees became even more sparse, the vegetation mostly weeds and overgrown vines that swallowed everything. They blanketed huge, irregular shapes. Asra assumed the shapes were more trees or hills until they stepped into what was clearly the remains of a city. The vines hid buildings and houses. They curled all over what looked like metal carriages. A few more animals crossed their path, just as thin and bedraggled as the deer.

Asra was no longer sure what they were looking for, but they kept walking.

An hour after they'd descended the mountain, they caught the attention of two people who began to follow them. Their pursuers had originally been roaming around a hollowed-out building filled with more of the rusted machine corpses. They moved swiftly to each one and chattered loudly in a language Asra didn't recognize. Since they weren't attempting to be quiet, Asra assumed they didn't need to worry about anything too dangerous here.

Asra and the others made themselves obvious, magic and weapons stowed to be as non-threatening as possible. They followed for another hour or so, during which they knocked several things over and even accidentally ran into one another, seriously testing Asra's ability to pretend she hadn't noticed them. When one of them audibly stubbed their toe, cursing in the universal language of pain, Brigid shook her head, her eyes wide. There seemed to be little point to this charade. They didn't seem scared or inclined to run off at the sight of them, anyway.

Asra, Brigid, Elwin, Connery, and Solvan stopped and sat down on a decrepit stone staircase, the building it led to gone entirely, and took out some food. Finally, Brigid looked directly at the two and waved, giving them the smile you'd give a child. They startled, and Asra could hear them whispering. Eventually they approached, slowly.

"Hello," Brigid said kindly when they were close enough. Connery and Elwin looked wary, both of them with their eyes on the surrounding buildings, ensuring this wasn't a trap. Brigid waved a bit of last night's venison toward them. "Care for something to eat?"

Both of them were thin, their faces gaunt, and they had the skittish energy of prey. They both carried packs, presumably filled with whatever they'd been scavenging. Their clothes were threadbare and a bizarre mismatch of style and material. There were words printed on the male's shirt that Asra couldn't read, and the female wore two different shoes.

The male approached first. He said something in his language we couldn't understand.

Connery responded. "We've just arrived here from Trevesten. What is this place?" The two of them gave equal looks of confusion. Connery tried several other dialects from other parts of Trevesten.

"Show off," Solvan muttered.

"Doesn't seem to be doing much good," Connery replied, rubbing the side of his face, which now sported a heavy layer of stubble he'd not bothered to remove. He pointed to himself. "Connery." He did it once again and then pointed toward the male.

The male exhaled, understanding, "Oh-wen," he said, pointing to himself and exaggerating the sounds. He pointed to his companion, "Lor-ah." She gave us a tight smile. They all gave their names. Owen and Laura repeated them several times for good measure. Connery motioned with his arms to the buildings, touching the ground at our feet, and then holding up his hands and giving Owen a questioning look. Owen briefly conferred with Laura in their language before he said, "App-lasha."

Owen and Laura gratefully ate the food. Through a combination of facial expressions, playacting, and drawings, they learned a bit about the place Asra was fast losing hope was Sverresen. If they hadn't made it that far, this must be Laloten. She glanced at the sky. It couldn't be Makome. Almost as little was known about the fifth world, but they knew it had dragons.

She shared a look of concern with Solvan, her eyes acknowledging that not only had they apparently failed to find the place of wild magic, magic they'd planned to sell back in Trevesten, but also that they were likely stuck here. All that planning, the daranas she'd created, the powers they'd procured...the blood Connery had given them, wasted. It fell like a weight into Asra's stomach. How could she have gotten this so wrong?

Laura, who had the gentle voice of a mother and was much friendlier on a full belly, drew a picture on a page of Elwin's notebook, a map of a large place with many people. She drew angry lines to show large storms and terrible winds. She crossed out nearly all the people on the page. At the group's distraught faces, she shrugged and waved her hand behind her. This happened a long time ago. She drew a smaller area within the map, closer to the coastline, and put a few people inside it before pointing to herself and Owen.

Elwin drew a map for them of Trevesten and explained as best he could that they had traveled here from there, looking for something.

Not having a better plan, the five of them joined Laura and Owen as they traveled through the dilapidated city. Navigating around giant pits of sand and water and scaling small structures, occasionally stopping so Laura and Owen could gather things they deemed useful. They made their way down a long trail, vegetation to either side but no structures.

Two metal beams ran on the outside of their trail, which often disappeared beneath piles of rocks or large puddles before emerging on the other side. Elwin and Brigid documented the oddities in their notebooks, listing all the questions they planned to ask. Laura and Owen tried to explain the beams, making an odd sound and moving their arms as if they were stirring a sideways pot. At the group's collective looks of bewilderment, the two shook their heads ruefully and gave up.

They walked for another two hours before some signs of civilization appeared. Disembodied voices floated toward them. Children murmuring to one another. A small girl ran past them into the vegetation before immediately running back, stopping to stare at them with curious eyes. She yelled something, and several more heads popped out of the tall grasses, scampering over the beams and speaking rapidly to Owen and Laura. The children also wore tattered, mismatched clothing, and there were more than a few with thin, sallow faces.

During the walk, Owen and Laura had taught them a few rudimentary words.

"Haylow," Asra said, sounding out the word in their language. The children said nothing.

Brigid and Elwin joined her attempts at a greeting, trying to coax the children into a less timid response. Connery's eyes were still suspicious, but he bowed his head to them politely. The children were drawn to Solvan, likely because of his diminutive height, but Solvan, who'd grown up with children who could fight and steal as well as any adult, only smiled warily.

The trail grew into a wider road, the children all joining their procession. They climbed uphill for another twenty minutes before finding themselves in a settlement.

Asra stopped, and her mouth fell open. The inhabitants were as varied as any of the fae in Trevesten's bigger cities, but they all shared the same drawn, sinewy look. Some were peeking out of crumbling stone buildings. Others stood beside new but simply built wooden structures.

"They all look so...defeated," Brigid whispered. And she was right. Asra had never seen expressions like these. She had never been inside Tarkana, but she imagined it was what the long-term inmates might look like.

"Where in the Allmother are we?" mumbled Solvan.

Connery moved to her side, his arm brushing against hers as he took in the space. His presence was overwhelming. Asra wished she had never allowed him to come. She was ashamed he had to witness this absolute failure of a job. There was no wild magic and no way out. At least not unless she could fix the kunli.

She turned away from the hundreds of pairs of eyes staring at her, away from Connery, toward a female off to her left. She was fiddling under a large pot. The female sat down beside it and was twisting a small stick, her hands quickly rubbing it back and forth. A skinny wisp of smoke went up, and Asra realized the female was trying to light a fire.

Asra walked over and, without thinking, flicked her wrist and sent sparks flying under the urn. The fire immediately gained momentum, licking up the sides of the metal. She turned back to the crowd, who were now all staring at her with wide, fearful expressions.

"Ah," Brigid said out of the corner of her mouth, "so not just no wild magic, no magic at all."

Asra's head snapped to Brigid in alarm. The crowd surged forward, and Elwin and Connery immediately assumed defensive stances. Several tense moments passed where nobody moved.

Suddenly, a male ran toward them, holding a listless toddler. He held the child out to them, his eyes pleading in desperation. The child's skin was waxy. Her eyelids fluttered open and closed.

He shouted at all of them, frantically begging. Asra could see Solvan's expression go from suspicious to understanding. He dropped his pack, reaching inside for one of the daranas filled with healer's magic. He paused and looked up at Asra in question.

There were so many hungry, pitiful faces, and for the first time, she had no idea what to do. He pushed the child toward them again as he and the others spoke rapidly in their language. Her fingers heated, pushing to defend her.

Asra's eyes cut to Solvan, and she nodded.

20

LIM

LASHIA, PRESENT DAY

We were supposed to be listening to a lecture.

The library held events for authors and scientists to give presentations about their work. The focus of today's lecture was on art restoration. Half a dozen paintings were displayed on the stage in varying degrees of recovery. I had salvaged a few paintings myself, intending to hang them in The Peregrine, and was hoping to pick up some tips.

But seeing those cool blue eyes roam over me was making it very difficult to concentrate. I cleared my throat, and he reluctantly turned back to the speaker. Our legs were nearly touching as we sat side by side with the other guests. A breeze blew in from the open window. The scent of him floated over to me, mixed in with the smell of ancient paper and ink.

We clapped softly when the presentation was over. Bastian's hand found the small of my back as he led me out the front door and into the sunshine.

"Thank you. I hope it wasn't too boring for you." I smiled, mourning the loss of his warmth as he dropped his hand. We walked side by side down the street, occasionally nodding or waving to people we knew. It was all very normal and civilized and entirely unfamiliar to me. Irritation

flared through me at how long I'd settled for nothing but Leo's inconsistent flirtation for company.

"Don't be ridiculous. I was mesmerized." He smiled at me. There was
no game in it, just honest appreciation.

"Me too," I responded as he opened the door to the cafe. We stepped
into a quiet interior.

A girl no older than fourteen and skinnier than a toothpick led us to
our table. Without a word, she placed two glasses of water down before
ducking back into the kitchen.

"How are things at the restaurant? Sydney and the others still leaving
you alone?" Bastian leaned toward me. I liked the way he looked at me,
like there was nothing else worth his attention.

"Good, yeah. Not a peep since her delightful artwork."

Bastian nodded solemnly. "She doesn't seem the type to get her hands
dirty. Probably had someone else do it for her."

"Probably not," I mused. "Also, 'whore' is over four letters, so I'd be
surprised if she knew how to spell it."

Bastian chuckled, his eyes twinkling.

I sighed. "That wasn't fair of me. Sydney isn't stupid."

Our server chose that moment to reappear. She again said nothing but
simply looked at us expectantly.

"What do you recommend?" I hadn't even glanced at the handwritten
menu.

She jabbed her thumb at a chalkboard hanging on the wall behind her.
"Special's nice."

Bastian and I both craned our necks to see behind her. The board said
only 'fish cakes and salad.'

We shared a look, and I shrugged.

"Two, please," Bastian said, giving her a polite smile. She vanished almost instantly back into the kitchen.

He cringed. "Sorry, I come here all the time for lunch, but I haven't seen her before."

I waved it away. "It's fine. I've had to pull Elias away from tables when he's been chatting too long. This is a refreshing change of pace."

He scanned the restaurant and lowered his voice. "I have to confess, I've failed as your attorney."

My eyebrows shot up. "Oh?" I couldn't help scanning the restaurant, alarmed. Was his 'failure' going to lead to my arrest?

"I couldn't find anything on your particular situation. It doesn't look like there's been any precedent for such a thing since the origin of the registration."

I let out a breath. "I see. Well, that's better than knowing it has happened and the punishment is life in prison."

Bastian put his hand over mine. His skin was soft, and I couldn't help but think about how it might feel caressing other parts of me.

"I will let you know if I hear anything else. But probably best that I take off my lawyer hat so I can continue to enjoy your company socially."

I grinned and shook my head. "I take it you're not good at multitasking?"

"It's not that. Previously, lawyers weren't really supposed to date their clients. Not currently a requirement given our meager population of both people and lawyers, but it's not a bad rule."

"Ah, well," I said, motioning with my eyes to my arms, "if you hadn't noticed, I'm a bit of a rule breaker."

Bastian gave me a smile that made my skin pebble. Tiny bolts of electricity moved down my body. He opened his mouth, but the server interrupted him by unceremoniously dropping two plates of food in front of us, the faint outline of her blue cuffs glowing through the thin material of her shirt. She hustled away without a word. What was her ability? Maybe she never wondered about it at all.

After lunch, I strolled back to the restaurant, enjoying the late afternoon light filtering through the clouds. It had been a perfect date. The food was surprisingly good despite the service. Bastian still made me nervous. There was something about him that intimidated me a little—probably just the expensive clothes. I browsed through a few window displays, thinking maybe I'd buy some new things for myself.

There was a gorgeous red dress in the shop window. It was far too fancy for anywhere in Marais, but maybe Eudora. I pictured walking arm in arm with Bastian as we made our way into one of the bigger theaters. Him in his black wool suit, the red dress swishing around my hips.

My smile fell as my eyes landed on the elbow-length sleeves. I looked at every other dress in the window and those on display in the next store over.

I wouldn't be able to wear any of them.

On Sunday, two weeks after the riot, I was sitting with Sasha, Celeste, and Priya in the park. The weather was perfect, cool enough for blankets but still warm enough to sun ourselves. I'd brought a picnic, and the three of us sat near a thriving willow tree. We were happily munching away on some crustacean salad (I'd never caught enough to get more than a few cups of meat at a time) and spiced potato chips. Priya snoozed in her carrier. With everything that had been going on, I'd been neglectful in my duties as honorary aunt.

Priya began to fuss, and Sasha quickly unwrapped her and brought her to her chest to feed. She stroked her hair, soothing her.

A piece of paper flew by and stuck to the outside of the picnic basket. Celeste plucked it off and her face immediately soured.

"What is it?" Sasha leaned over, her face transforming as well. Her hand went protectively to Priya's head.

"This is getting really out of hand. I don't know why they can't do anything about these nutjobs." Celeste handed the paper to me in disgust, but I'd already guessed what it was. It was more or less the same flyer Sydney had shoved at me, but now it had a different time and date for the meeting.

"They can't do anything to them unless they break the law," I muttered a little pathetically. I crumpled the paper up and put it with the rest of our trash.

"Setting fires is breaking the law! Damaging property is breaking the law!" Sasha said indignantly.

"Yeah, but arresting them for that won't stop them from believing all of this nonsense," Celeste replied. "I don't want them to go to jail for vandalism. I want them to pull their heads out of their asses and stop baiting everyone with this bullshit."

"Do you think it's bullshit?" I asked quietly.

They wore identical looks of surprise. Sasha's mouth popped open, but Celeste got there first.

"They think we have magic, that we're going to turn them all to frogs or something. They're horrible to all of us for no good reason. That is bullshit."

"I think"—I avoided their eyes—"that some of them believe it would be possible for us to get our magic back." I rubbed a little green weed between my fingers, hoping I sounded casual. "And if that happens, we'll be out for revenge."

"What?" Sasha's eyes widened. "How do they expect us to get our magic back?"

Celeste rubbed a thumb across one of her cuffs, pushing into the skin as if it would finally budge. "Yeah, tell them if they find out to let us know." Her words were bold, but I noticed they'd both dropped their voices to near whispers despite us being the only people in the park.

Guilt squirmed inside me. There was really no reason for me to be the judge of this, to decide that I was the only one 'worthy.' The Sun Guardians were getting worse every day. If they did something truly awful, shouldn't I give us a chance? Could I live with myself if something happened and I did nothing to prevent it? The conversation with Indie and Simon came back to me. Which was the more responsible choice?

I just shook my head at Sasha and said, "No idea," like the liar I was.

"What do you think your magic would be, Sasha?" Celeste asked, her irritation deflating with the lack of information. She helped herself to some small shortbread cookies I'd packed.

Sasha sat up straighter, grinning. "I hope it's flying. Flying would be the best."

"No way. I'd want to shoot fire." Celeste made little pew-pew sounds as she pretended to inflame the world around us. Sasha looked alarmed and Celeste laughed. "Or maybe something less violent. What about you, Lim?"

"Oh, um, I don't know. Maybe heal people?" I nibbled some shortbread.

They sported identical looks of derision, and I laughed.

"Way to make us both feel bad, Lim," Celeste deadpanned.

Sasha threw a napkin at my head. "Seriously, very rude. You're supposed to say something selfish and fun."

I chuckled again, popping the whole cookie into my mouth. "Okay, I'd want the ability to control everyone's mind and make all of you do my nefarious bidding."

Sasha barked out a laugh but smothered it to a snort, trying hard not to disrupt Priya's meal.

"That's better," Celeste said approvingly. "What if we all had really pathetic powers? What if you just had the power to... control pencils."

"Or turn yourself into a cushion," Sasha replied.

"Or talk to spiders. Which would be cool, but nobody would want to be around you. You'd just be 'spider-gal,' with all the spiders stopping by your house to visit all the time and tell you their weird spider gossip. And forget about showering alone." Celeste's eyes widened with feigned horror while Sasha and I both laughed so hard tears sprang to my eyes.

I considered for a moment that it wasn't completely out of the realm of possibility. Not all the Jinns had terrifying power. Some could change into a certain animal or could hold their breath and exist underwater for long periods. Some could clean or make clothing; some were just stronger than average. I couldn't control minds or the elements.

Maybe if I uncuffed the Jinns, it wouldn't be as dramatic as it was before. Maybe just give us a bit of an edge or powers that would be normal talents in time, like being a fantastic artist or excellent swimmer. Just enough so that the Sun Guardians and people like them would calm down and leave us alone, and we could go back to living in peace...well, relative peace.

"Would you really, though?" I asked, wiping my eyes. "If the option was there, would you uncuff yourselves, and Priya?" I folded up the napkin in my lap so they couldn't see the earnestness in my face.

"Of course," Sasha replied while Celeste said, "Absolutely. You wouldn't?"

I let out a breath and shook my head. "Maybe I would, but you don't think it would make things awkward with the Tals?"

Sasha considered it, a shadow of grief passing over her heart-shaped face. "I know my father loved me, but he always treated me like I was kind of...defective. Like a favorite teddy bear that's missing an arm. Leo's somewhat better, but he too seems to love me despite it—as if it's not part of me." She stopped and looked down at Priya, a look of love replaced suddenly by anger. "When I got pregnant, one of the other teachers said, "Wouldn't it be great if she was 'normal?' You know, not a Jinn." Defiance filled her eyes when they met mine again.

Hurt twisted deep in my belly. Sasha had known no family but Emir and Leo. She'd never known the mother who could have helped her understand that having magic made her special, not broken or abnormal. Her coworker probably thought they were being nice. Then again, her mother also could have been one of those Jinns who thinks magic was a curse.

Sasha's observation also brought my feelings about Leo into sharp focus. Leo treated it like it was an incurable illness, something to be pitied as opposed to something that made us who we truly were.

Celeste kissed Sasha on the temple before turning back to me. "I think you forget, Lim, that you spend a lot more time with Tals than we do because of the restaurant." Sasha nodded next to her. "Like Sasha said, other than Leo, I don't have meaningful Tal relationships that would be affected by me being able to electrocute people at will." She winked and mimed lighting our surroundings on fire again.

I rolled my eyes and smiled, but inside, my heart fell a little. It was true that other than Leo, Elias, and now Jake, I didn't really have any other close Tal friends. I couldn't think of any others my parents knew either. Ayla and Keen had Tal friends in their class at school, but the children who came to the house to play were almost always Jinns.

After lunch, when I was sure I was out of sight of anyone, I willed myself to my parents. We'd agreed after the riot that I should always appear in my old room in the attic. Since it was highly unlikely that anyone would be there and I could claim to have been upstairs if there were any visitors.

I found my mother in the living room with Ayla. They were playing a game with far too many pieces for my liking. Ayla stared at the board, boards actually, with intensity. She held a figurine in one hand and she placed it with all the gravitas of an army general. I cleared my throat.

"Oh, Lim, I didn't hear the back door," my mother said for Ayla's benefit.

"Hi, Mom. Hi, Aye-Aye." Ayla stuck her tongue out at me. She didn't appreciate the ridiculous nicknames I came up with for her. "I just came"—I motioned with my empty picnic basket—"to get some greens. I'm running low."

"Wasn't today market day?" Ayla asked dubiously but without taking her eyes off the game. My mother's eyes slid to mine.

"It was. I forgot to buy some." Ayla said nothing, presumably satisfied. I gestured to my mother, and we went to the kitchen. I filled her in on my lunch with Sasha and Celeste.

"What are you thinking?" My mother filled and put the kettle on to boil.

"I am thinking," I said slowly, drawing out the words like I could never take them back, "that I will offer to uncuff my friends. And you all, of course. Everyone should choose for themselves." I tacked on at the end to lessen the guilt from potential repercussions.

She said nothing for a moment. She seemed almost resigned like she'd been waiting for me to say it. "What did Bastian say?"

Bastian and I had been on two more dates since our visit to the library. I shook my head at her. "He never found anything." I rubbed my palm nervously. "I wasn't 'chosen' or anything. I just found a plate. I don't deserve to keep it from them. Especially if it could keep them safe." That part at least felt true. It should be as much their decision as if they'd found the plate.

My mother was quiet for a long time. She pulled the kettle off the stove and poured it into a teapot. She added a few spoonfuls of a dark blend. Pine needles and something sweet rose in the steam. Finally, she turned to me. "I'm not sure about this, Calimea. It feels like we'd be painting a target on our backs."

"I know. But if something happened, and I knew I could've saved them, or they could have saved themselves? I'd never forgive myself for not giving them the chance." I shuddered, thinking about how my date could have ended up if I hadn't been able to get us out of there. They would have injured us and possibly done worse. Her face mirrored my fear as she thought about the possibilities.

My mother looked into the living room at Ayla, carefully maneuvering her players around the board and moving them back again.

She gave me a reluctant nod. "I suppose people have to be free to make their own decisions."

21

LIM

LASHIA, PRESENT DAY

Later that night, I sat down and carefully wrote out invitations to Indie, Simon, Sasha, Celeste, Audre, and, after debating about it for a moment, Aiden. The notes told them to come to the restaurant tomorrow at one for a special lunch. I did not invite Bastian, figuring I could at least give him plausible deniability if things went wrong. A runner appeared to deliver the messages a few minutes after I'd put out my flag. I paid the kid extra to make sure he put them directly into hands as opposed to leaving them at the door.

The next day, I stood in the kitchen staring at my ingredients. What did one make for this kind of event? Recreating the odd meal I'd eaten off the plate was a possibility, but I dismissed it as the symbolism would be lost on people. I checked the pantry. I went down into the cellar. I went back into the pantry. This was ridiculous. I was a starsdamn chef. I could make lunch for a dozen people in my sleep.

I diced some cured pork and put it into a cold pan. I turned on the heat and let it slow cook, rendering out the fat. Once it was nice and crispy, I pulled it out of the pan and threw in some finely minced onion and garlic and sauteed them in the pork fat before pouring in some wine to deglaze the pan, scraping up all the bits on the bottom. In a separate bowl, I whisked some egg yolks with some grated sheep's milk cheese and lots of black pepper. When everyone arrived, I would cook some pasta and mix it all together until I'd combined them into a silky consistency. People could serve themselves and top their pasta with crispy pork and bright green herbs I'd put out. I'd also make a bitter salad with oil, some of that same cheese, and lots of tart lemon juice.

When I had just finished setting the long table, Audre arrived.

"Hey." She eyed the table with a suspicious smile. I had gone slightly fancy. "Is this a nice way to tell us we're all getting fired?"

I shook my head and gave her an "are you kidding me?" look. Audre still looked a little discomfited, but I could tell she was reserving judgment until later.

The others started wandering in. It was an odd group and everyone knew it. Audre didn't say it, but I could see she noticed that Elias and Jake were not there. Indie and Simon arrived, both of them with one thousand questions on their lips. And everyone seemed a little surprised Aiden was there, and based on his expression, so was Aiden. He took it in stride and began greeting people and chatting. My parents arrived and brought Keen and Ayla. I guess they didn't think it was right to keep this from them anymore.

But the odd group aside, people sat down and relaxed as they poured themselves and their neighbors wine, passed the giant bowls of pasta and salad, and dipped warm bread into a thick mixture of oil, herbs, and spices. When the food was mostly gone, and everyone had forgotten the odd makeup of the group and were just enjoying themselves, I stood up and clinked my glass for attention. The room immediately went deadly silent—they hadn't forgotten after all.

I could have made a speech but figured I might as well get it over with. So, instead, I just rolled up my sleeves.

Sasha gasped.

Aiden put it bluntly and said, "Fucking stars."

It broke the tension, and people laughed nervously. Ayla wasn't laughing but struggled between excitement and annoyance. She hated to be the last to know anything.

I grabbed the plate from the sideboard where it had sat innocuously all during dinner. I held it, with a napkin per Simon's instructions, and let everyone take a good look at the wondrous artifact.

Taking a deep breath, I said, "I fell asleep touching this—after finding it in the swamp. In the morning, the cuffs were gone." Short and to the point. Nobody said a word as I paused. "You all know what's happening right now with the Sun Guardians." At this, there was much grumbling and a few curses. "If you touch this and it removes your cuffs, you may be a target. They could arrest you. I asked Bastian, and he said he still couldn't find any current cases like mine—so I really don't know what could happen." The faces around the table were a mix of hope and wariness. "It should be up to you. My magic saved me when the riot broke out at The Brixton. It could save you, or it could make your life much ...much worse. But it's your choice. I won't make it for you."

You could have heard a flea sneeze. Brax made an appearance and leapt from the balcony to sit next to me. I put a hand on his head and stroked him while the group continued to stare at me.

"Did you say 'your magic?'" Ayla whispered at last.

I sent myself just to the other side of the room. This time, I didn't want to miss the reactions. I was appropriately rewarded. Celeste spit out her drink. Ayla ducked her head under the table. Aiden stood up, but it was Keen who turned and spotted me first.

"She's right there!" Everyone turned, and I disappeared again, this time going to the balcony. They found me faster this time, so I moved again and again until Ayla and Keen were coming out of their skin with excitement, and the adults weren't far off. I went back to the head of the table.

I picked up the plate with the napkin and put it on an otherwise empty round table next to us.

"Why aren't you touching it?" Celeste asked.

"It seems to nullify magic. It removed the cuffs and released her magic, but we're not sure what it will do once the cuffs are gone," Simon responded.

Indie took a sip of her wine and said, "So how long do we touch it for it to work? Do you think we need to stay here all night?"

"Probably not. I thought my cuffs were paler after I'd found it and I'd only held it for a short time." I shrugged. "Then again, I'm no expert."

The room was silent as everyone seemed to ponder their decision. My mother and father looked at one another in resignation. Clearly, my parents' need for their children to be able to protect themselves, and possibly the persuasion tactics Ayla had begun the minute I disappeared, had won them over.

The scraping of Aiden's chair was deafening. He strode over to the plate and touched the center. There was a collective and audible intake of breath. Nothing happened. Several long minutes went by, but then, slowly, the blue glow dimmed. Aiden's eyes widened in amazement. The look of joy transformed his face, the part we could see anyway, as he watched his cuffs slowly, ever so slowly, fade away into nothing. It took about twenty minutes, during which nobody moved or spoke, not even the children.

"I never really thought I would see it," he murmured. "They're really gone." His eyes were almost misty as he held out his arms and flexed his fingers.

"Do you feel anything?" Simon cocked his head at Aiden.

"It feels weird." His eyes darted to me. "Should I try to disappear too?"

I smiled. For a moment, he looked so different. It might have been the first time I'd seen him completely sober. "Sure, you can try that. I spent several hours in the garden trying every damn thing I could think of, and nothing happened, so it might take some time."

"Here." Sasha got up and brought Aiden a candle. "Try to light this."

Nothing.

"Can you fly?" from Ayla.

Aiden squinted as he attempted to levitate, "Hmmm, nope."

"Are you really strong?" asked Keen, inspecting him. Aiden walked over and picked him up with ease, but that was probably normal.

"If you try to control my mind, I will punch you in the face," Celeste said conversationally.

Aiden just stared at his arms, turning them over, flexing them. He scanned the room, and I could tell he was going through the same mental gymnastics I had. I could practically see the ideas and attempts running through his mind. At least he didn't have a judgmental balara staring at him the whole time.

"Anyone else? You don't have to decide now. It's not a one-time offer, but I'd like to put this somewhere safe if we're not using it."

The group shifted nervously, some with excitement, others with nervousness, but one by one, everyone except for Priya ("It's harder to hide her arms and I'm not sure I'm prepared to have a child with the power to melt things if she doesn't get her way") and Audre stood up and made their way to the table.

I didn't question Audre's decision, but she volunteered. "I'm seeing...a Tal. I wouldn't want to hide this from him. But I've forgotten this evening already." She put her hand over her chest.

"Would that Tal be a certain sous chef we both know?" I whispered to her as I walked her out.

She sighed dramatically. "What can I say? All that cooking together in close quarters. How could he not fall for this?" She mimed fluffing her hair.

I laughed and hugged her. "That's wonderful news." She waved me away in embarrassment.

"Good luck, okay? Be safe." Concern filled her face, but I didn't miss her quick look of longing at the others.

"We will." I closed the door behind her. Honestly, she'd made the right decision. I'd meant what I'd said about not choosing for anyone, but it did not escape me that everyone in this room was now in a much more precarious situation than they had been before they'd walked in. I tried to push away the thoughts of trials and jail cells and focus on the looks of awe and excitement on the faces in the room.

They looked at me expectantly as they huddled around the table. My parents, Keen, Ayla, Indie, Simon, Sasha, and Celeste each placed a finger on the plate.

Indie discovered her power first. As soon as she stepped away from the table, she grabbed a knife and pricked her finger. She merely had to glance at the blood and the wound dried up and disappeared. Her eyes gleamed in triumph. It should have been obvious. Her predisposition for healing had to come from somewhere.

"That will come in handy!" Simon said as he inspected her finger. "Do me now."

"You never need to ask, sweetie." Indie grinned and aimed at Simon. But before she could touch him, Simon rose, almost involuntarily, into the air and out of her reach.

"Coward," she said as she watched her husband, but pride filled her voice.

"No way," breathed Keen and Ayla at once. Simon's eyes calculated the size of the room before shooting away. My mother shrieked. Aiden and I cheered. After several crashes into the balcony, causing Brax to hiss in annoyance, he managed to more or less get the hang of it. He still crash-landed multiple times, laughing every single time, but caused slightly less damage each time.

"At least I'll always have someone to practice on," Indie muttered to me under her breath after he slid into the wall again. After healing Simon's bruises, she moved around the group looking for other injuries—my father agreed to be Indie's pincushion, and he winced as she nicked him and healed it over.

I shook my head at his martyrdom as he said, "It's for science."

But his lips didn't move.

"What did you say?" I said at the same time he said, out loud, "Did you hear that?"

My brow furrowed. "Do it again."

Indie paused, her knife poised to strike again at the mere suggestion of concession.

"Derek could beat Brax in a fight."

I barked out a laugh, and everyone turned to us. I tried it in reverse and said only in my head, "You could never say that to Brax's face."

"What is going on?" My mother looked at us in confusion.

He could speak mind to mind but could not, thank all the stars in Lashia, read thoughts that were not intentionally spoken to him. He could also transmit a thought to all of us at once. Testing this made it look as if we were all playing a very weird, silent game of 'Simon Says.'

At the other end of the table, Keen was listing off any kind of power he could think of while Ayla scrunched up her eyes and tried each one.

"Can you see through solid objects? Tell the future? Why don't you go jump in a lake and see if you can breathe underwater?" He laughed as Ayla scowled at him. She threw a piece of bread at him, and he was gone, the bread bouncing off an empty space.

My mother jumped up. "Keen!"

Keen reappeared in the same place, his face bewildered. The group all turned to look.

"Show me again!" Ayla demanded, hands clasped in front of her.

Keen disappeared. The room broke into applause.

"Interesting," I said. "Can you turn me invisible too if I'm with you?" He took my outstretched hand. Suddenly, a film covered the world, like I was looking through a slightly smudged glass. "Now let go." When his hand fell away, he remained invisible, but I was not.

Aiden gave a low whistle. "Now that is cool."

I didn't miss the look of yearning on Ayla's face. She spun in a slow circle, concentrating. My mother looked as if she was performing a very poor ventriloquist act as she, too, thought through all the possibilities.

Celeste turned out to be telekinetic. She was throwing things into the air so Simon could catch them. Sasha didn't seem too bitter about not getting the ability to fly, although she had been testing out her power, the power of air, by attempting to knock Simon down mid-flight, so maybe she hadn't truly gotten over it.

The remains of the food lay abandoned. Napkins littered the floor and chairs had toppled over in the excitement. Perhaps someone would develop the ability to clean up? A napkin flew into a pile with another. Celeste was still practicing.

"Are we immortal now?" Sasha said, bouncing a smiling Priya on her hip.

"I don't think so. I don't believe any of the old Jinns were immortal. Because of their ability to avoid trouble"—Simon tipped his head at me—"or heal"—he bowed to his wife who gave a regal wave, "they might have lived longer than others at the time, but they did die."

By the end of the lunch, my mother, Aiden, and Ayla still had not discovered their powers. But they all seemed fairly confident that they would manifest in time. We agreed, for one another's safety, to keep our powers secret (there had been a lot of pointed looks at the kids and Aiden, all three of whom looked incredulous and offended at the suspicion). Everyone knew Bastian was aware of my power, but I agreed he would not know theirs or that I had uncuffed anyone else.

There was a tacit agreement between my parents, Indie, and Simon that my ability to move others without being with them didn't need to be brought up. My father's ability to send thoughts directly into the minds of others, even without their permission, had started a fairly spirited debate about consent, so it was probably best to keep that to myself for now.

22

ASRA

LASHIA, ~ 500 YEARS AGO

Asra dragged herself over to the small stone hearth. She wrapped the fur blanket tighter around her shoulders. The original power from the daranas was long gone. They'd started draining themselves to distribute magic to each new group of the humans that joined the settlement. It was enough. Some of them seemed to have better natural aptitude, but they could still hold on to only one distinct ability. Their level of base magic was non-existent.

She was glad to see that despite these limitations, the magic seemed to affect the environment a little, too. The animals were getting bigger, less sickly looking.

After donating her magic to the darana, she was so cold. Her fire was only smoke in her veins, and her bones felt brittle, like the smallest fall would break her. For weeks afterward, she wouldn't have the strength to float a leaf, let alone send messages to the others or do any of the things she'd taken for granted at home.

And it got worse each time for all of them.

Someone had lit the fire while she'd been sleeping. She scoffed at how pathetic she'd become. In Trevesten, nobody would have been able to sneak up on her, sleeping or not. Asra would have had a knife to their throat before they'd gone two steps. The day after a donation, though? She would have slept through her throat being slit.

But murder was apparently not the plan because whoever it was, they'd brought food. A small pile of flat bread, broth, and a bit of dried meat and fruit. She gratefully drank the broth, occasionally dipping the bread in and chewing mindlessly. The flames reached out to her, lending her their warmth.

The door opened, and she was too weary to even startle at the sound. But her exhaustion quickly turned to confusion.

Connery stood at the door with a pile of firewood. "I'm sorry. I thought you would still be asleep."

Asra mustered the strength to frown. "What are you doing here?"

Connery stacked the firewood by the hearth. "I heard you were drained. I brought you some food." He tipped his head to her nearly finished meal. "I lit the fire but figured you wouldn't keep firewood handy like the rest of us."

"You say that as if any of those things are the kind of things you normally do." She calmly cocked her head at him. But her heart began beating faster, and she nearly cried when her flames, always so dependable when her emotions were high, remained dormant.

Connery didn't respond to her tone. Instead, he tipped his head at one of the two chairs in the room. "May I sit down?"

"I really can't stop you," she shrugged. Asra turned back to the fire. The broth was nearly gone, but she sipped it to give herself something to do.

Connery was sitting behind her, but she could sense his every breath. She always knew when he was nearby, had become so cognizant of his movements and expressions over the years. The wind bent to his will and he could join it, rush away with it, or slow a spinning storm. She pretended he just caused those subtle air shifts that made her capable of feeling him so keenly. How she knew when he glanced her way, even when she wasn't looking.

She felt him now, hesitating, working up the courage to say whatever it was he came here to say. Because despite his casual demeanor, he didn't do things like this for her. Not anymore.

"I've been speaking with one of the villagers." His voice was calm, the royal voice. Asra cringed. He sounded like a stranger. "They don't live as long as we do. They've never had magic before."

She knew where this was going. She'd gotten a little fed up last week. Every day was about survival here. It was a rough life. One man apparently thought things weren't hard enough for his wife. It was a little impulsive, but she didn't regret it. He was abusive trash. And now he was dead trash. His wife and child would be better off.

"You can't expect to live as long in a world like this." Asra didn't care how callous she sounded. The broth was gone, and she picked up the fruit. She tried to toss it into her mouth, but each movement was painful. Solvan was still sleeping it off in the other room, and he'd donated before her.

"No, I don't. What I mean is we cannot expect that they'll have what we have—that they'll have seven lives." He paused. "And there's so few of them as it is."

Asra twisted toward him, a weak warmth struggling through her veins. "So, this is a lecture? Forgive me, Lord Connery, I meant no offense. But if you insist, take me away." She held out her arms to him, wrists bent like he might put manacles on her. She smirked at him, but there was no feeling behind it.

Connery didn't get angry. He looked at her thoughtfully as if he was trying to find the female he knew under this new, hardened exterior.

Indignation burned inside her. Her exterior had always been tough. She'd let her guard down for him, and it had been a huge mistake.

Her smile dropped, and she stood, hiding her wince as she did so. He rose to meet her. Inside Asra, that warmth grew, pulled at her. His scent filled the air, and it made her feel all of those things again that she shoved down inside her. Her body strained to be nearer, her fire was traitorous, flushing through her skin at their proximity. She wouldn't give him the satisfaction of stepping back.

"They've never come back." His eyes were intent on hers. "If that was a natural part of this world, we would have seen it by now."

They'd been in Lashia now for over fifty years and nobody ever remembered. But these people were not fae. Surely the five of them would still experience their rishivals, even with the drag this place had on their power?

Asra scoffed, aware she was being childish. "That doesn't mean they don't have other lives, just that they don't remember them."

Connery gave her a sad smile. "If they don't remember them, then how will Lily's husband remember the lesson you taught him if he returns?"

She'd walked into that. "It's not like we can throw them in Tarkana. He could have killed her." Was it her imagination or had Connery gotten closer to her? Or had she moved toward him?

"I know." His breath was warm against her skin. She was tipping her head up.

"Do you think we'll come back?" She whispered the thought that had invaded her mind more than she cared to admit. Late at night, when she tossed in her uncomfortable excuse for a bed, she obsessed over what other torture she might have brought upon her friends. Would this place let them come back? Would it give them back their memories? Or would they be like these people? Doomed to forget everything they'd learned and continually repeat the mistakes of their past?

Who would even want to come back to this awful place?

"I don't know. Maybe it would be better if we didn't. If we all get a completely fresh start." Connery's eyes were stormy, more gray than blue as he searched her face. "Would that be so bad?"

Asra swallowed. He didn't want his memories back. Their time in Lashia, jobs they'd pulled, that last night. Days of holding him while he sweated out the last of the hush. Cleaning up after him and forcing him to eat. After all that, he still wanted to forget everything.

She stepped back, her voice going cold. "That would be nice for you, wouldn't it? You'd never have to wrestle with any unwanted memories or feelings. Maybe you'll get lucky, and you'll come back as a powerless human who never has to look further than his own short, singular existence."

Connery flinched like she'd hit him. He shook his head and gave her that look again. Like she'd turned into someone completely unfamiliar.

Maybe he just hoped he'd one day look at her and not know her at all.

He put more distance between them. "Asra... I'm sorry."

Her face heated. "You have nothing to apologize for. I'm the one who should have known better, right?"

His chest fell, and she had the overwhelming urge to reach out to him, to touch him. It was pointless. She would not go down this road with him again. She forced away the memory of his lips on hers. He clearly had. She was surprised he wanted to forget Sabine as well. Then again, plenty of other willing females here.

Connery paused but then gave her a tight nod before walking out.

Asra stared into the fire for a long time. Long enough that she could relight it herself.

Two days later, she and Solvan were up and about. They stood in one of the large open buildings, mostly used for communal meals or meetings. They had five full daranas. Another wave of humans had come while Asra was sleeping, and they lined up before her and the other four. They'd already been here for hours, but all of them waited patiently to receive their allotted slice of power.

A young woman gave her a look of reverence that made Asra's insides recoil.

"Please don't look at me like that, I'm not the Allmother," she mumbled under her breath. Next to her, Brigid laughed. The girl widened her eyes but said nothing.

"What's the Allmother?" an older gentleman in front of Brigid asked.

"The giver of life and all magic." Brigid, Asra, and Solvan, on her other side, all intoned automatically.

The man bobbed his head. "It's like your god?"

Asra had heard the word before from the humans. She was fluent in their language now, they all were. Asra considered it. "She gives us our power, our lives. We build statues and give her offerings. So yes, that fits."

"She will reward you for doing so much for us," the girl whispered. Her tone made Asra's skin prickle uncomfortably.

"Reward us? What do you mean?" Solvan asked, smiling encouragingly at the next woman whose hand he placed on his darana.

"If you are good, they have a god that will send you to a place of everlasting happiness. If you are bad, you go to a place of endless torment," Elwin answered. He spent a lot of time teaching in their makeshift school and had clearly picked up a few things. Connery was beside him as they both walked up next to Brigid, having drained their daranas already.

Asra sighed, looking at all the humans still left. Solvan would try to donate again soon. She could probably get him to go a few more weeks to fully recover. After that, he'd need to wait months, maybe even a year, for another donation.

"That's interesting," Brigid said politely. "The Allmother doesn't interfere with our lives. When we have our ultimate death, our magic returns to her, and she provides it to the new fae."

"If she doesn't reward you, what are the offerings for?" the man asked. Brigid removed his hand from the darana.

Elwin raised his eyebrows and pulled his lips into his mouth. Connery looked slightly aghast.

"They're not bribes," Solvan said slowly, shaking his head. "We just give her stuff to say thanks."

Asra gently removed the girl's hand from her darana.

"So she's like a really powerful darana?" The girl said, reaching out her hands and flexing them.

The five of them broke into laughter. Asra was uncomfortably conscious that it had been a long time since that happened. The girl blushed.

"I've never thought of it like that, but it's not a bad way to put it." Asra smiled at her. Again, it felt as if her facial muscles were out of practice. That wasn't right. She used to laugh and smile all the time. At Solvan's quips, Elwin's excessive explanations. She remembered giggling with Brigid over their combined attempts to teach Connery to eat like he wasn't at a formal dinner. At one point, Brigid threatened to cut off his pinkie if she saw it sticking up again.

"Well, I don't think of you all like gods," the man spoke again. "More like those stories about the ghosts that grant wishes."

They shared a look of confusion.

"You know, rub a shiny metal thing"—he gestured to the darana—"and a ghost pops out and grants you three wishes? What were they called again?" He looked to the girl for help, but her face was blank. He tapped his forehead. "It'll come to me. It was an old story even before the Weakening."

"It's too bad we can't grant you exactly what you ask for." Connery's voice startled her. She didn't want him so close again after their last conversation.

But he was right. Since they could only give their own power, they had to be judicious. This group of humans was getting smaller, but still useful, amounts. Connery's wind allowed them to keep the worst of the weather off if they worked together. Asra's power kept them warm and able to light their own fires. Elwin's power was still probably the most useful out of all of them, but those who received Brigid's or Solvan's were always grateful.

"I think you do more than enough," the man said before the two humans moved aside for the next people in line.

23

LIM

LASHIA, PRESENT DAY

My body was still buzzing with the excitement of so many of us having our magic back. I was trying to expel the electric energy by cleaning the kitchen when a knock sounded at the backdoor.

"Hey." Bastian was smiling, but he looked exhausted. "I hope I'm not intruding. I finally got a break and just wanted to see you." He gave me a look like seeing me was the only good part of his day and butterflies filled my chest.

Outside, only the light from my windows illuminated him. His black suit was still impeccable, but he'd undone his top button, and his hair was mussed, as if he'd run his hands through it more than once today. Considering what I'd spent the day doing, I felt a little guilty as I held the door open for him to come inside. Under the brighter lights of the kitchen, the toll of the long hours showed on his face. There were faint dark circles under his eyes and a soft layer of stubble grazed his chin.

"Please sit. Have you eaten?" I asked.

He smiled ruefully. "No, but that's not why I'm here." I raised an eyebrow at him and smirked. I must have still been feeling a little bold from the afternoon's recklessness. Color rose up his neck. "I mean, that's not the only reason I'm here." My smirk turned into a full grin, and his blush deepened. "Ah damn it, I just mean, I didn't come here to guilt you into feeding me."

I laughed. "I enjoy cooking for people, remember? I'll make you something, and you can tell me why you look like me the morning after I accidentally made some very potent mead."

Bastian laughed and gave me a grateful smile, but his expression was still strained. I quickly grabbed him a drink and some bread to snack on while I fixed him a bowl of spicy tomato stew filled with pulled chicken and herbs. Bastian drank deeply and buttered a piece of bread, his eyes never leaving me for long as I moved around the kitchen. I might have over-exaggerated the sway of my hips just a little.

He took a breath and said, "A registrar in Eudora is dead." My hips stopped swaying immediately. "We're not sure if she did it herself or if someone murdered her."

I set the bowl down in front of him, my head reeling. "Why do you think someone killed her?"

Bastian stirred his stew and let out a sigh that showed how much this had been hanging on him. "She was poisoned, but it's unclear whether she did it to herself or whether someone did it to her because of her...activities." In response to the question in my eyes, he said, "In the weeks leading up to her death, she allegedly removed several people's cuffs. The borough will withhold her death benefits if she committed suicide. I know the family. They asked me to look into it."

"Stars..." I sank down into a chair as I tried to process everything he'd just said. "They can remove cuffs too?" That probably shouldn't have been my first thought at this horrific news. I'd never really thought about it. But if the magic was not infinite, then it would make sense to take them back.

Bastian nodded. He took a bite of stew and briefly closed his eyes, opening them to say, "This is wonderful and exactly what I needed."

My heart caved. I'd always enjoyed feeding people. It made me feel like needed, like I improved their lives in some small way. I gave him an understanding look, and he took another bite before continuing.

"Yes, the registrars can add or remove cuffs. Trainees start out by removing cuffs from the dead."

"They remove our cuffs after we're dead?" I scrunched my face in disgust. "Why?" Emir had a closed casket and checking wouldn't have occurred to me.

Bastian shrugged, chewing. "I don't know whether it's just practice for them or whether it serves some greater purpose. I've been in the morgue twice on two different cases when a registrar has shown up.

"With their creepy accompanists, no doubt." My shudder was half mocking and half serious.

Bastian gave a short, soft laugh. "They are strange. I've been introduced to at least half a dozen now and it's always like speaking to a blank piece of paper."

I laughed and then tipped my head to the side as I tried to remember anything about the accompanists that had come with Chiwel. They really selected the dullest people for that job. "What happened to the people she uncuffed? Did they... do anything to them?" I couldn't help looking away, but when I glanced back, Bastian's eyes were serious.

"Nothing has happened...yet." The word 'yet' punched a hole in me. Bastian reached out and took my hand. "They're still investigating whether she was working with any of them. They were a mix of Tals and Jinns, which would make the theory that it was against their will more viable. But I haven't been able to interview any of them. I promise to let you know as soon as I hear anything."

My heart hammered in my chest. "How did they find them?" I whispered. Bastian's thumb began stroking the back of my hand.

"The accompanists. They apparently didn't see her do it, but they could provide detailed information on all of her movements, everyone she met with..." he trailed off.

My heart slowed marginally. Having not had my cuffs removed by a registrar, at least they wouldn't be able to find me the same way. 'Or any of the people you just uncuffed,' an annoying voice in my head whispered. I blew out a breath. "Well, I can see why you needed a good meal."

Bastian pulled his chair around until our knees were touching. "That's not the only thing I needed." I couldn't help it. My eyes widened comically, and he huffed a laugh and groaned. "That is not what I meant." But he leaned forward and pressed a kiss to each of my palms. Suddenly, I was really hoping that was exactly what he meant. He raised his head, wearing a look that he wasn't at all opposed to things moving in that direction. "I like you for more than your food."

My breath caught at the intensity in his voice. I stroked the side of his face, my nails weaving into his hair. His hands began a gentle caress just above my wrists, and his eyes floated to my mouth. My fingers continued their exploration, sliding down his chest as he leaned forward and brushed his lips across mine. It was only the hint of a kiss, but heat blossomed inside me. His hands moved to my shoulders, drawing me up with him as he stood, our faces only a breath apart.

"You really are beautiful." He reached out and let his thumb graze over my bottom lip. "I remember the first time I saw you at the market."

My eyebrows rose, and I gave him a half smile. "Oh? How come you didn't introduce yourself?" I ran my hands over his shoulders and back, trying to drink in the feel of his skin.

"I was talking to some vendors about"—I pressed myself against him, he groaned and continued in a more strained voice—"about something important, I'm sure, when you rode by on your balara. He kept trying to eat the things the other shoppers were carrying, and you were swearing at him under your breath." He gave a small laugh at the memory. "Like he was a misbehaving child. One of them told me who you were." His fingers tangled in my hair. "I couldn't believe a woman that gorgeous was in the same borough and I'd never seen you." He tugged my hair lightly and slid his mouth along my throat. I could feel the warmth of his breath and imagined how it would feel on every part of me. "When I saw you again, I couldn't believe my luck."

His earnestness threw me, but I wasn't immune to compliments. I kissed him deeply in thanks, my teeth grazing along his lips, and that scent I'd been chasing since that night at the bar filled my senses. "You made quite an impression on the rest of the staff. Do you want to hear how gorgeous everyone in my restaurant thinks you are?"

Bastian gave a low chuckle, and all the most sensitive parts of me ignited. "No. I only want to hear if you think that."

I pointedly assessed him from under my lashes. The butterflies were practically dancing as my nerves set in. It had been a while. "I think that."

He leaned in and pressed a long kiss to my lips. I luxuriated in the feel of his mouth on mine, the taste of him on my tongue. His hands moved to my back, holding me hard against him.

The butterflies disappeared, but I was still conscious of my every breath. He'd removed his jacket, and I ran my fingers over his arms and chest. His hands ran down my waist, thumbs running into those sensitive indents that led south. My breath caught, and he captured the sound with his mouth. His kisses became harder, more insistent. We backed up against the kitchen table. Bastian's hands lightly gripped my thighs, lifting me until I was sitting, my legs wrapped around him.

As if they had a mind of their own, my fingers went to the buttons on his shirt. I groaned at the feeling of his bare skin as I pushed the material off him.

Cupping my face, he leaned back. "Is this okay?"

I smiled, my fingers circling his forearms. We both glanced down to see the contrast, my bare skin next to his glowing blue cuffs.

"Do you ever wonder what you can do?" I wrapped my legs around him tighter so he knew I wasn't backing out. My eyes closed briefly as I felt him hard against me.

He ran a thumb over my bottom lip. "I thought about it when I was a kid. I was scrawny." He laughed at my look of disbelief. "I wanted to be strong, invincible maybe."

My mouth twisted into a smile. "That would be fun." My voice lowered. "Would you ever want to find out?"

Bastian's hand dropped to my shoulder before running down my arm. He was silent for so long I thought maybe he hadn't heard me.

"No." His voice wasn't hesitant, and he leaned back a little. "Lim, you said this happened to you by accident?"

"Yes," I nodded, relaxing my legs so they fell off him. Guilt flowed through me, reminding me that while I hadn't done it on purpose, I'd allowed the others to do so.

"But you'd be able to repeat that accident?"

The kitchen was suddenly colder. Several of the candles had gone out.

"I might be able to do that, yes," I said slowly. "I told you I worked backward to figure out how I'd done it."

Bastian stepped back further and ran a hand down his face. "How much do you know about the time before the treaty?"

"It was a time of great suffering for the Tals. They were enslaved and mistreated." I crossed my arms and regurgitated the line that teachers had drilled into all of us.

"It was. By all accounts, Jinns were merciless. They used their magic to fight one another over the very few resources we had, and Tals barely survived. It was absolutely a time of 'might makes right.' The most powerful Jinns were the ones in charge, and Jinns without strong powers, or powers that couldn't be weaponized, did no better than Tals. Eventually, the latter joined up with the Tals to defeat the more powerful Jinns. They all agreed that the removal of the Jinns' power was the only way to ensure peace between the two peoples."

"Doesn't really seem like a fair trade," I murmured. An understanding crept over me and something inside me deflated. Bastian was a Jinn, but he didn't want us to have our power either. I'd never asked him whether he thought Jinns should be uncuffed. But it was clear he considered registration a necessary part of our world. He would not condone my choice to offer the plate to others. And he would definitely not support their choice to remove their cuffs intentionally.

"I wasn't aware you felt that way about the cuffs," I said. "I always assumed that all Jinns were putting up with them, but you, you believe in them."

Bastian's shoulders slumped. He looked out the window, as if he was seeing all the separate lives there, Jinns and Tals. "It's not that I don't want you to have magic," he said carefully, "it's that the magic doesn't have a moral compass. It assigns these incredibly dangerous powers arbitrarily, and that's too much risk. Especially when we already know how it would turn out."

That earnestness again. It would be so easy to agree with him. To go back to hiding and pretending I didn't know what it was like to know myself. I gave him a dejected smile and got down from the table. What he said made sense, but it didn't change my mind.

"This is a part of me, Bastian. Like you having blue eyes, or me having freckles. It's all me." I motioned up and down my body. "It's a part of the package." My voice became stronger with every word.

"I know. And I can accept that. Like you said, it was an accident."

Was he testing me? I frowned. "It *was* an accident. But I'm happy about it." The realization that Bastian would never celebrate my magic made my heart sink. "I'd want anyone I was with to be happy about it, to feel the same way I do about the registration."

Bastian swallowed and nodded. "I see."

A tear threatened to fall from my eye and I hurriedly wiped it away as he put his shirt back on. Since when did I have principles? Things certainly were simpler in a relationship that lived only in my head.

He lowered his head over mine, his hand sliding down to hold mine. "I'll still help you. However, I can."

My chest tightened at his decision, and I nodded. "Thank you."

The fire in the woodstove lasted a long time, throwing warm shadows on the walls as I sat in the kitchen, alone, wondering what I'd done.

24

ASRA

LASHIA, ~ 450 YEARS AGO

"Humans are remarkable, honestly," Solvan said, pushing a mound of earth toward an advancing group of those humans. They fired rudimentary weapons at us, arrows and rocks, from the valley down below. The earth stopped their movement but not their projectiles, and Asra casually threw up a gust of Connery's donated air to sweep them away. Behind them, Connery directed a group on how best to use their power together to protect the settlement from this latest batch of angry neighbors.

"Right now, they're remarkably getting on my nerves," Asra replied, but she knew what he meant. The magic had become like any other resource in this place, something else to fight over. The settlement to the south attacked this morning. They used mainly sharpened sticks and those pathetic horse-like creatures.

They apparently didn't care that this settlement, at over five thousand people, vastly outnumbered them. Asra and Solvan had easily thrown off their assault all day. They kept them back while trying not to hurt them, not to do anything to decrease their paltry numbers. And yet, still they came. They were remarkable in that they would do anything to improve their luck in this dismal place.

Asra didn't know whether they understood that the magic was trans-
ferable or whether they simply planned to take those with magic as
prisoners. All attempts to communicate had been met with silence.

Solvan just laughed and sent up a wall of trees using the flora magic
he'd gained from the darana. Asra noticed the sweat beading on his
forehead and the paleness in his face but said nothing. He sat down and
took a long drink of water from his canteen.

"Do you think there's a world where there are fae that have even more
magic than we do?" He cocked his head at Asra. She narrowed her eyes
at him. Solvan held up his hands as if he was readying to block a punch.
"I'm not talking about Sverresen." Even the sound of the name made
Asra wince in embarrassment. "I just mean, it seems likely that if there's
a world like this—there might be a world that looks like ours, but where
the fae have even greater gifts."

Asra exhaled in irritation. They all had an unspoken agreement not
to discuss Sverresen or other worlds. Especially since their last and final
attempt to repair the kunli had failed. Asra would never be able to find
what she needed in this place. Connery had thrown out the possibility
that when they died, they might be reborn in Trevesten but had no basis
for his theory.

It felt like giving up because it was. Every time she tried to make a plan
for anything, to better this world a little, a bitter voice in her head told her
there was nothing she could do. The voice would hiss at her to shut up
before she doomed her friends even further. Brigid, Elwin, Connery, and
Solvan had invested and become leaders among the humans. Whereas
Asra had faded into the background. People looked to her now only
because of her power and her association with the others.

Brigid and Solvan had attempted to talk to her about it several times,
but each time they had, her mind closed down and she considered head-

ing off on her own. Finding a place where she could live out her days in peace. Somewhere their faces didn't constantly remind her of her failure.

"I don't know, I think if there is, they're probably very lazy," Asra said as she floated away a few arrows that had made it through the trees. She'd become a coward, a far cry from the fae who'd tackled Connery to the ground and convinced him to join up with a group of criminal misfits.

Her eyes involuntarily flashed to him where he was leading his group in different exercises. They'd only grown further apart over the years and now barely spoke. He'd go off for weeks at a time. Merging with the wind and flying to faraway locations looking for other people or better resources. The further he flew, the longer it took for his strength to recover. He held onto hope that he would find a portal, like the ones to Tulo or Kysalt.

She didn't have any such faith.

He'd be leaving again soon. Despite their strained relationship, the thought made her heart twist painfully, even after all this time. He was taking a group of humans east, toward the coast, where he'd seen some better soil for farming. So much of the surrounding area was uninhabitable, shallow swamps or cracked barren desert.

She'd replayed their last moments together in Trevesten so many times. Asra could no longer tell what really happened and what her memory had produced to soften the impact of their estrangement. For a moment, his eyes met hers across the muddy field before she turned away.

Bringing Connery on had changed her. Solvan was always willing to go along with her plans. The more difficult and ridiculous, the better. Brigid and Elwin were more circumspect. They grounded her, refined her ideas to something achievable. But her motivation always centered on simple gain. When Connery showed up, she felt the need to show him they were more than petty thieves, that they were special, worth it. That she was worth it.

She'd been wrong.

"That's what I mean! Without necessity, there's no invention. If you have everything, you stop trying. Maybe they just lie around slowly turning into amorphous goo because they never need to move." Solvan stood and stretched, his arms reaching up and fingers splaying toward the late morning sun.

Asra bit back her retort, which was that if you have nothing, you can also stop trying. Instead, she just huffed a weak laugh at the ridiculous image he'd painted.

"You could go with him, you know." Solvan tipped his head toward Connery.

Asra's brows knit together, surprised. "Why would I do that?"

"Hasn't it been long enough? I know we didn't die yet, but couldn't you both just decide on a fresh start? Somewhere else?"

She chewed her lip. "It doesn't work like that." Asra couldn't believe Solvan, of all people, was trying to get her to repair her friendship with Connery. He and Connery had become friends, but in all their years together, Solvan had never once offered an opinion on Asra's love life. He'd always accepted that whatever went down between them was her business. Now his words opened an old wound, not nearly as healed as she'd thought.

"Tell me how it works. Because we've been here for almost eighty years. And the two of you both still look at each other like you're bracing yourselves. The effort just doesn't seem worthwhile. Can't you just, I don't know, talk to one another?"

In spite of the seriousness of his tone, Asra couldn't help but smirk. "Open communication? You've certainly evolved."

Solvan scoffed. "Don't try to deflect, it's insulting." He mimed finger-ing the lapel of a jacket.

Asra shook her head and let out a breath in exasperation. She expected this from Brigid and Elwin. The two of them had pried. There needed to be reasons, specifics, for the breakdown between her and Connery. They were frustrated when she couldn't give them more precise answers.

"We don't avoid each other. We don't resist talking. This is not some-thing we're doing." She ran two hands down her face. It was ridiculous to have this conversation. Connery did not think of her. There was no fight, nothing between the two of them anymore.

She could still sense when he was nearby. Whether he was sitting across the room or across the field like he was now, his emotions seemed to flow toward her like the wind he controlled.

But it still amounted to nothing.

"Relationships take work, intention." She waved her hands toward Brigid and Elwin. "They don't live until you kill them. All it takes is for one or both of you to stop taking care of it. You stay silent when you should speak, sit when you should stand." She struggled for the words, and Solvan pursed his lips in confusion. "You can't just expect things to happen."

Asra walked toward an arrow that had sunk into the mud some fifteen feet away. She yanked it out just to give her something to do.

"I'll always be second choice." The words were so quiet that she barely heard them above her own heartbeat. At first, it had all seemed so romantic. But Connery's words when they'd first arrived still stung. And although this place crushed her pride along with her magic, she didn't want to be a consolation prize. And she understood, finally, that he didn't want that for her either.

Solvan said nothing. His jaw had gone slack and his hair was rapidly thinning. Deep lines appeared around his face and mouth. His knees suddenly buckled, and Asra only had enough time to grab him as they both collapsed onto the ground.

He did not cry out, did not make any sound at all. The mouth that had always been ready with a quip, hands that moved like lightning, both were terrifyingly still. His milky eyes stared unblinkingly at the rusty-hued sky.

She was too shocked to speak, to yell for help. Her mouth dropped open in a silent scream. Someone ran toward them, and the scent of cool water and comforting herbs swirled around her. Connery knelt down next to Solvan, across from Asra. This was as close as they'd been in years, and she suddenly wanted him to get away from her.

Brigid fell to her side, her hands reaching out to Solvan's peaceful face, her magic running through his motionless body to find any sign of life.

Brigid pulled back her hand and placed it over his heart, tears rolling down her cheek. "He gave them so much," she whispered.

Connery's face drained of color. "How old was he?" His eyes found Asra's for a moment before she looked back at Solvan's lifeless form. She tried to catch her breath. Her chest was building with pressure and her tears fell unbidden, making small indents in the mud beneath her.

"One hundred and forty-five," she choked out.

Each time they drained their power into the darana, it took a year off their life. In the seven odd decades they'd been in Lashia, Solvan drained and distributed half of his life's power for the humans.

The rest of them were not far behind.

Asra traced a pink flower on Solvan's coat. A woman in the settlement had sewn it on for him after learning of his affection for tea made with the same flower. He'd brewed beer, built houses, and become a favorite storyteller among the children. Their favorite was when he performed Clyde, that ridiculous song about the overly ambitious dragon. They shrieked in delight when he used his abilities to turn himself into each character. He'd become so much more than a thief.

Another arrow landed about ten feet away from them. It made a soft thud as it landed harmlessly on the ground.

Asra stroked her friend's peaceful face. "In alia vita Solvan."

She raised her palm toward their attackers and sent up a wall of fire so long and so tall that even Connery and Brigid startled next to her. It had been a very long time since any of them had managed such a display of power. Even the small things were difficult now. But for Solvan, she would reach, gathering the dregs of her flames to send him on to his new life.

If he came back.

25

LIM

LASHIA, PRESENT DAY

Fall turned cooler, and it was the end of October before I knew it. Halloween wasn't really like it was before. I'd read all about the elaborate parties, haunted houses, and costumed children going door to door. Keen and Ayla had loved that part, and the children of Marais occasionally tried to revive the practice. But when the houses were far apart and unlikely to have any sort of treats on hand, it had always been an unsuccessful effort.

Marais, like the other boroughs, had a Halloween festival, though. Vendors and entertainers would congregate in the area in front of the library. Some people donned simple costumes, there were games and prizes for the children, and the traveling acts seemed to get better every year.

Indie and I were looking forward to the acrobats. Although I enjoyed their incredible ability to flip, climb, and twirl through the air, Indie wanted to be there in case one of them fell. Her medical school, like a lot of our education, had to make do with books that detailed techniques and procedures we didn't have the technology to perform. She and Simon shared the minimal technology they had with the other doctor in Marais.

Most things had to be relearned through a combination of trial and error and hand-written notes passed down from after the Weakening. It always excited them both when novel injuries came in because it gave them a chance to learn something. Now that she had the power to heal, she was even more restless to watch what her magic did to fix a particular injury.

"Nothing terrible, maybe just a nice compound fracture," Simon said, musing over the large chalkboard that listed the day's entertainment.

"I'd love to see another stomach injury myself," Indie replied casually.

"I think you both have a head injury," I said out of the corner of my mouth, hoping nobody had heard their bizarre exchange. We were early. Most people wouldn't show up before noon. But I had to set up, and Indie and Simon joined me before their office opened.

"Squeamish?" Indie's mouth quirked. "You have your experiments"—she tipped her head at my cart full of food and drink—"and we have ours."

Emir had never taken part as a vendor, but I was trying to get more people to make the trip to The Peregrine. My parents had built me a small booth. With help from Aiden, Keen had painted on the restaurant's name and a beautiful and detailed rendering of the namesake falcon. Indie and Simon helped me unload the booth before agreeing to meet me later.

I'd brought three casks of beer and cider, an assortment of handheld pies, as well as cookies, brownies, and hard candy. I piled the brightly colored sweets into a bowl that I hoped would attract children and their parents. Once I had a small fire going in the makeshift grill, I threw on some pies to get toasty and sat back to wait.

I'd seen a bear, a witch, two fairies, and a lot of ghosts. My sweets had worked like a charm. Children dragged their parents to my booth. I let them leisurely pick out a piece of candy before sending them and their parents away with hot pastries and desserts. My grin was wide as I chatted to people about the food, the festival, and clever costumes. It wasn't so hard. I wasn't sure why I'd been so resistant to doing it at the restaurant. And unlike Emir, I stuck to iced tea.

From where I sat, I had a perfect view of the acrobats towering above the crowd on stilts, magicians doing impressive card tricks, and the acts on the main stage. The crowd oohed and ahhhed for a woman who made a child's toy disappear.

Halloween seemed to be some kind of exception to the general rule against discussing magic. Perhaps because it was so obviously pretend, but more likely because the Tals could take part, too. It made me a little giddy knowing my friends and family were walking around with real magic, hiding in plain sight.

I hadn't seen Bastian in a few weeks. I resisted reaching out to him. Indie had been disappointed in him. Audre had been angry. Neither of them had been surprised.

"After all, what are the chances the first guy you date after having your head in the sand for so long would be a keeper?" Indie had said when I told her.

I had let myself wallow a bit before redirecting most of my energy to work.

From the booth, I had a great view of most of the festival. Audre and Jake were eating popcorn and trying their luck at the ring toss. My parents had already come by with Keen and Ayla, who had immediately dashed off to find their friends. Even Leo had stopped by to buy a brownie. I'd rolled my eyes at his hangdog look as he'd eyed the bowl of sweets. I'd tossed him a piece and shooed him away. Later in the afternoon, Aiden materialized from the crowd.

He gratefully tucked into a cinnamon cookie. "Booth looks great, Lim."

I gave him a wry smile in acknowledgment of the compliment he'd given himself. We both turned simultaneously toward a slight commotion happening on the other side of the street. We could hear a news hawker yelling headlines on the corner.

The crowd was responsive. There was a noticeable surge toward the kid, who was excitedly waving a newspaper. At some signal, his companions appeared with stacks of papers for the eager crowd. Aiden swiftly stepped over and bought one, opening it to see what all the fuss was about.

To anyone else, he would have looked interested, normal. But something about the way he refolded the paper and walked purposefully over to me set off alarm bells in my head.

Aiden put the paper down on the booth for me and then turned so he was facing the street, smiling casually at people, while I read quickly behind his back.

A registrar from Eudora, Sloane Mailer, has been found dead. Several people have been arrested in connection with Mailer's death. A source confirms Mailer removed the cuffs of the accused, and these activities may have played a role in her demise.

I swallowed. The crowd was glued to their papers. I had already told the group about the registrar. Now, I wouldn't need to ask Bastian to tell me what happened to the people she'd uncuffed. There's no way the trial wouldn't be front page news for weeks.

My eyes caught those of several other Jinns. I didn't know many of them well, but we were all feeling the crowd's scrutiny. There was a moment when everyone collectively paused, unsure of what would happen. There were nervous glances, shifting feet. Even the fire behind me seemed to have stopped crackling. Aiden continued to act as if nothing momentous had happened. He caught a sweet in his mouth after throwing it into the air—the picture of indifference. A few people around us responded to his demeanor, turning their eyes back to the stage or chatting with their neighbors.

I took several slow breaths.

Fire erupted, and the crowd gasped. A woman shrieked, her shrill voice carrying over the crowd. The main act had started. Two people stood to the side of the stage, blowing onto lit torches that exploded into fiery streaks. A woman rolled onto the stage, her legs curled backward until her toes touched her forehead. A man arrived from the other side, his yellow cuffs gleaming as he picked her up. He played to the crowd as he held aloft in all her circular glory. The crowd cheered, and I exhaled.

Several of the Jinns who met my eye made their way surreptitiously to the exits. The crowd was distracted, but I didn't miss the mistrustful looks being thrown around.

"Calimea—are you okay?" My father's voice echoed in my mind.

"Yes, you?"

"We're leaving. I'll bring the wagon back to get you." My father's voice sounded strained. He and my mother were no doubt having a difficult time convincing Ayla and Keen to leave the show without drawing too much attention to themselves.

"No, just get home safe. I can take care of myself if anything happens."

Aiden must have noticed my strange look—the same as we'd all worn when my father had discovered his power. "Want me to get my wagon and help you pack up?" Aiden asked, his eyes turning back to the crowd.

I sagged a little in relief. "Yes, thank you."

Aiden melted back into the crowd, cheerfully nodding to people as he made his way to his wagon. It was a struggle to pack up my things calmly, to wear the facial expression of someone who has heard some interesting but otherwise irrelevant news. I had just smothered my grill when a familiar voice spoke beside me.

"All sold out?" Chiwel, the registrar who had cuffed Priya, stood in front of the booth, a friendly smile on his face. His accompanists lurked a few feet away. I was relieved to see that their eyes kept darting toward the stage. Perhaps they weren't completely devoid of interest and personality.

"I have a few things left, just trying to get out before the departing crush. What can I get you?" I wiped my hands on my apron and gave him the best smile I could muster.

Chiwel asked for a cheese pie and a brownie. "Big news day around here. People normally avoid me. I'm not used to looks of sympathy."

"Oh"—I put my hand to my chest—"did you know her, the registrar?" I felt a sudden stab of pity for him. Not just because of the registrar's death but because being a registrar was a lonely occupation. People probably didn't look at him any more than was strictly necessary. And that Whitmore man had been awful. How many times did that happen, with Jinns or Tals?

"Not well," he said conversationally as he took a bite of his pie. "Delicious." He wiped his mouth with a handkerchief. "I'm a little surprised the Sun Guardians haven't shown up."

A chill went down my spine. Despite his rather imposing stature, Chiwel seemed kind. Was he threatening me? I couldn't help looking around to see who was watching this interaction. I hoped Aiden would stay away until he was gone.

"Maybe they wanted to dress up like ghosts and witches and have a night off from their typical nonsense." I shrugged impassively while my heart sped up.

Chiwel laughed softly, and I noticed that he'd been speaking softly for this entire exchange, as if he didn't want the accompanists to hear. "Maybe. They seem especially riled up right now. All this new talk of getting their own cuffs removed."

I remembered Sydney's bitter words about the Tals being punished for our crimes. "And this really isn't going to help," I grumbled, my smile dropping.

Chiwel pulled some coins out of his pocket and placed them in front of me. "It's weird though, that they didn't mention it was both Jinns and Tals?"

I frowned, looking down at the paper. He was right. It didn't mention that the uncuffed group had included both Jinns and Tals. The only reason I knew was because Bastian had told me. But how did Chiwel know I knew that?

"That is...weird." I held his gaze, willing him to say more.

"Certainly makes things awkward for the council." Chiwel smiled, selected a sweet from the last few left, and unraveled it. He popped in his mouth and turned around. He pretended to notice the accompanists behind him and took an exaggerated step back.

"Stars, guys, don't jump out of nowhere like that."

He walked away, the two accompanists trailing him from several feet behind.

Aiden came up behind me.

"Seems pretty calm about the whole thing," he said, watching Chiwel walk away.

I turned toward him. "He said he didn't know her well." Aiden picked up my grill, and I held out a hand. "Wait, isn't that still hot?"

"Feels fine to me." He carried the grill over to his waiting wagon while I collected the rest of my things.

On the way back to the restaurant, I told him everything Chiwel had said.

"Do you think Bastian told him? Or maybe he saw the two of you together and made an educated guess?"

"I don't know. Maybe he didn't expect me to know—maybe it was some kind of test." I shuddered, wondering if I had passed.

We continued down the road, pointing out the children in costumes and avoiding the eye of anyone with a newspaper.

Aiden cleared his throat. "Audre told me it didn't work out with Bastian. Sorry about that." He gave me a sympathetic smile before turning his eyes back to the road.

I rubbed my legs, warming them. "He's stuck in the middle. He wants to help me, but he also wants us to be cuffed." I pulled on my sleeves, nodding politely to the occupants of the wagon that passed ours.

Aiden scoffed derisively, and my eyes snapped to his face. "There should never be a middle with you, Lim. The decision between you and anything else should be easy. You deserve that."

I blinked, speechless for a moment. "Thank you."

He just nodded. "Anytime."

We passed by a group of people talking in front of the newsstand. They caught sight of us, and their looks were venomous. One of them spit on the ground while another opened his mouth to say something I was certain wouldn't be "Happy Halloween."

Aiden leaned closer to me, and I drew from his strength, willing myself to be calm. A cool breeze brushed my skin as I held my breath for several long beats. The entire group seemed to huff in resignation as we slowly passed them. They turned back to their newspapers.

I averted my gaze and exhaled.

"How about a drink?" I asked as we approached The Peregrine.

Aiden's beard shifted as he grinned in response.

Indie and Simon were making a chart.

The two of them used my menu board to write every possible scenario for the unfortunate Ms. Mailer.

"She either," Indie said, taking a sip of tea, "uncuffed them all willingly and they murdered her. Uncuffed them all willingly, and then committed suicide. Uncuffed them unwillingly, and they murdered her, or uncuffed them unwillingly and then committed suicide." She tapped the piece of chalk against the board and pursed her lips.

I widened my eyes but said nothing as I continued prepping for Saturday lunch and dinner. There was no sense in trying to interfere when the two of them were on a roll.

"Of course, my beautiful-brained wife, we also have to consider that her willingness was only for the Tals or only for the Jinns." Simon waved a piece of buttered bread at the board.

"Hmm," Indie replied, "you're right. What if she willingly uncuffed the Tals because she sympathizes with the Sun Guardians' desire to remove their cuffs? Then, the Jinns found out and forced her to uncuff them too? And then the Tals murdered her for uncuffing the Jinns? Or the Jinns murdered her so she wouldn't tell the Tals?"

"Or"—Simon rose to add his own notes on the chalkboard—"she voluntarily uncuffed the Jinns. The Tals found out and made her uncuff them, and then either group killed her for uncuffing the other?"

I hid my look of revulsion as they continued to dissect the registrar's death as thoroughly as they might dissect her body. They were both really leaning toward murder, and I was inclined to agree.

"Tell me again *exactly* what Chiwel said?" Indie leaned into my view.

"I have told you repeatedly what he said. I'm concerned about your memory at this point."

"My memory is excellent, thank you." Indie took a slow pull of her tea. "Chiwel approached you for a reason. I'm positive about that. It could have been an innocent reason—"

"Like he was hungry?" I said half-heartedly. Even I didn't believe that.

"Maybe," Indie said, annoyed at my interruption. "But I don't think so. Approaching you at the end of the day, after the paper had come out, but when everyone was distracted..." She looked at Simon knowingly. He nodded his head vigorously, his mouth full of scrambled eggs.

The backdoor opened, and Audre appeared. Her eyes went right to the board.

"Ooooh, okay, you wanna hear my theory...."

26

LIM

LASHIA, PRESENT DAY

About thirty minutes before we opened for lunch, a runner appeared at the front door. She was no older than Keen, her curly hair pulled back under a cap. She peeked through the windows, her energy palpable as I made my way to the door. I had barely pulled it open when she demanded,

"Calimea Revin?"

I nodded and smiled in response. She said nothing but pushed an envelope at me and sprinted back to her bike, off to her next recipient. Runners often hung out in groups around the more populated areas, waiting for jobs, laughing, and playing card games. I never understood the hierarchy they had between themselves. How did they decide who would take the job whenever someone appeared, waving an envelope or package, or using the little yellow flags the businesses used?

I opened the envelope,

Lim,

The Lashian council is concerned the illness we discussed the other night might spread. They are considering having everyone get checked out by a professional. No reports of it here, yet. Might be a good idea for you and yours to take some precautions for your health.

Speak more soon,

B

Something heavy sank in my stomach, and my thoughts all crashed into another at once. Did they find more people uncuffed? How could I not have realized something like this might happen? What would they do if they found all of us? The weight turned to roiling nausea as I thought back to the dinner, all of us happy and excited about our little rebellion.

My skin flushed as I read the note again. Anyone who read this from the council could figure it out, but not a random runner if they looked. My heart gave a little tug as I read his warning. True to his word, Bastian was still protecting me.

In a moment of panic, I pulled out the plate and went to the woods behind my parents' house. I made my way through the bald cypress and pine trees, counting my steps as I went. When I was far enough in, I dug a hole near one of the bigger trees and buried the plate. Then I dug it back up. I doubled my original number of steps and found another tree. This one was next to a large rock. I climbed up on the rock to see if I was truly secluded. It was not exactly a dense forest. But there were enough trees, shrubs, and hillocks that I was confident nobody would accidentally stumble upon my hiding place.

I wasn't sure whether I was hiding the evidence of my crime or keeping anyone from taking the plate away from me.

A large bird screeched to my left, startling me. I slid ungracefully down the rock. When I hit the bottom, my foot struck a root, and I went flying. The plate came out of its wrapping and out of my hand. I reached for it instead of trying to break my fall and ended up face down in the dirt, my hand slapping hard on the bottom of the overturned plate.

My hand burned from the impact. Self-pity, sadness, and regret coursed through my veins as I turned my head to the side and lay there.

Somehow, I thought we'd have more time. If I was being honest, I naively thought that nothing would happen. The Sun Guardians seemed to be more active, but the government never did anything about it before, so I assumed they'd ignore it now. Figures their response would be to inconvenience all of us instead of telling them to back off.

Squeezing my eyes closed, tears rolled off my nose and into the dirt. I never should have shown anyone the plate. A mature, responsible person would have taken responsibility and turned it and themselves in.

I stayed there, wallowing for several more minutes, waiting for a solution to present itself. When I'd been pathetic long enough, I clawed the plate back to me through the mud, pushing it into the ground a bit as I struggled to my feet. I hadn't gotten so used to "jumping," as I now thought of it in my head, that I instinctively used it yet. Probably for the best, considering.

I took a sharp rock and marked the large boulder where I buried the plate in a not so shallow grave, covering it with layers of leaves and moss. As I stood, I stumbled a little, it felt like marbles swirled in my head before coming to rest. I shook out the pins and needles in my arms and rubbed my hands together, strangely conscious of the roughness I found there.

I arrived back at the restaurant dirty, confused, and scared. I took out my feelings on the mud as I scrubbed myself clean in the shower. The absolute stupidity of believing that we would just be free to break the law without repercussion, a law every other Jinn still had to follow. What had I been thinking?

At my request, my father conveyed the contents of the note to the rest of the group. I didn't want to risk sending anything with a runner. To be on the safe side, I also told my parents how to find the plate.

"Please tell your dad," said Aiden as he walked into the restaurant later, "he needs to throw in a joke with his bad news. I need something cheerful next time, or I'm going to cancel my subscription to this service." He gave me a bracing smile.

Had several customers not walked through the door immediately after, I would have thrown my arms around him. As it was, I could only grin to show him how grateful I was for his positivity and lack of judgment.

Later that night, after the customers slowed enough that I could leave Audre, Jake, and Elias to close up, I went to Indie and Simon's.

When I arrived at their house, in the closet they'd reserved for that purpose, they were sitting in their garden. It wasn't terribly cold yet, but they had a fire going and had blankets wrapped around their legs, willing the fall air to come at last. I settled down in a chair that held another blanket and stared into the fire.

Indie handed me a drink, and Simon got up to put some things on the grill. After twenty minutes where none of us said a thing, Simon handed me a plate. Neither Indie nor Simon could cook, and my plate contained a plain roll filled with some grilled meat, no sauce, no vegetables.

"Stars at night, is this what you eat?" I examined my depressing dinner. Both Indie and Simon looked at me in surprise.

"Why? What's wrong with it?" Simon examined his roll as if he expected to find a rat tail.

"Nothing. I'm just in a bad mood." Rummaging around in their kitchen, I found a jar of mustard and half an onion. Dipping the onion in a little honey first, I grilled it and the rolls. I spread some mustard on my bread and topped it with the sweet grilled onions and meat. Indie and Simon both followed my lead, Indie slightly more begrudgingly.

"Hey, this is fancy!" Simon exclaimed, making himself two more.

I nearly choked on my sandwich at that, but it made me laugh. Indie once told me that if she could take a pill every day and never have to worry about eating again, she would. It was about efficiency. She had better things to do than worry about what to put in her mouth. I found her statement so disturbing she'd had to find me a chair to sit down.

"So you've come to tell us more bad news, or was what your dad said all of it?" Indie put her plate on the ground and clutched her drink.

"I'm sorry. I really am."

Simon had a mouth full of food, so he just shook his head. Indie leaned her head all the way back so she was staring into the night sky. "That treaty is hundreds of years old. I did think about it. But I talked myself into believing that they wouldn't take it seriously or that they wouldn't notice. But the truth is, we were all too excited to care." She bundled herself further into her blanket.

I thought of all the work the two of them had done to build their practice and a strange well of resolve began to fill me. "I don't have more bad news. I've come for information."

Indie brushed some stray crumbs off her blanket but said nothing. Simon was making himself a fourth sandwich. He applied his mustard and onions with careful precision before piling on the meat. His eyes slid to Indie, and I had a feeling they had already discussed their response before I'd even asked the question.

She exhaled. "You want us to help you get to Chiwel?"

"Yes. Any chance one of your patients is having a baby in the next few days?"

Indie snorted. "No such luck. Not any of mine, anyway. There might be at the other practice, but it's doubtful he would tell you."

"Can you think of any reason you could contact him, get him to come back?" My eyes found hers in the night, the fire making tiny dancing reflections in them as she looked at me. I didn't want to contact Chiwel myself. After our conversation on Halloween, I didn't trust him yet.

"And figure out a way for him to volunteer his services?" she asked, eyebrow raised.

"Baby steps." I turned to the fire, flexing my fingers in the heat.

The next morning found me eating breakfast with my family. Afterward, while I was washing the dishes, a rider came galloping up the drive. I immediately recognized him, out of a suit this time, but there was no mistaking that dark hair and those broad shoulders. I hurried out of the gate to meet him. Bastian stopped his horse in front of me and hopped down.

We stood awkwardly for a moment before he said, "It's good to see you."

"Likewise." I laughed nervously. "What are you doing here?"

"I went to The Peregrine first. I need to talk to you."

"About the mass checkup?" I gave him a sad smile.

"Do you mind if we go inside and talk?" His blue eyes were bright with worry.

The weight inside me doubled and grew teeth, gnawing at my nerves. I nodded.

"Have you told your family what I told you?" he asked.

I nodded again as we walked inside.

When we got into the living room, I introduced him to Ayla and Keen, who made their hellos quietly. Even they could feel the strain of this meeting.

Taking advantage of the loaded silence, Ayla wasted no time. "Are you in charge of Marais?"

He laughed, caught off guard. "No, I'm just a lawyer." My mother looked like she might interject at his use of the word "just," but Ayla continued.

"Are you a Jinn?"

"Yes."

"Do you like my sister?"

"Yes."

"Have you kissed her?"

"Yes."

"Ayla!" I groaned. "Can you stop with the interrogation?"

Ayla just shrugged. Bastian cocked his head at her before shaking it and reverting to seriousness.

"I understand Lim told you of my message, about the census?"

"Potential census?" I asked. I sounded pathetic, even to my own ears.

Bastian's expression was grave. "That's what I came to tell you. It's not potential anymore. They are making plans to ensure that every Jinn is checked for cuffs."

The room was silent, all of us looking anywhere but at Bastian.

"That's ridiculous." My mother fluffed her hair and smiled. Just another irate farm customer for her to handle. "One errant registrar and half of Lashia's population is under investigation? Really?" She gave him a look that said the Lashian council was just being silly.

"They are quite firm on the decision." Bastian's voice cut through all of us. My parents and I shared a look. This couldn't just result from one registrar and a few uncuffed people. A tiny spark of hope seemed to pick up its head at the thought that maybe there were more of us.

"When?" I asked.

Bastian kept his eyes on me, and I saw the fear there. "A month, maybe longer."

I sucked in a breath and wiped my palms on my dress. "Any more information on what might happen to me if they discovered I don't have my cuffs anymore?"

"There has been no discussion of any revised punishments." That was the most lawyerly thing Bastian had ever said to me. He grimaced a bit as if he heard it, too. "I'm sorry. Nothing new. I expect that if they find you, you'll be recuffed and imprisoned. They'll also likely interrogate you regarding the plate and whether you've used it to uncuff anyone else."

I didn't dare look anywhere but at Bastian. If I looked at my family, he would see their panicked expressions, and not just for me. He would notice my mother touching both her young children, ensuring herself they were still there.

"I also heard something else. It's unverified, so I'm hesitant to even say it." Bastian glanced at my siblings.

"What is it?"

"The Jinns and Tals that were allegedly uncuffed by Ms. Mailer. They were reportedly recuffed and have been imprisoned awaiting trial. But nobody has actually seen them. I don't know who is representing them. And there are rumors that the trial won't be public."

"What? Can they do that?" my father said from his chair.

"There has been a lot of concern for their safety. That could be why, but it's still concerning."

"You won't go to prison, right?" Keen asked me shakily. His face was still round with youth. Ayla stood beside me, her arms crossed in defiance. My fingers reached out to stroke her soft hair. A knot lodged in my throat. I had stolen a part of their youth with this, forced them to worry about the law and imprisonment. They were still young enough to be overjoyed at the promise of ice cream or wake up scared of a nightmare.

Ayla jumped in again, undeterred, "If you like my sister, don't you want her to have magic?"

Bastian immediately opened his mouth to answer when both me and my parents raised our voices in unison, "Ayla, please go to your room." We smiled a bit awkwardly. It was clear we all had the same understanding regarding Ayla's power.

"What? Why?" Ayla reeled on our father. "Why do I have to go to my room? I haven't done anything wrong!" She crossed her arms indignantly.

My father forcibly clamped his mouth shut.

Bastian raised his palms. "No, it's fine. I'm sorry. I should go." He looked at me, the apology in his eyes clear.

I walked him outside in silence. When we got to his horse, I could tell he was still struggling. Was he suspicious of Ayla? Or was he too wrapped up in confronting his own thoughts on the matter?

"Thank you for telling us what the Council is planning."

"What are you going to do?"

"I don't know." I really didn't. Even if I did, it was dangerous to keep involving him. Keeping everyone safe had to be my primary concern.

"I'll let you know as soon as I hear anything else." His hand twitched like he might reach for me but stopped.

A mixture of sadness and apprehension swirled inside me as his figure retreated into the distance.

"What do you mean I can't use my power? You all use your powers!" Ayla was yelling when I came back into the house.

"Ayla, you cannot force people to do things against their will." My mother was standing over Ayla with her hands on her shoulders, her red hair creating a curtain around her face.

My father joined in, "It's not just that baby. You heard him, we're not safe right now. None of us should be using our powers," My mother looked pointedly at my father, who nodded in resignation.

I walked toward Ayla and leaned down so I was at her eye level. "I want you to ask me a question without using your ability."

Ayla was on the verge of tears. Of all of us, she'd had no fun time to experiment. Although I'm not sure how much the group would enjoy being interrogated by a ten-year-old who could force you to tell the truth.

"Are you a big meanie?" She crossed her arms and threw daggers at me with her eyes.

I smiled sadly. I did not feel compelled to answer. It also occurred to me I wasn't sure of the answer to that question, and that made me even more apprehensive about my sister's power.

"Again."

"What is your favorite color?" she asked dully.

"Good." I moved forward and hugged her. She didn't push me away, but she wasn't about to hug me back. "I'm so sorry. This is all my fault."

"Hey, enough of that." My father clasped me on the shoulder. "We all had a choice. You're not responsible for what we chose."

"I think it's all your fault," grumbled Ayla.

"Don't be a baby," Keen responded, but his face was heartbroken.

I had a sudden vision of Keen and Ayla as powerful adult Jinns. Keen attacking her while invisible but unable to resist her demands. The vision swirled in my brain, mixing with images of Simon falling from the sky or Indie trying and failing to revive a lifeless body.

27

ASRA

LASHIA, ~ 400 YEARS AGO

Heavy mist, thick with the scent of pine, surrounded them. Visibility was so low the three of them didn't risk moving more than a few feet from each other. They could have been walking across a flat field or on the edge of a deep crevasse. Asra placed each step carefully. Every few feet, one of them left a small magical signature to mark the path. At least that still worked. The rest of their base magic had dwindled significantly.

Her strength was waning more than the others. She was older, and she'd done the math. Asra brushed a hand through her hair, shot through with gray streaks she could no longer hold at bay. It didn't require a huge amount of power, but all of them were showing wear from this difficult life they'd found.

A vision of Solvan's aged face flashed through her mind.

She glanced over and couldn't help a laugh from escaping as she watched Connery and Elwin's strange and hesitant movements. Like a bunch of blind baby deer. They looked over at her questioningly, but she just waved away their attention. The motion made the mist swirl around her fingers, like ghosts of her flames.

They'd been gone two days, scouting for more humans or resources. Connery's trips to the east had revealed some promising areas but also

more humans in need of magic. He was planning to settle there permanently. She, Brigid, and Elwin had refilled two daranas for him to take.

She'd accepted it. Accepted that his presence would always affect her,
that her skin would always prefer his, even after the others she'd found
here, men all too willing to slake their lust with her heat.

So far, they'd found nothing but the same bald cypress trees reaching
out of the muddy water, meager wildlife, and this endless damp veil.

"Why are we being so quiet?" Elwin practically shouted, making her
jump.

"Sweet Mother, was that necessary?" Connery held a hand to his chest.
But his lips quirked in a smile.

Asra couldn't help giving him one of her own. "I was just picturing
how stupid the three of us must look, slinking along like this. As if
anything is out here to see or hear us."

"There are probably hulking beasts lurking just beyond our vision.
Waiting to pounce on us as soon as soon as we try to walk normally."
Elwin took out his sword and slashed the air, causing more ripples to
eddy around him.

"There's nothing hulking out here. Not enough food for any beast to
bulk up," she said.

"What about those snakes that eat the air? Bet they live pretty well,"
Connery said, using his own sword to make foggy designs. His eyes
darted to hers and there was an awkward beat. They both seemed to recall
the last time they'd seen such a thing, and what had happened afterward.

"Yeah, air being the only abundant thing out here." Elwin picked up
a rock and tossed it forward. Asra picked up another and tossed it to her
left while Connery did the same to their right. All three of them landed
with soft thumps.

"No elevation change, but at least we aren't about to fall off a mountain," Elwin muttered.

All of them hoped the path would start heading downward. To a place they might see more than an arm's length in front of their faces. She'd tried heating the surrounding air, but it did nothing but turn the mist to steam, which then condensed, soaking their hair and clothes.

The ground became soft and spongy. Connery prodded the dirt with a long stick.

"Feels like flesh." He gave a small shudder.

The soil beneath them began rapidly sinking.

Asra held out her hands for balance. "What the stars?" She moved toward Elwin, but her next step hit nothing but air. She twisted just in time to see Connery disappear into the mist with a loud shout. The world tipped and Asra careened into him. He reached out and grabbed her hand, the two of them pushing against the dirt with their heels. Elwin shouted in panic from behind them.

They tried to grab with their free hands, but couldn't find purchase. Mud coated their skin and clothes, making traction impossible. Further and further down, her body slammed into rocks and tree roots. Connery rolled over her to avoid a large boulder. He cried out in pain as he landed on her other side.

Then, for several terrifying moments, they were airborne. Wind rushed to meet them, Connery's attempt to slow their descent.

A mist-filled scream caught in her throat.

Asra let go of Connery's hand as they rolled into the landing. Her ankle slammed into something sharp. Pain raced up her leg as she sat up. The healing power she sent out wasn't enough. The pain receded, but it would be back with a vengeance. It wasn't broken, at least.

She crawled over to Connery, who was flat on his back, his eyes shut tight. He moaned, his arm bent at a terrible angle.

"Damn it, that doesn't look good. Can you heal yourself?"

He took a few stuttering breaths before touching his fingers to the break. He exhaled, and under all the splattered mud, his skin regained some color.

"Can't fix it completely. It'll hold for now, though."

Connery had more of an ability than she did. They'd received the same amount from the darana, but his royal blood gave it a bit of a boost.

Asra was crouching over him, their faces so close she could have easily kissed him.

"Are you dead?" Elwin's voice sounded from far above.

"No, just injured," she yelled back, scooting away and holding out a hand to help Connery up. His skin was rough and filled with as many tiny cuts as her own.

"That's a relief. You see any way out?"

"Is it me, or does he sound concerningly far away?" Connery squinted at the gaping opening above us.

"Nope, it's not you."

Elwin's voice was barely audible, and they couldn't see him at all. She took in their surroundings. It was dark, but at least there was no mist. The walls were uncommonly smooth and even for a cave. Too precise to be natural.

"We're in a building," Connery shouted up to Elwin. "Might be able to climb up. But I've got a broken arm and Asra has a sprained ankle."

Elwin didn't bother asking Connery to become the wind. Shifting into anything when injured was asking for trouble. Trying to navigate blindly out of a winding hole was asking for further injury, as neither of them could float anything for more than a few minutes anymore.

Possessing no significant healing ability, they were better off finding an alternative.

"I'm going to look for something I can use as a rope," Elwin yelled, his voice already fainter.

"Stairs would be better!" Connery yelled back, fashioning a sling from his belt. Her pack had made it down, but his had slipped off in the descent.

They walked further into the cavernous space, aided by the fiery ball she held suspended above them.

As their eyes adjusted to the light, they could make out the walls of the structure. There had been a landslide. A mountain of dirt had covered the building, but it was surprisingly intact. Aside from the ceiling where they'd crashed through.

The mud on the floor thinned, exposing an intricate tile floor. Their steps echoed in the silence. An enormous circular fountain dominated the space. Whatever figure had once adorned the center had long since crumbled into the pool. The water was gone, but hundreds of dull coins blanketed the bottom.

A note appeared in the air in front of them and Connery grabbed it. He snorted.

"No luck on the rope. He wants to know if we've found any grappling hooks."

Asra pulled out a pencil and wrote a response, feeling the strain on her power to do so. They might find something they could use, but Connery was in no state to climb a rope.

She sent it back, and a moment later, another note from Elwin appeared.

Connery opened it. "He thinks he should go back for Ciran. He's got enough power to at least shift the dirt into something scalable."

Turning, she assessed the hole above them. "We could try getting to the top, then alternatively floating one another up the hole? If there is enough to grip while we rest?"

"Let's see if we can get there and take a look. No harm in him getting Ciran, though. We may get stuck."

Asra nodded, resigned. "I'll tell him to walk back to meet him halfway, make sure the signatures are holding. He can borrow a balara to get here quicker." Unlike them, Elwin could afford to waste his power on the notes. He could tell Brigid everything through their bond. He probably already had.

The building was unlike anything she'd ever seen. It had ten further stories above the ground floor, each of them with deep, open balconies. In some places, pale marble streaked with gold was visible under the debris.

Brittle wood littered the floor, remnants of paintings, the canvas little more than pulp now. Connery moved over to rub off a square metal plate adorning the wall. It was engraved with a range of numbers and a word they didn't recognize.

She pushed lightly against a wooden door, and it splintered at the touch, large chunks falling to the floor. Asra stood back as the rest of it fell apart before the two of them peered inside. The mud had poured in through a window, nearly filling the space.

A grand staircase appeared as they moved toward the end of the hall. It was made of the same cool stone. Several of the balustrades had golden figures perched on top. Asra rubbed her hand over one of them, a tiny figure with wings and a long horn.

Connery went first, testing it with his weight. They took tentative steps, avoiding the more damaged areas, marveling at the intricate details frozen in time.

The second floor contained dozens of empty wooden shelves, most of which had collapsed onto their sides.

After passing a dozen more rows of shelves, a massive pile of dirt forced them to stop. It had pushed its way in through glassless windows that took up three entire stories. She floated the fireball up, focused on the top to see if there was a way they could climb the internal mountain to get to the roof.

Connery's hand gripped her arm a moment before she screamed.

Hundreds of skeletons reached out from the mountain. Their jaws agape and thin fingers clawing through the soil. One of them wore a bracelet, the metal tarnished but the jewels twinkling in her firelight. Another had a near-perfect hole in the top of its skull, small gray cracks radiating outwards. Scraps of decaying fabric twisted around them, pulling their limbs into unnatural angles.

Asra stumbled backward, the bones sinking into the darkness as her fear snuffed out her fire.

Connery turned her away from the bones, pulling her back down the stairs.

"Oh fuck, oh fuck, why are there so many?" Asra stuttered as she closed her eyes and tried not to vomit on the floor.

He wrapped his arm around her as she took deep, shuddering breaths. "They could have been caught in the landslide, or the landslide might have taken a graveyard with it when it moved." His words were rapid, trying to fill the suddenly oppressive silence.

She raised the fireball again, but now the edges of the light were threatening, filled with hundreds of watchful, dead eyes.

Asra took another breath and inhaled Connery's familiar scent. Streams and delicate green plants, sweetness and life. She didn't back away, and he didn't let her go.

Finally, her breathing slowed. His hand slowly slid down her arm before dropping. His eyes found hers, and a different sort of apprehension replaced her fear.

"How about some tea?" The low tone of his voice made an unused part of her stretch. The creak of a door long since closed.

Eager for the distraction, she dropped her pack and dug around inside for the tea.

They sat on the fountain's ledge, drinking and nibbling on the provisions she'd packed. Luckily, they all carried food, but she made a mental note to be better prepared next time. This would be enough for two days, but it would be tight. Hopefully, if they couldn't find their own way up, Ciran could get here in one.

Recovered enough from the heinous discovery, they went back to exploring the rooms. Asra braced herself each time she opened a door, and Connery refused to move from her side. At every corner, his good arm was poised, ready to pull her back.

After decades of barely being in the same room together, it was driving her to distraction. His hand brushed against hers as they reached for the same doorknob. She felt his breath on her neck, against her hair, every time they crouched down to see if something was salvageable. His chest touched her back when they leaned into a room to inspect it.

Instead of calling out, Connery's fingers grazed her hand when she nearly walked past a small underground stream meandering through the rocks of another cave-in. Asra boiled some water until it was safe enough to drink, and Connery cooled it so they could wash.

She caught him watching as she rubbed the dirt from her face and neck. How was it that after all this time, he still just had to look at her for her pulse to quicken? For heat to ignite under her skin as if he controlled her fire?

Sleep was going to be difficult.

They found a place that looked safe enough, far away from the poor souls on the second floor. The temperature was dropping rapidly. All the wood was damp or rotted, and Asra could no longer hold a flame while she was asleep. They tacitly acknowledged the inevitability of their sleeping arrangements as they laid her blankets on a large metal table.

She sat cross-legged on the makeshift bed, her flame hovering above. Asra pulled out her notebook to document the experience while Connery distributed the food for their paltry dinner. He gave himself five pieces and her six.

"Stop that," she said, arching an eyebrow at him.

"What?" He gave her comically innocent eyes, and she laughed. That door opened a little wider.

"You obviously need more food than me." Besides him being bigger, he needed to maintain the power up to keep his arm pain free.

He grimaced. "I don't know how to tell you this," he leaned forward and whispered, "but this amount of food won't make much of a difference for either of us. So maybe you should just be quiet and thank your stars I'm so chivalrous."

She mimicked his posture and tone. "Maybe you should be quiet and learn how to count." Asra leaned back again as she flicked the extra piece of meat at him.

After they ate, when she could avoid it no longer, she extinguished the light, plunging them both into absolute darkness. Even with her slightly enhanced vision, she could barely make out the shape of him. But his arm and leg were warm as they pressed firmly against hers.

Their breathing was the only sound until Connery shifted and winced.

"What's wrong?"

"The belt really doesn't work in this position." He fumbled around beside her.

Asra climbed off the table. "Sit at the edge." She unwound her scarf and stood in front of him.

She could have relit the room. She braced her palm against that door, knowing she should shut it, push back against the wind that was rushing in.

He scooted to the edge, and she stepped between his legs. Asra's fingers trembled slightly as she put her arms around him, wrapping the scarf so his arm was tight against his chest. Another loop around his waist brought them nearly nose to nose. She pushed up on her toes, letting her thumb graze the back of his neck as she pulled the scarf around.

Was his heart beating as fast as hers was? They'd been friendlier in the last few years, if not friends. Her last conversation with Solvan had weighed on Asra, and while they'd kept their distance, it felt less intentional. She still stuck to the shadows behind the others, but she was comfortable there. The bitterness she'd once felt had melted into something more calm.

Resignation.

Her voice caught in her throat as his hand curled at her cheek. She could only just make out the shape of his jaw, the curve of his shoulders. It didn't really matter. She knew his face by heart. Had she his talent, she could've drawn it down to the last freckle and scar.

Asra's hands tightened on his waist even though a voice told her it was stupid. She was asking to be rejected all over again.

"Being alone with you is pure torture." His voice was like a wave washing over pebbles on the beach. She felt it roll through her body, sinking into every crevice. "I can't stand not being able to touch you."

"You are touching me," she said, her voice breathless.

His thumb traced her skin, running a path down to her lips. "But I shouldn't be. And even now, I can't touch you in all the ways I want to." He shrugged his shoulder with the injured arm to make his point.

That faint reminder of why they didn't spend time together. And how the last time they'd been alone, she'd snapped at him. Angry at his desire for a fresh start.

She was afraid to speak again, to break whatever spell allowed this moment away from the reality of their lives above ground.

Connery's lips found hers in the dark, and they both stilled, relearning how they fit together. He pressed harder, his hand reaching back into her hair and pushing her closer. It was a relief to run her hands over his body again. Her blood sang at the touch, her fire licked up her insides, racing to be near him.

Asra flung the door wide open.

She wrapped her arms around his neck, her nails dragging through his hair. His hand dropped to her waist before sliding around and crushing her body against his.

He was hard against her center, and she moaned as he pressed himself against her with obvious need. Slowly, as if he was giving her time to back away, Connery slid off and turned her around to face him, pushing her back against the table.

She could practically feel his frustration with his arm as he fumbled with her clothing. His voice dropped to a growl.

"Take off your shirt."

Swallowing, she complied, removing her shirt and underthings. He didn't ask her to use her flames, feeling the same freedom she did in the darkness. Even though he couldn't see her, his breathing quickened. Asra could easily remember the way he looked at her when she'd lain beside him in that tent in Solbaina, like she was dinner.

He was so close, but he didn't move to touch her. "And the rest."

Asra tossed aside the rest of her clothes and her boots. Nothing would make her light the room now, not while she felt the dark air move around her skin, slide around her neck, and between her legs.

"Sit down." Connery's tone had become softer but no less demanding.

Stars, she would come undone. Asra pushed back onto the table, the blankets rough against her legs.

Still, he didn't touch her. She leaned back onto her hands as he moved further into her space, down her body, mouth hovering over her skin. His breath caressed her throat and her breasts until she was shivering.

She cried out when his mouth closed around her nipple, her hands grasping his hair. His tongue teased one hard peak, then the other. She wrapped her legs around his waist to bring his mouth to hers, pushing her tongue against his while his hand moved lower.

Connery's fingers found her wet and ready. He toyed with her, making slow, lazy circles with his thumb. Asra ground herself against him in demand. He gently pushed a finger inside, and she shamelessly rode him, her thighs clenching around his hand. She pulled her mouth from his and tasted the skin on his neck, savoring the scent that followed her even in sleep, while he continued to build the pressure inside her. There was nothing but the sound of their need, skin against skin.

"Connery, please," she whimpered, grabbing at his shoulders.

He undid his buttons with one hand. Her fingers circled him, gliding along his soft skin. She scooted closer to the edge of the table, guiding him toward her.

Asra dragged the length of him along her wet center and he groaned, his hand slamming down on the table before gripping her ass, pushing himself deeper inside. His head fell to her shoulder.

"Such sweet torture," he murmured, his breath hot against her ear.

She sank her teeth into his skin as he pounded her with slow, deliberate strokes. The heat from their bodies was enough to make their skin slick with sweat as they writhed in the pure darkness.

Her pressure climbed until it was almost unbearable and Asra could no longer form a coherent thought. Her cry echoed in the empty rooms as wave after wave broke over her. He drove into her faster and faster until he whispered her name and release shuddered through him.

They didn't talk afterward. Both of them afraid to ruin it.

But he curled around her, relishing their shared warmth. Later in the night, he'd reached for her again. She'd climbed on top of him, careful of his arm.

But when gray light filtered through the cracks of the room, they remained silent, unsure of what they'd done.

As she dressed, Asra remembered what he'd told her all those years ago. That she deserved someone who chose her first. He'd pushed her away so she would find someone worthy. Instead, she'd languished, forming little connection to anyone new. Asra refused to think about where he got his comfort over the years. It didn't matter.

There was only one Sabine, and if they were reborn in Trevesten, she'd be right there waiting.

He stirred behind her, and she waited for him to say something.

A note appeared, and Asra lunged for it too quickly to be casual. "Ciran is here." He must have ridden all night.

Her voice shattered whatever spell they'd been under. Behind her, Connery struggled to dress. She marched over and helped him with his clothes. He searched her face, but she kept her focus squarely on buttons, his makeshift sling, anywhere but him.

He cleared his throat, but she interrupted him. "If you apologize, I will gut you." There was no feeling behind the words. "Use what you have on the pain. He's going to grow a ladder for us."

The sound of creaking, snapping limbs reached them. Ciran had already started. It would be a lot for him. He was only fifteen but had the strongest flora power in the village.

Asra put on her pack and walked toward the door. Connery grabbed her elbow and swung her back to him. The blue of his eyes swallowed her whole, and she immediately met his lips as they crashed into hers. The feel of his skin reminded her of everything they'd done, every place he'd touched her in the dark. But the tear that rolled down her face knew it was a goodbye kiss.

Connery's forehead met hers. "You are my greatest weakness."

She caressed the soft edges of his hair, feeling a bittersweet satisfaction from his words. "I've been called worse."

He chuckled and kissed her once more before they left the darkness behind.

28

SABINE

TREVESTEN, ~ 175 YEARS AGO

The bickering was really beginning to get on her nerves. They'd been at it for hours. Being Trevesten's closest neighbors, the Ambassadors from Eloisha and Boralta were here, of course. But there were others from all over Malan. Some of them were hoping to make a deal or foster a relationship between their nation and hers. Others just were here to enjoy the party, and report back on how amenable Morgan might be to a political marriage now that she was on her third life.

All of them loved to hear themselves talk.

After an imperceptible look of exasperation at Antonio, Sabine raised her hands. The ambassadors politely stopped talking. A few of them had the decency to look embarrassed that Sabine had to silence them like a schoolteacher.

"We don't need to solve everything this morning. You are all invited to stay for the next few weeks until Princess Morgan completes her rishival. Today is a day of celebration, after all." Her light tone dropped. "However, I would encourage any of you who are attempting to strengthen your trade agreements with Trevesten to discuss any roadblocks presented by your neighboring countries before bringing it to me again."

She hoped she was clear enough. Work out your own petty squabbles before bothering her.

"Apologies, Your Majesty. However, I think there is something we should discuss—perhaps discuss is too strong—think about over the coming weeks, so we are prepared to discuss it after the Princess' rishival is over." Ambassador Venten smiled placatingly at her.

Sabine raised an eyebrow at the male. Venten looked younger in this life, but he still sported the traditional Boraltan dress. Sabine appreciated that he'd avoided conversing with Morgan regarding their prior knowledge of one another even though, having already gone through his most recent rishival, he was well aware of their history.

"Go on."

"There has been an increasing number of scouting trips to Kysalt." Venten mentioned the first world, two layers below Malan. "Malan may need to create a unified set of import/export regulations."

The Ambassador from Eloisha scoffed. "Seriously? There are fae willing to go there? Are they trying to import frostbite?"

Mild laughter rippled through the crowd. Kysalt was the first of the seven worlds that the fae from Malan had been able to reach. It hadn't been difficult. There were several portals that existed in Malan, and it required little in the way of magic or effort to get there. The same was true for the seventh layer, Tulo. The other worlds were much more challenging, if not impossible.

But the world was nothing but snow, mountains, and more snow. Still, Sabine had sent her own scouting trips. So far, there had been little to report.

"Who knows what treasures lay beneath the ice?" Venten said.

'Clever,' thought Sabine. Everyone would be much more invested in regulations if they thought there still might be something of value there.

They wouldn't want the others to get an unfair advantage. But if Venten was already pushing for regulations, the Boraltans had clearly already found it.

"Fair enough, Ambassador Venten. I agree. We'll add it to the post-rishival agenda."

Venten and the others bowed to her before filing out, leaving her and Antonio alone.

"You think he's being up-front?" Antonio asked, referring to Venten's motivations for the regulations.

"I never think anyone is being up-front. But who knows? Perhaps the Boraltans simply need another place to torture the entrants in their contest for the crown."

Antonio chuckled. "Maybe. They're always entertaining."

"Fine. But if they hold a trial in Kysalt, you better bring an army of fire wielders for us."

Later that evening, Sabine brushed her fingers down the long row of leather-bound books before finding the one she had pulled out so many times. She placed the book on the podium, and it fell open to her touch, to the page she returned to again and again.

Connery's name was listed at the top. Below, his original date of birth, hundreds of years ago now, but with no date in the death column. It had been three hundred and twenty-five years, and he still scorned her. It was actually rather impressive, being able to block her in so many ways for this long. Although it hurt less now than it once did, it was still there, the dull ache of regret.

Sabine closed the book. She inhaled the deep scent of wood polish, leather, and thousands of pages of paper that surrounded her in the library. She took down a different book and found Morgan's name, making a few notes on her impending rishival. They would both come back when it was over to add further commentary.

With a sigh that seemed to come directly from her bones, Sabine returned the book and walked out. Her heart was heavy as it always was on these days, but her footsteps were quick as she made her way down the hall and toward the music.

The Princess's third rishival was well underway. Most of the attendees were several drinks in, and the mountain of presents for Morgan's twenty-fifth had finally stopped growing. Glittering balls of light filled the room. The revelers waded through them like giant unpoppable bubbles. Rainbows appeared, then arced and melted into a pool of gold before appearing somewhere else in the room. Music flowed in from every direction, the tempo seeming to increase with each passing hour.

Morgan made her way toward Sabine from across the room, smiling and hugging well-wishers as she passed. She had once again grown into such an amazing fae, strong and clever, but more importantly, kind and just. As Morgan made her way out of the balcony doors to where Sabine stood against the stone railing, she snagged two glasses of wine from a passing server.

"Don't tell me you're out here reminiscing about changing my diapers or something?" Morgan handed her a glass, her face crinkled into mock disgust.

Sabine laughed. "I've never had to change a single one of your diapers, thank goodness, but yes, I was feeling a little nostalgic." Sabine clinked her glass with Morgan's and they both drank.

Morgan leaned down next to her, her forearms on the railing. She didn't speak for several minutes but absentmindedly rubbed the small tattoo on the inside of her wrist.

"Are you nervous?" Sabine swirled her wine, a small smile on her lips. They'd had this conversation before.

"A little"—Morgan blew out a breath—"I suppose everyone wonders whether they will remain someone they like, how many amends will need to be made." Morgan gazed out at the night sky, and a sweet breeze blew across them, bringing the promise of winter.

"They do." Sabine idly traced the rim of her wineglass.

"And, of course, I'm not looking forward to all the vomiting."

Sabine huffed a sympathetic laugh. "No, but I'll make it as comfortable as possible for you. I'll confine you to your room and won't let you see anyone or send any messages until it is completely over and you have processed it all. And, of course, the healers will be standing by."

"Two weeks?" She turned her head and grimaced up at Sabine.

"Give or take." She gave her a sympathetic look and brushed the hair from her face.

"What is the longest rishival you've heard of?" Morgan asked, her eyes still on the sky.

Sabine smirked. "I would never tell you that—what good could come of it?"

Morgan grinned, rose, and turned to her sister. Her eyes were like black diamonds and framed with long lashes. Her hair was dark and curly in this life. It made them look more like sisters, although Sabine's hair was now straight. She used those eyes to scan the room, smiling at friends and relatives who gave her hearty words of encouragement. There were even a few less cheerful warnings about what was in store for her over the coming weeks.

"It is the last night we will know one another like this," Sabine said a little wistfully. She missed the Morgan she'd known before, but she adored watching Morgan grow up again.

Morgan gave her an odd look. "Sabine, you know I'm still going to be me, right? I'm still going to be your sister who loves you and occasionally does things that embarrass you?"

"Promise?" There was a note of vulnerability in Sabine's voice that she would only ever let her sister hear.

"I promise." Morgan hugged her tightly, and Sabine relaxed into her embrace.

In this life, Morgan had been born at four am. At two, the guards escorted out the last of the partygoers. They called their well wishes behind them as they stumbled out of the palace and into the dark stillness of early morning. Sabine led Morgan up to her room, where she bathed and put on loose, comfortable pajamas. She climbed into bed and Sabine tied the restraints to her arms and legs—she'd be able to get up from the bed but would not get far. It was a necessary precaution. The memories returned in a flood and it drove one to madness. It was too much to cope with all at once. People screamed and raged, broke things, and lashed out at their loved ones.

The healers now had tonics and elixirs that would dull the worst effects. The madness and the illness would come, but it would hopefully be manageable.

Sabine noticed her palms sweating a bit as she picked up such an elixir and uncorked it. She held the lavender-colored vial out to Morgan and smiled.

"In alia vita, Morgan."

"In alia vita, Sabine." She gave her a light but confident smile.

Morgan tipped the vial back, and the contents began working immediately. Her eyes became unfocused and she let her head fall to the pillow.

Sabine walked over to the chair in the corner where she'd gathered her books and some tea and sat down to wait.

29

LIM

LASHIA, PRESENT DAY

A few days later, I awoke to heavy snores beside me. Perhaps sensing my dismal attitude, Brax had curled his immense body around mine and his head lay heavy on my stomach. I made to get up, but he didn't move an inch, although I was pretty sure he was only pretending to sleep at this point. I struggled for several minutes in vain before I mentally smacked myself in the forehead—because my hand was still trapped under Brax—and jumped to the bathroom.

As I showered and dressed, I let myself pretend for a moment that it was a normal day and I was a normal girl, waking up with her gorgeous boyfriend instead of a clingy pet, with nothing more to worry about than whether I had enough bread for today's lunch service.

I continued to indulge myself by physically walking out of my rooms, but when I glanced out the windows, a strangled cry escaped me. The street beyond The Peregrine, the main avenue, was burning. The wind must have been moving in the opposite direction. I couldn't smell anything, but I could see the smoke, thick black plumes rising from building after building.

What the hell had they done?

I was so focused on the fire I didn't notice him at first. The angry Tal who'd thrown the rock through my window was back, wearing that same mean and purposeful expression. He and two other men stared into the windows. My lungs constricted painfully in my chest. Fear paralyzed me as he took a hammer from his bag and, with one casual movement, smashed my window and any feeling of safety I'd once had in this place. The sound of a hundred shards of glass tumbling onto my clean floor brought me back to my senses. I ran back to my room where Brax was instantly on alert.

I pulled open the wall panel where I kept the safe, thanking the stars I'd already hidden the plate. I grabbed the coin I kept on hand and a few other valuables while also attempting to shove my clothes on. In the time it took me to grab my meager belongings, they'd smashed three more windows, the splintered glass creating a rainbow effect as the morning sun glinted off of it. Hot tears sprang to my eyes at the destruction they had wrought in only a few moments.

The man climbed through the window, carefully avoiding the glass still stuck in the frame. The other two followed, but one of them wasn't so careful and sliced open his hand on the exposed glass. Revulsion roiled in my gut as he dripped blood onto a stack of bread plates.

"Damn it!" he snarled. The other two looked back at him, which is probably why they didn't notice when Brax sailed over the balcony and landed directly on top of the leader, the man's body collapsing under several hundred pounds of feral intent. I inhaled sharply and gripped the balcony railing.

"I fucking told you she had a chimera!" the one with the bloodied hand yelled.

Brax's target was screaming, his hands gripping Brax's rusty fur and using all his strength to push the chimera's head away from his. The heels of his boots made a pathetic squeaking sound as they pushed uselessly against the floor in an attempt to dislodge Brax's giant form. The other two barely hesitated before running back through the window, slipping on glass and earning several more serious cuts.

"Br—" I didn't even finish the word. Brax bent his head down, exposing his razor-sharp teeth, and ripped out the man's throat.

I blinked, my hand going involuntarily to my mouth, covering a scream that did not come. The wind changed and the smell of smoke filled the restaurant. I remembered to breathe and immediately began taking quick, shallow breaths. Brax just sat back on his haunches, looking supremely pleased with himself while a man, albeit a terrible one, bled out in my dining room.

I tripped down the stairs in a stupor, haphazardly clinging to my belongings. I couldn't think straight. The police would arrest me, they'd find out I wasn't cuffed. What if they put Brax down? The thought seized me with more panic than the thought of my arrest, and my heart pounded in wild panic. I tried to slow my breathing. My hands shook as I made a motion to Brax, and he jumped off and sauntered away.

I approached the near-decapitated body, and I briefly had the ludicrous thought that I should try to stem the bleeding. Could Indie do anything when it was this bad?

I doubted even her magic could reattach a person's head.

My eyes fell on the pool of blood now seeping through my floorboards, the heavy coppery tang filling my nose. I made myself turn away from the body, sure that if I looked too long, I might be sick. Instead, I broke away and ran around, grabbing a few more things. I had to get out of here. I had to make it look as if I hadn't been here for this. They might understand Brax protecting his property, but not me failing to call the police.

I paused again, looking at the corpse. I could move him somewhere, hide him. But there was so much blood. And since he was no longer a living thing, I would need to touch him to move him. In the end, I brought him to the door. He wouldn't be visible from the street. His head slumped precariously on the last remaining sinews of his neck as it pointed toward the door. Almost like he'd tried to crawl himself to safety. I forced down a wave of nausea. Tipping a table over, I blocked the rest of the blood from sight.

Once I had Derek loaded up with as many of my possessions as I could grab, I led him away through the back. The smoke was stronger now. I could see tiny bits of ash flowing through the air. Everything reeked of burning wood and an acrid smell that I doubted would ever come out of my clothes.

From a few streets over, there was a terrifying keening sound and a deep boom that rattled my remaining windows. It was still early. But in the gaps between my building and the others, there were a few people running toward the sound or staring mesmerized at the blackening sky. I could only hope it would distract them from looking too close at The Peregrine.

I called for Brax, who came leaping out the second-story window. I got into the saddle and trotted toward my parents' farm. This was likely the fastest that Derek had ever gone, but I was mad with impatience. Could I risk moving all of us right now? There wasn't a soul in sight. I made sure that the cart was tied securely to Derek and held onto one side of it for good measure.

I moved us to the trees beyond my parents' house. Brax immediately took off running. He would probably snag a chicken on his way in, although was he hungry? Was arsonist throat a sufficient meal or purely an appetizer? A hysterical giggle burst out of me. I was very close to losing it, and I listed the things I could hear to try to pull myself together.

The creaking of the wagon's wheels, Derek's hooves on the ground, my own blood pumping furiously in my ears.

Derek, who did not seem to have noticed anything at all, ambled out of the woods. My mother came running out the back, her red hair streaming behind her in a ponytail. Once I'd hopped down, she helped me unsaddle Derek, and the two of us began bringing my things inside.

"Your father has gone to help," she said as she lifted out a crate of some of my more precious dishes. "He was trying to speak to Sasha. To see if there's anything that she could do without being noticed."

"And?" I grabbed a bag I'd haphazardly filled with clothing and flung it into the house.

"She's gone with Indie and Simon. They're trying to do what they can, but the fire is still getting bigger and there are so many of them." My mother's eyes were round with worry, and it made her look younger somehow. But her hands were on her hips, and there was still strength in her movements. Ayla got her stubborn determination from her. Delia Revin would not wilt.

We abandoned the rest of my things in the court and went inside. "Wait, do you know your power yet?" My head snapped at her.

She shook her head. "I've been trying things all day." At this, her eyes darkened. She and Aiden were the only ones left who didn't know.

Keen suddenly materialized beside me.

I screamed and nearly jumped out of my skin. I put my hand to my chest, "Stars at night, Keen! Don't do that!"

He spoke as if my fear was inconsequential. "I can help!"

I frowned at him. I put my hand out, and he grabbed it without hesitation.

"Wait!" My mother pulled us apart, grabbing Keen close to her. He was nearly as tall as her shoulder already. "You're not taking him. He's a child!"

"I'm not taking him...yet." Didn't we have a responsibility to help? Wasn't this why I'd given everyone this choice? We couldn't just sit here with magic at our fingertips and do nothing. But I was terrified. What if we couldn't help at all, and all this power was worthless?

Keen's face was determined. Black smoke billowed up in the distance. This was the right decision. My mother's head shook at the resolve on my face.

"He can help. He can save people. We both can."

My mother looked at the two of us, her eyes suddenly wide with panic. "I can't stop you, but he's not going!"

"You could stop me, but do you really want to? When I could help those people?" Keen hugged her tightly. My mother's red hair pooled on the top of his head, matching his own shiny locks.

I swallowed. I'd already screwed up his childhood. At least now, the loss might mean we could save someone else's. "You don't need to go. You are still a kid, and that doesn't last forever." I thought of the corpse on my floor. "You might see things you can't unsee." I was nearly talking myself out of taking him, but he was just staring at me with a sweet but patronizing look. There was no changing his mind. There were tears in the corner of my mother's eyes, but suddenly they went unfocused.

"Calimea is here," she said. She raised a hand to her mouth in shock at whatever my father had told her. Keen grabbed my hand in determination, staring her down. She looked at him and closed her eyes. She didn't open them as she responded to my father with a shuddering breath. "She's going to bring Keen. The two of them can help." There was a pause. "I'll tell her."

The unfocused look was gone from her face. "They've destroyed entire buildings; a whole block is just gone." Her voice became angry, the color rising in her face, making it look as if even her hair was redder. "Damn them! After all we've done to rebuild!" She took a breath, raised her chin. "Your father says to come to the toy store on 8th street. That's where they are."

I nodded. The store was one of Keen and Ayla's favorites. The thought of all the beautifully carved wooden figures, board games, and toys being burned to ash made my throat constrict in anger.

"I'll take care of him, Mom." At least he was taking it seriously. Genuine fear filled his eyes at my father's report. Gripping him tightly by the shoulders, I bent down to his eye level. "Listen to me. I will send you back here the minute you ask. I will also send you back if I think it's too dangerous. You are not to leave my sight. Do you understand?"

Keen swallowed but nodded. My mother hugged us both. "Take care of each other."

And we jumped.

30

LIM

LASHIA, PRESENT DAY

The toy store was dark and suffocating. The air wrapped around my skin, warm and dense. My father and Sasha were by the window. She was sweating, her hands fisted at her sides, her eyes on the fire in front of us. I could see the strain on her face. The flames were too much and in too many places. She saw me out of the corner of her eye.

"It's not making any difference. I have to focus all my energy on one fire to contain it and then try to move to the next, but it's moving too fast. And I can't take the air away completely without killing everyone." Her eyes were bloodshot, and her dark hair stuck to her skin. When she unclenched her fingers, I could see them shaking.

"You are making a difference. If it weren't for you, it would have consumed the center of town already." She gave me a nod, but it didn't look like she believed me. "Where are Indie and Simon?" I turned to my father. His eyes were glazed, and I assumed he was having several conversations at once.

"There's a medical tent halfway up the street. They're both there. Simon is taking care of the minor injuries and burns. Indie is 'operating' on the more serious injuries in a private area."

There was movement everywhere in the street as people escaped with their more precious belongings. "What about Aiden?"

"Aiden is right there." My father pointed to a firefighter climbing, no, racing would be a more accurate word, up a ladder. He deftly swung to the side to allow another firefighter to get out the window and down the ladder before going in himself. How did I not know that Aiden was a firefighter? At the question in my eyes, my father said, "He doesn't know his power yet."

"Can you tell him I'm here and that I can get people out with no one seeing? Tell him to tell me if he cannot get to someone." My father went quiet while he relayed the message. Clearly, there would be no more hiding my ability to move people without touching them. At least from my friends and family.

"He wants to know if you can get to the corner of Third and Sommerville? There's an apartment building, and people are still being evacuated."

I grabbed Keen's hand, and we landed next to the apartment. We were invisible but still solid, and we had to jump suddenly to avoid people and firefighters as they ran through the smoke. I examined the building from the street. The flames were consuming it at every point, again that sour smell, but there appeared to be a safe route on the right side. Firefighters had a ladder up and were pulling people out and climbing down. The left side was about to collapse, already blackened to soot.

Screams went up as several of the windows blew out and rained glass onto the street. With much of the building gone, I could see the roof. There were firefighters coming up with people so they could descend a ladder—the interior stairs must not be usable at some point below.

I jumped to the roof; my feet faltered as the fear that I might fall straight through gripped me. Now was not the time to figure out I couldn't jump in midair. Keen squeezed my hand, steadying me. We took a beat to gather our bearings before running down the stairs into the building. It was a heat like I'd never experienced. The toy store had been stuffy, the air on the roof had been hot, but now we were inside a smoking oven. I gripped Keen's hand harder, the sweat already becoming a problem, and kept him close to me, prepared at any moment to jump back to the toy store.

There, on the far left side, a family was looking through a hole in what used to be their living room. A firefighter was trying to get to them, but the ground wasn't stable. The father held out an infant and passed her through. Just as the firefighter grabbed the child, the floor beneath her front foot collapsed. I moved her back about six inches, and if she noticed, I couldn't tell. She clutched the baby and ran back toward the stairwell. A woman, a man, and two small boys were still on the other side—their blue cuffs illuminating their flushed skin. Of course, they'd picked a neighborhood with mostly Jinns.

One boy was crying and holding his mother, and the other just stared wide-eyed. His father had gathered him up after getting the baby out. A flash of flame burst up a wall, throwing Keen into stark relief. Keen's profile was a dark outline, and for a moment, he appeared so much older. I couldn't wait for the firefighter to come back—the whole place was seconds from splintering into fiery ash.

I pulled them across the six-foot gap to our side.

The adults' eyes went wide, but the boys seemed too distraught to notice. They didn't pause long. The father herded his wife up the stairs with the youngest while he followed behind with their other son. The firefighter met them on the stairs and kept them moving. I moved us back to the roof, and they exited the stairwell and climbed down the ladder. Keen looked at me, and I gave him a small grimace. We were invisible, but our use of magic certainly was not. How could we ever do this without being noticed?

We went back to the street and started backtracking to the toy store. I was carefully scanning the buildings, trying to see if there was anyone I could retrieve. Some fires had gone out. I could see what my father had mentioned, the charred cavities of shops and restaurants. I immediately thought of my restaurant and had to refocus.

"There!" Keen said, pointing at a rooftop where more people waited to be rescued by firefighters. But the ladders were already going up, and we jogged on, searching for people who didn't yet have help.

Twelve times.

Twelve times, we went into buildings and pulled people from near incinerated rooms to safer positions, places they could either escape themselves or were accessible by firefighters or volunteers. Keen's hand nearly slipped out of mine at least that many times.

We moved an elderly gentleman and his two cats, a couple who got pinned against their wall by a fallen beam, and multiple children who had been separated from their families by the fire. Each time, I tried to do what I could without being too obvious, but each time, I failed a little more. I could have sworn a woman thanked us as she escaped. By the time we returned to the store, both of us had suffered minor burns. Our eyes were watering with pain, and my throat felt caked in ash. I dreamed of cool blue-green water; the image forcing itself into my mind in desperate suggestion.

Sasha threw her fists to her side. "I can't. It's not working. I'm exhausted."

It was exhausting. While Keen and I had been somewhat physical in our rescues, the use of the magic itself was draining, like a boat slowly filling with water until it capsized.

I got her a chair, and Keen went to the back to find her something to drink. He returned with several bottles of soda, and we all seized on them, downing each of them without drawing breath.

The rain started.

First a few drops, but within five minutes, it had become a torrential downpour. Sasha only had enough energy to focus it on the more serious fires, but it was enough. The four of us watched in wonder as the flames became smaller and weaker. Sooner than I would have thought possible, the street was quiet and in the safety of darkness.

Sasha collapsed into her chair again and cried with relief. My father handed her a handkerchief and another soda.

The rain did not let up. It lasted another hour before it slowed and then stopped completely. We all shared a look. There was no way that was a coincidence.

I was too afraid to go back to check on The Peregrine. My father had already let me know after I'd sent him and Keen home, that all was well at theirs. I walked to the medical tent and helped Simon dress burns. I tried to give Indie a bracing smile when she spotted me, but I think it just came out as a wince. She and Simon looked even worse than I did—for they wore the hallowed look of people who have seen too much suffering. My throat closed, but I think I was too dehydrated to cry.

The other doctor and his nurses were in the tent. Simon said Indie used the magic sparingly and discreetly, just to stop large bleeds or make serious burns more superficial. The wounded kept coming, and the medical tent became a hub for the displaced victims. It was only this that made me return home—to see if I had any room to spare.

I did not.

The Peregrine had never been so dark or so quiet. There was no cheerful light spilling from my windows. No sound of a guitar or fiddle drifting through the night. There were no stars in the sky to hold up the dark and keep it from crushing me.

The fire did not look like it had burned long, but it had ripped through the side of my restaurant, the oil in my beautiful chandeliers no doubt giving it a bit of a boost. My bathroom and bedroom were mostly gone. The guest room was slightly better off, but the balcony and the stairs were brittle and unscalable. The body of Brax's victim lay blackened on the floor, barely visible among all the other debris.

A spark of pure violence went up inside me as I thought of the renovations I'd done, the possessions I'd lost, the food that would be wasted and ruined. I wanted to find those pieces of shit that destroyed my life and transport them beneath the waters of the swamps, where they'd be food for all my tiny crustaceans.

A practical voice in my head interjected to say that this would probably not make the crustaceans taste very good. I let out a long breath. It appeared I was still a cook first and an angel of vengeance second. So I buried my face in my hands and cried racking sobs. I couldn't stop. I gulped for air and let my tears fall freely onto my soot-stained clothing.

I had been crying for what felt like an hour when familiar arms reached out and wrapped me in a tight hug. In between the smoke and damp wood, I could still smell a hint of lavender. I continued to cry into Audre's shoulder, and she did not let me go until my breathing slowed. I heaved my last sob, and only a few more tears were left to run down my filthy face.

When I could finally look at her, she gave me a watery smile before rolling up her sleeves to show me her unmarred forearms.

I gasped. "It was you? The rain?" I tried to wipe off my face with my sleeves, but I'm sure it just made it worse.

She nodded sadly. "I'm so sorry, Lim. When the fire started, I was right there. I watched those assholes light fires in homes they knew were filled with people, with Jinns, yes, but with Tals too. They didn't care. I wasn't sure I could help, but I ran here, and you were already gone." She rubbed her arms, remorse filling her eyes. "I got to your mom. She helped me find the plate." She rolled down her sleeves. "I don't know why I thought I'd be able to help, honestly, but I just kind of knew. Once they were off, I tried the most obvious thing first."

It was my turn to give her a tear-soaked laugh. "You were amazing." I wrapped my arm around her shoulder. "I don't know what we'd have done without you."

She looked up at me from under my arm, her eyes stricken. "It wasn't the Tals, Lim. At least it wasn't those"—she waved a hand toward the avenue—"Tals."

"What do you mean?" I shook my head and stepped back, confused.

"I saw Tarik when I was racing to get to your mom's. He was heading toward The Peregrine, but I was too focused on getting to your parents'. I didn't put it together until now. I'm so sorry. I should have come back here right away."

Tarik, of course. He and his awful sister weren't just going to give up. My eyes found the body of the dead man again. It made sense. His friends wouldn't have come back and torched the place. They wouldn't want to destroy the evidence. They'd want me to be punished for this.

"Don't be ridiculous," I muttered sadly. "A few days ago, most of us wouldn't have been able to do much of anything, and now you're apologizing for not doing enough. You absolutely did the right thing, Audre. People before things, always. You saved so many lives tonight."

She nodded, brightening. "I did kind of feel like a superhero." I laughed. My heart mended the tiniest bit as I tried to take my own advice about what Keen and I had done tonight.

At the sound of a cart, we turned to see Aiden and another firefighter. Aiden climbed down, and before I could stop myself, I ran over and wrapped my arms around him, hugging him as tight as I could. There was a hint of something that reminded me of my kitchen, but it was hidden under a layer of cinders and sweat. Aiden's strong arms wrapped around me, but when he stepped back, he was shaking his head bitterly.

"I only just heard, Lim. I'm—"

"If one more person apologizes to me, I'm going to scream, and my throat already feels awful."

Aiden continued to shake his head, his beard so thick with ash it was white. His hazel eyes large and mournful. Aiden's eyes always seemed mature to me, but I was reminded now, looking at him, that he was only a few years older than us. After seeing him work tonight, going back over and over again without regard for his own safety, I saw the experience in his eyes differently. I certainly saw his drinking differently, too.

"Aiden, you can't be everywhere at once," I said sadly. "We can only do what we can"—I briefly looked to Audre—"when we can, with what we have. None of this is on any of us."

"Yes, it's on those psychotic Tals," Audre muttered under her breath, but I shot her a warning look as the other firefighter hopped down and began examining the outside of the building.

Aiden swallowed hard, but he nodded. He leaned forward so he could whisper to me and Audre and said, "I figured it out."

Audre came to his other side, so we blocked him from view. "Well?"

Aiden cocked his head to the side, and suddenly, the best feeling in the world washed over me. It was the first day of summer and my birthday in one. Everything was wonderful. How could it not be when my heart was filled with so much joy and peace? I grinned at Audre and she bumped my shoulder. The two of us almost started laughing when I noticed Aiden's grimace.

The bubble on our joy popped, replaced by our true emotions.

"Oh. My. Stars." I put my hand over my heart, reeling from the sudden pain of reality. "That is unreal. Please never do that to me again."

Audre too was rubbing her chest as if she couldn't figure out where the happy feeling had gone. She gave Aiden a wary look.

"I didn't realize I was doing it tonight. Nobody was in hysterics, nobody was panicking. Everyone followed my instructions calmly, like it was all just pretend. I thought at first they were all in shock." A flash of something like recognition passed over Aiden's face, and he rubbed a hand across his beard, dislodging some of the ash. When he continued, his voice was quiet, thoughtful. "It was pretty useful in such an awful situation."

"So you saved even more people. Nobody made any rash decisions." I gave him a grateful smile. His smile was hesitant, a look of almost surprise in his eyes.

His colleague returned to us after walking around and assessing the structure.

Her jacket said, "M. Tanner." Aiden gestured to her. "This is Lt. Tanner."

"Marie," she added, but her look was somber. "I'm sorry, Ms. Revin." Apprehension filled her eyes as they darted to Aiden. "I hate to be the one to tell you this, but I think someone was inside."

Aiden looked over to where she was pointing and then back to me with pure alarm. I put my hand on his arm. "It was one of them. I was here when he and his friends bashed in the windows. Brax injured him, and I ran. Apparently, his friends didn't think he was worth saving." I left out the part where he couldn't have been saved. Aiden put his hand over mine and nodded. The shadow of panic receding.

"Ah, well." Tanner cleared her throat, possibly hearing what I didn't say. "I suppose he got what was coming to him." Her eyes were understanding, and I'd put good money on her being a Jinn.

I turned back to the blackened building. Staring right at us were the remains of the room where Emir died, the bedroom where Bastian had stayed, and the place where Sydney had said such hateful things. My insides ached as I thought of my relationship with Bastian dissolving so quickly. He'd made it clear that while he cared for me, he still thought I should be cuffed, which angered me more than it probably should. He wasn't wrong to feel that way, but did that make him much better than Leo? He expected me to put my feelings aside in the name of safety. Right then, I didn't feel very safe.

I shook Tanner's hand and asked her to show me any safe points where I might get into the building—some things in the kitchen might be salvaged. She beckoned for us to follow her, and the four of us went around the back. Aiden went first, shining his light and checking the soundness of the entrance before allowing us to peek in.

The kitchen wasn't in terrible shape, but I wasn't sure how much of the food could be used now that it had been exposed to so much smoke. I let out an audible sign of relief that my shelves were still intact, all the jars and bottles patiently waiting for me. At least anything in a sealed container stood a good chance of being alright.

I started toward my shelves when Aiden's arm reached out and wrapped around my waist. He pulled me back just as the second floor caved in. The beams in the ceiling split with a sickening crack before crashing down. The contents of all my jars and bottles smashed and shattered to the floor, letting out bursts of scent, licorice, oregano, thyme. Hundreds of tiny pink petals floated to the floor like ash.

31

LIM

LASHIA, PRESENT DAY

The morning after the fire, I awoke at six. I didn't want to get out of bed. Instead, I lay there for hours, staring at the ceiling of the bedroom I'd had since childhood. I wondered if this was some sort of payback for Emir. Not just payback from Tarik but the universe refusing to allow me to profit from his death. Self-pity drowned out all logical thought. I morosely pictured a future where I repeatedly rebuilt The Peregrine, only to have it destroyed each time by some new event. Serves me right for keeping the name. Who names their restaurant after a long-extinct bird?

I eventually made my way downstairs to the kitchen. My parents had kept Keen and Ayla home. Their school had been a few streets away from the fire, and we suspected some of the other families would have been affected. My mother was in the kitchen, washing the dishes with her back to me, when I came in.

She held out a wet plate next to her and dropped it. "Mom!" I dove to retrieve it and slammed into a solid body. Keen and I tumbled to the ground, only barely saving the plate from cracking on the floor.

"Sorry!" I said, helping my little brother up. My mother leaned against the sink, looking exasperated. Her face softened when our eyes met. I probably looked like death. My eyes were puffy from crying and I hadn't bothered to shower yet.

"Do you need some help with your stuff?" Keen offered, putting the dry plate away and rubbing his shoulder where I'd slammed into him.

He and I spent over an hour organizing the things I'd grabbed before the fire, as well as what I'd salvaged from the wreckage last night. I tried to feel grateful for what I'd managed to save, but the feeling wouldn't come. Maybe I'd ask Aiden to compel me until I could manage it myself.

We came inside afterward, and Keen made himself a sandwich. I tried to eat, but nothing sounded appealing. I sat at the table, feeling sorry for myself. My father came into the kitchen, bringing the smell of soil and animals. He said nothing as he washed the dirt from his hands and put the kettle on to boil. He poured me a cup of strong tea, filling it only halfway so I could fill the rest with milk he'd warmed up.

"I'll go with you after I finish in the yard, and we can figure out how to fix it."

Shaking my head, I didn't meet his eyes. "I don't know. It's pretty badly damaged." The milk in my mug eddied and twisted in on itself among the dark tea.

"We don't have to decide anything now, Calimea." He put his callused hand over mine.

I just swallowed and nodded.

My mother came back into the room, holding the book she used to track farm orders from the people in Marais. Ayla shuffled in after her, watching me like I was a bubble that might suddenly pop.

"We'll all go with you." My mother took the seat next to me.

"Thank you," I mumbled. "Ugh," I shook myself, trying to dislodge the weight on my shoulders. "Thank you for helping Audre, too. Way to work under pressure, Mom."

"I was terrified I'd do it wrong." She shrugged, and I noticed for the first time that my mother looked different. I couldn't put my finger on it. She was... brighter? Or maybe like she'd had the best night's sleep ever, but that couldn't be true after last night.

"Did you do something different with your hair?" I squinted at her.

My father chortled.

"No." A smile played at the edges of her lips as she dabbed her napkin against them.

Ayla perked up. "Tell her, Mom!"

I raised my eyebrows, understanding dawning on me.

My mother fluffed her hair, which I could tell now was uncommonly shiny. "I can change my appearance."

"What? Why didn't you tell me?" I searched her face again, trying to see the differences.

She huffed a laugh. "There was a lot going on and it seemed the wrong time to be excited about it."

"Mom"—I looked at her in exasperation—"don't be ridiculous. Show me!"

"Okay!" She had clearly been dying to demonstrate. One minute, my mother sat in the chair, the next minute, two of my father sat at the table.

"Amazing," I said, examining her face for any sign of her beneath the image of my father.

"I wish you'd stop doing me. It is the weirdest thing." My father shuddered and took a bracing drink of his tea. She changed into Ayla, Keen, and finally me. It was, as my father said, the strangest thing and mostly unpleasant. My mother returned to herself, but she now had black hair and violet eyes.

"That's my favorite," Ayla said around a mouth full of pancakes, and her enthusiasm was a little too exuberant. I smirked a little at her. All talk of not using our powers had ceased, and it was clear Ayla had no plans to revive that conversation.

My mother reverted to her original form, but with, I noticed, fewer wrinkles.

"That's amazing! Have you ever seen someone with violet eyes? Do you have to have seen it in real life to imitate it?"

As she considered my question, she turned her hair violet and her eyes black. "Guess not. I think I would have to see the person to turn into them though. I don't know how useful it would've been last night, but it seems like it would come in handy." She toyed with the necklace around her throat.

My father gave her an indulgent smile. "Well, I think you are breathtaking, no changes necessary."

Ayla rolled her eyes, and Keen pretended to gag on the sandwich he'd made of two leftover pancakes and some bacon. At the mention of last night, I just let out an exhausted breath. I know Indie and Simon had done some good work, but there had to have been fatalities. And I wasn't the only one without a home to go back to. At least I had somewhere to go.

Three days later, the head council of Lashia, which managed both Eudora and the issues applicable to all the other boroughs, announced the census. A grainy photograph of the three councilors ran alongside the government's heartfelt plea. The photo was in black and white, of course, but everyone knew that while the individual councils of each borough might be a mix of Jinns and Tals, all three of the head councilors were Tals.

The peaceful state of our society is in peril. Hundreds of years ago, Jinns agreed to separate themselves from their unique abilities. Abilities that caused the death and oppression of thousands. For those individuals who have broken this sacred law, the punishment will be severe. However, since we know every Jinn wishes to return our society to its ideal state and mend the division between Tals and Jinns, we are instituting a census. All Jinns will be required to submit themselves, and their cuffs, for inspection. We know these uncertain times are at the root of the undesirable interactions of late, and are hopeful this solution will strengthen and reaffirm Lashia's commitment to unity and justice.

"Severe? What does that mean? They haven't even held a trial?" Indie asked.

"And since when is it only our responsibility to 'mend the division?'" Simon added.

"Undesirable interactions," Audre spat. "Really dancing around the word 'arson,' aren't they?" She tossed the paper aside.

We stood inside the remains of the restaurant. We'd been cleaning it since early this morning. Indie, Simon, Audre, and Aiden were all either shoveling or salvaging. Indie and Simon had arrived with the news that they'd been able to contact the registrar, under the pretense of misplacing Priya's paperwork, and Chiwel had agreed to come back. Now, we just needed to figure out how to get him to recuff us all and keep quiet about it.

Aiden picked up the paper from where Audre had dropped it. "And no mention of the uncuffed Tals or the Sun Guardians. It's unbelievable how willing they are to lie to us." He looked at me.

I arched an eyebrow and pursed my lips in agreement. Talking about sentencing without mentioning a trial was deeply suspicious. I expect-ed that even if the accused had made a deal, it should have also been front-page news. Another brick of worry and distrust lodged itself on top of all the others I was carrying.

All they had to do was keep playing it as if the Tals were mainly upset about the breach of 'our most sacred law' and they would cement this period forever as Jinns being the problem, of us being the reason for our censure, regardless of the fact that the Tals had hated us for as long as I could remember and the council never did anything to stop it.

It was almost ironic that unstoppable displays of power were what the Tals always seemed to be afraid of, but when it came down to it, they were the ones who had destroyed everything. They were the ones responsible for the four people who'd lost their lives in the fires. It was our magic that stopped it.

"Ungrateful bastards," I said, the anger in my voice a living thing.

There was a soft "hey" from the door. Leo stood in the doorway, his face distraught. His eyes bounced from the dining room to the bar and up to the balcony where his father's apartment was nothing more than a hole in the sky now. He hadn't been in town when the fire broke out.

Even though it was mine now, I had to acknowledge that Leo had spent a huge portion of his life in this place. With the amount of rebuilding it would require, it would never truly be the last place he saw his father again. I walked toward him and wrapped him in a hug.

"I'm sorry, Lim." He pressed a kiss to my forehead. "We are going to find the people who did this."

"You and everyone else in Marais," Audre muttered. Leo looked up at her, and she stopped sweeping to lean on her broom. She let out an exasperated huff. "We know who did this, Leo."

I quickly gave her a warning head shake. I didn't want to bring up Tarik to Leo. We weren't sure he had done this, and I didn't want it getting back to Tarik that Audre had seen him.

Audre gave me a look of understanding but also shook her head. She wasn't talking about Tarik. "The people that burned the avenue? They give out flyers, they have meetings, for fuck's sake!" Audre's eyes blazed. "Now one of those guys is thankfully a blackened skeleton." Leo winced a little at that. "But one of his friends is out walking around Marais with a big ol' obvious cut on his hand and probably gonna be the guest speaker at their next damn meeting!" She took a breath and Leo had the good sense to be quiet. "And do you know how many arrests they've made?"

Leo's eyes searched the rest of us for help. Aiden crossed his arms. Simon leaned against the bar, shaking his head. Indie frowned at Leo like he was a particularly inept student. I had to step back to look and see if he was truly not getting this.

"Zero," Indie provided, making a circle with her hand. Simon held out a hand as if to display his wife's brilliance, and Audre just glared.

"It's only been a few days, but I'm sure they're doing what they can." Leo pouted, looking around like he didn't recognize any of us. There was a general murmur of exasperation. "Look, I'm sorry." He threw up his hands. "I'll go to the people I know on the council. Emir lost money to all of them at some point. I will make sure they're interviewing the Sun Guardians." He put his hands on his hips, looking at each of us. "Okay?"

Everyone grumbled an assent. Leo blew out a breath. "Okay, good. Now, how can I help?" He rubbed his hands together, assessing the room.

Aiden turned toward Leo. He'd just gone back to picking up the remains of a chair, and even under the hat and the beard, I could see him give Leo a look filled with contempt. His voice was a low growl. "I'm pretty sure we all just made it very clear how you can help."

Leo took a step back, as surprised as I was at Aiden's tone. "Right, I'll go right now then." He meant it, but I could hear the undercurrent of annoyance in his voice.

I gave him a tight smile. "Thank you." His face softened, and he nodded before walking away.

32

SABINE

TREVESTEN, PRESENT DAY

Sabine concentrated on the scene, willing it to yield more details, to make the fuzzy edges and faces come into focus. Ash-covered faces, buildings reduced to cinders. So much pain. Something terrible had happened. Frustrated, Sabine let herself fall out of the vision. She took a small sip of coffee, frowning into its depths.

"Anything interesting?" Morgan asked from the other side of the breakfast table, where she was smothering a piece of bread with soft cheese and an excessive amount of deep red preserves. She'd pulled back her curly black hair with a trio of gold bands that twinkled in the pink morning sunlight.

"Interesting, yes. Comprehensible, no," Sabine said in irritation. Her visions were sometimes not as clear as she would have liked them. Distance occasionally made them muddled or blurry, but they usually contained something she could go off of in terms of location or purpose. This place was different. She'd already had two visions similar to this one in the past few weeks, and neither made sense.

Morgan waved a hand, and the coffee pot floated over to her, refilling her cup. "Really? A wise old goat like you?"

Sabine tried to give Morgan a look of disdain, but her lips quirked. "No, it's off somehow. It's almost like it's...underwater." She put her coffee cup down and bit into a buttered piece of bread.

Seeing the present had seemed like a strange gift when it had manifested after her most recent rishival. It had proved quite useful for keeping the queendom safe. She could spy on anywhere in Malan, but of course, its usefulness depended on something relevant happening while she was spying.

Sometimes, she could simply focus on where she wanted to see. Other times, like this morning, she would get a vision that swam in the edges of her mind, begging to be let in but refusing to clear.

The visions were helpful, warnings, or less dire things, just tidbits that were interesting to know. There was a common theory that the fae's powers manifested based on the desire of our past lives. She certainly would have killed for this ability when she had rescued Morgan all those years ago. Thinking of Morgan as a bright-eyed toddler made her think of Connery. She held onto a secret and somewhat pathetic belief that this power would somehow allow her to see him again, even if he didn't want to see her.

The doors to the dining room opened, and Antonio strode in, his gray hair swept back from his deeply tanned and lined face. He clearly saw no reason to waste his power on erasing those frown lines or returning his hair to the golden brown of his first hundred years.

"Good morning, Your Majesty, Your Royal Highness." He stopped short of the table and bowed briefly to them. He wore the casual uniform today, no armor, no weapons, save the sword which was so permanently attached to his hip, Morgan had bet her ten marks he slept with it on. Not that either of them really had any way of verifying that claim without grossly overstepping their authority.

"Good morning Antonio, coffee?" Morgan floated a cup over to him, and he plucked it from the air.

"Thank you." He took a sip and made a satisfied sort of sound.

"Any issues with the raid?" Sabine asked. Antonio was nothing if not detailed. Left to his own devices, he would have started from the beginning and provided every bit of information down to the position of the moon when the raid commenced. Several centuries of service and they'd finally reached the point where he understood she would ask the questions she wanted answered. He would provide additional information only if it were truly pertinent.

"No issues." He took another sip of his coffee, but she could tell he was itching to speak more.

"How many daranas did you find?" Morgan asked.

"Twenty-seven." He gave a satisfied nod.

"Twenty-seven!" Morgan and Sabine shouted together. Antonio did not flinch at the outburst, his expression was thoughtful.

"It's more than we expected, but we knew the number would be significant. This was an organized group, not low-level criminals. They were still small, only able to hold one or two powers at most. We'll start running the tests. See if we can track down the sellers."

Morgan and Sabine shared an exasperated glance. Sabine didn't bother telling Antonio to make sure there were no daranas left in the raided building. He and his soldiers would have torn the place apart, to be sure. This was more than they'd ever found before, and her stomach churned at the thought that this problem didn't seem to be going away, only getting worse.

Daranas were notoriously difficult to make and could explode if their creators attempted to store too much magic inside them. If they didn't combust, they could be uncontrollable, bleeding out too much magic all at once, killing the recipient or turning their mind to mush. But no matter how many laws she put in place or sting operations she executed for the dealers, they continued to pop up all over Trevesten.

Sabine stood from the table, rubbing her temples. That annoying vision was still pulsing at the edges of her mind. Antonio wouldn't track the sellers down for arrest but to find out why they had to sell their magic in the first place. Things couldn't be that desperate, could they? She hated feeling like she wasn't in tune with Trevesten's needs.

"Thank you, General." She moved toward the doors that would take her to her office, but Antonio did not move to leave. She and Morgan shared a look. Had something gone wrong after all?

Antonio paused, clearly considering his words. "I have some other news." He stopped abruptly as if he now dreaded telling her. Gathering himself, he quickly recovered and his eyes softened. "I have some new information about Connery."

Her heart dropped, and the blood rushed from her face. She staggered back slightly and put her hand on the high back of an armchair. It had been so long, with nothing, not a whisper of his whereabouts. She still couldn't help searching every crowd but had accepted that she wouldn't find him unless he willed it. The three of them hadn't discussed her mate in decades, maybe even longer.

It still hurt. She understood she'd driven him away, and this was the consequence she was meant to suffer. But another part raged at such a punishment. Who was he to torture her like this, to give no sign, no word of his well-being, nothing but this empty pit where her heart had been? On those nights when her thoughts turned truly dark, the latter part won. She would drown herself in drink and the touch of another, the anger in her blood a potent, living thing. But the former now hoped when she had not dared to hope before. Antonio would not have bothered to say anything unless he thought the information was promising.

"Tell me everything." Her voice sounded weak, and she immediately took a breath to steady herself. A queen is never weak.

Morgan, who had dropped the piece of bread into her coffee in surprise, composed herself and turned to look at Antonio. He put his coffee down, spread his legs slightly, and put his hands behind his back. Nothing but a soldier giving a standard report.

"We interviewed all the fae we found during the raid to determine the extent of their activities. There were five males and two females. Their interviews were performed by the following officers—"

"Antonio." Morgan squeezed the bridge of her nose between her fingers and made a circling motion with her finger to make the general speed up.

Sabine wasn't sure she wanted Antonio to speed up. Her heart was racing like a wild thing. Fear seized her lungs and squeezed painfully.

Antonio cleared his throat. "Of course, Ma'am. The second male, a rat shifter by the name of Baldrick, told us he had learned how to make the daranas from a female named Asra. When questioned as to where we could find this 'Asra,' he said that we could not, that she and her crew had completely disappeared hundreds of years ago. Baldrick expressed bitterness at the memory as he had paid Asra to help him create stronger daranas, ones that could hold even more magic, but she had taken his money, and he'd never seen her again."

Sabine's knuckles were white as they gripped the back of the armchair, and her breathing had become shallow. Morgan came to stand at her side, taking Sabine's other hand in both of hers.

Antonio continued, fully aware of the trauma he'd unearthed but politely ignoring Sabine's stricken look. "They put Baldrick through the standard protocol and asked him to disclose all known associates, including what he knew of this Asra and her crew: names, histories, abilities, etc. Baldrick claimed that Asra's crew had comprised herself as well as four other fae: Solvan, Elwin, Brigid, and Connery. Connery, he said, was not like the others. He spoke and acted differently, and that, along with a comment one of the crew made about him being a 'royal pain in the ass,' made him think Connery had some connection to royalty or perhaps been a servant in a royal household."

Morgan looked at Sabine, her eyes round. "The pain in the ass part sounds true," Morgan said, trying to lighten the mood. "He did think pretty highly of himself."

Sabine couldn't even manage a weak smile. "Did this Baldrick have any idea where they'd gone?"

"He said that he didn't know but that Asra had hired him to procure some defensive objects as well as several items that indicated to him she was planning on making numerous daranas. He also said that when he delivered the items to their location, it appeared to him that they were packing quite extensively, and yet Asra told him to come back in two weeks for the lessons for which he'd paid. When he returned, she was still not home. He claimed he nor anyone else he knows has heard from them since. He assumed their job, whatever it was, went... poorly."

Sabine's mind raced. Was it possible that Connery was dead? Had he been dead all this time? Her heart cracked wide open at the thought. She would have felt it in her soul, no matter how long they'd been apart. But if what this shifter said was true, if Connery and this group had simply vanished, she had to consider it.

"I need to sit down." Sabine pulled herself around to the front of the armchair and collapsed. Morgan pulled up a footstool and sat before her,

her eyes filled with sympathy. "Did he say anything else useful?" Sabine choked out.

From behind her, "He suggested Sverresen as a possible destination for the group."

She groaned and closed her eyes, letting her head fall back against the chair. Sabine could practically hear Morgan roll her eyes as her sister scoffed, "unbelievable that people will really believe that ridiculous tale regardless of the complete and total lack of proof for thousands of years."

Sverresen was meant to be a world where magic was wild and untamed. A place where it didn't belong to any person but filled the world and was there for wielding by anyone, at any time, in any way. It was a children's tale; she'd heard it herself from several of her parents, but it was especially comforting to children born with only minor power. While she didn't doubt the existence of the sixth world itself, she seriously doubted it contained fluffy pink pillows of magic or flowers that could speak.

Antonio was suspiciously silent behind them. Sabine leaned forward in her chair and looked at him. Morgan did the same, her eyes shrewd and narrowed.

"What is it, Antonio?" Sabine's voice took on a hard note that she'd not used in lifetimes. The beast within her stretched, looking around hopefully.

He opened his mouth to speak and immediately closed it. "I don't wish to speak out of turn."

Morgan and Sabine shared a surprised look. They'd never once prohibited Antonio from speaking his mind, speaking the too many details of his mind, yes, but they did not enforce any sort of protocol where he could not freely give his opinion.

"We'll allow it," Morgan said dryly as she waved a hand and made a cup of tea appear, pushing it into Sabine's hands. She drank from it gratefully.

"We know Sverresen exists. Whether the tales of its power are true are unsubstantiated, but this is not the first time I've heard of such an expedition. Otherwise sane fae have spent lifetimes researching it, and many have attempted to get there."

Morgan frowned. "These 'sane fae' you speak of. Did they come back?" It was a rhetorical question. Nobody ever came back. That's why the legends lived on, for Sverresen as well as Laloten and Mokame. The last documented attempt to visit any of the those worlds was hundreds of years ago. The people of Trevesten now only studied them safely from classrooms.

Antonio made a gesture she had not seen him make in all the many long years they had known one another. He shifted on his feet. From Antonio, it was the equivalent of someone else nervously and unrelentingly chewing their nails. She glanced at Morgan, whose eyes were rounded in surprise.

He cleared his throat. "No, of course not." Morgan opened her mouth, but Antonio uncharacteristically interrupted her. "But the fact that we don't know what happened to them is a piece of information in itself. They did not return even after thirty years, when they definitely should have if the journey turned out to be fatal... within our world."

And there it was. Even if Connery and this group had attempted such an ill-advised thing and died in Trevesten, Eloisha, Boralta, or any of the lands in Malan, he should have returned about twenty-five years later. That knowledge had always been a source of particular pain. It would sneak up on her when she wasn't even thinking of him, gutting her from behind. That he should be reborn and, despite all the perspective that usually gave a fae, continually decide against reuniting with her.

But the thought now sidled up to her, like a lover, a source of comfort. If he didn't die here, he could be in Sverresen. And if he was there, was it possible he wasn't given the gift of rishival in his next life? What if he didn't remember her? What if his death there was final?

Her shame at driving Connery away had eaten away at the confidence she had in their relationship. It had picked it apart until there was nothing left, until every look, every caress, every time he told her he loved her was suspect. It was all diluted by his abandonment until it forced her to believe that he'd never cared for her at all.

Sabine had to admit that despite being mates, it wasn't enough. The connection was between the magic, and most of the time, it was a solid enough foundation. But it wasn't unheard of for mates to choose others or to wait a lifetime or two until both fae had matured. That was the official statement she'd given when Connery left. People may have bought it at the time, but Sabine was over two hundred years into her third life. She doubted anyone believed it had anything to do with maturity now.

As she listened to Antonio, a spark rose within her that she'd quashed for hundreds of years: hope. But was it the good kind of hope or the baseless kind that restrains and blinds? Antonio was one of the most practical fae she knew, if not the most practical. If he had suggested this, she would allow herself to consider it.

She would let herself dream that Connery had not rejected her but had voyaged to Sverresen, or whatever place was out there, and, by magic or death, found he could not return.

33

LIM

LASHIA, PRESENT DAY

It was Audre's idea to go out.

I tried to clean myself off as best I could, but the soot staining some of my fingertips would not budge. I couldn't muster the effort to do anything more to my wet hair than braid it down the back. And the clothes I'd saved from the fire weren't exactly festive.

But I arrived at Duluth's, a lively little place near Indie and Simon's, as promised. They'd gotten a table near the window, and as I walked in, I could see that everyone but Aiden was already there.

There were quite a few people I knew from The Peregrine, and they waved to me with smiles of support. I stopped to chat with several people who offered various aid, spare glassware, or extra plates. Two people pushed drinks into my hands, and I was carrying both of them, my heart and feet a little lighter, as I made my way through the crowd. I was so touched that by the time I'd gotten to the table, I didn't even mind that Audre had invited some random man to sit with us.

I sat down, letting a grin take over my face, and handed my bonus drink to Sasha. I smiled at Audre's stranger. Had she given up on Jake so soon? I suppose I couldn't blame her. Jake was certainly good-looking, but this man was something else. Strong jawline, broad shoulders, a head full of soft dark hair. I averted my eyes before she could accuse me of ogling her date and sipped my wine.

The table was strangely quiet.

"What?" I said to Indie. "Did you run out of things to talk about before I got here or something?"

Indie opened her mouth but then snapped it shut. Sasha and Celeste said nothing. Simon piped up and asked, "Lim, you wanna play some darts?"

"Hey, that's cheating," Celeste cried.

"Yeah, you can't distract her to win." Audre flicked a peanut at Simon.

"We didn't establish any rules about distraction," Simon scoffed.

I wasn't so dense that I didn't understand I was the butt of some joke but couldn't tell what it was. My eyes narrowed at each of them, but they said nothing and avoided my glare. Whatever, I could talk to the new guy. I turned to him and smiled a smile I hope conveyed that this group wasn't always as weird as they were being now. Up close, I could see a scar running up his neck from under his shirt. It stopped just below his ear. Upon closer inspection, it wasn't a scar but a burn. He had another small one just below his left eye.

I blinked. And blinked again. His hazel eyes.

The man tucked his lips like he was trying not to laugh.

"...Aiden?"

He exhaled. "Oh, good. I was afraid there for a moment."

The noise that erupted from the table momentarily distracted me from my staring. Celeste pulled out a piece of paper, her silver bracelets tinkling as she used her finger to read down the list. "Two minutes and thirteen seconds. Damn it. It's Indie." There were groans and cheers as money made its way down to Indie's beckoning palms.

My brain was moving at the speed of molasses. Each moment I'd ever had with Aiden slowly replayed in my head, replaced with the version sitting before me. This very...impressive version. Exhaustion always made me think a bit more with my lady parts, and I had to mentally shake myself.

"I...you shaved," I stuttered.

"Yes." He rubbed the side of his face absentmindedly. "I was never really supposed to have a beard. Fire hazard and all. Captain made an exception for me. But after the fire, I realized how stupid it was. Dangerous," he amended.

I had the sudden urge to smooth my hair down, but I caught myself. I gave a quick glance to Indie, who was sipping her drink with barely contained glee. "So," I said, finally catching up, "you were all betting on how long it would take me to notice?" My cheeks flushed as they all nodded and grinned in response. "Wait just a minute. Don't tell me all of you noticed right away?"

"Hell no," Audre said. "I stared at him for a good minute and was about to tell him to get the hell away from my table. Simon knew right away, and Celeste wasn't far behind him." Simon fist-bumped Celeste. Aiden continued to look cheerful but slightly uncomfortable at being the center of attention.

"But I took the longest, I take it?" I said, rubbing a hand down my face and turning apologetically to Aiden, whose face was still arresting. There was a general murmuring of assent. "Great." I grimaced at Aiden. "Sorry, buddy."

I turned and hid my face in my drink. When I looked up, both Audre and Indie were mouthing the word "buddy?" at me with comically wide eyes. I hoped the dim lighting hid the embarrassment that crept up my cheeks.

Scrambling for some dignity, I turned to Aiden. "Do you like it? Do you feel weird?" I asked, grabbing a handful of peanuts from the communal bowl on the table.

"It feels very weird. I haven't seen my face in so long I forgot what I looked like." Aiden pulled a little at his shirt and I could see the scar extended down past his collarbone.

"And?" I smiled. "How do you like yourself?"

He actually blushed a little. Perhaps he blushed all the time, and I couldn't tell before, but it suited him. His eyes twinkled. "I think I look alright." He gave a lopsided grin and sipped his drink. I could certainly see his lips better now.

I laughed and diverted my eyes. "How about those darts, Simon?"

As the evening wore on, the crowd became livelier, and when the tipsy singing started, even I joined in.

Audre had ducked out an hour earlier to go meet Jake, and Sasha and Celeste had gone home to relieve Celeste's mother, who'd been watching Priya. They'd put on a brave face, but the thought of losing Priya, of being imprisoned and unable to watch her grow up, was consuming both of them. I'd recklessly promised them I'd find a way to convince the registrar. Instead of filling me with dread, the promise I'd made to them seemed to give me hope as well.

That tiny hope and quite a few rounds of drinks had made us all a little more relaxed.

"Where did you get those?" Simon said, his chin propped on his hand, his voice slow and careless. He pointed with his eyes at Aiden's face, and Indie and I turned to look at what I'd been studiously avoiding mentioning all night. Mostly because I did not want Aiden to think I'd been staring at his face for too long.

"Simon," I said in warning.

"What? He doesn't mind? You don't mind, do you?" Simon asked, his head a little unsteady on his shoulders.

"Okay, I think that's our cue," Indie said, standing up and gathering her coat. "Up, you." Simon allowed himself to be collected by his wife, an arm draped over her shoulder. He whispered something suggestive into her hair, and she rolled her eyes. "Yeah, good luck with that." She ushered him out the door, and they ambled back toward their little blue house.

I played with my wineglass. "Sorry about that."

"No. It's fine." He rubbed the right side of his face absentmindedly. "Do you want to know?"

"I do if you want to tell me." A tipping feeling, like balancing on a ledge, gave way to pride. I was someone he trusted.

"I was fresh out of the academy—full of ego and not much sense." A smile tugged at his lips, remembering his past self like it was a long-forgotten friend. "My dad was a firefighter, so were my brothers. My mom died when we were young and it was just a house full of one-upping and stupid pranks.

"I'd been on the job for about a year when there was a fire that broke out among a group of shops. Until then, I had handled nothing bigger than a few small kitchen fires, basic first aid, and monitoring tar pitching for the bigger buildings in town." He took a sip from his drink. Simon had bought him a beer earlier, but now he was drinking iced tea.

I was already sure this story was going to get much worse.

"I was working with my brothers, my dad, and several other firefighters, but it was impossible. The wind was moving quickly and we just couldn't get it under control. We'd evacuated all the surrounding buildings, but there were still people in the upper levels of the shop. I went up on the roof and cut a hole. The fire and smoke immediately blew out, and I could hear people inside. It wasn't safe, but I was so convinced I could do it.

"I dropped in and tried to fight my way to the people on the other side." He swallowed and rubbed a spot on the table with his finger. "I got four people out before my brother Kiran started yelling at me from above, telling me to get out. I'd already inhaled a bunch of smoke, but I was convinced there were more people that needed help. Even after I knew it was pointless, I kept searching. I was frantic and scared. I know that now; it's like a paralysis, but you can't stop moving. Kiran jumped down to get me out. He grabbed me by the jacket and shoved me out the window onto the ladder. The floor collapsed beneath him. He didn't make it."

Aiden downed the rest of his tea and put the glass on the table. "My father and my other brother couldn't even look at me. They treated me like a ghost in the house." His voice had gone very quiet, but he seemed to recover as he spoke the next part. "Marie, Lt. Tanner, had already moved to Marais, but she came to the funeral. She visited to check on me six months later and told me I was going back with her. I haven't been back since."

Something cracked in my chest. He'd been all alone. "You haven't seen them? Do you write to them?"

Aiden just shook his head in response to both questions. "They know where I am. I don't believe they want to see or speak to me." He absent-mindedly rubbed the side of his face with his hand.

Unbelievable. For him to lose his brother and lose the rest of his family. It filled me with anger for people I'd never even met. How could they abandon him when he must have been so broken?

I reached across the table and put my hand on Aiden's. That look of surprise again, just like after the fire. "That wasn't your fault."

He put his hand over mine and squeezed it. His hazel eyes, usually so full of merriment, were uncharacteristically serious. "I appreciate that, Lim, but I'm not a kid anymore. It was my fault. I panicked and made a bad decision. It just resulted in something much worse than most people's bad decisions. But"—he went to rub his face again and settled for putting a hand through his hair—"I know that hiding and getting drunk every night is not the answer. I can still do a lot of good." He looked at me pointedly and lowered his voice again, "With or without my power."

The two of us were silent for several minutes, but I didn't remove my hand. My voice was a weak whisper, "My decision has made my family and closest friends wanted by the police, possibly subject to lifelong imprisonment, and ruined my first real adult relationship before it even started." I gave him an exaggerated grimace. "Not exactly winning in the good decision department myself."

Aiden squeezed my hand again, his eyes like a caress. My face softened. "And you had to make your decisions in a life or death situation. I just"—I blew out a breath—"made a lack of decision." I frowned at my poor wording and pulled my hand away, letting my fingers trail down my face. "What is that? What do you call the absence of a decision?"

"Complaisance?" Aiden said quietly.

My eyebrows rose and my skin flushed a little with shame. But he was right. I hadn't decided to uncuff everyone; I had just allowed it. I didn't decide to open a restaurant. I sat around making excuses until one was given to me. The grim realization of my ways nearly overwhelmed me. I didn't date anyone. I just let whatever was between Leo and me be an excuse for being alone. Even when I knew, deep down, that a relationship between us was never going to happen. And even when

Bastian appeared, I let Aiden move things along instead of encouraging Bastian myself.

"Why did you help Bastian ask me out?" I blurted.

Aiden stretched his long legs out in front of him. He pushed his hands into his pockets. "Because guys came in and hit on you all the time, and you never noticed. Bastian was the first guy you seemed to see besides Leo. I thought it would make you happy."

I crossed my arms over my chest, my brows knitting together. "People always hit on the bartender. The promise of free drinks is very attractive."

"No." He gave me a wry smile. "People hit on you because you've got the kind of beauty that's almost painful to look at, with a body that makes the pain worth it." My mouth fell open. "Of course, you rarely let them get to know you well enough for them to find out you're kind and clever, too."

My face turned three shades of red and I was very conscious of the intensity of his gaze.

He shrugged. "Even when you have black fingertips and appear to be wearing some kind of potato sack." He gave my outfit a curiously horrified once over.

I covered my face as I laughed. "Thank you. That's the nicest and weirdest compliment I've ever received."

He leaned back, saving me from further speech, before pushing back his chair and standing up. "C'mon, it's late." He looked around at the remaining patrons in the bar. "I live just around the corner. You can jump home from my house."

We gathered up our coats and made the short walk to Aiden's. The air had turned crisp. The leaves were all red and brown now. We could smell fires in the surrounding houses, giving off their heady scent. I was grateful I still associated the smell with good memories instead of sadness and terror. It was the kind of night that made me wonder what it would be like to be Indie and Simon, going home to their own little house, knowing they'd wake up together.

Aiden lived in a skinny house that was squeezed between several others. He had a small porch with a table, two chairs, and a small lantern. Who sat out here with him? Marie? He walked up the stairs and lit the lantern. The light threw his face into shadow, making him look like the Aiden from before, the darkness hiding all but the brightness of his eyes. We both stepped into a small entryway.

He turned to me, and I was about to say goodnight when something caught in the corner of my eye. I rotated slowly toward a small framed drawing of a building. The house was a simple thing, two stories, the bottom of brick and the top of wood. There were fluttering curtains in the windows and overflowing flowerbeds, even a small cat basking in the sunlight outside.

"Did you draw this?"

Aiden shrugged. "I'm not great, but I have drawn that house a few times. It's one of my better ones," he said with no false pride.

Something overwhelming was happening in my chest. A flood or a balloon filling me up, struggling to get out. "Why do you draw it so often? Is it your childhood home?" My voice was high and strange in my ears.

"No," Aiden said, noticing my discomfort. "No, I started drawing it a few years ago. I don't know where the idea came from. It started kind of basic and then I kept adding details as I thought of them."

"I know this house," I whispered almost to myself. I couldn't understand why, though. It wasn't any house I'd seen in Marais. I didn't recognize it from Eudora. Something inside me knew it wasn't in either of those places.

"Lim, are you okay?" His voice filled with concern.

"Yes, fine. Sorry." Shaking myself, I tore my gaze from the drawing. "It just looks really familiar." I leaned in, and Aiden didn't startle this time as I hugged him but wrapped his arms around me. Rosemary, mint, and something that reminded me of river rocks beneath my feet. "I'll see you later, and Aiden?"

"Yeah?"

I grinned. "I think you look alright too."

I turned to jump when the sound of something being thrown against Aiden's door stopped me.

"It's probably just the newspaper." Aiden gently pulled me behind him as he reached for the doorknob. "Usually shows up by dinner time. Must have been a big news day."

The street was empty and quiet in the darkness. He leaned down and picked up the paper.

He turned so we could both see as he opened it to the front page. The two of us huddled together to read.

A strangled gasp left my throat.

UNCUFFED JINNS SENTENCED TO DEATH, EXECUTION AT DAWN

My hands flew to my mouth as Aiden's eyes rounded with horror.

"Fucking stars," Aiden whispered.

34

LIM

LASHIA, PRESENT DAY

I gripped Aiden's hand as we arrived in the alley behind my old apartment in Eudora. It was four a.m., and neither of us had gotten any sleep. I cursed silently as my knee slammed into a stack of wooden crates in the dark. But no lights appeared in the few windows facing the alley. It was eerily silent as we made our way to the street.

I had never jumped so far. And I hadn't been to Eudora in years. But my old apartment remained the same. I'd chosen it because it wasn't centrally located. It used to take me over thirty minutes to walk to culinary school each day.

Back then, I'd enjoyed the long walk into the city. The rare electric lights buzzing with energy. Streetcars that ran on suspended cables, their bells clanging loudly as they lumbered down the busy streets. Buildings that were wholly new, not just repaired ruins like in Marais. I used to love looking in the shop windows, browsing through the amazing boutiques. Not today.

I didn't even consider asking Keen to come with us to increase our chances of going unnoticed. I didn't want him to see this. My parents would see the paper and the note I'd left on top of it when they got up.

But I didn't want to go alone.

I led us toward the location noted in the newspaper. Our coats pulled tight and hats low over our faces. It wasn't likely that anyone would recognize me here, but it wasn't impossible.

Execution, *public* execution. No imprisonment, no slap on the wrist. This was beyond anything I had imagined, anything Bastian had ever found. Anger surged inside me at Bastian for not telling me. I shook it away. It was doubtful anyone in Marais knew about this yet. That was the point.

The empty streets felt poised, waiting. A sick feeling in my stomach replaced the anger. My friends and my family, the man at my side, I'd condemned us all to death. My throat threatened to close as Keen's and Ayla's innocent faces filled my mind.

I stumbled, and Aiden wrapped his arm around my shoulders.

"Stay with me. None of us are up there today." The wind twisted the sound of his voice as the gallows came into view before us.

It looked like a stage. The ropes were already there, waiting for their gruesome marionettes.

I'd never known of anyone being executed in Lashia for anything. The Lashian council was sending an obvious message. I pulled my coat tighter as I leaned into Aiden's side, knowing I'd feel just as vulnerable with my cuffs as without them right now.

A light was on in a bakery across the street. The sweet smell of baking bread seemed so out of place with what awaited us. But we needed something to do. Dawn was over an hour away, and while I didn't expect us to be the only ones watching, I didn't want to draw attention.

The owner, a curvy woman with muscular arms and bright blue cuffs, let us sit at a table near the window. She noticeably didn't ask us what we were doing up so early. She gave us a tight smile as she brought out steaming cups of tea and two beautiful croissants. I didn't want to eat them. Didn't want to associate her incredible talent with such a horrible memory. But I pushed the buttery delicacy into my mouth anyway, relieved when it didn't turn to lead in my stomach.

She had a newspaper lying open on the counter. Aiden and I had both memorized the article at this point. After we'd been sitting nervously for half an hour, she spoke.

"Why do you think they don't mention their names?" There was fear in her voice but also anger.

My eyes found hers. "Could be for their families' safety. But more likely because it humanizes them. They want us to know we're all alike and they'll treat us the same." My voice cracked a little at the end and Aiden's hand reached out to cover mine.

"Monsters." She breathed. She cast her eyes downward as if she regretted being so forthright with two complete strangers.

Aiden tipped his head to her in agreement. "Announcing it the night before to keep the crowd down. No public trial. 'Monsters' isn't strong enough."

She gave him a delicate nod before returning to the morning's baking.

Between the two of us, we ate six croissants and drank four cups of tea while we waited. Other people came in and out of the bakery, but we avoided their eyes.

We chatted a bit as we waited, about his job, the restaurant. It was almost normal, almost like a date. I scoffed internally, but Aiden saw it.

"What is it?"

I shook my head. "Nothing."

He tipped his head and gave me a small smile.

I blew out a breath. "It's stupid and callous. I was just thinking that if it weren't for this"—I waved at the gathering crowd outside—"this would feel almost like a..." I trailed off, hoping he wouldn't make me finish the sentence.

"A date?" He gave me a sweet smile, like he might let me down easy. "I promise if you ever let me take you out on a real date, neither of us would be getting up this early the next morning."

"After only one date? Someone's confident." I joked, but tiny fireworks went off inside me.

Aiden said nothing, just gave me a look like we were already there, tangled up somewhere quiet.

I held on to that tiny bit of light, that better things might still come.

The shop bell broke us from the moment. The shrill ringing reminded us of why we were here.

An enormous crowd had grown outside.

I briefly grasped the baker's hand as I silently handed her the money.

We slipped outside into a world awash with pink and orange. Aiden and I chose a location with a side street to our back. Plenty of places to hide if we needed to leave quickly.

The crowd was a mix of people. There were Jinns and Tals here to see the spectacle. It shocked me to see parents with sleepy-eyed children. Who would willingly subject their child to this nightmare?

"Calimea?" My father's voice was strained but strong even at this distance.

"I'm here," I said internally. I tapped the side of my head, and Aiden nodded in understanding.

"Your mother and I don't think it's safe for you to be there." I pictured the two of them in the cold early morning kitchen. Perhaps the kettle hadn't even boiled yet.

"We plan to leave as soon as it's over." I swallowed, looking around. There were people watching from the windows in the surrounding homes. Several runners were perched on the streetlamps. "I promise we'll be safe."

Aiden's fingers curled tighter around my shoulder as a man stepped onto the platform. The crowd, which had been filled with nervous chatter, hushed.

"It's starting." I could picture my father, his hand reaching for my mother's.

The man didn't smile or say good morning. His voice was loud as he addressed us. "Three Jinns were found guilty of murdering Sloane Mailer after forcing her to remove their cuffs. Their sentence, death by hanging, will be carried out this morning."

The entire crowd gasped. I wasn't sure I believed him, but if they claimed she was murdered, at least her family would get the death benefits.

Aiden's breath warmed my ear. "On your right."

I let my head slowly turn to see a group of Sun Guardians. They were in the back, holding another banner with 'Go home Jinns' on it. The surrounding people looked nervous. A few of them surreptitiously moved away from the intimidating group. My stomach churned when others gave the Sun Guardians looks of support.

"See anyone we know?" I turned my face up at him. Without the beard, it was easy to see his eyes, clear and razor-sharp.

"No." He didn't look at me as he pulled my hat lower on the right side, his fingers grazing the skin of my neck. But then his eyes found mine and his voice was so low I could barely make out the words. "Do not risk your safety or exposure for me if this goes sideways. I can handle a crowd."

I'd never been so close to Aiden in my life. His face was only a breath from mine, closer than the bar last night. It felt wrong. Not wrong, like I wanted him to step back. Wrong, like I was breaking a rule by seeking comfort in the touch of his skin on mine. "I'm not leaving you here. If we get separated, meet me back in the alley."

His eyes caught mine briefly, and with a look, we both acknowledged this strange newness between us. Was it just the sudden trauma? I had no further time to contemplate it when six people marched onto the platform. Three of them were wearing hoods over their heads. The others led them by ropes attached to the ones wrapped around their wrists. My breaths became quick and shallow and my fingers pulsed with heat despite the brisk morning air.

Only the Jinns. Neither the paper nor the man had said anything about the Tals, who presumably received no punishment. They weren't just monsters; they were corrupt fucking assholes. Again, that prickly heat skittered across my skin.

The crowd seemed to hold its breath as nooses were placed around their necks. They didn't call out or struggle but seemed oddly calm. Was that what the hoods were for? To hide their faces and subdue the crowd's compassion?

I tipped my head up to Aiden and gave him a pointed look. Was he helping them? Soothing their fear?

He shook his head, brow furrowed. Their reaction confused him as well.

Wasn't anyone going to say anything else? Did they have no family, nobody who cared to say goodbye? The man at the front of the gallows nodded.

Three sickening cracks carried through the crowd.

I gripped my stomach as I tried not to vomit at the sound. A young man next to me couldn't hold it back and was sick on the sidewalk. The crowd barely stepped back from it, too focused on the swinging bodies before us.

There was a moment of silence. Then grotesque cheers rose from the Sun Guardians. They raised their banners and pounded their feet. Others joined in, their voices rising from the crowd and the surrounding buildings. To their credit, the Jinns in the crowd didn't hesitate. They fled immediately down the side streets or into the surrounding buildings. The chants from the Sun Guardians and their supporters grew louder as they surged toward the gallows, toward the hanging Jinns.

"Let's get out of here," Aiden said.

We turned around and a terrible thought occurred to me.

I brought us to his apartment, where I collapsed on the floor, heaving.

"I could have saved them," I garbled through gasping breaths. "I could have pulled them away. I didn't even think about it." I grabbed at my coat, trying to relieve the growing heat. My nails scratched at my neck, struggling with the suddenly oppressive material.

Aiden pulled my face up, forcing me to look at him. Concern filled his eyes, along with firm resolve. His determination was palpable.

"Yes. You could have. You also could have made yourself a bigger target. If those three Jinns disappeared, the Sun Guardians would have burned down Eudora in response." He gave me a mournful smile. "You can't save everyone, Lim."

My heart broke for him all over again as his words sunk in, absorbing my regret.

35

LIM

LASHIA, PRESENT DAY

The execution was all anyone could talk about. For the first time, I was grateful I wasn't open. I wouldn't have to hear it discussed and dissected all night. Wouldn't have to listen to anyone's hateful opinions on the uncuffed Jinns. I overheard more than enough just walking through the borough. So many people claimed to have seen it firsthand, one would think half of Marais had been there.

I still saw it every time I closed my eyes. Heard the cracking sound. I tried to keep busy, cleaning and repairing what I could in the restaurant, but panic was my constant shadow. I was no step closer to avoiding the census or reapplying anyone's cuffs. Visions of my friends and family hanging from those same gallows plagued me constantly.

I wasn't sleeping well.

The runner knocked on the doorjamb since I was still missing a door. The afternoon sun was spilling through, so I could only just make out the shape of a person. I squinted at them as they checked my name and handed me a book-sized parcel. It was from Simon. I read the note,

I found it! I knew I had something better than a history book. I haven't been through it yet. Figured I'd send it along now and you could get reading.

I unwrapped the parcel, which did indeed contain a book. It wasn't as hefty compared to some books I'd seen Simon read, but it was positively ancient. I was almost afraid to touch it. The green cover was barely holding on, and some pages looked like they were moments from becoming dust. Still, it was odd that Simon hadn't yet read it.

I opened it and immediately understood why. The book was written in an entirely unfamiliar language. Someone had printed that language in the world's tiniest but neatest print I'd ever seen. What was I supposed to do with this? I set the book on one of the two tables that had survived the fire and pulled up a chair. I gingerly opened the cover to reveal an interior inscription that was nearly obscured by water damage.

Connery of Ta—

It was a diary. The entries bore numerical entries that seemed to have started at one number and then changed to different numbers halfway through. I flipped through the pages of precise handwritten entries and groaned. Grabbing the book, I went back to the remains of the kitchen where I could be sure I was in private, and jumped to the supply closet in Indie's office.

I carefully listened at the closet door before slipping into the room. Easing her office door open, I peeked into the hallway. It was only a few moments before Simon walked toward me with a patient, a heavyset man who was limping. Simon let the man go in first, but before he could close the door, I hissed at him,

"Psst!" Simon whipped his head around. "What am I supposed to do with this?" I waved the book at him through the crack in the door. Simon opened his mouth to speak, then shook his head and motioned with his hands to tell me to wait. I sat down at Indie's desk, my chin resting on top of my crossed forearms, staring at the book.

Simon walked in, making me jump. "Getting a little cavalier, aren't we?" he said before picking up the book.

"Getting a little desperate, more like. And I currently don't have a lot to do with myself," I deadpanned.

Simon gave me a sympathetic grimace. There were dark circles under my eyes from my constant nightmares.

He cleared his throat and forced excitement into his voice. "Well, watch and be amazed, young Lim." He opened the book carefully to a page halfway through before turning it toward me. The drawing was some kind of diagram, like an engineer might use. Despite the scientific-looking nature of it, including labels in words I didn't understand, it was definitely my plate. Or one just like it.

I grabbed the book out of his hands. Hope filled me before it quickly died, and I let out a groan. "This seems great, but can you read this? Because I certainly can't."

"Well, no, I can't, but maybe if we studied it, we could work it out. I've got other books at home and some of them have references to a language the original Jinns used. Maybe they could help."

Simon might be able to learn a long-dead language in that time, but I didn't have the same confidence in myself. The doubt I had at this insurmountable task was clearly written on my face.

Simon gave me a bracing look. "Do you have any better ideas?"

"No." I stood up and held the book to my chest, swaying a bit with exhaustion.

He was right. I did not have any better ideas. The census was on Sunday, that was less than a week away. Chiwel would be here on Wednesday. The original faith that had filled me when I'd promised Sasha and Celeste that he would help was quickly evaporating. Other than a half-baked idea to use Ayla's powers of coercion to get him to tell us something we could use as blackmail, I still wasn't sure how to convince him to help us.

"Mind if I go to your house?"

I thought learning the language was going to be difficult. I was wrong. It was impossible.

I'd started by pulling any book I could find off of Simon and Indie's shelves that had anything remotely to do with the original Jinns. I separated them into piles based on how useful I thought they would be and started trying to skim the first pile for any reference to the Jinn language. There were references, for sure, but nothing like a helpful dictionary or even a short story translation. There were no more sketches of the plate, but I re-read all the same horrible things we'd learned in school. Powerful Jinns who enslaved Tals and weaker powered Jinns. All the terrible crimes that made Bastian believe the cuffs were necessary.

The sun was setting and Indie and Simon still weren't home. My stomach was growling, but I couldn't bring myself to get up. My heart was heavy with the threat looming over all of us.

They wouldn't execute Keen and Ayla. Who executes kids? And if they didn't, who would take care of them? A bitter taste coated my throat. Despite everything, the person who would have most likely taken them in was Emir. I didn't even realize I was crying until a fat tear dropped onto the cover of the diary.

Poor book. It had survived all these years, just for me to ruin it with my tears. I put my finger on the drop and tried to rub it away. It faded as I moved my finger back and forth. Soot still lightly stained my fingertips.

I thought I'd gotten all of it off, and now I was going to leave a mark on this book from that as well.

I stopped moving my finger when the soot started moving over my skin. I quickly pulled my finger back and examined it. It wasn't soot; it was ink. And it was swirling onto my finger before fading back into my skin. I had the sudden, alarming thought that I'd absorbed all the ink—Simon would absolutely kill me, even if he couldn't read it. But the contents of the book were unchanged. I put my finger back down on the book and made slow circles on the cover. Again, the black swirls reached up my finger, like a cloth absorbing water. The black stain did not go higher than my knuckle before disappearing into my skin.

Finally, it stopped. I flipped open the book. The tiny handwriting was still intact, written in the strange language.

But I understood it. I more than understood it. It was as if I'd read it cover to cover many times.

The author was a Jinn, a powerful Jinn named Connery. There were endless accounts of him presiding over meetings, settling disputes, even officiating marriages. He was clearly some kind of leader. His entries ranged from boring administrative stuff to accounts that portrayed the darkness of the time.

He described a meeting with a woman named Lilly. Lilly had come to him about the actions of one of the other Jinns. This Jinn, Asra, had seen Lilly's husband beating her. Asra had strode into Lilly's house and, without a word, incinerated her husband on the spot. Lilly and her young son, who had been there too, had been in shock at the small pile of ashes that had only moments ago been causing them so much pain. They'd both been stunned into silence, neither one of them sure of what Asra would do next.

But, according to Lilly, Asra had been entirely unaffected. She hadn't stormed into the house in a rage, either. What had struck Lilly was the lack of emotion from the Jinn. She hadn't seemed angry or sad or anything. Lilly told Connery that Asra had only said, "he won't do that again," as she casually walked out. Connery mentioned Asra a few times. It seemed as if he tried to steer clear of her and I could see why.

Connery sounded like an extremely capable and driven person. But there was an undercurrent of sadness in his words I couldn't attribute to just their situation. There were mentions of others in the group. He referred to jokes they shared, successful hunting trips, and meals they'd prepared together. Peppered among all of this were allusions to mistakes he'd made and references to a woman named Sabine, who was apparently no longer with their group.

His diary didn't mention how she had died, but it was clear it had deeply affected him. He'd even tried to make some sketches of her face, but they were always scribbled over, an artist unhappy with their work. One drawing he allowed to remain, but it was not of the woman but of a house. A house with two stories, fluttering curtains in the windows, and a small cat basking in the sunlight outside.

I sucked in a breath. Had Aiden seen this book before? I wasn't even sure where Simon had gotten it. If he'd bought it in Eudora, it was possible Aiden had seen it in passing, and the little drawing had stuck with him.

I put the book down, my breath shaky. It was possible, but it made little sense. Especially not with the way I, too, had reacted to seeing the drawing. The way I reacted to it now, like if I just squinted hard enough, I could see inside those windows.

Connery's diary had given me more than a look at the early Jinns. It also told me why I could absorb knowledge from the book.

I picked up a book in the stack and slowly circled my fingers on it. Once again, the darkness crept up my skin and stopped after a minute or two. I picked up my finger and the contents of the book filled my mind.

I did it again, and again, and again. At the twentieth book, the power just dried up. Well, that was good to know. Couldn't have been that much in the darana in the first place. I could sense the different powers now—two separate energies distinct from my own ability.

Indie and Simon finally came through the door, bringing the smell of the chilly night air with them.

"Why are you sitting in the dark?" Indie said, going to light the lamps. I hadn't even noticed, but it was dark outside. The moon was high, casting pale shadows outside.

"Any luck?" Simon asked, sitting down on the arm of the chair beside me.

"Yes," I mumbled, my head still heavy with knowledge I couldn't quite make sense of. "Yes," I said in a stronger voice. I stood up and opened the page to the drawing of the plate, showing it to them. "It's called a darana, and it wasn't meant to nullify magic, only store it so it could transfer it to other people."

I pointed to the various labels. "This is where we all put our hands, to begin with, and it absorbed the power. If you put your hand here," I said, pointing to the bottom of the plate, "it will transfer the power back."

"It will recuff us?" Indie asked.

"No, I don't think so—just give us the power to recuff others. The darana can't do anything itself other than store and transfer. Someone still needs to wield the power."

Indie and Simon were somber. They'd maintained a strong facade after the execution, but their eyes now shone with the toll it had taken. They practically sagged with relief. But under it all, there was the dismal understanding that they would lose their magic again. The three of us grappled with the emotions swirling through us. The adrenaline drained away, leaving only sadness. Simon never even got the chance to fly outside.

"Wow," Simon said finally, his voice loud after the prolonged silence. "You really figured it all out that fast?"

I held up my finger, the inky stain completely gone. "I touched the bottom when I hid the plate originally, fell onto it actually. Besides the power to cuff everyone, it appears I also absorbed the power to 'read' by touch."

"What?" Simon said, his eyes filled with envy. "Show us!"

Indie grabbed a book from the shelf, hastily wiping a tear that had fallen. "Here, do this one. I've been meaning to read it forever, but it's never going to happen. You can give me a summary."

"I can't." I handed her back the book with an exaggerated grimace of apology. "Based on what I know now, the darana must have been near empty when we gave it our cuffs. There was only a little left of this power. I made it through about twenty books"—at this, Simon put a hand to his chest and gave a pained cry and Indie patted him on the arm—"before it stopped. It's not my natural power, so it'll always be weaker. Probably work again tomorrow, though."

"Do you think this is how the registrars get their power?" Indie asked, putting the still-unread book back on the shelf.

"Makes sense." I shrugged.

"That would explain why they remove cuffs from the dead. Have to get as much back as possible," Simon added.

"Wait, you said 'cuff all of us.'" Indie looked at me. "What about you?" Her eyes filled with wariness, and she put her hands on her hips, preparing to fight with me about any ideas I had about sacrificing myself.

"Don't worry," I said, going to their kitchen with an eye toward finally satiating my hunger.

A strange relief stole over me, like when I finally perfected a recipe.

"I have a plan."

36

SABINE

TREVESTEN, PRESENT DAY

Oderon was a puzzle of crisscrossing streets and tiny alleyways. This was a place that had sprouted up around a port with no forward planning. There were countless dead-end roads, houses that were pressed together like the pages of a book, and many precarious looking, elevated walkways. Bridges that allowed people to make their way quickly from one part of the town to the other without using the crowded streets. The people of Oderon somehow traversed them with ease. Built on bizarre stilts that were nailed into buildings or tied to chimneys and hung with lanterns to light the way. There might be only a single plank or two on which to walk. Sabine eyed them from the carriage thoughtfully. This was a place where the people moved quickly, safety a secondary concern to speed.

Sabine had been to Oderon before, but not for decades. She recalled seeing these walkways only near the port, designed to allow sailors and fishers to get to the town while avoiding the heavily trafficked areas around the dock. It was handy if you only had a few hours in port to shop, eat, or visit one of the many brothels sandwiched in between apothecaries, bakeries, and taverns. Now they were everywhere. Her driver glanced up nervously at the many people who passed over the carriage, ignorant of the guest in their midst.

She'd taken a normal merchant's carriage, and they'd arrived at night. This wasn't a royal visit. She was only here to see for herself if the rat shifter had been telling the truth about Connery's last whereabouts. Antonio sat across from her, his eyes like razors on the people in the street and his hands glued to the two knives sheathed on his thighs. He'd sent ahead several plainclothes guards who would monitor her surreptitiously, available only if she needed them. Looking out, she couldn't tell which ones were hers and which were true inhabitants, and she complimented Antonio for how well he'd trained his men.

Antonio's lips gave a small curve upward. He nodded toward a male on a horse, swigging from a bottle and looking as if he'd just come off a three-day bender. "Some of them really do like to commit."

Sabine's eyebrows shot up. The fae was undeniably convincing. But now that she knew he was a guard, she could spot the tiny inconsistencies. The clear, watchful eyes, the fine, albeit dirty, horse. His show of being unbalanced on his horse could not quite hide the strong frame poised for action. Her gaze met his for a moment. He gave her an excessively flirty smile as he took another drink, spilling much of the contents of the bottle down his front. Sabine and Antonio laughed as the carriage pulled ahead and she made a mental note to commend the actor/soldier when she was back in Adnatia.

The house they were looking for belonged to Asra, the reported leader of the crew Connery had joined. It was tucked down a skinny road, not wide enough for the carriage. She and Antonio stepped down and, along with two other guards, made their way down the dirt-packed road. The house was two stories, the top of wood and the bottom made of red clay bricks. There were vibrant flowerbeds in the front, their sweet scent mixing with the smell of the sea.

Sabine knocked, pulling her hood close around her face. Her covering wasn't out of place here where it seemed many people didn't want to be recognized.

"Got nothing better to do with your pretty hands?" Sabine's head turned at the voice. An older female with smile lines and a voice like syrup stood on the other side of the street. Sabine pegged her for a shapeshifter; she had that look of someone used to regularly inhabiting more than one form. Sabine would know. The female cricked her neck in silent confirmation.

"I beg your pardon?" Sabine asked. Beside her, she could feel Antonio cataloging every minute detail of the female and her home. A green clapboard house with faded white shutters, cast yellow by the lamplight. There were lace curtains adorning her windows which were open to catch the evening breeze.

"Nobody living there for lifetimes." The female leaned in the doorway, her hands crossed over her chest.

"Who is taking care of it then?" Sabine motioned to the flowers.

"Those are my flowers. I planted them so I wouldn't have to look at the dirt anymore." She massaged her palms with her thumbs, her eyes never leaving Sabine.

"Did you know the person who lived here last?"

The female's face clouded for a moment. "Asra and her people."

"You've lived here a long time then?" Antonio asked, giving her a friendly smile. Her eyes slid to him and she didn't hide her gaze as it roved over his body. "What is your name?"

"Natalia. Me and mine have lived here since before the first ship ever docked in Oderon. I was born here, and seeing as I'm on my last life, I'll die here too." She grinned inwardly at memories they couldn't see, her watery gray eyes crinkling. She felt familiar to Sabine, but nearly everyone did. It was hard to recognize people from life to life unless you knew them well. As queen, she'd met so many people, looked out into so many crowds. It was nice but also discomfiting sometimes.

"Do you know where she went?" Antonio adopted a languid pose, noticing Natalia's interest and leaning into it.

Sabine marveled at how her straight-backed general could disappear like this, but he wasn't great at getting information from people for nothing. One would think she'd be adept at interrogation, but her magic was nothing compared to his skill. He just became the person they wanted to speak to. She supposed that's why he got lost in the details of his reports. He thought everything was important; it was just a question of when it would reveal its usefulness.

"Sverresen," she said. "Spelled the place before she left and haven't seen anybody in there since." She finished massaging her hands and now idly rubbed her forearms.

Sabine suppressed a wince. It was so jarring to hear people speak of Sverresen like it was just another town, some place you could ride to and not a child's dream. But hope still stirred inside her like a whirlpool.

"May I?" Antonio motioned with his head toward her arms. She seemingly couldn't afford the power to keep the arthritis at bay.

"Be my guest, but I'm pretty used to it." She held out her hands and Antonio strolled over to her, taking her hands in his and letting his power flow through her. His healing power was weak, meant for temporary battlefield mending. But it was enough that she'd be pain-free for at least a month. He could not heal her completely. It would take someone with that specific gift to do so. But she smiled in thanks.

"How did they plan to get there?" Antonio asked as he let his hands slide down hers, his voice personal, like a friend she'd known forever.

"Went through Solbaina." Natalia cocked her head at Antonio like he was pretty but perhaps not so bright.

"Why do you suppose they didn't come back?" Sabine interjected. She hoped Natalia didn't hear the desperation in her voice.

She pushed her lips upward, feigning confusion. "Why would anyone come back from Sverresen?

Something with claws or talons. She must be some kind of sharp-toothed predator to be able to gut Sabine with her words. Why indeed? An image of Connery lounging upon a ship made of clouds, pops of magical light bursting all around him, a beautiful fae cradled in his arms, Asra. Sabine hurled the image from her mind.

"But she spelled the house, right?" Antonio let a sly smile grow on his face. "So they must have been planning to come back at some point."

Natalia shook her head at him. She put a hand up as if to ward off Antonio's advances. "Asra was a good friend to me. They all were. Connery, too, even if he was a bit of a stick in the mud sometimes."

There it was again, thought Sabine. A sharp scrape at her insides, hearing Connery's name said casually by someone who did not know what it did to her.

"Maybe it was so wonderful they decided to stay once they got there." Natalia paused. "Or maybe they stayed because he knew it was the only place you wouldn't find him." Natalia's voice had become lethal and her smile dropped. She raised an eyebrow at Sabine. "My eyes see just fine in the dark, Your Majesty."

Antonio didn't leave her side. Instead, he circled her, like another beast would, sniffing out the threat. He kept the smile on his face, and she matched it, enjoying his watchfulness.

"Maybe," Sabine said. She knew the shifter wasn't completely confident about those theories.

Sabine turned to the house and called upon her own magic, letting it build in her fingertips. She placed her hands on the door and tiny tendrils slipped through the cracks, seeking the spelled objects this Asra female had concealed within her home. The protective trifles were strong enough for common thieves but not for the reigning queen. They crumbled to dust beneath her power.

Sabine put her hand on the doorknob and turned it. The door groaned open into the darkened room. A rush of feeling consumed her, the feeling of him. She could almost hear Connery in this place. All the bitterness and doubt she'd carried for hundreds of years fell away. Connery would never have left her wondering like this. Even if he rejected their bond, he was still himself. And he was not a cruel male.

"But you know what"—she turned to the female, her voice firm but kind—"I think not."

37

LIM

LASHIA, PRESENT DAY

Indie and Simon sat at my parents' kitchen table with Aiden and Audre. Indie was giving Aiden a frank clinical assessment. Before Aiden had arrived, I'd told them about my conversation with Aiden at the bar. How he'd supported and comforted me in Eudora. True to form, Indie demanded the minutia of Aiden's every breath and eyebrow raise. Everything had to be noted, analyzed, and stored for future comparison. Neither of them seemed remotely surprised at this turn of events.

"I don't understand. You knew Aiden thought about me like that?" My head shook in disbelief.

"He didn't tell us or anything," Simon said, piling cheese onto the pasta I'd made for us.

Indie tossed her eyes as she pushed her curls back from her face. "He obviously had some interest in you. I mean, he came to the bar practically every night."

"But that's because...." I fidgeted in my seat. I didn't want to say 'that's because he had a drinking problem,' but Indie and Simon gave me a look that said they'd heard it all the same.

She cleared her throat, "There are plenty of bars, Lim." But then she said in a softer voice, "I also think he came so he wouldn't have to be alone."

I knew what she meant. After everything I'd learned about Aiden and his family, the rejection he'd felt from the people who should have loved him the most, put all our interactions in a different light. The conversations with people at the bar, helping me with the cleaning, recommending Indie to people anyone who complained of any kind of illness. My heart cracked at the memory of his surprise at being invited to the dinner when we'd regained our magic.

"Why didn't either of you say anything?"

"Would it have mattered?" Indie asked bluntly. Shame filled my cheeks.

"Yeah, what would be the use if you were just going to ignore him like every other guy? Until Bastian came along. By the way, any concerns he might sell you out?" Simon's voice was relaxed, but from the way he stopped devouring his dinner, he was genuinely worried.

I appreciated the abrupt change of subject while I pondered my friends' less-than-generous opinion of my treatment of men, especially since they were right. As Aiden had recently helped me understand, I wasn't great at going after what I wanted, even when it was right in front of me.

"No. I think, regardless of what his opinions are on the matter, he'll keep quiet." Being the upstanding citizen he was, he'd done an interview for the paper where he'd subtly explained away the oddities of the fire. After all, freak weather was a cornerstone of the Weakening, and it had never truly returned to the same patterns as before. The people who Keen and I had helped also appeared to be keeping quiet about their unusual rescues.

We had waited until the second day of the census to be sure of a larger crowd headed to volunteer themselves for inspection. As soon as accompanists and the police began knocking on doors, many people had decided they'd rather get it out of the way than suffer such indignation in their homes. Indie had said they no longer needed him, that they'd found Priya's paperwork. The registrar seemed friendly, but he also unnerved me.

"What a bunch of morose-looking people. What kind of party is this?" My father grinned at us all as he walked into the kitchen and there was a weak ripple of laughter. Ayla was clutching a book, her face one of pure devastation. She'd perhaps taken the news harder than anyone. Keen moved in next to her, his face downcast but resigned.

"Well, might as well get it over with." Audre stood up from the table and held out her arms for me.

I took a deep breath and put my hands on her exactly as I'd seen Chiwel do, exactly as I'd done with Celeste and Sasha the night before. It was fascinating. I could feel her magic inside her, bouncing and crackling like lightning or fire. Did it just feel like there was nothing there when Chiwel cuffed a Tal? Or did they simply have a different signature? I focused on what I needed to do, which power I needed to call, and as my fingers dimmed, two blue cuffs appeared on Audre's forearms.

It shocked me when a tear rolled down her normally unflappable face, but she wiped it away. "No big deal."

Keen and Ayla went next. Ayla sobbed but at least didn't express any anger at me. I wish she would have. I wish everyone would have yelled at me for disrupting all their lives with this, all because I didn't want to keep a secret, because I didn't want to have to bear the responsibility. Aiden gave me a crooked smile, as if he knew what I was thinking. He gave my hands a squeeze when I was done.

When I'd finished everyone but my mother, I held the plate out to her. She placed her hand on the top while I held the bottom. The room waited in absolute silence for over fifteen minutes. Finally, I placed the plate back in its now extremely dirty wrapping.

I held out my arms and sifted through the foreign powers. It surprised me I could so easily distinguish between my power as well as the three additional ones. The cuffing power wasn't unpleasant; it was almost familiar, like a favorite sewing needle. That was likely why I had not noticed it before. My mother's magic was running a hand across bubbled glass.

As I concentrated on that specific slice of magic, two glowing blue bands appeared on my forearms.

There were two places in Marais where one could voluntarily submit for inspection: the library and the post office.

Our carriage moved quickly, my father's balaras trotted alongside others headed in the same direction. It was now getting quite cool, and many people were wearing long sleeves, but I kept mine pushed up. I needed to keep an eye on the glamor.

Another wagon filled with my parents' friends, the Bretons, pulled up alongside us. They had twin boys a year older than Keen.

"Do you believe this, Tobias?" The man puffed out his cheeks in annoyance. "What a bunch of nonsense." His wife nodded in agreement.

"Waste of a perfectly fine day is what it is," my father exhaled. "I'm gonna drop these two off at the library, and the rest of us are going to head on over to the post office. We've got a bet on who can get done quicker."

Mr. Breton laughed. "That's one way to make it interesting. What does the winner get?"

"I get to choose dinner!" Ayla called out, probably louder than was strictly necessary, but she played it well.

"Oh, is that so?" Mrs. Breton responded. "I suppose when you have a chef in the family, you can choose something pretty amazing." She smiled at me, and I grinned in thanks, hoping my smile appeared natural and didn't reveal my rising anxiety. I'd been growing steadily more apprehensive as the day approached, but now my panic rose like something insurmountable.

The road divided, and we had to turn to get to the post office. We could already see a line of people outside. I checked my arms for the hundredth time to ensure the cuffs were still there.

"See you there then!" Mr. Breton called to my father as he turned. My father waved cheerfully as we rode away.

When we got to the library, we said our goodbyes quickly, paranoid about drawing attention to our division. I'd wanted to keep away from the rest of my family if something went wrong, but we'd debated on whether me being completely alone would look more suspicious. In the end, Ayla surprised us all by declaring that she would go with me, as they'd be far less suspicious of her. As Aiden, Indie, and Simon would also be at the library, my parents agreed.

I joined the line with Ayla. Further up ahead, I glimpsed Aiden standing with several of his fellow firefighters. He caught my eye, and I tried to look calm. He gave me a look that promised better things to come, and I relaxed a bit, giving him a small, but at least genuine, smile. It would be fine. It had to be. Suddenly, Indie and Simon appeared from within the library. They were stopping to chat with people, pulling on their coats as they stepped into the brisk sunshine. My sigh of relief was more of a groan, like a breath I'd been holding for days. Ayla just stared at her shoes, bored, nothing like a long line to entertain a ten-year-old.

Indie and Simon made a beeline toward us. Their relief was a balm to my frantically beating heart. "At least it was quick," she blew into her hands.

"Yup, just a quick glance and checking a box," Simon said, smiling bracingly at a few people around us who had heard. They gave strained smiles back, somewhat relieved but still nervous.

"You want to grab lunch afterward? We could meet over at The Green Man?" Indie asked. This had already been our plan, but she said it anyway, to fill the nervous energy that was still flowing through us. And to let everyone around us know that this was just a minor inconvenience for us, nothing to ruin a perfectly nice day out.

"Sounds good. Save us some seats." I hugged her tightly. Simon gave me a squeeze on the arm, and they both said goodbye to Ayla before walking away.

Despite Simon's assurances, the line seemed to move impossibly slowly. My stomach was sour, and I focused on counting the pillars in front of the library, the sound of the people chatting around me, the feel of Ayla's hair as I played with it. Aiden walked out laughing and joking with his friends, and I closed my eyes and sent up another thankful prayer to the stars. He saw them off with pats on the back and handshakes before coming to stand with us.

"I'll wait for you slowpokes." He waved at a few other people in line, asking after people he knew from work, from the good parts and the bad. I wanted to lean into his solid frame and feel my nerves melt away, but I resisted. It was one thing for him to comfort me during the execution, quite another to make a public declaration of this strange shift in our friendship. I pushed my toes into my shoes and willed my breathing to calm.

"Lim, can I go play with those kids?" Ayla was eyeing a group of children playing on the steps while their parents waited in line.

My chest tightened, but I said, "Fine, but when I pass you, you come with me."

The line moved and the girls Ayla had been playing with were called back by their parents. I called to her, but as I did, the girls' parents turned around and smiled at me. Through a combination of gestures and noiseless shouting one does in a quiet place, they asked to take Ayla in with them so she could stay with the girls. I nodded and gave them a thumbs up. It could only help Ayla to be with other cuffed Jinns and not next to me. The two of us held our breath as she disappeared into the library.

After several painstaking minutes, Ayla came skipping out with her friends, talking animatedly and looking like she was about to ask for a favor.

She ran up to me, and I nearly cried with relief, but for the sake of the other family who were watching, forced my expression into one of pleasant calm.

"Can I go to their house to play?" She pointed behind her and the parents smiled to show they were good with this plan.

"Ayla, we have a family lunch after this," I said, knowing my parents would want to lay eyes on their youngest child. "Could we possibly arrange for it to be on Monday? The girls would also be very welcome at ours." I was too stiff and overly formal, but they didn't seem to notice.

Ayla pouted, but the mother of the girls said, "We're okay with that. How about after school? We could take Ayla home with us and we'll bring her back after dinner?" The mother was smiling at her girls placatingly.

Ayla let out a resigned sigh. "Okay fine. See you then," she sang to her friends, and they responded in kind. I gave the mother an exaggerated eye roll, and she chuckled as she led their family away.

"Ayla, go across the street and stand with Aiden while I go in." Despite her being far too old for such things, Aiden picked her up and put her on his shoulders. She squealed in delight, still very much a child for all her serious demeanor sometimes. Aiden gave me a look like he might say something but just lightly brushed my hand and watched as I walked into the building like I didn't have a care in the world.

"Next!" I approached an older man with deep frown lines.

"Name?"

38

LIM

LASHIA, PRESENT DAY

"Calimea Revin." I pushed up my sleeves, willing my hands not to shake.

He grunted and flipped through the papers in his chart. When he got to my name, the frown lines deepened, and he said, "Sorry, I've got to take you aside, Ms. Revin."

"What?" The floor fell out beneath me, and my heart started hammering in my stomach. "Why?"

"I don't know." He sighed. "That's just the note they've got. Can you come with me?" He sounded bored, like the panic attack he was giving me, and the suspicion that was now rapidly spreading through the crowd was positively mundane.

"Is this to do with the fire?" I thought quickly. "Did they find the culprits?" I asked loudly, hoping to convince the others in the crowd who were now craning their necks to see what was happening.

He cocked his head, confused. "Oh, maybe. Did you file a report?" He beckoned me deeper into the library. I didn't roll my sleeves back down but lifted my arms and pulled my hair into a bun so everyone I passed got a good look at my bright blue cuffs. We exited out the back door, where a police carriage pulled by two strong-looking horses waited by the curb.

He signaled for me to sit inside, in the space for people who were detained.

"Really?" I lowered my eyebrows and injected my voice with disdain.

He rolled his eyes and closed the carriage door, motioning for me to sit beside him up front.

As we approached the station, a strange sense of resolve came over me. At least I wouldn't have to wonder anymore about what would happen to me. But I wouldn't jump, not until I could be sure this wouldn't work.

I climbed down from the carriage and walked through the doors as nonchalantly as I could. Officer Planck, my driver, spoke briefly to the Officer at the front desk. She raised her eyebrows and ducked down to whisper to him.

"What?" He leaned back in confusion and looked over at me. "Are you blind? They're right there." He motioned to my arms.

She just shrugged and jerked her head to the right.

He walked back over. "Sorry, I've been told I need to put you in a cell, Ms. Revin."

"What?" I hoped I was conveying both shock and innocence.

"Apparently there has been a request"—he waved his hand toward the front desk—"that a registrar examine you personally. Follow me."

My heart was now pounding in my chest and my head. Nausea sloshed in my stomach. I kept my gait even though my legs were like wet noodles. The urge to jump was overwhelming. I could feel my magic straining to be used. My body hummed with impatience as I failed to either fight or flee.

Officer Planck led me to a cell. He looked mildly apologetic but still locked the door behind him.

If the word 'depressing' had a smell, it would smell like this, I thought. It was dank, rust and moldy clothes permeated the air. There was a slight echo. No other prisoners in here with me to absorb the sound. I didn't hear any rats though. That was a small favor.

"I expect they'll be here soon," he said as he walked away. I briefly wondered how much time Officer Planck had before retirement.

There was a hard bench, and I sat primly, looking irritated. It occurred to me that someone still might be watching me, so I continued to act exactly as I would have if the cuffs I wore were real. Who had requested I be examined by the registrar? The only Tal who'd ever known was Emir. Several people had carved their initials into the bench, and I traced the letters, trying to distract myself.

It had been over an hour, during which I constantly checked that the blue bands had not faded, when footsteps sounded toward my cell. I tried to swallow but my throat was dry—where's the bread and water when you need it?

Bastian walked through the doors. He was as sharply dressed as always, the full suit today. He glanced back and then strode to my cell door. I stood up as he approached, finding comfort in the sight of those blue eyes.

"The registrar was in the next borough, but he'll be here any minute." His voice dropped. "Please tell me those are real." He glanced down at my arms.

I pulled my lips to the side in a grimace.

"Stars." He ran a hand through his hair. "A registrar in Asheville disappeared. That's why the registrar is coming from there—he's doing their inspections, too."

"What?" I hissed. "I thought they kept track of them? What is the point of those creepy suits?"

"Yeah, the creepy suits disappeared too."

"Oh," my mouth popped open, "sorry."

Bastian just shook his head. "They're supposed to call me if anyone is brought in. In case they want a lawyer. When I heard your name..." he trailed off, his eyes full of worry.

I couldn't plausibly deny that I'd forced a registrar to remove my cuffs, if I couldn't give them the real reason I didn't have any. I frantically tried to think of a believable lie but came up empty. I pushed my fingers against the bars, trying to stop the bile rising in my throat.

"You think more people are going to turn up uncuffed?"

Bastian glanced quickly at the door and then nodded. "Maybe. But I'm guessing that's why they took the accompanists too this time."

I nodded. "To keep them from tracking anyone down." My brow furrowed. There were definitely other Jinns out there who would do anything to have their cuffs removed. I could be in danger from them too if they found out about the darana. If I survived this inspection, that is. "How is her family?" I asked, referring to the late registrar.

"Coping. I got them to pay the benefits." Bastian said the last part with a flicker of irritation. He was angry that he'd had to fight—that her family had to go through all of that after losing her. I smiled forlornly. He was a good man. He'd been kind to me right from the beginning. His hand covered mine where it held the bars, and his face held pure, unguarded concern. "Do you have any ideas?"

I examined the ceiling as if I were thinking. "Running away?" I brought my head down and leaned it against the bars. With much more confidence than I truly felt, I pulled back and said, "As long as it's just me, I'll be fine." I had to believe that everyone else had made it through the inspection without scrutiny.

Bastion squeezed my hand again in understanding. "I'll do whatever I can to help."

I almost told him I couldn't ask him to defend me, knowing the way he felt about cuffs, but Betty interrupted us. She popped her head through the doorway and gave me a supportive smile. I wondered what Bastian had told her. If the police arrested me, she'd hear all about it, anyway.

"They're here."

Bastian gave my hand a squeeze before walking out without a word.

I stepped away from the bars and listened to the sound of several pairs of feet heading toward me. My lungs contracted, and I struggled to breathe. My skin was hot and too tight for my body. What if he tried to cuff me now? Would I have time to jump before that happened?

Two identical accompanists arrived, along with Officer Planck and Chiwel. Planck stopped near the entrance and crossed his arms as if he had somewhere better to be. The accompanists stood on either side of my cell door.

"Can you open the door, please?" Chiwel asked politely. He did not give any indication of us ever having met before.

The accompanists might have raised their eyebrows a fraction but said nothing. Officer Planck walked over, unlocked the door, and then backed away to his original spot. The accompanist clearly made him uncomfortable.

Chiwel raised his eyebrows meaningfully, but his voice came out cheerful and calm, just like it had been with Priya. It did nothing to calm the hammering of my heart. My palms began to sweat.

"Well, now, let's just see, shall we? This will only take a second."

I frowned. Chiwel was continuing to give me a look I couldn't interpret. He placed his thumbs over my wrists before sliding them down to my palms.

"Why would anyone want to go without these baby blues? I think the best thing to do is to keep them on."

Chiwel said the last three words with careful deliberation. My eyes widened in understanding before I rearranged my face into a sort of righteous indignation—I was, after all, an innocent citizen being grossly maligned here. I threw all my concentration into maintaining the glamor.

He'd blocked the view of my arms with his body, and it surprised me that the accompanists didn't lean forward to see. Officer Planck, however, had an unobstructed view from his place beside the door. Chiwel's fingers glowed, and I could feel the cuffs go on under the glamor.

But my magic was still intact. There was something else there now too, something that reminded me of winter, snow covering the landscape.

He pulled his hands off me.

"Same ol', same ol'." He said as he backed away. The accompanists barely looked at me. One of them pulled out a piece of paper and handed it to me. It was similar to Priya's paperwork, only it had today's date and my name with the words "Registrar Verified."

"Sign here, please." The accompanist handed me a pen.

I signed the piece of paper and the identical one beneath it.

"That one's yours to keep, in case this happens again," Chiwel explained as he opened the door to let me out.

"I really hope it doesn't," I said as haughtily as I could. Then I pulled on my coat and tried not to run out of the cell.

Chiwel and the accompanists turned down a different hallway while Planck led me out of the station. I stopped and turned to him, intending to be polite but really hoping to the stars I would never have to see him again.

"Did you need something else?" His eyes were a little unfocused, and he frowned as if this waste of time had been my fault.

"Nope." Screw courtesy. I raced down the steps and away from the station.

As I strode toward The Green Man, I caught sight of several new Sun Guardian symbols on the walls. One symbol had been hastily applied to a storefront of a beauty shop, the dried red paint reminding me of Sydney's artwork. I knew for a fact the place belonged to a Jinn. Angry heat built behind my eyes, but I pushed it down and tried to focus on being grateful for Chiwel's intervention, despite not knowing why he had helped me.

"I don't understand, he knew you were"—Indie looked around surreptitiously—"unadorned?"

We ensconced our little group of twelve in the back of the large pub. The atmosphere was dour, the other Jinns had little to celebrate at being forced to parade their cuffs around, and the place was near empty. Aiden, Audre, and I were hidden behind a low pony wall between our table and the next booth. But we huddled our heads together and kept our voices low anyway, everyone trying to make sense of what Chiwel had done for me.

"Yes." I thought back to when I'd first met Chiwel, the way his eyes had slid to my arms. Had he known then that something was off about them? If he'd known when they hadn't been fully removed, when I'd only just touched the darana long enough for them to flicker, he would have absolutely known on Halloween.

"And you didn't make him do it?" Ayla asked, eating her way through a giant slice of lemon cake. We'd all ordered dessert in our collective relief. The remains of carrot cake, cinnamon beignets, and pumpkin pie lay scattered around the table.

"No." I snorted, grateful that she seemed okay, even after today.

"Any idea who tipped him off?" Aiden asked quietly.

Everyone still living who knew about my cuffs was at this table, except for Bastian and Chiwel. I shook my head at the thought of Bastian betraying me. He wouldn't do that. Chiwel himself was a possibility if he was willing to uncuff people and wanted to know if I was an ally.

"I'm not sure."

"But you're sure he didn't recuff you?" Simon asked, pulling my unfinished cake toward him. On either side of him, Indie and Celeste stole a bite.

"Yes. I can still feel my magic." We all glanced around like criminals again, except for my mother, who smiled cheerfully and waved to someone she knew across the room. I carefully rolled up one sleeve and released the glamor.

My mother's smile turned into a gasp. My father let his hand fall to the table, the beer spilling a bit, as he stared openmouthed.

"What the stars are those?" Aiden frowned with concentration at my arms, which now had glowing red cuffs. My mind was scrambling, but I quickly reapplied the glamor and rolled down my sleeve.

"They're accompanist's cuffs," Indie responded. Simon nodded, but he scrunched his face and turned it to the side as if he were trying to recall everything he knew about accompanists.

"What?" Several of the others echoed my response.

"Once, an accompanist who was at my office for registration cut himself on a nail getting out of the carriage. Sliced his sleeve right open," Indie explained.

"Four stitches," Simon added.

"They have red cuffs, just like that. I don't know what they do, though."

"Jinns have blue cuffs that restrict magic. Tals have yellow cuffs that do nothing but prove they're registered. Registrars have green cuffs to show they have magic they're allowed to use. And Accompanists have red cuffs." Aiden ticked off the options on his fingers. "But I've never heard of an accompanist doing anything."

"They do something. I can feel it." I flexed my arms. "It feels as distinct as the other powers that aren't mine." I tipped my head at my mother, who looked crestfallen at the mention of her now-restricted power. "But I'm not sure how to use it safely without knowing what it does."

"Can you fly?" asked Ayla, grinning.

"Are you really strong?" asked Keen, catching on.

"If you try to control my mind, I will punch you in the face," Celeste announced in sing-song.

I joined the rest of them in their laughter, feeling the last of the weight that had plagued me since Emir's death melt away.

39

SABINE

TREVESTEN, PRESENT DAY

Sabine stood in the center of Asra's home—she refused to consider it Connery's home too. Morgan and Antonio stood beside her. The plainclothes guards were outside again, patrolling in and around this little corner of the town. She'd seen the one from before. This time, he dressed as a fisher, his wide hat pulled low. He gave her that lascivious smile again. She wondered if he had a mate somewhere, wondered if they worried about him when he was off guarding his queen on these strange missions.

It had taken less than a month to gather the items she needed. Being queen had the advantage of giving her access to all that had been confiscated from the queendom's criminals. What she was doing was illegal. There was no other way to say it.

Summoning people required a large amount of magic, four different artifacts, and a bevy of ingredients, half of which were illegal just on their own. Summoning a person against their will was kidnapping, plain and simple, and that, of course, was illegal. But her father had outlawed summoning someone willingly too, because of the high potential for improper use. The palace and Tarkana were spelled against such a thing, but fae were nothing if not resourceful.

They'd pushed back the couches and the chairs to make room, and Morgan had drawn a large circle on the floor with chalk blessed by a Visarian priestess. Antonio had broken the vials of powder at each quarter point of the circle. He, out of all of them, seemed rather excited by this obviously criminal and completely unpredictable activity. Perhaps the strait-laced general had no opportunities to let loose. Sabine made a note to herself to find him a hobby when they got home.

Sabine straightened her shoulders. When they got home *with her mate*.

In the corner, Morgan's eyes were worried. Her lips pursed, and she drummed her fingers against the sword at her side. They'd all come armed this time. Sabine was hopeful, but she wasn't stupid. She couldn't be completely sure she could bring Connery to them or what he would be like when he got here.

Nightmares about uncontrollable magic had plagued her, giant dust clouds of power filling the house and suffocating them all before bleeding out into the streets. She shook her head—this would work. The instructions she'd pieced together for this spell were vague, but she'd followed them carefully. Sabine had a begrudging respect for Asra. According to Natalia, she'd been a master at such things. She'd have to be if she'd created such capable daranas as Baldrick had claimed.

Sabine had returned to the house three more times before this, what she hoped would be the last time. Each time, she'd tried to bring forth another one of those blurry visions, suspecting that they were the place where Connery now was. Why else would they be sent to her? But they'd yielded nothing of use.

As she continued her visits, she met with Natalia, who turned out to be kind and helpful. For some reason, Sabine unburdened her long-repressed emotions to the shifter. She allowed herself to voice all her thoughts and fears for Connery and for their bond. Thoughts she'd even hidden from Morgan, afraid that her sister would wonder why she had not yet gotten over it. Morgan had no mate yet. Once she did, Sabine was sure she'd understand.

As Sabine predicted, Natalia was not as confident as she'd seemed the first time they'd met that Asra, Connery, and the rest of the crew had willingly stayed in Sverresen. "They loved a challenge, but it would take a lot for her to leave this place. She had so much ambition." She stalled a little. Sabine nodded to show that she understood. Asra's ambition did not always involve being on the right side of the law. "She would have made a good royal, with all her plans." Natalia fiddled with her coffee cup, rolling the heavy ceramic between her hands.

Sabine had made an unqueenly snort at that. A lot of the royals she knew had no plans other than to live off their continuing wealth and growing magic.

"Promise me you won't do anything to her—to any of them. They didn't kidnap him, he came to them of his own free will. I'm not saying he was happier here, but he had time..." Natalia trailed off, but Sabine understood. Connery had time to think, to get over her. Natalia surprised her by finishing with, "...to handle his demons." Sabine didn't know what that meant. Natalia didn't seem to be referring to her. Other than her broken promises, Connery had never appeared to be tortured by anything.

"I'm not planning on bringing them all. I couldn't anyway, having never even met any of the others. The spell requires a connection with the person summoned." Even if she could bring any of them, a dark, mean part of her wasn't sure she would bring back Asra or any of the group that had spent so much time with Connery. She hated herself for the jealousy, the bitterness, but from the moment she'd heard Antonio's report, it had sunk its teeth into her and would not let go.

Natalia nodded. "Promise it anyway," she said wryly. Her arthritis was back and she flexed her fingers absentmindedly.

"I promise I will pardon them for whatever they've done up to now, as long as they have not hurt him or kept him against his will." Sabine reached out and placed her hands on Natalia's, willing her magic to search out and calm the angry joints. Sabine's power was stronger than Antonio's and would keep the female free of pain for at least six months.

Sabine had sent a healer after that last visit. Now Natalia stood watching them all from Asra's kitchen, wringing her hands not from pain but from apprehension. Antonio shot her a bracing smile, and Natalia tried to return it.

"It's time," Sabine announced.

40

LIM

LASHIA, PRESENT DAY

The mood at my parents' house turned somber in the days following the census. I was sure everyone had now come down from the high of surviving. Now, they were mourning the loss of their power, feeling it just below the surface of their skin but unable to reach it. But everyone was safe, and that was the most important thing, wasn't it? Even if we all felt a little worse off, knowing what was possible.

Keen walked into the room and plopped down in a chair to read. I could hear Ayla in the kitchen, telling our parents about her playdate. Brax butted his head against me to encourage me to continue my head scratches, and I obliged him half-heartedly. He gave me up as a bad job and slunk out of the room and into the night.

"I'm going out," I announced before the thought had even fully formed in my mind. Abruptly, I stood and pulled on my coat. My parents only nodded, and my father raised his cup of tea in acknowledgment. With every step I took, my mood seemed to sour. We'd been so happy at the Green Man, or at least deeply relieved. We'd all skirted actual death. That was a lot to be grateful for. But I didn't feel grateful. And I was still angry at myself for having created this horrific period in the lives of my loved ones.

As I passed the beauty shop with the giant red sun on it, I stopped. It was empty. There was a 'for rent' sign in the window. I looked around. There was nobody on the street but me. Looking back at the shop, my blood heated. I didn't know whether she'd been driven away. Maybe she'd found a better location. But I doubted it. My thoughts whirled as I marched away. Would things like this keep happening until all the Jinns left Marais? Where would we go? Somewhere else to be picked on and shunted aside?

When I passed Indie and Simon's street, I admitted to myself where I knew deep down I'd been going all along. I tried to shove away my bad mood as I knocked on Aiden's door.

Aiden opened the door wearing only loose pants, his hair damp from a shower. My melancholy evaporated, and I did nothing to hide my unabashed appreciation of his body. His skin was dark from the sun, and it emphasized his well-defined muscles. I would definitely need to find out where Aiden was spending time outside without his shirt. Tiny droplets of water dripped from his hair onto his chest. I had the overwhelming desire to press my lips to his skin and let my tongue catch one of those drops.

"I...thought you might want company," I stuttered. "Or," I amended, taking a breath, "I wanted your company, and I hoped you'd be okay with that."

Aiden opened the door wider, giving me a grin that sent heat dancing across my body. "Absolutely, come in."

My eyes darted to the drawing of the little house as I crossed the threshold. I diverted my gaze to watch Aiden's muscled back as he led me into the small living room. There was a fire sending off little pops and sparks, and something low was playing on the radio. As he helped me with my coat, the tips of his fingers slid down my arms. I swallowed a little as I turned to him and found myself inches from his bare skin. I could see the scars clearly now. They traveled down the side of his neck to just past his collarbone.

"What is that?" I pointed to a mark below his collarbone. "Did you used to have a tattoo?" I mentally slapped myself for bringing up his scars right now.

"I had a birthmark." He pulled back his head to look at his skin. "But the scar covered it. It's started to show through." He shrugged. "Didn't use to look like that, though."

It had a sort of teardrop shape with slashes through it. Brax's claws came to mind. I couldn't imagine a scar having that effect on a birthmark, but what did I know about scars, or birthmarks for that matter?

"Let me get you a drink, wine?" My eyes jumped to his, and I smiled, thankful for the distraction. Aiden went down the hall first and when he came back he was pulling on a soft gray shirt, his abs flexing deliciously as his arms reached over his head.

I sank down onto the couch and clenched my knees together. 'Down girl,' I thought. It might actually insult Aiden that after all the time we spent together, I was only panting after him like this now that he'd shaved.

His home was cozy but sparse. There were two other drawings, one of ships in a harbor, as well as a large hand-drawn map of Lashia over the fireplace. His books were stacked neatly on a bookshelf, and I spotted a bicycle I'd missed, propped against the wall near the entryway.

"Here you go." Aiden came back out of the kitchen and placed a glass of wine in my hand. I clinked my glass with his mug as he sat on the armchair next to me. My eyes fell closed as I took a sip and leaned back against the couch.

I waited for him to ask me what I wanted, what I was doing there. But he said nothing. I could feel his gaze on me.

"I'm back at square one," I said finally, without opening my eyes. "All of that fear and uncertainty, and I'm right back where I started. No cuffs and no restaurant. Well, half a restaurant." I opened my eyes. "How do you feel? Do you regret it?" I asked, not bothering to hide the vulnerability in my voice.

Aiden contemplated his tea. He made a gravely "hmmmm" sound that made me think of late night whispers. He looked up at me, his hazel eyes locked on mine. "I regret nothing. It was all worth it."

"We could have died," I whispered.

He put his mug down and moved to sit on the ottoman in front of me. "We could have. But we didn't. Thanks to you."

I leaned forward. "It was my responsibility. I put everyone at risk."

Aiden frowned at me. Was that disappointment in his eyes? I suddenly felt very small. Perhaps I'd made a huge mistake coming here. I swallowed.

"You didn't force anyone into this. We all made our own choices." His voice changed to the tone of a command. "You can't allow your guilt for giving us the choice to eclipse the pride you should feel for saving us."

I pulled my bottom lip into my mouth, biting it gently and evaluating the potential outcomes of this evening. Aiden's eyes fell briefly to my lips.

"I mean, technically, it was Simon's book."

He grinned. Aiden had an incredible smile, and it filled me with immediate relief.

"I don't want us to lose our magic," I blurted before I lost my nerve. "Any of the Jinns. I don't think it's fair and I want to do something about it."

It felt amazing and treasonous to say it out loud. I waited for him to tell me it was too dangerous, that we'd just escaped certain death. To tell me things would never change for the better.

His eyes met mine unflinchingly. "The execution didn't make me want to be good. It didn't make me want to follow the rules. For the first time, I thought about what it would be like to use my power as a weapon." His words were slow and deliberate. They moved over me like fingertips.

I hoped the fire in my eyes matched his. "I'm sorry," I said, leaning toward him.

His lips quirked. "I thought we just established you have nothing to be sorry for?"

"No, not for that. For not...seeing you sooner. After all this time." My cheeks heated with embarrassment.

The smile dropped from his face as he leaned forward. Our faces were so close, barely enough room for a thought between us. The rest of the room seemed to blur as he focused on me with searing intensity. "I didn't want you to see me. Not then. I needed to figure my stuff out." He ran a hand down the side of his face, considering something. "Do you think any of our power worked with our cuffs on?"

"I appreciate you trying to give me an excuse for being so dense." I smirked.

Aiden's answering smile was heated. "I don't know. I used it during the fire without noticing. And when I moved here, after what happened with my family, I didn't feel worthy. I didn't want anyone to see beyond the superficial, wanted to stay small, so they wouldn't look too close." He paused. "So you wouldn't look too close."

His fingers were splayed across his knee. The tiniest sliver of his skin touched mine. I couldn't think of Aiden as small. Even when he was trying to stay hidden, I was always aware of him. Could always sense where he was and what he needed.

"And now?" I didn't recognize the voice that came out of me, but I was glad it wasn't hesitant. I was even more glad I wasn't wearing another sack dress.

He reached down and gently pulled my shoes and socks off. I raised my eyebrows, but he just pulled my bare feet toward him, propping them up on his thighs. He dug his thumbs into the soles of my feet. My head fell back and I moaned indecently.

"That feels so good."

I was on my feet all the time. I had tried to massage them myself, but it was nothing like this. This was pure bliss. He alternated back and forth between them, pushing into the arches, then massaging the pads below my toes. He ran his large palm over my ankles and down my foot, pushing them into a point, stretching them in the sweetest kind of pain. My body had gone taut and loose at the same time.

He leaned in closer to me. I was acutely aware of my feet pushing into his abs as his hands ran over my ankles. His thumbs made circles as they moved slowly up my shin, his palms caressing my calves. Each circle pushed my dress higher until it was just above my knees, and my breathing had gone from relaxed to ragged. It felt familiar to be with him, like his skin already knew mine, but at the same time, strange and dangerous.

I was falling quickly, stumbling downward into the dark unknown. Aiden could not be a fling. There would be no sweet separation like Bastian, or sense of resolve like Leo. It was so easy to be with him, it felt almost deceptive. But I wanted him; my skin reached for his like I already knew how deftly he could wring pleasure from my body.

"Do you want me to keep going?" His voice was low and rough, and it reverberated between my thighs. He gave me a look filled with purpose, his eyes hooded. There was no mistaking the desire there.

I ran my eyes over him, his strong jaw, freshly shaved, his dark hair still damp and falling slightly over his forehead. I wasn't sure about a lot of things, but I was certain I did not want him to stop. There was a sense of satisfaction at seeing him look at me that way, even though it had been me who had missed the signs.

"I would like that very much." My voice was breathy as I let him see the truth in my eyes.

The corner of his mouth rose, and his face relaxed with relief. He continued his ministrations but did not take his eyes off me. When he couldn't reach any higher with my feet pressing against him, he pulled my legs to either side of him. Slowly, he leaned forward until his lips were inches from mine. His arms wrapped around my waist and he pulled me off the couch onto his lap.

I let out a little "oh" in response, a torrent of warmth filling my body. I could feel him beneath me, so close to where I wanted him to be. My hands gripped his shirt while his palms snaked up my arms to pull my face toward him.

My fingers stroked up his chest as he captured his lips with mine, teasing them open until we were tasting each other and my body was impatient with need. I did indeed pull my mouth from his and let my tongue glide over the skin of his neck until I trapped one of the warm droplets from his hair. Aiden's breath hitched in response and his hands traveled down to grip my hips, pulling me tighter against him. My tongue explored the ridges of his neck, and he stiffened when I reached the scar. He relaxed again, letting out a low growl as I let my nails drag down his back in what I hoped was a clear appreciation of every part of him.

I pulled his shirt back up over his head, desperate to feel his skin against mine. A small gasp left me as he picked me up and kept my legs wrapped around his waist, fingers gripping my thighs tightly, his mouth never leaving mine. The wall was hard against my back as he pushed me into it, driving me closer to him. I writhed against his body, eager for the moment I could make every part of my skin meet his, and I felt him groan in agreement.

Aiden pulled back suddenly to look at me, his grip weakening. Even in my lust-addled haze, I could see something was wrong. Aiden's smile faltered, he swayed on his feet.

"Aiden?" Grabbing onto his forearms as I slid out of his grip, I said, "What's wrong?"

He shook his head. "I don't know. It feels like I might be sick."

His skin flushed hot and cold against the back of my hand as I checked his forehead. "Just stay with me, okay? I'll help you." I threw his arm around my shoulder and held him by the waist, trying to lead him toward the bathroom. There was a strange sensation, something pulling on him, pulling him away from me.

Aiden let out another shudder and nearly keeled over. "I've got you. Just a few more steps. I'm with you."

He nearly slipped out of my grasp, and I tightened my grip, leaning into the jump, even though I hadn't been trying to move us. Panic ignited inside me. The fear that I would both lose him and myself in some in-between place.

I slammed hard onto an uneven wooden floor, pain radiating through my back as Aiden collapsed on top of me. He turned to the side and was immediately sick. The room was pitch black, but I could sense other people around us. There was barely enough time to register the familiar feeling of wherever we were when a voice spoke. I didn't understand why, but it filled me with dread.

"Connery?" A light flared in the room. Instinct had me scrambling to get up, my hand going over Aiden's heaving figure protectively. One of the most beautiful women I'd ever seen collapsed to her knees and looked at Aiden with unguarded joy.

41

LIM

TREVESTEN, PRESENT DAY

I was dead. They were burning my body.

My blood boiled and my skin melted off my bones over and over again as I writhed in agony. Every muscle ached. It hurt even to open my eyes. I vomited until my stomach muscles seized up.

Someone was tying me to the bed. Something that should have scared me or at least made me curious, but I could do nothing, nothing but endure this endless torture. I wanted to die; I tried to do it. I flung myself out the window, not knowing how high up I was, whether it would work, anything to end this. Ah, that must have been when they tied me to the bed.

I lashed out at my captors, begged them to kill me. My bones cracked and shifted beneath my skin as if they were trying to escape the hell that was my body. My nails dug into the surface, desperate to hold on while the room spun uncontrollably. Images and memories flew through my head, filling it until my skull would surely crack. Knowledge forced its way in like a steel spike, and I screamed, certain my brain would collapse and melt.

Cards fluttered to the ground before changing into flower petals, broken glass. Hundreds of feet pounding above my head. Hungry insects and the overpowering smell of flowers. Warm blue eyes rushed toward me like a tornado. I walked through fire and it didn't burn. A massive black cat grinned at me while a man disappeared into a wall.

How long had it been? This was home but this was not The Peregrine, and it was not my parent's house. With enormous effort, I raised my eyelids. The pain was less. It wasn't gone, slight aches ran along the length of me, but nothing as it had been. A warm body lay beside me. I lifted my hand and placed it on the soft fur. The vibration I felt there was soothing, and I felt it huddle closer to me.

I couldn't keep my eyes open for long. A glass tipped against my mouth. The scent of roasted vegetables filled my nose. I was dead. Why did anyone bother roasting vegetables for me? The broth slipped down my throat and I moaned. It filled the hollowness inside, and I cried in relief. But I had no tears, I was too thirsty for tears. I continued drinking and became conscious of a voice like honey murmuring to me.

"It's okay, Asra, the worst is over."

A familiar face swam in my vision. She had deep laugh lines and gray eyes that were round with affection.

"Yas?" My throat was hoarse from screaming. Was it filled with ash, or was that another memory?

She smiled in relief. "Thank the Mother! That was the worst rishival I've ever seen. They've got some good stuff now, for the nausea especially, but it's out of my price range." She blew out a breath.

I nodded. Marbles filled my head again. They swung back and forth as I tried to sit. I only made it as far as leaning against the headboard.

She brought the cup of broth to my lips again, and I drank carefully. "I'm Natalia this time around. I didn't catch your new name before you started puking everywhere." She put the cup back on the nightstand.

I couldn't manage a smile, but I found her hand over the covers. I held it gratefully. "Calimea Revin. Lim to my friends." Several of the marbles came to rest and I could think a little more clearly.

Suddenly, I shot up, "Aiden!" I searched the room even though we were the only two in it. My stomach lurched dangerously.

Natalia gave me a bracing look. "He's gone. The queen took him. She had his family's permission."

My thoughts and memories were like a flock of birds. I struggled to pick out what was relevant among the fluttering of long-forgotten names and places.

"She made him travel? When he was going through the rishival?" I couldn't believe Sabine would make him suffer like that.

"He didn't go through it. He stopped being sick almost immediately. But you only managed a few words before the rishival took you." She frowned at the memory. "He didn't know her or me."

I blinked, confused. "He still left?"

Natalia tilted her head and raised her eyebrows like I was being thick. "She's the queen. He didn't have a choice."

"The cuffs," I groaned. I rubbed the two bright red bands on my forearms. "Aiden won't go through his rishival, won't remember being Connery, until he gets his cuffs off. They're like the manacles they give the fae in Tarkana but applied to our skin."

Her lips pursed as she looked at my cuffs in suspicion. "But you still have yours?"

"These are different. Although I didn't ask for these either. I'm not sure what they do." The words came out of my mouth, but they were wrong. I clutched at one of the birds, trying to hold on to the thought. I knew what these cuffs did. This was power we'd brought to Lashia.

Chiwel and I were going to have a talk when I got back.

"Actually, I take that back. This is obahn power."

Natalia instinctively pulled her hands away.

"Don't worry." I sighed. "I'm not about to use it." A humid room beneath the bakery. A woman with mousy brown hair. My breath stuck in my lungs as I put it together. The accompanists had the power to erase memories. But why?

Natalia shuddered. "Where in the Allmother have you been?"

The question reminded me viscerally of Solvan. A wave of emotion crashed into me as I pictured my last moments with him. The sight of his pale face as I held him in the mud.

Not Solvan anymore, Audre.

Solvan, Brigid and Elwin. And Connery. Brigid and Elwin—Indie and Simon, I corrected myself, would always find one another. They were mates. But all of us, we'd stayed together, even without our memories, even after everything that happened. It had been hundreds of years and we'd still found each other. I had no memories of my time in Lashia after that initial life and now. I could probably blame the cuffs for that as well.

Something prickled in the back of my mind among all the other thoughts fighting for attention. The small group of humans that were attacking us when Solvan died. The thousands of people to whom we'd given magic. We all gave so much power.

I pulled my face out of my hands. A familiar doubt crept in. That voice that said I needed to leave it alone, that my plans were reckless and stupid. The feeling that had plagued me for so many years. Connery's eyes as he brought me firewood. As they watched me night after night at the bar. I couldn't believe the five of us were really still together after all this time.

Fire sprang to my fingertips, circling and twisting in my hand, begging to play. I shoved that cowardly voice down behind every thought and memory that was more deserving of my focus.

Natalia helped me stand. My body seemed to become less fragile with each step we took. By the time we'd reached the first floor, I no longer needed her help. My power rushed throughout my body, a child excitedly exploring a new home.

I pushed open the closet door and felt around in the dark for the hidden latch. The false back popped open. Natalia followed me down the stairs, humming tunelessly. My red cuffs glowed in the darkness.

With barely a curl of my fingers, flames burst to life in the fireplace, illuminating my workshop. My skin hummed in delight at the use of my fire. Row upon row of jars and bottles greeted me. Some had gone dark in the last several centuries, but most were still glowing with their captured spells and magic. Thick, viscous green elixirs, sparkling pink ether, and stones thrumming with power.

I ran my fingers along the row, and they caught on a square glass case containing the spent scales of a giant yellow snake. I pushed that memory away. The here and now was what mattered.

I pulled down several jars and set them on the long wooden table.

"What are you making?" Natalia asked, eyeing the ingredients with interest.

That old excitement sizzled under my skin, strengthening my resolve. "Amends."

If you enjoyed this book, please, please, leave it a review!

Will Lim be able to right the wrongs of the past? Will Aiden return to Lim and the crew or choose to remain with his mate? Find out in the sequel, All the Forgotten Things!

If you'd like a bonus heist scene and to find out about future releases, head on over to my website (www.lmdodds.com) to sign up for my newsletter.

Thank you so much for reading. I loved sharing this world with you!

Acknowledgements

Writing this book was an intense journey and I couldn't have done it without the love and support of so many people. Thank you Brendan, for saying yes to (almost) all my ridiculous ideas. And to my parents, and the rest of my family who have had to hear about this forever, love you. And you can read it now, just don't tell me.

Huge appreciation to my friends and beta readers, Savannah, Ben, Jeni, Cara, Mary, Whitney, Fielding, Aurelie, and Lou. Special shout out to Neeks — I cannot thank you enough for your consistent and thorough help. Thanks Martin for giving me the benefit of your musical knowledge and to Helen and Jenny for connecting me with Vanessa, Ariana, and Norah at Not Sorry Productions, who got me through my first NaNoWriMo.

Couldn't have done it without my editor, Amanda Oraha. Thank you so much for everything you've done to bring Lim and the crew to life. Much appreciation to Alexandra Purtan as well for the original cover design.

And of course, to anyone who took a chance on me and read this book, you have my unending gratitude!